**The black throng surrounded Erika Hernandez
and pressed inward.**

Then came the oppressive roar of a voice inside her mind. *We are the Borg. Resistance is futile. You will be exterminated.* It was as intimate to her thoughts as the gestalt once had been, but it was hostile, savage, and soulless.

A spinning saw blade cut away the front half of her rifle, and the weapon spat sparks as it tumbled from her grasp.

Hands closed around her arms and pulled her backward, off-balance. She flailed and kicked, lashing out with wild fury.

More hands seized her ankles, her calves. The sheer weight of bodies smothered her, and a sting like a needle jabbed her throat. Twisting, she saw that one of the Borg drones had extended from between its knuckles two slender tubules that had penetrated her carotid.

An icy sensation flooded into her like a poison and engulfed her consciousness in a sinking despair.

Pushed facedown as the Borg's infusion took root, she smelled the ferric tang of blood spreading across the deck under her face. Then a hand cupped her chin and lifted her head.

She looked into the eyes of a humanoid woman whose skin was the mottled gray of a cadaver. Hairless and glistening in the spectral light, the female Borg flashed a mirthless smile at Hernandez. "You are the one we have waited for," she said. "Surrender to the Collective . . . and become Logos of Borg."

STAR TREK®
DESTINY

Book III
LOST SOULS

DAVID MACK

Based upon

STAR TREK and

STAR TREK: THE NEXT GENERATION®
created by Gene Roddenberry

STAR TREK: DEEP SPACE NINE®
created by Rick Berman & Michael Piller

STAR TREK: VOYAGER®
created by Rick Berman & Michael Piller & Jeri Taylor

STAR TREK: ENTERPRISE®
created by Rick Berman & Brannon Braga

POCKET BOOKS
New York   London   Toronto   Sydney   Axion

Pocket Books
A Division of Simon & Schuster, Inc.
1230 Avenue of the Americas
New York, NY 10020

This book is a work of fiction. Names, characters, places, and incidents either are products of the author's imagination or are used fictitiously. Any resemblance to actual events or locales or persons, living or dead, is entirely coincidental.

This book is published by Pocket Books, a division of Simon & Schuster, Inc., under exclusive license from CBS Studios Inc.

All rights reserved, including the right to reproduce this book or portions thereof in any form whatsoever. For information address Pocket Books Subsidiary Rights Department, 1230 Avenue of the Americas, New York, NY 10020

First Pocket Book paperback edition December 2008

POCKET and colophon are registered trademarks of Simon & Schuster, Inc.

For information about special discounts for bulk purchases, please contact Simon & Schuster Special Sales at 1-800-456-6798 or business@simonandschuster.com

Art by Rick Berry; design by Alan Dingman.

Manufactured in the United States of America

10 9 8 7 6 5 4 3 2 1

ISBN-13: 978-1-4165-5175-1
ISBN-10:   1-4165-5175-1

For Lerxst, G., and the Professor, who inspired me to get on with the fascination; for Bryan, whose remarkable generosity humbles me; and for Randy, who made the introductions.

HISTORIAN'S NOTE

The main narrative of *Lost Souls* takes place in February of 2381 (Old Calendar), approximately sixteen months after the events depicted in the movie *Star Trek Nemesis*. The flashback story occurs circa 4527 B.C.E.

Death closes all: but something ere the end,
Some work of noble note, may yet be done,
Not unbecoming men that strove with gods.

—Alfred, Lord Tennyson, *Ulysses*

2381

1

It was the hardest decision William Riker had ever made.

He cast a suspicious glare at *Titan*'s unexpected visitor, a human-looking young woman with a crazy mane of sable hair and delicate garments that showed more of her body than they covered. She had claimed to be Erika Hornandez, the commanding officer of the Earth *Starship Columbia,* which had vanished more than two centuries earlier, thousands of light-years from the planet where *Titan* was now being held prisoner. Her tale seemed implausible, but she had offered to help his ship escape, and so Riker was willing to accept her extraordinary claims on faith . . . at least, until *Titan* was safe someplace far from here and he could put her identity to the test.

Hers had been a proposition he couldn't refuse, but freeing his ship from the reclusive aliens known as the Caeliar would come at a price: His away team—made up of most of his senior officers, including his wife, his *Imzadi,* Deanna Troi—would have to be abandoned on the planet's surface.

But there was a war raging at home, and above all,

he had a duty to protect his ship and defend the Federation. No matter what he did, he was certain his decision would haunt him for a long time to come.

"Take us home," Riker said.

Hernandez snapped into action and took command of the situation. Pointing at the display screen over the science station, she asked curtly, "Who set up this tap on the Caeliar's subspace aperture?"

"We did," answered Commander Xin Ra-Havreii, *Titan*'s chief engineer, gesturing to himself and the ship's senior science officer, Lieutenant Commander Melora Pazlar.

Hernandez stepped to the console and began entering data. The strange young woman's fingers moved with velocity and delicacy, as if she had mastered the Federation's newest technology ages earlier. "I need to change your shield specs to protect you from radiation inside the passage," she said.

"Our shields already do that," Ra-Havreii said.

"No," Hernandez replied, her flurry of tapping on the console unabated, "you only think they do. Give me a moment." Her hands came to an abrupt stop. "There." She turned and snapped at Riker's acting first officer, Commander Fo Hachesa, "Which station controls onboard systems?"

Hachesa pointed at ops.

"Thank you," she said to the stunned-silent Kobliad. Moving in rapid strides, Hernandez crossed to the forward console and nudged Lieutenant Sariel Rager out of her way. "I'm programming your deflector to create a phase-shifted soliton field. That'll make it harder for the Caeliar to shift the aperture on us while we're in transit." She looked across at Ensign

Aili Lavena, the Pacifican flight-control officer. "Be ready to go at your best nonwarp speed, as soon as the passage opens. Understood?"

Lavena nodded quickly, shaking loose air bubbles inside her liquid-atmosphere breathing mask.

Watching the youthful Hernandez at work, Riker felt superfluous on his own bridge.

"All right," Hernandez announced, "I'm about to widen the subspace aperture into a full tunnel. When I do, the Caeliar will try to shut it down. Be warned: This is gonna be a rough ride." She looked around at the various alien faces on *Titan*'s bridge. "Everyone ready?" The crew nodded. She met Riker's gaze. "It's your ship, Captain. Give the word."

Nice of her to remember, Riker thought. He led Hachesa back to their command chairs. They sat down and settled into place. Lifting his chin, Riker said to Hernandez, "The word is given."

"And away we go," Hernandez said. She faced forward, fixed her gaze on the main viewscreen, and lifted her right arm to shoulder height. With her outstretched hand, she seemed to reach toward the darkness, straining to summon something from the void. Then it appeared, like an iris spiraling open in space: a circular tunnel filled with brilliant, pulsing blue and white rings of light, stretching away to infinity.

Lavena pressed the padd to fire the impulse engines at full power. One moment, Riker heard the hum and felt the vibrations of sublight acceleration through the deck plates; the next, he was clutching his chair's armrests as the ship slammed to a hard, thunderous halt and threw everyone forward.

"More power!" cried Hernandez over the alarm

klaxons and groaning bulkheads. "I'll try to break their hold on us!" She closed her eyes, bowed her head, and raised both arms.

Riker had witnessed some of Deanna's psychic struggles in the past, and he knew that whatever Hernandez was enduring to free his ship, it had to be worse than he could imagine. "Give it all we've got!" he bellowed over the chatter of damage reports pouring in via the ops and tactical consoles.

Titan lurched forward, then it was inside the pulsating brightness of the subspace tunnel. Lieutenant Rriarr gripped the side of the tactical console with one paw as he reported, "High-level hyperphasic radiation inside the tunnel, Captain. Shields holding."

That's why she had to modify our shields, Riker realized. *Otherwise, we'd all be handfuls of dust by now.* Bone-rattling blows hammered the ship. "Report!" Riker ordered.

"Soliton pulses," Rriarr said. "From behind us."

"They're trying to bend the passage and bring us back to New Erigol," Hernandez said. "Keep that soliton field up!"

"Divert nonessential power to the deflector," Riker said.

"Belay that, sir," countered Ra-Havreii. "The gravitational shear inside the tunnel is rising. We have to reinforce the structural integrity field!"

Hernandez shot back, "Do that, and we'll lose control of the tunnel. We'll be taken back to New Erigol!"

"If we don't, the ship might be torn in half," replied the angry Efrosian engineer. Punctuating his point, a console behind him exploded and showered the bridge with stinging debris and quickly fading sparks.

Falling to her knees, Hernandez kept her arms extended and her hands up, as if she were holding back a titanic weight. "Just a few more seconds!" she cried in a plaintive voice.

The bluish-white rings of the tunnel began distorting as the black circle of its terminus became visible. "Lieutenant Rager, all available power to the deflector," Riker said. "That's an order." Another round of merciless impacts quaked the ship around him. "Hold her together, folks, we're almost out!"

An agonized groan welled up from within Hernandez as the egress point loomed large ahead of *Titan*. She arched her back and lifted her hands high above her head before unleashing a defiant, primal scream.

Outside the ship, in the tunnel, a massive ripple like a shimmer of heat radiation coursed ahead of *Titan*, smoothing the rings back to their perfect, circular dimensions and calming the turbulence. The shockwave rebounded off the exit ring as the *Luna*-class explorer hurtled through it.

Energy surges flurried the bridge's consoles, and displays spat out chaotic jumbles. A final, calamitous blast pummeled *Titan*, and the bridge became as dark as a moonless night. Only the feeble glow of a few tiny status gauges pierced the gloom in the long moments before the emergency lights filled the bridge with a dim, hazy radiance.

Smoke blanketed the bridge, and the deck sparkled with a fine layer of crystalline dust from demolished companels. The deck was eerily silent; there was no sound of comm chatter, no feedback tones from the computers.

"Damage report," Riker said. He surveyed the bridge for anyone able to answer him. He was met by befuddled looks and officers shaking their heads in dismay.

Ra-Havreii moved from station to station, barely pausing at each one before moving on to the next, growing more agitated every step of the way. When he reached the blank conn, he gave his drooping ivory-white mustache a pensive stroke, then turned to Riker and said, "We're blacked out, Captain. Main power's offline, along with communications, computers, and who knows what else. I'll have to go down to main engineering to get a better look at the problem."

"Go ahead," Riker said. "Power first, then communications."

"That was my plan," replied Ra-Havreii, heading for the turbolift. He all but walked into the still-closed doors before making an awkward stop, turning on his heel, and flashing an embarrassed grin. "No main power, no turbolifts." He pointed aft. "I'll just take the emergency ladder."

As the chief engineer made his abashed exit, Riker got up and walked to Hernandez's side. In slow, careful motions, he helped her stand and steady herself. "Are you all right?"

"I think so," she said. "That last pulse was a doozy. Guess I didn't know my own strength."

Riker did a double-take. "You *caused* that final pulse?"

"I had to," she said. "It was the only way to close

off the passage and destroy the machine at the other end once we were clear. That'll keep the Caeliar off our backs for a while."

"Define 'a while.'"

Hernandez shrugged. "Hard to say. Depends how much damage I did and how badly the Caeliar want to come after us. Could be a few days. Could be a few decades."

"We'd better get busy making repairs, then," Riker said.

She nodded once. "That would probably be a good idea."

Riker turned to Lieutenant Rriarr. "As soon as the turbolifts are working, have Captain Hernandez escorted to quarters and placed under guard." To Hernandez, he added, "No offense."

"None taken," she replied. "After eight hundred years with the Caeliar, I'm used to being treated like a prisoner."

Deanna Troi screamed in horror as Dr. Ree sank his fangs into her chest just below her left breast, and Ree felt absolutely terrible about it, because he was only trying to help.

The Pahkwa-thanh physician ignored Troi's frantic slaps at his head as he released a tiny amount of venom into her bloodstream. Then the half-Betazoid woman stiffened under his slender, taloned feet as the fast poison took effect.

Four sets of hands—one pair on each arm and two pairs on his tail—yanked him backward, off Troi, and dragged him into a clumsy group tumble away from her. He rolled to his feet to find himself confronted by the away team's security contingent, which consisted of Chief Petty Officer Dennisar, Lieutenant Gian Sortollo, and *Titan*'s security chief, Lieutenant Commander Ranul Keru. The team's fuming-mad first officer, Commander Christine Vale, snapped, "What the hell were you *doing*, Ree?"

"The only thing that I could, under the circumstances," Ree replied, squaring off against his four comrades.

Vale's struggle for calm was admirable, if unsuccessful. She flexed her hands and fought to unclench her jaw. "This had better be the best damned explanation of your life, Doctor."

A shadow stepped off a nearby wall and became Inyx, the chief scientist of the Caeliar. The looming, lanky alien tilted his bulbous head and permanently frowning visage in Ree's direction. "I am quite eager to hear your explanation as well," he said. The deep inflation and deflation of the air sacs that drooped over his bony shoulders suggested a recent exertion.

Ensign Torvig Bu-kar-nguv cowered outside the door of Troi's quarters and poked his ovine head cautiously around the jamb to see what was transpiring inside. Ree understood perfectly the reticence of the young Choblik, whose species—bipedal runners with no natural forelimbs—were descended from prey animals.

As Ree chose his words, Commander Tuvok, *Titan*'s second officer, entered and kneeled beside Troi. The brown-skinned Vulcan man gently rested one hand on Troi's forehead.

"I confess it was an act of desperation," Ree said. "After the Caeliar destroyed all of our tricorders—including mine—I had no way to assess the counselor's condition with enough specificity to administer any of the hyposprays in my satchel."

"So you bit her," Sortollo interrupted with deadpan sarcasm. "Yeah, that makes sense."

Undeterred by the Mars-born human's cynicism, Ree continued, "Commander Troi's condition became progressively worse after she went to bed. Based on my tactile measure of her blood pressure, pulse, and temperature, I concluded there was a high probability that she had suffered a serious internal hemorrhage." He directed his next comments to Inyx, who had moved to Troi's side and squatted low, opposite Tukov, to examine her. "She would not permit me to seek your help or request the use of your sterile medical facilities for the procedure."

"And *that's* why he bit her," Dennisar said, riffing on Sortollo's dry delivery. Commander Vale glared the Orion into a shamed silence.

Inyx rested his gently undulating cilia over Troi's bite wound. "You injected her with a toxin."

Menace was implied in Vale's every syllable as she said, "If you've got a point to make, Doctor, now's the time."

"My venom is a relic of Pahkwa-thanh evolution," he said to her. "It places prey in a state of living suspended animation. Its purpose in my species' biology was to enable sires of new hatchlings to roam a large territory and bring live prey back to the nest without a struggle, so that it would be fresh when fed to our young. In this case, I used it to place Counselor Troi in a suspended state to halt the progression of her hemorrhage."

Keru sighed heavily and shook his head. "All right, that does kind of make sense."

"What you did was barbaric and violent," Inyx said. A sheet of quicksilver spread beneath Troi like a metallic bloodstain. It solidified and levitated her from the floor. "Your paralyzing toxin, while effective in the short term, will not sustain her for long. If that is what passes for medicine among your kind, I am not certain you deserve to be called a doctor."

Inyx began escorting the levitated Troi toward the exit.

Tuvok lurked silently behind Inyx, his intense stare fixed on Troi's face, which was frozen in a look of shock even though she was no longer sensate.

Vale blocked Inyx's path. The security personnel regrouped behind her, fully obstructing the doorway. "Hold on," she said to Inyx. "Where are you taking her?"

"To a facility where we can provide her with proper medical care," the Caeliar scientist replied. He glanced at Ree and added in a pointed tone, "You might be surprised to learn that *our* methods do not include masticating our patients."

Ree was a gentle being by nature, but the Caeliar seemed committed to putting his goodwill to the test. "She needs the kind of medical care that I can provide to her only on *Titan*," he said to Inyx. "If you really were the beneficent hosts you claim to be, you'd let us return to the ship."

Inyx halted and turned back to face Ree. "I am afraid that is quite impossible," he said.

"Yes, yes," Ree groused. "Because of your sacred privacy."

"No," Inyx said, "because your ship has escaped and left you all behind." A gap opened in the ceiling above Inyx and Troi, who ascended through it into the open air of the starless night. Inyx looked down and added, "I will leave you to contemplate that while I try to save your friend's life." He and Troi faded into the darkness and were gone.

A shocked silence filled the room as the remaining away-team members regarded one another with searching expressions.

Dennisar asked no one in particular, "Do you really think *Titan* got away?"

Keru gave a noncommittal sideways nod. "The Caeliar haven't lied to us so far. Could be the truth."

Vale said, "If they did, good for them. And it's good news for us, too, because you know Captain Riker will send help."

Everyone nodded, and Ree could sense that they were all trying to put the most positive possible spin on the cold fact of having been abandoned by their shipmates and captain.

Torvig was the first to wander back to his quarters, and then Tuvok slipped away, his demeanor reserved and withdrawn. Vale left next, and Keru ushered his two men out of the room.

Ree followed the burly Trill security chief out of Troi's quarters into the corridor. Keru snickered under his breath. "I'm sorry, Doc," he said. "But for a second there, I really thought you were trying to eat Counselor Troi."

"I would never do such a thing," Ree said, affecting a tone of greater offense than he really felt. Then he showed Keru a toothy grin. "Though I have to admit . . . she was rather succulent." Noting the man's anxious sidelong glance, Ree added with a flustered flourish, "Kidding."

4527 B.C.E.

2

A fiery mountain fell from the sky.

Deep thunder rolled above the snowy landscape as the behemoth of scorched metal plunged through the low cover of bleak autumn clouds. Wreathed in flames and ashen smoke, its angle of descent shallowed moments before it caromed off the rocky mountainside. Eruptions of mud, splintered trees, and pulverized stone filled the air. The dark mass cut epic gouges into the alpine slope, and it broke apart on its descent to the rugged coastline of the ice-packed fjord below.

An avalanche rushed before it. Millions of tons of snow, dirt, and ice moved like water and then set like stone as they buried the shattered crags of blackened metal. The ground shook, and the roar of the collision and its consequences echoed and reechoed off the surrounding peaks and glaciers, until it was swallowed by the deep silence of the arctic wilderness.

Twilight settled on the fjord.

And there wasn't a soul to bear witness.

"Stand back," MACO Sergeant Gage Pembleton said. "I'm almost through. One more shot ought to do it."

He stood, wedged in a jagged rent in the foundation of the Caeliar city-ship Mantilis. He aimed his phase rifle into the gap he had melted, through the densely packed ice and snow that had entombed the wrecked vessel after its calamitous planetfall on this unknown world, tens of thousands of light-years from Earth. A quick tap on the rifle's trigger released a flash of heat and light, and then he saw open sky. Frigid, pine-scented air surged through the new opening, and his whoop of celebration condensed into wisps of vapor in front of his face.

Waiting inside the remains of a laboratory complex, behind and beneath Pembleton, were the other five human survivors of Mantilis's hard landing. Three of them were privates from the *Columbia*'s MACO company: Eric Crichlow, a bug-eyed and large-nosed son of Liverpool; Thom Steinhauer, a German with chiseled features, close-shorn hair, and little sense of humor; and Niccolo Mazzetti, a handsome Sicilian with olive skin, black hair, and a reputation for never being lonely on shore leave.

Huddled between the MACOs was Kiona Thayer, the only woman in the group. She was a tall, raven-haired Québécoise with distant Sioux ancestry—and a bloody, hastily bandaged mess where her left foot once had been. Pembleton found her wound hard to look at—chiefly because he'd been the one who'd inflicted it, on orders from his MACO commander, Major Foyle.

At the front of the group was the *Columbia*'s chief engineer, a broad-backed Austrian man named Karl Graylock. He asked, "Is it safe to move outside?"

"I'm not sure yet," Pembleton said. He set the safety on his weapon and rubbed his brown hands together for warmth. "But I can tell you it's cold out there."

Graylock raised his eyebrows. "Coming from a Canadian, that means something." He glanced back at the others briefly before he added, "Maybe you and I should have a look first."

"Aye, sir," Pembleton replied. "I'll test the footing." Taking careful steps, he felt that the gravity was stronger than he was accustomed to. He made a careful climb through the icy passage he had carved one shot at a time. A few meters shy of the top, he called back to Graylock, "It's safe, Lieutenant."

The chief engineer followed Pembleton up the slope and out into the needle-sharp cold. The air was thin. As they stepped ankle-deep into the snow outside, Pembleton was awed by the sheer majesty of the vista that surrounded him: towering cliffs of black rock streaked with pristine snow; placid fjords reflecting a sky that glowed on the horizon with pastel hues of twilight; a few brilliant stars shining high overhead. It was so beautiful that he almost forgot that his fingers and toes had started going numb from the cold. "Quite a view," he said, his baritone voice reverentially hushed.

He looked sidelong at Graylock, who had turned to face in the other direction. The beefy engineer stared up the slope, his jaw slack. Pembleton did an about-face and beheld the swath that Mantilis had cut down the mountainside, through the upper half of the tree line. The devastation was impressive—in particular, the wounds that had been hewn into the mountain's rocky face—but it paled before the sight that filled the heavens above it. Ribbons of prismatic beauty wavered behind the distant peaks, against a black sky peppered with stars. The aurora was breathtaking in its intensity and range of colors.

"Wow," Pembleton muttered.

"*Ja,*" said Graylock, his voice barely a hush of breath.

Pembleton pushed his hands inside the pants pockets of his camouflage fatigues. "We should probably wait until it gets a little brighter before we bring the others out here," he said. Pointing at the fjord, he added, "Then we can head for low ground, by the shore. I'd suggest we make camp there and sort out the basics—shelter, fire, potable water, and as much food as we can stockpile. Then, if anything like spring ever comes, we can head for warmer weather near the equator."

"Why go so far, Sergeant?" Graylock asked. "Shouldn't we hold position until we figure out how to call for a rescue?"

Pressing his arms to his sides to quell his shivering, Pembleton said, "There's never going to be a rescue, sir."

Graylock folded his arms across his chest and tucked his hands under his armpits. "We can't think like that, Sergeant," he said. "We can't give up hope."

"With all respect, sir, I think we can." Pembleton tilted his head back to look up at the stars. He remembered what the Caeliar scientist Lerxst had told him just before Mantilis made planetfall. "We're almost sixty thousand light-years from home, and the year is roughly 4500 B.C." He turned his head toward Graylock and added, "This is where we're going to live the rest of our lives . . . and this is where we're going to die."

This nameless world had turned but once on its axis, and already Lerxst and his eleven fellow Caeliar felt the ebb of their vitality. "We should conserve our strength," he said to his colleague Sedín. "Reducing our mass will lessen the effects of this planet's gravity on our movement."

"Shedding some of our catoms is only a short-term solution," she replied. "Unless we find a new source of power, we'll weaken to the point where we can't recorporealize."

A pang of guilt impeded Lerxst's thoughts; he had decided to jettison the city's main power source and much of its mass into subspace, rather than risk inflicting its devastating potential on an unsuspecting world in the crash. But divorced from the gestalt, and with their city in ruins, he and the other Caeliar of Mantilis had no means of rebuilding their lost generators. Without them to power the city's quantum field, the Caeliar's catoms would swiftly exhaust their energy supply.

"At this extreme polar latitude, solar collection will not be a viable alternative until after our reserves have been depleted," Lerxst said. "Do we have enough strength to tap and develop this world's geothermal resources?"

Sedín's gestalt aura radiated doubt. "The bedrock here is deep, and we're far from any volcanic activity." She shared an image of the mountain atop which their city had been sundered. "There is a greater likelihood of mining fissionable elements."

"Not enough for our needs," Lerxst replied. "I am also concerned that their use might risk introducing toxins into this world's ecosphere." It had been aeons since he had felt so vexed. "If only we hadn't lost all of the zero-point aggregators, we might have had time to build a new prime particle generator."

Another Caeliar, an astrophysicist named Ghyllac, entered the darkened control center from behind Lerxst. He was followed by two of the human survivors, Gage Pembleton and Karl Graylock. Ghyllac said, "Visitors for you, Lerxst."

Lerxst turned to greet their guests. "Welcome, Gage and Karl," he said. "Have you reconsidered our invitation to use what's left of Mantilis as a shelter?"

"*Nein,*" Graylock said. "There is no food for us at this altitude on the slope. We need to move down to the fjord."

His statement seemed to perplex Sedín, who replied, "There is no greater variety of flora along the shoreline, Karl."

Pembleton said, "We'll try our luck at fishing."

Sedín was about to apprise the humans of the folly of such a labor, but Lerxst cut off her reply with a gentle emanation through their tragically reduced gestalt. He asked Graylock, "Then to what do we owe the privilege of this visit?"

"We need batteries," Graylock said. "Large ones for charging equipment and smaller portable ones."

Apprehension passed like an electrical charge among the dozen Caeliar inside the demolished control facility. Parceling out any of their already scant stored energy to the human survivors would only hasten the Caeliar's fade into oblivion.

"We'll share what we can, limited though it is," Lerxst said, shutting out the swell of anxiety from his colleagues.

The humans nodded. Graylock said, "As long as we're here, we might as well ask if we can salvage parts and materials from the city's debris."

Lerxst bowed and spread his arms slightly. "Be our guest."

"Thank you," Pembleton said. He lowered his voice as he looked at Graylock and asked, "Anything else, sir?"

Graylock shook his head. "No." To Lerxst, he added, "You'll let us know when the batteries are ready?"

"Of course."

"*Danke schön,*" Graylock said with a nod. He turned and walked out, and Pembleton followed at his side.

After the humans were far from the control center, Sedín asked, "Was that a wise promise to make, Lerxst?"

"I obeyed the dictates of my conscience," Lerxst said. "Nothing more."

Ghyllac interjected, "We need that energy to live."

"So do the humans," Lerxst said.

The survivors' first full day on the planet barely deserved to be called a day at all, in Pembleton's opinion. The colorless sun barely edged above the horizon, turning the arctic sky marble gray above a wide, slate-colored sea.

One by one, the rest of the group followed Pembleton from the rifle-cut tunnel, out onto the wind-blasted mountainside. Everyone was garbed in warm, silver-gray hooded ponchos provided by the Caeliar. Their backpacks were jammed with blankets, a smattering of raw materials, and battery packs of various sizes.

Lieutenant Thayer lay on a narrow stretcher. The task of carrying her was shared by the MACO privates. At any given moment, two of them were handling the stretcher while the third rested between turns of duty.

To what Pembleton had decided was the west, an advancing storm spread like a purple-black bruise. "We'd better move if we want to reach low ground in time," he told Graylock.

"In time for what?" the engineer said.

"To build shelters and get fires lit," Pembleton replied. "Before the storm hits." Surveying the sparsely wooded slope, he added, "We sure don't want to get caught in that up here."

"Good point," Graylock said. "Lead us down, Sergeant."

The group trudged wearily toward the fjord, far below. In the slightly heavy-feeling gravity, each step gave Pembleton a minor jolt of shin-splint pain.

He glanced back to confirm that everyone else was faring all right. Crichlow and Mazzetti had the stretcher steadily in hand, and Steinhauer and Graylock were chatting amiably about something in rapid-fire German.

Along the way, the one resource whose supply exceeded demand was fresh water. According to Graylock's hand scanner, the snow that blanketed the landscape was remarkably pure and undoubtedly safe to drink. "At least we won't dehydrate," he said, trying to muster some optimism.

"That just means it'll take us longer to starve to death," Pembleton replied, in no mood to have his morale boosted.

Within less than two hours, they were far enough down the slope that other nearby peaks blocked out the feeble sunlight. Crossing into the steel-blue shadows, Pembleton felt the temperature plummet several degrees. His every exhalation filled the air ahead of him with ephemeral plumes of vapor.

It was late in the day and quickly growing dark by the time they reached the water's edge. "Steinhauer, help Graylock set up by those big rocks, up on that rise," Pembleton said. "It'll give us a break from the wind and keep us dry when the runoff comes down the mountain. Mazzetti, you and I will dig a latrine on the other side. Crichlow, take your rifle and a hand scanner. Hunt for any kind of small animal—bird, fish, mammal, I don't care. Anything edible."

"Right, Sarge," Crichlow said. He stripped off his backpack, tucked a hand scanner into a leg pocket of his fatigue pants, grabbed his rifle, and stole away into the sparse brush.

By the time Graylock and the MACOs had finished building the group's shelter—a tenuous structure of hastily welded scrap-metal supports overlaid by more of the Caeliar's wonder fabric—the sky was pitch dark. A vicious wind howled like a demon's choir between the cliffs that bordered the fjord, and the air was heavy with the scent of rain.

A snapping of twigs and crunching steps on snow turned Pembleton's head, and he aimed his rifle as a precaution. He lowered it when he recognized Crichlow, who emerged from the brush looking tattered, scratched, and dejected.

"Nothing out there?" Pembleton asked.

"Oh, they're out there," Crichlow said. The young private met Pembleton's disappointed gaze and shook his head. "But the little buggers are so spry, I can't get a bead on 'em."

Pembleton fell into step beside Crichlow as they walked toward the shelter. "Don't worry about it," he said. "Tomorrow, switch to snares. See how that goes."

"Right, Sarge," Crichlow said. "Will do."

They pushed through the front flaps that served as a door for the shelter. The ground had been covered with large squares of the Caeliar fabric, except for a circle in the middle, where large stones had been piled and heated to a bright red glow that filled the enclosure with smokeless warmth.

"Tighten your belts, folks," Pembleton said. "Looks like bark soup for dinner." Groans of dismay were his reward for honesty. "Look on the bright side," he continued. "After we enjoy our tasty broth, you'll all get to sleep, because I'll take the first watch, till 2100. Mazzetti, second watch, till 0100. Steinhauer, third watch, to 0500. Crichlow, last watch. We'll rotate the schedule nightly."

Mazzetti asked, "Can't we just set a hand scanner for proximity detection?"

"We're trying to save its power cell for things like finding food and figuring out what's toxic," said Graylock.

"Exactly," Pembleton said. "And Mazzetti? For asking that, you just volunteered for bark-collection detail."

The bark soup was hot but also bitter, like a raw acorn. Despite having drained his canteen twice in the hour after dinner and spitting furiously, Pembleton still hadn't expunged the taste from his mouth. *Fortunately, I have the rain to keep my mind off it,* he brooded.

Driven by brutally cold gales, a freezing spray slashed through the night and found every gap in Pembleton's salvaged-fabric poncho. His phase rifle was slung across his back, and his hands were tucked inside his camouflage fatigue jacket and under his armpits for warmth.

After Mazzetti had gone out for bark, Graylock had run a scan for any kind of edible plants near the shelter. Nothing had registered on the hand scanner. No berries, fruits, or nuts. Not even simple grasses. Just poisonous fungi and lichens.

The weather's only going to get worse, he predicted. *The nights'll get longer, and the cold'll get deeper.* He looked at the mediocre shelter that he and the others now depended on, and he frowned. *If that thing survives a winter in this place, it'll be a miracle.*

A short time before the end of his watch, the downpour was borne away on the shoulders of a biting wind. In minutes, the precipitation abated to a drizzle, and then it stopped. The air cleared, and as a parade of fast-moving clouds transited the sky, he saw the hypnotic radiance of the aurora behind the peaks.

Then something beneath it, on the slope of the mountain, caught his attention. Pale glows of movement.

He fished his binoculars from his fatigues and trained them on the light sources high above his position. Magnified, the details of the scene became clearly visible. The Caeliar had come out from their buried, broken metropolis and were gathering atop a blackened crag that once had been part of its foundation.

Pembleton wondered what they were up to, so he increased the magnification of the binoculars to its maximum setting and looked again. Then he realized they were gazing back at him.

They looked different—sickly. There was a spectral quality to them, an otherworldly radiance and a lack of opacity.

He lowered the binoculars and thought of the millions of Caeliar who had willingly sacrificed themselves to send Mantilis through the subspace passageway, and through time, to this barren place; their city had become a necropolis.

Lifting the binoculars again, he saw the Caeliar for the ghosts that they'd become, and it filled him with despair.

I guess we're not the only ones dying here.

2381

3

"Hail them again, Commander," Captain Picard said to Miranda Kadohata, the *Enterprise*'s third-in-command and senior operations officer.

Her lean, attractive Eurasian countenance hardened with frustration as she worked at her console. "Still no response, sir," she said, her accent redolent of a Londoner's inflections.

Medical and security personnel worked with quiet efficiency around and behind Picard, clearing away the evidence of the ship's recent pitched battle with Hirogen boarders, two of whom lay dead in the middle of the *Enterprise*'s bridge. A thin haze of smoke still lingered along the overhead, and its sharp odor masked the stench of spilled blood on the deck.

On the main viewer, framed by streaks of warp-distorted starlight, was the *Vesta*-class explorer vessel *U.S.S. Aventine*. Under the command of Captain Ezri Dax, it was racing at its best possible warp speed toward Earth. They were in futile pursuit of a Borg armada that had, only hours earlier, slipped through a previously unknown—and since collapsed—subspace passage from the Delta Quadrant. Picard feared that at any moment Captain Dax's crew would activate their ship's prototype quantum slipstream drive and rush headlong into a suicidal confrontation.

Lieutenant Jasminder Choudhury, the *Enterprise*'s chief of security, directed four medical technicians entering from the main turbolift to the Hirogen's corpses. "Get those into stasis," she said. "We'll want them for analysis later."

"Aye, sir," said one of the technicians, and the quartet set to work bagging the enormous armored bodies.

While they worked, another turbolift arrived at the bridge, and four engineers stepped out. They carried tight, tubular bundles that unrolled to reveal long sheets covered with tools tucked into fabric loops and magnetically sealed pockets. In moments, the engineers all were at work, repairing ruptured duty consoles and bulkhead-mounted companels.

Commander Worf finished a hushed conference with junior tactical officer Ensign Aneta Šmrhová and returned to the command chairs to take his seat next to Picard's. Speaking at a discreet volume, he said, "Sensor reports confirmed, Captain. There are more than seven thousand Borg cubes deployed into Federation, Klingon, and Romulan territory. Several targets have already been engaged."

"Thank you, Number One," Picard said, though he was anything but grateful for the update. He raised his voice and asked the flight controller, "Mister Weinrib, time to intercept?"

"Actually, sir, the *Aventine*'s lead is increasing,"

Weinrib said. "They're now point-eight-five past our top rated speed."

Picard admired the sleek lines of the *Aventine* as it slipped farther away from the *Enterprise*. He was almost ready to abandon hope of reasoning with Dax when Kadohata swiveled her chair around from ops to report, "*Aventine* is responding, sir."

"On-screen," Picard said.

Captain Dax's face appeared on the main viewer. *"Changed your mind about joining us, Captain?"*

"Far from it," Picard said, rising from his chair and walking forward. "I urge you to reconsider this rash action."

The young, dark-haired Trill woman seethed. *"The Federation's under attack,"* she said. *"We have to defend it."*

"We will," Picard said. "But not like this. Sacrificing your ship and your crew in this manner serves no purpose. Going into battle against great odds can be brave or noble—but going into battle without a plan is worse than futile, it's wasteful."

She heaved an angry sigh, and he sensed her frustration, her desire to do anything other than stand and wait. *"So, what do you propose we do?"*

"We'll contact Starfleet Command and request new orders," he said. "They may not even be aware that our ships are still in service after the loss of the expeditionary force."

A smirk tugged at one corner of Dax's mouth. *"Contact Starfleet Command? No offense, Captain, but that's not exactly the answer I expected, given your reputation."*

"I'll admit that when my orders have contradicted

common sense, morality, or the law, I have followed my conscience," Picard said. "But at the moment, Captain, we haven't any orders at all—and I think we at least ought to see if Starfleet knows where it needs us before we commit ourselves to a potentially fatal course."

Dax relaxed her shoulders. *"I suppose it can't hurt to ask,"* she said.

"Then might I suggest we drop out of warp?" Picard said. "At least until such time as we know where we ought to go?"

She narrowed her gaze for a moment, and then she nodded to someone off-screen. *"We're returning to impulse,"* she said. *"Can you patch me in when you're ready to talk to Starfleet?"*

"Of course," Picard said. *"Enterprise* out." The screen switched back to the exterior view of the receding *Aventine.*

Picard nodded to Worf, who said to Weinrib, "Match their speed and heading." The conn officer nodded his confirmation.

On the viewscreen, the streaks of light shrank back to gleaming points as the *Aventine* and the *Enterprise* returned to normal maneuvering speeds.

Another guarded victory for common sense, Picard mused. "Commander Kadohata, raise Starfleet Command on any secure channel, priority one."

"Aye, sir," Kadohata replied.

He turned toward his ready room. "I'll take it in my—" He stopped in midstep and midsentence as he saw the burned and smoke-scarred interior of his office, which had been set ablaze during the assault by the Hirogen hunting pack. Picard frowned. The sight of his flame-scoured sanctum resurrected unpleasant memories he'd hoped were long buried.

Time is the fire in which we burn.

Looking back at Kadohata, he said, "I'll take it in the observation lounge, Commander." He walked to the aft starboard portal as he added, "Commander Worf, you have the bridge."

4

"Battle stations!" roared Captain Krogan. The bridge lights snapped to full brightness as the *I.K.S. veScharg'a* dropped to impulse one million *qell'qams* from the Klingon world Morska. Following close behind the *veScharg'a* was its battle partner, the *Qang*-class heavy cruiser *Sturka*.

A firestorm of disruptor blasts raged up from the planet's surface and hammered the two Borg cubes in orbit. The impacts seemed to have no effect on the cubes except to silhouette them and give them blinding crimson halos. Then the Borg returned fire and wrought blazing emerald scars across the planet's surface.

Krogan's first officer, Falgar, bellowed, "Raise shields! Arm weapons! Helm, set attack pattern *ya'DIchqa*."

"Ten seconds to Borg firing range," answered the helmsman.

"All reserve power to shields," Falgar ordered.

Time to find out if Starfleet's secret torpedoes work for us, Krogan brooded, watching the Borg cubes grow larger on his viewscreen. His foes would have several seconds of advantage over his *Vor'cha*-class attack cruiser, whose effective firing range was a few hundred thousand *qell'qams* shorter than that of the Borg cubes. The *veScharg'a*'s goal was to survive the Borg's initial barrage and get close enough to target the cubes with the transphasic torpedo, which Admiral Jellico of Starfleet had just ordered to be distributed to ships of the Klingon Defense Force.

"The Borg are firing," Falgar said, sounding perfectly calm. Then explosions shook the battle cruiser with the ferocity of *Fek'lhr* himself. The bright battle lights flickered. Fire and sparks erupted from aft duty stations, and the stink of burnt hair assaulted Krogan's nostrils.

Qonqar, the tactical officer, shouted over the clamor, "Weapons locked!"

Krogan slammed a fist on the arm of his chair as he pointed at the Borg cubes on the screen. "Fire!"

A trio of blue bolts shot forth, spiraling erratically through the Borg's defensive batteries. As they closed on target, Falgar called out, "Holm! Break to starboard! Qonqar, all power to port shields!"

More blasts shook the *veScharg'a*. Krogan grinned as he watched the viewer and saw the aft-angle view of the torpedoes hitting home and blasting one Borg cube to pieces in a sapphire flash. As the blue fire cloud dissipated into the vacuum of space, another cerulean blast filled the starscape behind it, as the second Borg cube was annihilated.

The bridge officers cheered and roared at their victory. Krogan permitted himself a satisfied smirk and a nod of his head. *It is a good day to die . . . for my enemies.*

The warriors' revels were ended by the shrilling of an incoming subspace message. Communications officer Valk covered his in-ear transceiver for a moment, then looked up at Krogan. "Signal from General Klag."

"On-screen," Krogan said, lifting his chin to project pride and confidence to his commanding officer.

The visage of General Klag, commander of the Fifth Fleet, filled the viewscreen. *"Report,"* said the general, who was now also hailed as a Hero of the Empire.

"Our foes are vanquished," Krogan said.

"Excellent," Klag said. *"Your vessel is needed at a new battle. What is your status?"*

Krogan replied, "Minor damage but still battle-ready."

Klag nodded, and then he asked, *"What of the Sturka?"*

Qonqar routed an after-action report from the *Sturka* to Krogan's command monitor. "Captain K'Draq reports they've taken heavy damage," Krogan said, reviewing the details.

The general's brow creased beneath his scowl. *"We need every ship. Can they continue?"*

"Doubtful," Krogan said. "They've lost warp drive."

"Leave them, then," Klag said. *"Rendezvous with the fleet in three hours, at the coordinates I'm sending you now."*

At a glance, Krogan knew that the meeting point lay on a direct line between the Azure Nebula, source of the Borg scourge, and the Klingon homeworld. "The Borg are coming for Qo'noS, then," he said.

"If they do, they come to die," Klag said with an

eager grin. *"Get under way now. That is an order. Klag out."*

The screen returned to the wounded orb of Morska and the smoldering, battered hull of the *Sturka*, adrift in space. Krogan relayed the rendezvous coordinates to the helmsman's console. "Set a new course," he said. "Maximum warp. Go." Stars swept across the screen and then distorted into streaks as the *veScharg'a* jumped to warp.

Though Krogan would never say so—not to his crew, to his family, or to his superiors—he knew that it had been sheer luck that had preserved his ship even as the *Sturka* had fallen to the Borg. And if there was one truth that every warrior knew, it was that no one's luck lasted forever.

Chancellor Martok stepped off the transporter padd and was glad to be back aboard his flagship, the *I.K.S. Sword of Kahless*. General Goluk, a high-ranking member of the Order of the *Bat'leth* and the commander of Martok's venerated Ninth Fleet, gave him a nod of greeting. *"Qapla', Chancellor."*

In his cutting growl of a voice, Martok replied, *"Qapla',* General. Report." He marched out of the transporter room, in a hurry to reach the bridge.

The gray-bearded general followed him and said, "Khitomer and Beta Thoridor have fallen. Beta Lankal and the Mempa system are under attack, as are several dozen smaller colonies."

"And Morska?"

"Defended by the *Sturka* and the *veScharg'a,*" Goluk said. "The Borg are also laying siege to Rura Penthe."

"Who cares about Rura Penthe?" Martok said. "Is Klag gathering his fleet?"

"Yes, my lord," Goluk said, following Martok up a steep crew ladder to the command deck. "Our forces will assemble in three hours and engage the Borg in four."

Martok bounded up from the ladder and strode down the passageway toward the bridge. Despite the absence of his left eye and his limited depth perception, Martok knew the steps and corners of his ship so well that he could navigate its corridors blind. "Has there been any word from our forces at the nebula?"

"Not yet," Goluk said. He remained close behind Martok's shoulder as they walked.

The two grizzled warriors arrived on the bridge. The command center of the *Sword of Kahless* was packed with warriors, all of them intently busy preparing for rapid deployment. Deep, muted voices mixed with the comm chatter and the ambient hum of the ship's power-distribution systems. On the viewer, dozens of *Vor'cha*-class and *K'vort*-class cruisers moved in tight formations, turning in unison like flocks of birds.

Captain G'mtor, a seasoned officer who proudly bore a deep facial scar from his right temple to his chin, approached the chancellor and the general. "New reports from Federation and Romulan space, Chancellor," G'mtor said. "Battles have begun at Nequencia Alpha, Xarantine, and Jouret. The Borg armada is destroying all stray vessels it encounters."

"We'll find strength in numbers, then," Martok said. He took his place in the command chair. "How many ships are ready to follow us into battle, Captain?"

"One hundred seventeen are gathered here at Qo'noS," G'mtor said. "Another three hundred sixty-one will meet us at the rendezvous coordinates."

General Goluk asked, "And how many Borg vessels have we detected inbound?"

"Four hundred ninety-two," G'mtor said. He flashed a sharp-toothed grin. "So already we enjoy an advantage."

Immediately, Martok could tell that Goluk was performing the arithmetic in his head. Then the general inquired of G'mtor, "How did you arrive at that conclusion, Captain?"

Martok loosed a short roar of laughter and answered for G'mtor, "Because we are *Klingons*!" Encouraging roars came from every warrior on the bridge. These men were sharp and ready for battle, and it filled Martok with pride to be among them. He stood and said to G'mtor, "Open a channel, all ships."

G'mtor nodded to another officer, who carried out the order with haste and nodded in reply. "Channel open," G'mtor said.

In a breath, Martok gathered himself and declared, "Warriors of the Empire! A great hour is upon us, a foe to test our mettle. The Borg have come not to plunder us but to destroy us—to leave our empire in flames, our bodies broken, our spirits disgraced at the gates of *Gre'thor*.

"This is a mistake they will not live to regret. We will meet their armada with our own and show them what it means to fight with honor. We shall whip the Borg from our space and crush them. Our empire has risen by the sword, and one day it might be felled by it. But if such a fate awaits us, let us fall to warriors— not to these *petaQpu'*.

"Today is a good day to die, for a warrior—but not for a way of life. The Klingon Empire *will not fall* today." He slammed his fist and forearm to his chest. "Fight well, and die with honor, sons and daughters of Qo'noS! *Qapla'*!"

A roaring *"Qapla'!"* came back to Martok from his bridge crew, who broke without preamble into a throaty and spirited rendition of "Soldiers of the Empire." Their proud voices echoed off the bulkheads and rang through the corridors, where new choruses of singers picked up the tune and carried it on.

General Goluk nodded to the communications officer, who closed the channel as the singing continued. Martok settled into the command chair, which sat on a dais above the rest of the bridge. The general placed himself at Martok's right side. Over the hearty song, he said, "All ships ready to deploy, my lord."

"Break orbit," Martok said. "As soon as the fleet is in formation behind us, coordinate our jump to maximum warp."

Goluk let Captain G'mtor handle the details of marshaling the fleet into warp speed. Martok, meanwhile, savored all the sensations of shipboard life: the gruff singing voices, the warm aromas from the galley several decks below, the rumbling of the impulse engines pushing the ship out of orbit, the chimelike echo of boots stamping across duranium gratings.

This was not the war he would have chosen, but it felt good to be leading his people into battle, all of them united under one banner. The Kinshaya and the Elabrej had not been enough to give the far-flung worlds of the Empire common cause. But the Borg were a menace without equal in known space. The Collective's attack had galvanized the noble families and the common people, and it had quelled the resurgent internecine struggles of the High Council.

Barked commands across the bridge were followed by the flash of warp-distorted starlight across the main viewscreen.

When this war is over, Martok ruminated, *the Empire will be stronger than it's ever been . . . or it will lie in ashes.*

5

———◆———

Starfleet's reports to the Palais de la Concorde grew worse with each passing hour, and President Nanietta Bacco had tired of reading them. She winced as her intercom buzzed, and her elderly Vulcan executive assistant, Sivak, announced, *"Admiral Akaar is here to deliver your midday briefing, Madam President."* Bacco was about to concoct an excuse to send the admiral away when Sivak added, *"Ms. Piñiero and Seven of Nine are with him."*

She sighed. "Send them in."

Bacco got up from her chair and turned around to look out the panoramic floor-to-ceiling window. Outside, the Tour Eiffel gleamed in the afternoon sunlight above the sprawl of Paris. Wispy clouds raced low along the horizon in the distance.

She pressed a padd on her desk to tint the window against the glare. As the electrochemical shade descended between her and the City of Light, the moment felt to Bacco as if it might be a tragically prophetic omen of the hours to come.

One of the doors behind her opened. It took all of her resolve to turn back and face her visitors, who she knew came bearing bad tidings. Leading them in was Bacco's chief of staff, Esperanza Piñiero, whose black hair and olive complexion contrasted with those of the two people who were following her.

Starfleet's liaison to the Federation president, Fleet Admiral Leonard James Akaar, was a tall, barrel-chested, and broad-shouldered man of Capellan birth. His pale gray hair fell in long natural waves on either side of his weathered face.

Beside him was Seven of Nine. She was fair-skinned and blond. Her striking good looks were marred by the presence of residual grafts of silvery gray metallic Borg technology on her left hand and eyebrow.

Seven, whose name had been Annika Hansen before her early childhood assimilation by the Borg, had been liberated from the Collective by the crew of the *Starship Voyager* during their long journey home from the Delta Quadrant. Now she was Bacco's top security adviser on all matters concerning the Borg.

"Good afternoon, Madam President," Akaar said, resembling a talking bronze statue in the honeyed light of her shaded window.

"Admiral," Bacco said with a polite nod. She offered one as well to her security adviser. "Seven."

Piñiero feigned offense. "No greeting for me?"

"I see you all day, every day," Bacco grumped.

Before Piñiero could continue their verbal volley, Admiral Akaar interrupted, "Madam President, we have important news."

"None of it good, I'm sure," Bacco said, easing herself back into her chair. She made a rolling motion with her hand. "Continue, Admiral."

A despairing frown darkened his expression. "The

Borg are moving even faster than we could have imagined," he said.

Seven added, "They likely assimilated new propulsion technologies while replenishing their strength."

Bacco asked, "How fast are they moving, Admiral?"

"We have confirmed attacks on Yridia, Hyralan, and Celes," he said. "We project the Borg will siege Regulus in two hours, Deneva in three, Qo'noS in five. At this rate, they are only nine hours from Vulcan and Andor and twelve hours from Earth. By tomorrow, they will be able to hit Trill, Betazed, Bajor, and dozens of other worlds. Most of our simulations suggest the collapse of the Federation in ten days, and the fall of most of our neighbors in local space within a month."

Bacco let her head fall forward into her hands. "Dear God."

Piñiero pushed her fingers through her hair, back over her scalp. "We have to evacuate those worlds," she said. "Now."

"Actually, Madam President," Akaar interjected, "that will not be feasible. It would entail trying to move tens of billions of people in a matter of hours."

Seven added, "It would be a futile effort. Any ships that fled those worlds would be hunted down by the Borg."

The ex-drone's calm certainty only inflamed Piñiero's anger. "So? Should we just tell our people to sit quietly and wait for the end to come? What kind of plan is that?"

Akaar's shoulders slumped. "I agree in principle, Ms. Piñiero. But we no longer have enough ships at our disposal for an evacuation effort. All civilian ships that are able to flee have already done so, and all armed vessels and their crews have been pressed into service for core-systems defense."

Bacco lifted her head and said to Akaar, "How many lives have we lost so far, Admiral?"

"Ma'am?"

"How many civilian lives, Admiral?" She hardened her anger to hold her despair at bay. "Do we even know?"

The admiral looked ashamed. "We have estimates."

"How many?"

He asked, "Since the first Borg attack?"

"Yes," Bacco said. "Since the beginning."

"Including non-Federation worlds . . . approximately thirty billion."

It was too vast a number for Bacco to grasp. Thirty billion was too large even to be a statistic; it was an abstraction of death writ on a cosmic scale. "Can Starfleet muster enough ships to intercept the Borg armada?"

"It is not that simple, Madam President," Akaar said. "There are no isolated thrusts of enemy forces to intercept. The Borg have dispersed on thousands of vectors across known space. We had organized Starfleet's defenses to shield the core systems. Unfortunately, the Borg have committed enough ships to attack all our worlds at once." He cast his eyes downward. "I regret to say we have no defensive plan for that scenario."

Fixing her weary glare on Seven, Bacco said, "Care to offer any strategic or tactical advice?"

"Our options are limited," Seven said. "I have been unable to help Starfleet pinpoint which cube is carrying the Borg Queen, which limits our ability to launch a surgical counterstrike. Fortunately, none of the ships in the Borg armada has displayed any of the absorptive properties of the giant cube we faced last year. That suggests the *Enterprise*'s mission to stop the assimilated vessel *Einstein* was a success."

Piñiero threw a sour look at Seven. "Good thing," she said. "Otherwise, the Borg might have presented a threat." The snide remark drew a stare of cold fire from Seven.

Bacco frowned at Akaar. "Admiral, do you have any news to report *besides* the end of the Federation as we know it?"

"Yes, Madam President," he replied. "We have re-established contact with the *Enterprise* and the *Aventine*. They were in the Delta Quadrant on a recon mission when the Borg armada attacked. They've returned and report that all subspace passages have been collapsed. Admiral Jellico is cutting them new orders now."

At that news, Bacco leaned forward. "Can you pass along a message for me to Captain Picard?"

"Of course, Madam President."

"Tell him that if he has *any* idea how to stop the Borg, no matter what he has to do, he has my unqualified authority to do it. If he has to toss Starfleet regulations and Federation law out an airlock, so be it. If we're still here when the dust settles, he can count on full pardons for himself and his crew, no questions asked. The same goes for anyone working with him. Is that clear, Admiral?"

Akaar nodded once. "Exceptionally clear, Madam President."

"Then let's all hope Picard has one more miracle up his sleeve. Because God knows we need it."

6

"The truth, Captains, is that Starfleet no longer has a plan."

Picard didn't remember Edward Jellico looking so old. In the scant months since Jellico had ascended to Starfleet's top flag office, he seemed to have aged a decade. His already white hair had thinned, and the lines in his face had deepened into gorges carved by the never-ending anxieties of command. More alarming to Picard was that he sympathized with how he imagined Jellico must feel. Standing in the ready room of a captain less than half his years, Picard felt like a relic of a bygone age.

Captain Dax replied, "Admiral, are you saying that Starfleet has no new orders for us?"

"Not unless one of you has a bright idea," Jellico said.

The two captains traded apprehensive looks across Dax's desk. Picard looked back at Jellico's visage on the monitor and said, "We're still weighing our options."

Dax interjected, "Should we set a course for Earth, sir?"

Jellico shook his head. *"You won't make it in time. You're four days away. The Borg'll be here in twelve hours."*

"Actually, sir," Dax said, "my chief engineer tells me she can bring our prototype slipstream drive online within a few hours. There's a chance we could beat the Borg to Earth."

Holding up one hand, Jellico replied, *"One more ship won't turn the tide, Captain. We're past that now."*

Picard tried to mask his profound frustration, but hints of it slipped into his tone all the same. "Admiral, certainly Starfleet hasn't conceded the war already?"

"Of course not, Jean-Luc. We've distributed the schematics for the transphasic torpedo to all ships and starbases, and we've given it to the Klingon Defense Force." Dax glanced nervously at Picard as Jellico continued, *"It might be too little too late, but we're not going down without a fight."*

"Admiral," Dax said, "isn't it dangerous to send those schematics via subspace with so many Borg ships in the region? What if they've intercepted and decoded them?"

A frown thinned Jellico's lips almost to the point of making them vanish.

"It was a calculated risk," he confessed. *"It's not what I wanted to do or the way I wanted to do it . . . but at this point, not doing it is tantamount to surrender. I gave the order to override Admiral Nechayev's security directive. If it turns out to be the wrong call, there's no one to blame but me."*

Hearing such humility from Jellico surprised

Picard. He didn't know whether it was because Jellico, having reached the top of the Starfleet career ladder, had finally relaxed or because crisis brought out the most human facets of his persona.

"Admiral," he said, "with your permission, I'd like to take the *Enterprise* and the *Aventine* back into the nebula to search for survivors from the expeditionary group. We've confirmed that half of *Voyager*'s crew is still alive; there may be others."

Jellico nodded. *"By all means, Captain. Proceed at your discretion. But make certain you have an exit strategy."*

Again, the admiral's pessimistic turn of phrase captured Picard's attention. "An exit strategy?"

"Jean-Luc, if Earth falls . . ." Jellico choked on his words for a moment, and then he continued, *"If Earth falls, the war's pretty much over. The fighting might go on for a few more weeks, but the Federation as we know it will be gone. If it comes to that, take your ship and anyone you can carry, and try to get to safety. Don't launch some quixotic mission to liberate the Federation, because there'll be nothing left. Just save your ship and your crew."* A melancholy gloom settled in his eyes. *"Don't die for a lost cause, Jean-Luc."*

Then he blinked away the sentiment and added, *"Wish us luck, Captains. Godspeed to you both. Starfleet Command out."*

The Federation emblem replaced Jellico's face on the desktop monitor. Dax deactivated the screen and sighed. "Nothing like a pep talk from headquarters to boost morale." She stood and turned to her replicator. "I'm having a *raktajino*. Can I get you something?"

"Tea, Earl Grey, hot," Picard said.

She turned to the replicator and said, "*Raktajino,* hot and sweet, and an Earl Grey tea, hot." The drinks formed in a whorl of golden light and white noise. When the machine had finished, she took the drinks from the nook and handed the tea to Picard.

He took a sip and savored the bitter flavor. "Thank you."

"You're welcome," she said, easing back into her chair and taking a sip of her caffeinated Klingon beverage. "Sorry to hear about your ready room."

"Not as sorry as I am," Picard said. He enjoyed another sip of his tea, then added, "We should set course back to the nebula as soon as possible."

Dax said, "All right, but I don't think we're going to find many survivors beyond the *Voyager* crew."

"Perhaps not," Picard murmured, even as he was distracted by an awareness of something new—something different—shining in his thoughts like a beacon in the darkness of mere being. "But we need to get under way, soon. There's something there, and I need to know what it is."

Slowly shaking her head, Dax replied, "If you say so. I just hate feeling like we're running for cover when everyone else is fighting for their lives."

"Running for cover?" Picard said.

She called up a short-range starmap overlaid with tactical data about the Borg armada's deployment into the surrounding sectors. Pointing at the Azure Nebula, Dax said, "It's the eye of the storm, Jean-Luc. All Borg ships are moving away from it. It's the safest spot in known space."

He studied the star chart and nodded. "Indeed.

Which makes it the ideal location from which to plan our next move."

"I wasn't aware that we *had* a next move," Dax said.

The sense that something was drawing him back to the nebula intensified. "We don't—at least, not yet. But I have a feeling that's about to change."

7

———

Walking through darkened corridors, Riker felt like a shade haunting his own ship. Two hours after returning to Federation space, most of *Titan* was still without main power. The bridge and the main computer were back online, but little else was.

He turned a corner into a small stampede of pressure-suited bodies and was forced to step clear of the team of damage-control engineers, who were quick-timing it to their next crisis du jour. All the way down from the bridge, from deck to deck and from one emergency ladder to another, Riker had seen similar frantic scrambles of activity by the ship's engineers.

They're earning their pay today, he mused.

"Ra-Havreii to Captain Riker," said the chief engineer, the richness of his voice flattened by being filtered through Riker's combadge.

Riker stepped to the side of the passage and stopped. "Good to hear your voice. Are all comms back up?"

"No, sir," Ra-Havreii replied. *"I'm talking to you from the shuttlecraft* Gillespie. *We're currently rout-*

ing all shipboard comms through the shuttles' transceivers."

"Good thinking," Riker said. "Can we use them to get a signal to Starfleet Command?"

Ra-Havreii said, *"Not yet, but soon. I'm interplexing their comm systems now to boost their range. I expect to have it ready in a few minutes. But that's not why I hailed you, sir."*

Stepping down a short, dead-end side passage for a bit of additional privacy, Riker said, "What's on your mind?"

"We have some fairly systemic damage in a number of critical areas, Captain," Ra-Havreii said. *"Without main power, we can't replicate new parts—but without replacement parts, we can't restore main power. So I need your permission to acquire the necessary components, sir."*

It took Riker a moment to pierce Ra-Havreii's unusually subtle wording. "You want to salvage from the wrecked ships in the nebula," he said, nodding with grim understanding.

"Aye, sir. I know it must seem a bit ghoulish, but we need those parts. We've opened the shuttlebay doors using manual controls, and the Armstrong, *the* Holliday, *and the* Ellington *are ready to begin recovery ops—on your order, sir."*

As distasteful as Riker felt it would be to plunder a fresh starship graveyard, he knew that the chief engineer was right. It was an absolute necessity. "Proceed, Commander. Do what you have to do, and keep me posted."

"Aye, sir. Ra-Havreii out." A barely audible click signaled the closing of the comm channel.

Riker walked out of the dead end and back to the corridor, turned right, and continued toward his destination.

The two female security guards posted outside the door watched Riker as he approached. To the left of the door was Senior Petty Officer Antillea, a Gnalish Fejjimaera. Aside from resembling a human-sized bipedal iguana, her most noticeable physical characteristic was the prominent fin on the top of her scaly, olive-hued head.

On the other side of the door was Lieutenant Pava Ek'Noor sh'Aqabaa, a statuesque and breathtaking Andorian *shen* who preferred to let her flowing white hair frame her blue face. The only parts of her that looked remotely fragile were her antennae, but Riker pitied the person who dared try to lay a finger on them without permission.

He looked to sh'Aqabaa as he arrived at the door. "Any trouble, Lieutenant?"

"None, sir," sh'Aqabaa said.

Riker nodded. "Good. I'm going in to talk to her." He keyed in a security code to unlock the door to the guest quarters. The portal slid open ahead of him, and he walked in.

Once he was a few meters inside the compartment, the door hushed closed behind him, and he heard the soft confirmation tone of it returning to its locked state. He remained still for a moment while his eyes adjusted to the dim illumination into which he'd stepped. Noting the cyanochrome hues that surrounded him, he realized that all of the artificial lighting was off. The only light came from the glow of the Azure Nebula outside the row of rounded-corner windows that sloped along one side of the living area. Silhouetted in front of them was *Titan*'s latest guest, Erika Hernandez.

She didn't look in his direction as she said with serene courtesy, "Don't bother to knock, Captain. Come right in."

He felt abashed at his faux pas and slightly wary of this peculiar stranger who had appeared without warning on his bridge. True, she had done him and his crew a great favor, but it still felt too soon to trust her. Feigning a casual demeanor, he sidled over to her in front of the windows. "Now that my crew is able to work on repairs, I thought it was time we talked."

"I figured as much," Hernandez said.

Outside the windows, in the middle distance, shuttlecraft from *Titan* maneuvered through the roiling cobalt mists and snared large hunks of starship debris in tractor beams. "We've been forced to scavenge, I'm afraid," Riker said.

"Don't feel you need to apologize," Hernandez said. "Out there, it's just wreckage. In here, it's survival. That's just the way it is. If this had happened to my ship, I'd have done the same thing.'"

Riker cleared his throat. "Since you've brought it up, let's talk about your ship," he said. Gesturing toward the sofa beneath the window, he asked, "Can we sit down?"

"Of course," she said. She settled in at one end of the couch, and Riker took a seat at the other end. She asked, "What do you want to know?"

"You said your ship was the *Columbia*," Riker said. "You were talking about the twenty-second-century Earth starship?"

Hernandez nodded. "Yes, the NX-02."

"That ship went missing more than two hundred years ago," Riker replied. "And according to our records, its captain was in her forties. You look a bit young for the part."

The youthful woman flashed a bright, wide grin. "I've had some work done," she said with a playful lift of her eyebrows.

"Apparently," Riker said, returning her smile with one of his own. "Starfleet also discovered the wreck of the *Columbia* in the Gamma Quadrant, more than seventy thousand light-years from here and even farther from where we found you."

She sighed. "Yes, I know. When Erigol's star went supernova and created this nebula in 2168, the Caeliar took off in their city-ships. Most of them didn't make it. I was in the capital, which did escape, but it wound up a few hundred years in the past. My ship stayed in the present and entered another passage; it got tossed across the galaxy, and my crew was probably incinerated by the radiation inside the subspace tunnel."

Riker was about to ask another question when she cut him off. "Why the third degree, Captain? Can't you just take a sample of my DNA and use that to see if I am who I say I am?"

"I did," he confessed. "My chief nurse recovered traces of your DNA from the bridge consoles you touched and from some of your hairs we found on the deck. I already know you're the real Erika Hernandez—and the way you turned Lieutenant Rriarr's phaser into dust when you came aboard tells me you're also something more. What I want is to know more about your history, so I can understand why you helped us escape."

Her disarming smile returned. "You could have just asked."

"What fun would that be?"

They laughed for a few seconds, and then Hernandez looked away and became serious. "You really want to know why I helped you? The truth is, there's no one reason. I've wanted to get away from the Caeliar pretty much from the first moment they told me I couldn't leave. I also spent the last several hundred years feeling I let down all the people I was supposed to protect. The convoy the Romulans ambushed . . . my crew . . . Earth . . . my friends in exile." Hernandez became quietly introspective for several seconds, and Riker let her collect her thoughts.

She continued, "Anyway, when the Caeliar took your people on the planet prisoner, it was like seeing it happen to myself all over again. Then I saw those black cubes destroy your fleet, and I remembered how much I wanted to be there for Earth when the Romulans attacked. I figured you'd feel the same way about this." She looked up at him, and her expression conveyed a deep sadness. "I'm so sorry I couldn't save your landing party. Especially your wife. But there was no other way."

"It wasn't your fault," he said, and he meant it. "I made the decision. You have nothing to apologize for." He hesitated to ask what he really wanted to know, but his need was too great to be denied. "Can you just tell me . . . is Deanna all right?"

"She was pretending to be, but I noticed signs

that she was in pain—and when I listened in on the Caeliar, I heard them say she was in some kind of medical distress."

Riker wrapped his left hand over his fist and clamped down, focusing his thoughts on remaining calm. Hernandez cast her eyes toward the floor, away from his obvious emotional turmoil. She said, "I'm sorry the news isn't better."

"I'm all right," he said, and he pressed his fist over his mouth for a second. It was an effort to lower and unclench his hand. "One more question: If you were able to open a passage and bring us here, why couldn't you take us back to Earth?"

"Because I didn't create the passage we traveled through," she said. "I only widened it, by amplifying the power to the machine that generated it. If I had tried to open a new passageway, the Caeliar would have detected it and shut it down. As it was, the gestalt was about to collapse the tunnel that pointed here. So it really was this or nothing."

"Good enough," Riker said. He stood. "Thank you for your patience, Captain."

"My pleasure," she said. He started to leave but turned back as she asked, "Now that you're home, what's your plan?"

He flashed a rueful smile. "I plan to call for help."

Jean-Luc Picard stepped back onto the bridge of the *Enterprise,* expecting an update on the ship's repairs. Instead, Worf rose from the command chair and said, "Captain, we are being hailed."

"By the *Aventine*?" Picard wondered what could

have happened in the minutes since he had left Captain Dax's ship.

Surrendering the center seat to Picard, Worf replied with an uncommon gleam, "No, sir, by the *Titan*."

The name of the ship was enough to provoke a double-take by Picard, who cast an incredulous stare at his first officer. *Titan* was supposed to be thousands of light-years away, months from Federation space. "What is the signal's point of origin, Number One?"

Worf said, "Directly ahead, sir. Inside the Azure Nebula."

"Do we have a visual?"

"Affirmative."

Picard stood tall and smoothed his uniform. "Onscreen."

Sickly colors fluctuated on the main viewscreen, and an oscillating whine stutter-scratched through the speakers. Then the signal resolved into an unstable image with mildly garbled sound, and Picard recognized the haggard face of his old friend and former first officer, William Riker. *"Captain Picard?"*

"Yes, Captain," Picard said, unable to suppress a discreet grin. "It's good to see you again."

Riker returned the smile. *"Likewise, Captain. I wish it could have been under better circumstances."* He nodded to someone off-screen and continued, *"We're pretty banged up over here. My people are working a salvage mission in the nebula, but if there's any way you can lend us a hand, we'd be grateful."*

"I think something can be arranged," Picard said. Out of the corner of his eye, he caught Worf's confirming nod. "We're on our way back to the nebula with the *Aventine*. Have your people found any survivors during your salvage?"

Frowning, Riker replied, *"Only on* Voyager, *and they refused to abandon ship or be rescued. They're doing the same thing we are, scrounging for parts, except they have to rebuild an entire warp engine, one coil and bolt at a time."* He shook his head. *"You have to give them credit—they've got spirit."*

"Indeed," Picard said. "Will . . . don't think I'm not glad to see you, but your arrival is rather *unexpected*. How did *Titan* come to be in the Azure Nebula?"

The question pulled a tired sigh from Riker. *"It's kind of a long story,"* he said. *"Do you want the full explanation?"*

"I'm afraid we don't have time for that," Picard said. "Perhaps you could sum up?"

Riker nodded and lifted his eyebrows in mild amusement. *"Long story short: We followed energy pulses that we thought would lead us to a Borg installation. Instead, we found a species of powerful recluses called the Caeliar, who took us prisoner. A fellow prisoner helped my ship escape through a subspace tunnel, but I had to leave my away team behind."*

At the mention of a subspace tunnel, Picard's attention sharpened. His next question was driven not by logic but by a gut feeling, an intuition that the presence he'd sensed a short time earlier had to be connected in some way to *Titan*'s sudden arrival in the nebula. "Captain, by any chance, did the prisoner who aided your escape come with you aboard *Titan*?"

"As a matter of fact, she did," Riker said.

For a moment, Picard broke eye contact with Riker and concluded that his feeling had been right. The timing of the two events was definitely not a coincidence. Riker pulled him back into the conversation by inquiring, *"Why do you ask?"*

"Simple curiosity," Picard lied. "We'll reach you in just over an hour. If possible, have your chief engineer advance us a list of any parts or personnel you need to effect repairs."

"Will do, Captain," Riker said, looking utterly exhausted. *"We'll be looking forward to your arrival. Titan out."* The channel closed, and the nebula's distant blue stain on the starry heavens returned to the *Enterprise*'s main viewscreen.

Picard returned to his chair and sat down. Worf took his own seat at the captain's right. "Mister Worf," Picard said. "Please contact Captain Dax and let her know that I would like her and Commander Bowers to join us here on the *Enterprise* when we welcome Captain Riker aboard."

"Aye, sir," Worf said.

The captain added, "And instruct Commander Kadohata to coordinate with the *Aventine* in the creation of spare parts for *Titan* and the assignment of emergency crews."

"She has already done so, sir."

"Very good." From his chair, Picard had an all but unobstructed line of sight through the still-open door of his ready room, which remained a darkened, carbonized cave just off the bridge. Nodding to his scorched sanctum, he said to Worf, "I want that door closed, Mister Worf."

Worf scowled at the open portal. "We have tried,

sir. A plasma fire warped the interior bulkhead. The door is stuck."

Unable to rein in a surge of irrational anger, Picard snapped, "No excuses, Worf! Get it done." Embarrassed by his own outburst, he got up and walked to the aft turbolift. "You have the bridge, Number One." He felt the eyes of the bridge crew on him as he made his exit. The lift doors closed, granting him sanctuary in the solitude of the turbolift car.

"Deck Eight," he said.

It took the turbolift less than ten seconds to descend seven decks. The doors parted with a soft hiss. Picard walked quickly and was grateful to return to the refuge of his quarters without encountering anyone else along the way.

He moved in light, careful steps through the living area and poked his head inside the bedroom. Beverly was asleep. Picard noted the time—just shy of 0500—and wished he had the luxury of slumber. *No time for that now,* he scolded himself. He undressed in the dark, kicked off his boots at the foot of the bed, and lobbed his perspiration-soaked, battle-soiled uniform into one corner, intending to put it in the reclamator later, when Beverly was no longer trying to rest.

Stripped naked, he padded into the bathroom and shut the door. The light faded up slowly, and he felt as if it were revealing him to himself, a figure taking shape in the shadows. There were fatigue circles under his eyes, darker than any he'd ever seen on his face before. Somewhere beneath the mask of years that stared back from the mirror, there lurked the younger man he'd remembered being not so long ago.

Keeping his voice down, he said to the computer, "Shower, forty-six degrees Celsius." Inside the stall, a fierce spray of hot water flooded the small compartment with water vapor. Overhead, the ventilators purred into action, drawing up the moist clouds to stabilize the humidity.

Picard stepped inside the shower and bowed his head under the pleasantly sultry mist. *If only I could just stay here,* he thought. But with his eyes closed, he continued to see the charred bulkheads and seared-bare deck of his ready room. He shook his head, trying to cast off the memory, which disturbed him for reasons he didn't dare to let himself name.

Instead, he focused his mind on the new presence. He didn't hear it the way he heard the Borg. Where the Collective spoke in a roar, this was but the faintest hush of a whisper, and it was all the more compelling for its subtlety.

As the *Enterprise* continued toward its rendezvous with *Titan,* Picard knew one thing for certain: Whatever this new intelligence was, every moment was bringing him closer to it.

And one word echoed unbidden in his thoughts. *Destiny.*

4527 B.C.E.

8

"The wind's picking up," Pembleton said with a wary eye on the gunmetal gray sky. He and the rest of the survivors huddled around the campfire, all bundled tightly against the frigid gale. "Smells like more snow."

"God hates us," Crichlow muttered. "That's what it is."

A week had passed since they left the wreckage of Mantilis and encamped near the shoreline below. In that time, at least sixty centimeters of snow had fallen. Temperatures had plummeted daily, and the fjord, which had been crowded with pack ice, now was frozen solid. Adding to the group's misery was the fact that the days were growing shorter. Soon the sunrises would cease altogether, and several months of night would be upon them.

Flames crackled and danced around a tiny, gutted rodent carcass, which was impaled on a scrap-metal spit mounted on a pair of Y-shaped branches. Evaporating water inside the firewood hissed as it escaped, and one of the logs fissured along its length with a sharp *pop*. The aroma of cooking flesh had Pembleton's stomach craving sustenance, but it wasn't his turn to eat. Every other meal was reserved for Kiona Thayer, who needed to maintain her strength to fend off infection and promote the healing of her wounded foot, which would soon be strong enough for her to walk.

Mazzetti, who had become the group's de facto cook, gave the broiled rodent another quarter-turn on the spit. "Almost done," he said to Thayer, who nodded.

A chilling gust made the taut ropes of their shelter sing with vibration. Graylock eyed the ramshackle mass of metal, fabric, and microfiber rope. Then he turned with a glum expression back toward the fire and scratched at his stubbled face. "We need to reinforce before we get more snow," he said.

The three MACO privates groaned, and Steinhauer hung his head in denial. The chief engineer had sent them on daily hikes back up the slope, to salvage everything they could carry back down from the debris of Mantilis. Between the thin air and the strain of fighting this planet's gravity, it would have been a miserable assignment even in good weather.

Crichlow sighed, frowned, and shook his head. "Right, lads. Time for another trip up Junk Mountain."

"Steinhauer, make sure you check the traps before we go," Pembleton said. To the two officers, he said, "It'll be faster work if I go with them to lend a hand. Will you two be all right here on your own for a few hours?"

Thayer harrumphed behind a cynical grin. "Sure," she said. "We'll have a grand ol' time. Maybe we'll go ice fishing."

Through chattering teeth, Mazzetti replied, "For what? More poisonous seaweed?"

"I think she was kidding, Nicky," Crichlow said.

Pembleton summoned all his willpower to stand and step away from the comfort of the fire. "On your feet, men, we need to move. We'll only have about nine hours of daylight today. Let's not waste them." Watching the privates lag and dawdle, he coaxed them. "Up, gents. With a purpose, let's go."

Getting his men in motion was always the hardest part of the day. Once they were walking, even uphill, they were fine. It was a simple matter of overcoming their inertia.

Two hours later, they had settled into a rhythm, trudging single-file up the easiest face of Junk Mountain. Their boots crunched through the thin, icy crust and sank almost knee-deep into the wet, heavy snow underneath. "We need snowshoes," said Pembleton. "Any of you know how to make snowshoes?"

Steinhauer replied, "I do, Sergeant."

"Consider yourself volunteered when we get back to camp."

"*Jawohl,* Sergeant."

Crichlow, walking point, lifted his fist and halted the squad. He looked back at Pembleton, made a V sign with two fingers under his eyes, and pointed to something several meters away, to the right of their position. Pembleton strained to pick out textural details in the vast swath of white.

Then he saw them: fresh footprints. Animal tracks. Something big. Maybe even edible.

Graylock's infusion of parts and materials would have to wait. Their shelter wasn't perfect, but it would hold for another night. Food was a far more pressing concern, one that needed to be dealt with as soon as possible.

Pembleton eased his phase rifle off his shoulder and into his hands. The three privates unshouldered their weapons and mimicked Pembleton as he released his rifle's safety. With a series of quick gestures, he gave the order to move out and follow the animal tracks in the snow.

Crichlow remained on point, and the four MACOs remained in single-file formation as they stalked their prey. The trail led uphill, along a more treacherous section of the mountain's face. Within an hour, it was clear that the animal had taken refuge in a massive formation of jagged, coal-black crags.

"Steinhauer," whispered Pembleton. "Scanner."

The private, whose formerly severe crew cut had started to grow out into ragged shocks of fair hair, retrieved and activated his hand scanner. On Graylock's orders, the survivors had been sparing in their use of the devices, and also their weapons, because recharging them in the weak arctic sunlight was problematic. The team was supposed to resort to the powered equipment only as an emergency measure.

Starvation counts as an emergency, Pembleton decided.

Thrusting and slashing with his arm, Steinhauer directed the squad through a narrow pass in the crags. The men braced their weapons against their shoulders and hovered their fingers over the feather-touch triggers. Every step of the way, Steinhauer directed them toward the animal's life sign.

Then he held up a fist. The group halted.

He checked the scanner again. Looked up and around. Held up two fingers and pointed in one direction, then another. Two signals, diverging. Retreating deeper into the crags.

Pembleton gave the signal to advance in pairs, with each covering the other. Steinhauer and Mazzetti pushed ahead, while Crichlow remained at Pembleton's side.

The pass grew narrow as the four men worked their way past several irregular switchbacks, trading the point position at each one. Inching around another corner, Pembleton saw the narrow trail open into a small clearing. It was somewhere in the middle of the towering rock formation, which jutted up on all sides toward the ashen sky.

In the middle of the clearing was a mound of gnawed-rough bones, half buried in the bloodstained snow. It took him only a fraction of a second to realize that he and his team were not hunters here in this frozen wasteland but prey.

He turned to give the order to fall back. Then he heard Mazzetti scream. The crags filled with the shrill echoes of a phase rifle firing on automatic. He sprinted back through the pass, his muscles burning with fatigue as they fought the gravity, his lungs screaming for oxygen in the thin mountain air. Stumbling through a hairpin turn, he found Steinhauer standing with his back to a slab of rock, snapping off short bursts of charged plasma into random gaps between the sawtooth stones. The man's entire body was shaking with the effects of adrenaline overload.

A few meters farther down the pass, all around Mazzetti's dropped rifle, there were massive splatters of blood on the snow. Red chunks of viscera dangled from rough edges between the crags, along a steady crimson smear on the rocks—the kind of stain that would be made by dragging a mauled man over them.

"Cease-fire!" said Pembleton. He laid a hand on top of Steinhauer's rifle, and the private relented in his pointless barrage. "Lead us out of here, Private."

Steinhauer regarded him with a horrified stare. "We can't just leave Niccolo to those . . . those *things*," he said.

Pembleton took the hand scanner from Steinhauer's belt, powered it up, and made a quick sweep for life readings. Then he turned it off and handed it back to the private. "Mazzetti's dead," he said. "Move out, back to camp. That's an order."

With a keen awareness of now being the hunted, Pembleton retrieved the dead man's dropped rifle and herded his two shocked-silent enlisted men back the way they had come, out of the pass, and back down the mountainside. One man short, the squad retreated into the coming night.

Graylock will have to make do without any more spare parts, Pembleton decided. *Because if the predators on this planet are anything like the ones on Earth, this isn't over.*

He feared it wouldn't be long before he faced these creatures again. It would be dark soon.

The line between existence and oblivion had become faded and permeable for the Caeliar exiles. Robbed of mass, Lerxst now recalled physical sensations only as abstractions. Texture and temperature were no longer comprehensible to him since he had given up his frame of reference in the material realm. Motion was all but imperceptible. Pressure had given way to an almost unbearable dispersion of his essential being.

All that remained real to him was the emotional landscape of the gestalt, his communion with the other eleven Caeliar.

"Time seems to move faster now," said Sedín, her thoughts instantly shared with the others.

Agreement resonated among them without words.

Ghyllac added, "I no longer sense a distinction between light and darkness. Everything has turned to twilight."

Assent came from Felef, Meddex, and Ashlok.

"I can't remember twilight," countered Denblas, drawing concurrence from Celank and Liaudi.

Ripples of concern came from their youngest, least resolute members—Dyrrem, Narus, and the trio's speaker, Yneth. "We three cannot remain coherent for much longer without an influx of new energy," she said. "Our thoughts are . . ." She submerged into a long pause. "Disordered," she added at last. "Entropic."

"Without the anchor of mass, we cannot risk traveling this world," Lerxst told her. "Outside Mantilis, we could become dispersed by natural phenomena such as wind or tides."

Sedín replied, "And if we remain in Mantilis, we will slide toward chaos without even trying to save ourselves." Cradling the psionic presences of Yneth, Dyrrem, and Narus in her gestalt projection, she continued, "We must act to save our own."

"There is nothing we can do," Ghyllac said. "Our grounding in the physical is now too fragile to tap this world's resources or to move toward stronger solar radiation at the equator."

Felef replied, "That is not strictly true. In the most extreme circumstances, there is always consolidation."

A mental shudder traveled through the gestalt.

Liaudi asked with pointed curiosity, "And how would we decide who was to surrender their energy to the gestalt? Would the strongest expire to sustain the weaker among us? Or would we claim the weakest to bolster the others?"

"It would be best if the selections were governed by dispassionate logic," said Meddex, "employing a calculation of how to achieve the greatest degree and duration of good from the least amount of sacrifice."

Ashlok said, "I have already made such an analysis. Despite the logic of it, the sacrifices it demands feel arbitrary. I think it might be best if we let ourselves be guided by our consciences rather than by a tyranny of numbers."

"Might that be because you find the verdict of the numbers troubling?" asked Celank. "Do they call for your divestment?"

"No, not at first," Ashlok said. "My concern is that, as Liaudi speculated, the physics of the situation suggest that the maximum survival rate is obtained by sacrificing the weakest for the benefit of those requiring the least aid."

"Regardless of whether we consolidate according to logic or to our charitable impulses, it still amounts to a slow death by dissolution," argued Dyrrem.

Narus added, "The humans sustain themselves by consuming the local fauna. Perhaps there is a biological solution to our dilemma as well. Symbiosis, perhaps, rather than consumption."

"Doubtful," Sedín said. "Except for trace molecules, we crossed the barrier from organic to synthetic aeons ago. It may not be possible to backtrack on the path of our evolution."

"Even if it was possible," Ghyllac said, "we would need a sentient life-form with which to bond, to guarantee sufficient neuroelectric activity to power our catoms. Such a fusion would be a delicate and dangerous undertaking. If it is mishandled, it might debase us or turn our hosts into automatons—or both."

Lerxst made it clear that his was to be the last word on the matter. "We have neither the strength nor the facilities to perform the necessary research for such a task," he said. "If we wish to propose it to the humans, we will need to have the ability to pursue it, and that will entail consolidation. If that is the consensus of the gestalt, then we should resolve now which few will donate their energy for the sake of the others."

The hesitation was brief. Dyrrem, Narus, and Yneth projected their intention to release their catoms' energy to the gestalt, condemning the last afterimages of their forms to chaos and expiration. Gratitude and sorrow came back to them threefold from those they were about to preserve.

It was a swift transition. Three minds withdrew from the gestalt, which diminished in richness but grew in strength as power flowed through it, restoring form to its remaining members. Dyrrem, Narus, and Yneth were gone.

Sedín asked, "Who will make our proposition to the humans?"

"I will," Lerxst said.

Ever the cynic, Ghyllac asked, "And if they refuse?"

Lerxst replied, "Then we have just seen the fate that awaits us all."

"Try bending it," Graylock said, over an atonal howl of wind that fluttered and snapped the fabric of the shelter's walls.

Kiona Thayer flexed her ankle backward and forward in slow, stiff movements. "It's still fighting me," she said, nodding at the motor-assist brace Graylock had fashioned to enable her to walk normally.

"I think it's just the cold," Graylock said. "Gumming up the lubricant. It'll be fine once it's been moving for a while." He nodded toward the glowing rock in the middle of the enclosure. "Keep it close to the heat, and we'll try it again in an hour."

The weight of snow on top of the shelter had caused an unsupported section to droop inward. Graylock ducked under it as he circled around the heated rock to look over Private Steinhauer's shoulder. The young German man worked with pale, calloused hands, twisting together lengths of separated wood fiber that had been soaked in hot water until they had become flexible enough to manipulate. Woven together into a tight grid, the fibers formed the walking surface of handmade snowshoes.

"Those are looking good, Thom," Graylock said.

Steinhauer shrugged. "They're all right."

"How many pairs do you have finished?"

The private leaned forward and pulled open a folded blanket that protected his finished work. "Two and a half pairs," he said. Holding up the unfinished, teardrop-shaped shoe frame in his hands, he added, "This will make three."

"Good, good," Graylock said with a satisfied nod.

He continued around the shelter's perimeter and kneeled beside Crichlow, who lay almost on top of the heated rock. The young Liverpudlian was swaddled in blankets, sweating profusely, and shivering with enough force that he seemed to be suffering a seizure. Graylock removed the damp but fever-warmed cloth from Crichlow's forehead and used it to mop some of the sweat from the sick man's face and throat. Wringing it out over the dirt near the hot stone, he asked his patient, "Do you prefer it hot or cold, Eric?"

"Cold," Crichlow said through chattering teeth.

Graylock stepped over to a bowl set near the outer wall. He used a tin cup beside it to scoop out a small amount of cold water and pour it with care over the cloth. Then he brought the cloth back to Crichlow, folded it in thirds, and set it gently across the man's forehead. "Feel better," he said to him.

As much as he was tempted to crawl inside his own bedroll and retreat into slumber, Graylock knew when he checked his chrono that sleep would have to wait. He pulled extra layers of Caeliar-made fabric over himself, and he was careful to wrap his face, cover his nose and mouth, and shield his eyes with lightweight goggles he'd borrowed from Crichlow. Before he parted the overlapping folds of the shelter's entrance, he warned the others, "Bundle up, everyone. I'm heading out." When the others had draped themselves under covers, he made his exit.

Stepping outside had become an act requiring great willpower. In the fortnight since Mazzetti had been killed, the days had grown noticeably shorter on daylight, and the average temperature had gone from the kind of cold that could give someone frostbite to the kind that could kill a careless person in a matter of minutes.

Graylock watched his breath condense in front of him, filtered through three layers of fabric. Underneath his scarves, the moisture collected on his skin and chilled instantly, making his face feel clammy. He followed a narrow path that Steinhauer and Pembleton had excavated from the hip-deep snow that surrounded their camp. The footing was slick and icy, and the fact that he was trudging uphill to the lookout position made the short trip all the more difficult.

At the top of the rise, Pembleton paced in a circle around a stand of tall boulders. From there, in clear weather, a sentry could see anything that might approach within seventy to eighty meters of the shelter. Even at night, with only starlight for illumination, it was possible for one's eyes to adjust and pierce the darkness to keep watch for predators.

The sergeant nodded to Graylock as they met at the mound's peak. "Evening, Lieutenant," Pembleton said.

"I'm here to relieve you, Sergeant."

Pembleton replied, "I wanted Steinhauer to cover Crichlow's shift, sir."

"Too bad," Graylock said. "Steinhauer's making good progress on those snowshoes. I want him to rest and keep working. The sooner we have five pairs of shoes, the sooner we can move out."

Nodding, Pembleton said, "I understand, sir. But you're in command—we need to keep you safe in the shelter. Let me take the late watch."

"You've stood two watches today already," Graylock said. "It's a wonder you aren't frozen solid. Go inside. I can spot motion and shoot a rifle as well as anyone."

A larger-than-usual plume of breath betrayed Pembleton's frustrated sigh. "Yes, sir," he said. He removed the rifle that was slung over his shoulder and handed it to Graylock. "How's Crichlow doing?"

"Worse," Graylock said. "I don't know if it's a medical issue, like a congenital disease, or a virus or a parasite."

Pembleton asked, "Can't the hand scanner tell you that?"

It was Graylock's turn to sigh, this time in dismay. "The power cell ran out this morning."

"Can we transfer power from one of the rifles?"

Graylock shrugged. "Not efficiently, and most of the rifles are getting low, too. A few more weeks, and we're unarmed." He looked up at the alpine peaks high above them. "Unless we want to make another trip up Junk Mountain and ask the Caeliar for more batteries."

"And risk running into our friends with the fangs and claws again? No, thank you." Pembleton leaned sideways and looked past Graylock, surveying the rolling, snow-covered landscape that ringed the mountain's base. "Besides, I think the mountain's coming to us." He pointed, and Graylock turned his head.

A single Caeliar moved quickly toward them, its wide, three-toed feet bounding over the fresh-fallen snow without leaving so much as a mark. The alien's pale, mottled skin seemed made to catch the weak starlight. Its bulbous cranium and long, stretched-frown visage became distinct as it drew within a dozen meters of the sentries' peak.

Pembleton asked Graylock with politic courtesy, "Are you planning on challenging it, sir?"

Chastened, Graylock lifted the phase rifle, aimed it at the Caeliar, and shouted, "Halt! Identify yourself!"

The Caeliar stopped moving a few meters away. Its ridged air sacs puffed and deflated with the deep motions of respiration. "Karl, it is Lerxst."

Graylock demanded, "What do you want?"

"To talk with your people, Karl—all of them. I am not exaggerating when I say that our lives may depend on it."

2381

9

—•—

Dr. Shenti Yisec Eres Ree paced back and forth on the terrace outside the away team's shared residential suite. It wasn't easy for him to negotiate such narrow turns with his therapodian build—semirigid tail extended behind him for balance, head thrust forward, torso almost level to the ground.

All around him, the Caeliar city of Axion was lit from within and reflecting itself in its polished, vertical surfaces. Overhead, the sky was perfectly black, unblemished by stars; only a few low-running clouds bounced back the bluish-white glow of the metropolis. Natural scents from the planet below traveled on the breeze, but Ree couldn't dispel the sensation of being caught up in a half-formed illusion of a real world.

Footsteps drew closer. Ceasing his perambulations, Ree turned to find Commander Tuvok stepping through the open portal to the terrace. "Good evening, Doctor," said the Vulcan.

"Commander," Ree said, watching Tuvok with a wary eye.

Tuvok continued past him to the low barrier,

stopped, and rested his hands on the wall's shallow ledge. To Ree's surprise, the tactical officer said nothing else; he seemed content to stare out at the cityscape in stoic silence.

Ree didn't buy it. "You're here to berate me, aren't you?"

"Quite the contrary," Tuvok said. "I feel that I owe you an apology. However, I was not certain whether this would be an appropriate time to express it."

With exaggerated swoops of his long head and sinewy neck, Ree scoped the entirety of their immediate vicinity. "No one here but us and the invisible Caeliar who spy on us," he said. "So speak freely, Mister Tuvok."

Turning about to face Ree, Tuvok said, "Very well. I should have arrived sooner to help you explain yourself to the others. I had been meditating and monitoring Commander Troi's mental state. Though I sensed her distress, I understood that you were trying to help her. Unfortunately, I did not realize that you were in danger because of the security team's misreading of your actions. By the time I extricated myself from my telepathic link with Counselor Troi, I was too late to corroborate your account of events before the matter got out of hand. So I ask your forgiveness."

Ree bowed his head. "Thank you, Tuvok. I don't think you owe me any such apology, but if you think it was called for, I accept it in the spirit in which it was given."

Tuvok nodded once, and then he pivoted again to face the needle-thin towers and the gossamer-like metal filaments that linked them. With the conversation apparently ended for the time being, Ree resumed pacing. He took care not to swat the Vulcan man with his tail while making his turn at the end of each lap. In the silence of the night, Ree's claws clicked with a sound like a low spark on the rough stone of the terrace.

He paused again when he heard more footsteps approaching. Commander Vale emerged from the main corridor, trailed by the loping figure of Inyx. Lieutenant Commander Keru followed them.

When the three were meters shy of the terrace, Ree flicked his tongue twice in quick succession to taste the pheromones in the air. Vale's biochemical emissions matched her demeanor: aggressive. Keru's scent suggested he was calmer than she was. As usual, the Caeliar scientist made no mark in the air, though Ree thought an odor of sulfur might have been appropriate.

Behind Ree, Tuvok faced the oncoming trio.

"Doctor," Vale said, "Inyx needs a sample of your venom."

Openly suspicious, Ree asked, "Why?"

Inyx stepped around Vale and walked a few steps forward. "I've had centuries to study human anatomy and biology in detail, but Deanna's heritage is of mixed ancestry. That made it more difficult for me to make a diagnosis and select a course of treatment. However, I am also unfamiliar with your species and its unusually complex venom. If I am to save your friend's life, I cannot afford to spend time separating your biotoxin from Deanna's bloodstream. A pure sample will enable me to sequence its properties more quickly and develop an antivenom."

"If you're treating her medically, I demand to monitor the process," Ree said.

Inyx straightened and took on an imperious mien. "Given the crudity of your methods, that is quite out of the question."

"She's my patient," Ree said.

Vale replied, "I'm pretty sure she fired you when she told you to keep your hands off her."

"That was hardly an enforceable dictate, Commander," Ree retorted. "The good counselor was clearly *non compos mentis.*"

"Doctor, just give Inyx the venom," Vale said. Beside her, Inyx proffered a small sample jar with a cover of taut fabric.

Stalking forward, Ree said, "If you want a sample from me, you can draw it in whatever facility you're holding my patient."

"Deanna is not being held," Inyx said. "We are trying to help her, but her condition has become critical. Though your venom may have preserved her fragile status for a few minutes, it has complicated her treatment. Your patient's best interest is now best served by your cooperation, Doctor."

Ree paused and reflected that Inyx's position was actually reasonable. His reluctance to comply with the Caeliar's request was rooted in the simple fact that he didn't trust them.

His ruminations were interrupted by the firm squeeze of a hand near the nerve cluster above his shoulder. He swung his head back along his flank to see Commander Tuvok. The Vulcan was clamping his hand and scrunching a fistful of the Pahkwa-thanh's leathery hide in his grip. Ree flashed a toothy grin at the swarthy humanoid. "If you're trying to render me unconscious with a nerve pinch, Commander, don't bother." Tuvok released his grip on Ree and backed off, his expression neutral. Ree added, "I presume all that business about making an apology was a ruse to put you in position in case I refused Commander Vale's request?"

"No," Tuvok said. "My apology was sincere."

"And I'm not making a request, Doctor," Vale said. "I'm giving you an order: the venom sample, now."

Taking a more conciliatory tack, Inyx said, "Had it not been for your comrades' recent attempt at escape, I might have been persuaded to permit you to observe Deanna's treatment. Under the circumstances, however, I am under orders from the Quorum to restrict your access to all information about our technology and methods. So I will ask you again, as one healer to another, help me save Deanna's life. I beg of you."

"Give me the cup," Ree said, holding out one clawed hand.

Vale transferred the container from Inyx to Ree, who impaled its fabric cover with one incisor fang and released roughly fifty milliliters of colorless, odorless venom into the cup. Inyx stepped forward, and Ree handed him the sample. "Keep me apprised of Counselor Troi's progress, please."

"Of course," Inyx said. "And thank you."

As the Caeliar turned to depart, Ree asked, "Why didn't you send your errand girl Hernandez to collect the sample?"

"Because she is the one who enabled your ship to escape," Inyx said. He walked out onto the terrace and levitated away into the night.

Keru shambled away, back toward his quarters,

followed closely by Tuvok. Vale lingered a moment and glared at Ree.

"Do you realize that every second you stood there arguing, Troi could be dying?" she asked once the others had gone. "Is that really a chance you wanted to take?"

"Not at all, Commander," said Ree. "But you know the details of her condition almost as well as I do, and you know what has to be done. But what will the Caeliar do after they assess the situation? What if their imponderable brand of moral calculus compels them to sacrifice Deanna to save her fetus?"

Vale rubbed her eyes, signaling that she was not only tired but also tired of their conversation. "Do you really think that if you were there, you'd be able to sway their judgment in the slightest?"

"Of course not," Ree admitted. "But at least I'd be in a position to bite one of *them*."

Rolling her eyes, Vale replied, "*Now* you tell me. If I'd known *that* was your plan, I would've taken *your* side."

10

———•———

Erika Hernandez felt queasy as she stumbled in a panic through her quarters on *Titan*. Screams echoed from the corridor, and she heard the sounds of energy weapons being discharged in the corridor outside her locked door.

Thunderclaps of impact shook *Titan,* knocking her to the deck. She scrambled to her feet and staggered across the heaving floor. Something had set upon the ship with such speed that there had seemed to be no time to react.

Through the windows, she glimpsed a fearsome black cube moving through the indigo fog of the nebula. It battered its way through the storm of starship debris, firing brilliant green beams at *Titan,* which pitched and lurched after every shot.

A direct hit rocked the ship. The lights stuttered out. Outside her quarters, the clamor of battle grew more intense. On a gamble, she dashed to the door, which opened ahead of her. One of the guards who had locked her in, an Andorian *shen,* lay dead on the deck, her nubile form butchered and bloodied. Hernandez grabbed the *shen*'s rifle and prowled away, through the dark, smoke-filled corridors, following the din of combat.

Everywhere she looked, biomechanoid components seemed to have sprouted from the bulkheads, as if the ship were diseased.

She turned a corner and stepped into a cross fire.

Emerald streaks screamed over her shoulder and seared crackling wounds into the chests of two of *Titan*'s security personnel. Hernandez hit the deck as two other security officers, of a species Hernandez had never seen before, returned fire at their opponents. Shimmering beams of phaser energy crisscrossed in the hazy darkness.

I should get to cover, Hernandez told herself, but she didn't dare stand to run, and her curiosity demanded to see who or what had boarded *Titan*.

She turned her head and saw the enemy. They were humanoid, clad in formfitting black bodysuits and festooned with cybernetic enhancements. Their optical grafts swept the corridor with red laser beams, and several of the boarders had one hand replaced with complex machinery, ranging from cutting implements to industrial tools.

They advanced into the phaser barrage at a quick march, moving with the kind of precision she had only ever seen from jackbooted thugs in old historical films. To her shock, the phaser beams had no effect on them—they simply deflected them with personal energy shields.

Mustering her strength, she coiled to spring to her feet and sprint toward the security team. Turning back, she saw that it was too late for that. They had been ambushed from behind by more of the cyborgs, who slashed and impaled with abandon. Cries of pain were swallowed by the cruel whirring of machinery.

She rolled and tried to turn back the way she had come. There was another squad of the malevolent invaders closing in from behind her. Pivoting in a panic, she realized she had nowhere to run. *Not without a fight,* she vowed, and she opened fire. None of her shots did any good.

The black throng surrounded her and pressed inward.

Then came the oppressive roar of a voice inside her mind. *We are the Borg. Resistance is futile. You will be exterminated.* It was as intimate to her thoughts as the gestalt once had been, but it was hostile, savage, and soulless.

A spinning saw blade cut away the front half of her rifle, and the weapon spat sparks as it tumbled from her grasp.

Hands closed around her arms and pulled her backward, off-balance. She flailed and kicked, lashing out with wild fury.

More hands seized her ankles, her calves. The sheer weight of bodies smothered her, and a sting like a needle jabbed her throat. Twisting, she saw that one of the Borg drones had extended from between its knuckles two slender tubules that had penetrated her carotid.

An icy sensation flooded into her like a poison and engulfed her consciousness in a sinking despair.

Pushed facedown as the Borg's infusion took root, she smelled the ferric tang of blood spreading across the deck under her face. Then a hand cupped her chin and lifted her head.

She looked into the eyes of a humanoid woman whose skin was the mottled gray of a cadaver. Hairless and glistening in the spectral light, the female Borg flashed a mirthless smile at Hernandez. "You are the one we have waited for," she said. "Surrender to the Collective . . . and become Logos of Borg."

The human part of Hernandez unleashed a defiant scream, a torrent of pure rage. But her body lay still and silent, submerging into the merciless grip of the Collective. Trapped inside herself, Hernandez was tortured by her memory's endless refrain of mute protest: *No!*

She awoke screaming. She covered her mouth with one hand.

The door signal was loud in the silence of her quarters. Lieutenant sh'Aqabaa asked via the comm, *"Captain Hernandez? Are you all right?"*

"Yes," Hernandez said. "Just a bad dream." *A dream,* she repeated to herself, unable to believe it. The padd by her side still displayed the file she had been reading—a declassified report about the Borg that Captain Riker had suggested she take a look at. *I must have drifted off while I was reading.*

It had been nearly eight hundred years since she had slept. After bonding with the Caeliar gestalt, her body had no longer required sleep, either for physical or mental rejuvenation. The catoms that infused her cells regulated her neurochemistry and biological processes. Axion's quantum field had been the only solace or sustenance she had needed since undergoing the Change.

Until now, apparently.

She recalled a threat the Caeliar had once made

to Inyx, in order to coerce him into thwarting her attempts at communication with Earth. They had warned him that if he could not control her, they would exile her to a distant galaxy, where, without Axion's quantum field, she would age normally and die alone.

I guess escaping from Axion has other consequences, she reasoned, rubbing the itch of slumber from her eyes. *I wonder what other surprises I have to look forward to.*

As if on cue, her belly gurgled loudly, its acid-fueled yodel resonating inside her long-dormant stomach.

Naturally, she mused with a sardonic grin.

Hernandez got up and walked to a device that her Andorian guard had called a replicator. "You can get your meals from here, and it'll even do the dishes," sh'Aqabaa had said. It was time, Hernandez decided, to put that claim to the test.

Standing in front of the machine, which resembled little more than a polished-polymer nook in the wall, she muttered aloud, "How am I supposed to use this thing?"

A feminine computer voice replied, *"State your food or beverage request with as much specificity as you desire or are able to provide."*

"A quesadilla with Jack cheese and black beans, with sides of hot salsa, guacamole, and sour cream. And a mojito."

The machine responded with a flurry of glowing particles and a thrumming swell of white noise. When both had faded, a tray sat in the nook. On it was a plate covered by a piping-hot quesadilla, some small bowls with her condiments, and a glass with her minty-sweet rum beverage. She removed the tray from the replicator and carried it to a small table.

The aroma of food awakened memories she had thought long faded—of her childhood home and family dinners; the delicate texture of a flour tortilla fresh from a skillet; the sublime flavor of stone-ground guacamole made from ripe avocados, fresh cilantro, salsa, salt, garlic, and a touch of lime juice; the cool, refreshing decadence of a perfect mojito.

With great expectation, she sampled her replicator repast.

The quesadilla was rubbery, the salsa was bland, the guacamole was greasy, the sour cream tasted like paste, and there was something subtly but undeniably wrong with her mojito.

She pushed the tray away. *Food that's not food, booze that's not booze,* she fumed. *This is why I had a chef.*

Sleep eluded Will Riker.

All he'd wanted was a short nap. He turned from his right side to his left, flipped and punch-fluffed his pillow in search of a cool spot, and slowed his breathing in an effort to cajole his mind and body into letting go of consciousness. Closing his eyes, he focused on the white noise he had requested on a loop from the computer, of a low wind rustling the leaves of a tree.

It was all in vain. Rolling over, he let his arm splay across the empty half of the bed. Deanna's half.

Her absence had pierced him like a needle; his

every thought was stitched with its doleful color. Worse still was the guilt. He kept picturing her expression when she learned that he and *Titan* had escaped from New Erigol, leaving her and the rest of the away team behind.

I deserted them, he accused himself.

In the hours since *Titan*'s return to Federation space, he had begun to second-guess himself. *What difference will one more ship make now? Especially one as beat-up as ours?*

Lying alone in the darkness, he examined his decision with an increasingly critical eye. On the face of it, it had seemed at first to be the one that served the greatest good: It had freed his ship and the hundreds of personnel still onboard. That was as far as his justifications could take him, however. He couldn't persuade himself that he had really done any good for Starfleet or the Federation. In the end, all he could say was that he had saved the many by sacrificing the few.

By sacrificing his *Imzadi.*

She would never have done that to me, he told himself. Vivid recollections of his month of brutal captivity on Tezwa paraded through the theater of his memory. In those dark hours, when he had been beaten and broken, tortured and terrorized, only two things had kept him anchored in himself. One had been the indelible memories of music, of melodies and virtuoso performances by jazz master Junior Mance; the other had been the unshakable certainty that his *Imzadi* would never give up her search for him, that she would never abandon hope. Now he had repaid her devotion with a hollow appeal to duty.

He threw off the covers and sat up on the side of the bed. Leaning forward, he planted his face in his palms and imagined himself returned to the fateful moment, hours earlier, when Hernandez had made her proposition. Replaying it in his mind, he tried to conceive of how he could have answered differently, of some case that he could have made for not leaving the away team. There were no answers.

Every time he asked himself the question again, he was forced to admit that no matter how futile it might seem to hurl his ship into a war that was already all but lost, he was being driven by instinct—and drawn toward something.

"Computer, cease white noise," he said, and the breathy whisper of air through leaves came to an abrupt end. "Unshade the windows." The sloped, rounded-corner windows above his bed lost their dark tint and became transparent, revealing the backlit blue radiance of the nebula. Several of *Titan*'s shuttlecraft were on their way back, their tractor beams towing large sections of hull salvaged from demolished starships.

Watching the recovery operations in the nebula, he felt as if abandoning Deanna had blasted him to bits and that he was now struggling to piece himself back together from broken parts. He would do a fair job of presenting himself as functional and whole, but he knew that without Deanna, he would be like a phaser rifle field-stripped by a cadet and then misassembled, with one vital component left out, forgotten on the ground.

In other words, he castigated himself, *useless.*

A comm signal filtered down from the overhead speaker, followed by the voice of Commander Hachesa. *"Bridge to Captain Riker,"* said the acting first officer.

"Go ahead."

"Update from the Enterprise, *sir,"* replied Hachesa. *"They and the* Aventine *will rendezvous with us in fifteen minutes."*

"Acknowledged," Riker said. "Tell Lieutenant Commander Pazlar and Commander Ra-Havreii to meet me in transporter room two in ten minutes."

"Aye, sir. Bridge out."

He stood and stretched. "Computer, fade up lights to one-half," he said, and the room slowly brightened. Shambling groggily toward the bathroom, he hoped that a shower would revive him before it was time to meet with his former captain. The chrono on his end table displayed the time as 0617 hours.

Not bad, he thought. *I almost got an hour of sleep. Except it wasn't quite an hour, and I never actually slept.* He tapped a padd next to the bathroom sink and turned on the cold water. He cupped his hands, filled them beneath the icy stream, and splashed his face, shocking himself to full alertness.

He blinked at his dripping-wet, haggard reflection in the mirror. *Who needs sleep, anyway?*

"Energizing," said the transporter officer.

Jean-Luc Picard turned to face the raised platform. The system powered up with a resonant hum. To his left stood Beverly and Worf, and on his right were Captain Dax and Commander Bowers from the *Aventine*.

In front of them, three columns of sparkling bluish-white particles surged into existence and adopted humanoid shapes. Even before the radiance faded, Picard recognized the welcome sight of his old friend and former first officer, William Riker, standing at the front of the platform.

The transporter effect dissipated. Standing behind Riker were an Efrosian man with long white hair and a flowing mustache to match, and a slim, blond Elaysian woman who wore a motor-assist armature over her uniform, from neck to ankles.

Riker descended from the platform, and Picard stepped forward to greet him. "Welcome aboard, Captain," Picard said, shaking Riker's hand and flashing a wide, friendly smile.

"Thank you, Captain," Riker said, his own smile guarded and ephemeral. He let go of Picard's hand and gestured to the two officers who had beamed in with him. "Allow me to introduce my chief engineer, Commander Ra-Havreii. And I think you know my science officer, Lieutenant Commander Pazlar."

"Indeed, I do," Picard said, nodding to the duo. "Commander Ra-Havreii, it's a pleasure. Your reputation precedes you."

Ra-Havreii lifted his snowy brows. "That's what I'm afraid of," he said, with a weariness that belied his jesting tone.

Dax stepped forward and met Riker with a smile. "It's good to see you again, Will," she said. Nodding over her shoulder, she added, "This my first officer, Commander Sam Bowers."

Riker reached out and shook Bowers's hand. "A pleasure."

Pazlar stepped around Riker and offered her hand to Dax. "Nice to see you again, *Captain*."

"Likewise, Melora," Dax said with a friendly smile. "You look wonderful, as always."

"Says the woman who gets younger *every* time I see her," Pazlar said, with a teasing roll of her eyes.

Worf stepped forward and greeted Riker with a firm and enthusiastic handshake. "Welcome back, sir."

Clasping the Klingon's hand in both of his, Riker replied, "Thanks, Worf. How're you liking my old job?"

"Too much paperwork," Worf said.

"Try being a captain," Riker quipped. He released Worf's hand and accepted a quick, friendly embrace from Beverly.

"Welcome back, Will," she said. As they parted, she added, "I thought Chris and Deanna were coming. Are they all right?"

The stricken look that paled Riker's face warned Picard that something terrible had happened and that Beverly's innocent question had salted an open emotional wound. A sidelong glance at Dax's sympathetic expression made it clear to Picard that she, too, understood what was being left unsaid.

Riker turned his eyes toward the deck. "I had to leave them behind to save the ship. . . . It's a long story."

It was a terrible strain for Picard, in the aftermath of such losses and tragedies as he had recently endured, to mask his own pangs of loss and grief at this revelation. Deanna Troi was almost like a daughter to him—even more so after her long-overdue (in his opinion) wedding to Riker. He'd developed similarly paternal feelings for Christine Vale, with whom he had suffered and been tested in several crucibles that had claimed the lives of many *Enterprise* personnel— the bloody Dokaalan colony incident, the planetwide riots on Delta Sigma IV, and, worst of all, the protracted carnage of the Tezwa debacle.

If it's this deep a wound for me, imagine how much worse it must be for him, Picard thought, trying to impose some perspective on the matter. *To lose his wife and his first officer, both at the same time. How could anyone bear that?*

Bowers broke the uncomfortable silence. "I don't mean to be callous, but we have a lot to talk about and not much time. Maybe we should adjourn to a more appropriate setting."

"Wait a second," Riker said to Bowers, and then he looked to Picard. "The *Voyager* crew has more experience with the Borg than anyone. Shouldn't they be part of this?"

"I wish they could be," Picard said. "Unfortunately, Captain Chakotay is in critical condition, and many of his officers and crew were killed. *Voyager* won't be mobile for several days, and Commander Bowers is correct, we can't wait." He turned to Worf. "Are the arrangements made, Number One?"

"Yes, sir," Worf said. He stepped toward the door, which opened with a soft hiss. Turning back, he said to the group, "Everyone, please follow me."

Dax and Bowers were the first to act on Worf's invitation, and Picard gestured to Riker and his officers that they should go ahead of him. After the trio had stepped out of the transporter room, Picard and Beverly followed them and remained at the back of the group.

Beverly didn't say a word as she took Picard's hand. She didn't need to explain why; he understood. In a crisis, Riker had made a decision that would likely haunt him, no matter how the situation ultimately resolved itself. It was a dilemma that could only be fully appreciated by another captain whose wife served with him aboard the same starship. She gave his hand a brief squeeze and then let it slip from her grasp.

Picard wondered if he could possibly have the courage to make the choice that Riker had made—to desert his pregnant wife in the name of duty, in the service of the abstraction known as the greater good. Then he thought of how much time's merciless fires had already taken from him, and he knew that he couldn't.

He walked in somber silence with Beverly . . . and wished that decorum had let him hold her hand just a little bit longer.

Sequestered in the *Enterprise*'s crew lounge—a.k.a. the Happy Bottom Riding Club—the three captains and their officers helped themselves to hot and cold beverages that had been set out on the counter by the lounge's civilian barkeep, Jordan. He had ushered out the other patrons before the officers' arrival. Now that the VIP guests were inside, Dax saw Jordan exit through the main portal, leaving the officers to confer in privacy.

Dax filled a mug with fresh-brewed *raktajino*. She took a sip of her piping-hot beverage and admired the lounge's many decorative touches. Among them were dozens of portraits of *Enterprise* personnel who had been killed in the line of duty, with small bronze placards denoting their names, ranks, and KIA dates; a map of California, with a star denoting the location of the lounge's twentieth-century-Earth namesake; a replica of that bar's liquor license; and memorabilia of past starships that had borne the name *Enterprise*.

Worf stepped up to the bar on Dax's left and filled a tall glass with prune juice. Captain Riker sidled up on Dax's right and poured himself a mug of piping-hot coffee. Noticing her wandering gaze, he confided, "Jordan spruced the place up, but I was the one who named it."

As soon as he'd said it, Dax was certain she noted a glower from Worf that was aimed in Riker's direction.

That's a story I'll have to ask Worf about later, she decided, while nodding politely at Riker.

Captain Picard raised his voice for the room and said, "Could we all gather, please? We haven't much time." The officers convened and sat down on either side of a row of small tables that Jordan and his staff had pushed together at the forward end of the lounge, along a wall of windows with a spectacular view of the nebula.

Dax only half listened as Picard summarized for Riker how the *Enterprise*'s efforts to halt the Borg's access to Federation space had led him and his crew to the Azure Nebula.

After Picard finished, Dax quickly apprised Riker of the link between her crew's investigation of the downed Earth *Starship Columbia* NX-02 in the Gamma Quadrant and the subspace passage that brought them to the nebula.

Then came Riker's brief but gripping account of *Titan*'s detection of energy pulses in a remote sector of the Beta Quadrant and the trap into which he and his crew had been led as a result. Dax saw the anguish in Riker's eyes as he related in detail the circumstances that had compelled him to abandon his wife and his away team. "I had to make a snap decision, so I chose to bring my ship home," he said. "But it was a rough trip, and if what Captain Hernandez tells me is true, the Caeliar gestalt put up a hell of a fight to keep us there."

Two words leaped out at Dax, who interrupted, "Did you say 'Caeliar gestalt'?"

Riker did a surprised double-take. "Yes. Why?"

"The alien that stole the runabout from my ship," Dax said. "The one who led us here. He identified himself as Arithon of the Caeliar. He was looking for something called the gestalt."

"Well, I'd say we found it," Riker said. "And the Caeliar."

Pazlar interjected, "Captain Hernandez's account of the destruction of Erigol and the recorded date of the supernova that made this nebula are a match. If the Caeliar created those subspace passages, it would explain why this was their nexus."

Bowers, whose body language telegraphed his impatience, replied, "I'll admit that's all fascinating, but is any of it relevant to stopping the Borg armada?" Unfazed by the group's many stares of reproach, he continued, "Seriously, what's the plan here? What's our next step?"

Captain Picard frowned but salvaged Bowers's pride by answering, "The commander has a point. We need to focus on the future, not dwell on the past. I'll open the floor to ideas."

"Part of the problem," Ra-Havreii said, "is that there's little chance we could reach any of the threatened worlds in time to make a difference. The Borg outpace us by a wide margin. By the time we reach Earth or Vulcan or any of the other core systems, the battles for their fates will be long over."

"Maybe not," Dax said. "The *Aventine*'s carrying a prototype quantum slipstream drive. We weren't scheduled to start testing it until next month, but I think we can bring it online now, with a few hours' notice. If it works, we could leapfrog past the Borg, maybe even beat them to Earth by a few hours."

With casual skepticism, Picard replied, "To what end? With all respect, Captain, that's not a plan—it's just a tactic."

"I was simply refuting Commander Ra-Havreii's assertion that we're too slow to make a difference," Dax said.

"I see," Picard said. "You're right. It's important to know what capabilities we have at our command. But before we deploy them, we owe it to ourselves to be certain of our objectives."

Dax summoned the calm confidence that her symbiont's lifetimes of experience granted to her. She quashed her initial defensive reaction and let herself hear the wisdom in what Picard had said. "You're absolutely right," she replied. "Before we make any plans, we need to take stock of our strengths and resources." Looking at Riker, she added, "Starting with Captain Hernandez. After eight centuries among the Caeliar, she might have knowledge of advanced technologies that could help us fight the Borg. Before we do anything or set any plans in stone, we should see if she's able and willing to help us."

Picard nodded. "An excellent point, Captain." He pushed away his mug of Earl Grey and stood up. "I think it's time you and I met Captain Hernandez." Then he asked Riker, "Can I impose on you to make the introductions?"

Riker nodded and said, "My pleasure."

"Very well. Meeting adjourned."

Everyone stood and moved in a loose group toward the exit. Bowers fell into step close beside Dax and said confidentially, "What if she can't or won't help us?"

Dax frowned as she pondered that scenario. "In that case," she replied, "I wouldn't make any long-term plans if I were you."

11

The shortest battle of Martok's life was rapidly becoming the costliest. In the few minutes since his fleet had uncloaked and engaged the Borg armada with a barrage of transphasic torpedoes, more than seventy percent of both forces had been annihilated.

"Keep firing!" barked Captain G'mtor, over the rumbling of shockfronts and debris buffeting the *Sword of Kahless*. "Set course, bearing two-six-one! Don't let that cube get away!"

Already, several Borg ships had broken through the line and were accelerating deeper into Klingon space, their trajectories gradually diverging as they zeroed in on different star systems. Just as they had in the Azure Nebula, they had rammed their way through the Klingon blockade, sacrificing a few cubes for the sake of the overall invasion effort. *Once they pass out of range, we'll never catch them again,* Martok knew.

He watched the image of the receding Borg vessel shrink on the main viewscreen. Then the tactical officer called out, "Weapons locked!"

"Fire!" snapped G'mtor. Six transphasic torpedoes slashed in blue streaks up the center of the viewscreen and converged with lethal alacrity on the cube. A sunflash blanched the viewer. When it faded, it showed a cloud of smoldering black wreckage being dispersed by the navigational deflector of the victorious *Sword of Kahless*. "Hard about!" bellowed the captain. "Tactical, acquire a new target!"

Fire and fury blasted through the bridge's starboard stations. A slab of metal struck Martok's chair and knocked it off its pedestal. The impact hurled him from the rushing jaws of spreading flame and slammed him brutally across the deck, where the bulkhead fragment pinned him and shielded him at the same time. Soldiers and parts of soldiers ricocheted off the port consoles and collapsed in smoking heaps on either side of him.

The bright white battle-stations lighting went dark, and the ruddy glow of standard illumination took its place. Gray static flurried on the main viewscreen, and the air was bitter with smoke from overloaded circuits and the stench of burnt hair. Martok spat out a mouthful of his own blood and tried to drag himself out from under the metal slab. Knifing pains alerted him to broken bones in his rib cage and left leg.

General Goluk stumbled over the rubble-strewn deck to Martok and yelled to a pair of nearby warriors, "Help me lift this bulkhead plate off the chancellor!" The tall, broad-shouldered duo did as the general ordered. With three pairs of hands and deep grunts of pained effort, they raised the slab high enough for Martok to free himself. Once he was clear, they let it fall to the deck with a resonant peal of metal on metal.

Martok reached up and took Goluk's offered hand.

The general pulled Martok upright and steadied him until he could balance himself on his unbroken leg. To the two warriors, Martok said, "Get me damage reports and a battle update." Once they had stepped away, Martok asked Goluk in a confidential tone, "G'mtor?" The general nodded at the smoking heap of rubble and bodies from which Martok had been extricated.

Around the bridge, bloodied and scorched soldiers of the Empire struggled to wrest data or responses from their consoles. A faint crackle of comm chatter permeated the hazy compartment like an undercurrent. The minute Martok spent waiting for reports from his crew felt like an eternity.

One of the soldiers who had aided him returned. "Engines, shields, sensors, and weapons are offline, Chancellor," he said. "Life support is failing."

"What of the rest of the fleet?"

The warrior's jaw tensed, as if he refused to let the words escape his mouth. Then he bowed his head and said, "Broken."

Goluk asked, "Do we have communications?"

"Yes, sir," the soldier replied. "General Klag reports the *Gorkon* has been crippled and is unable to continue pursuit of the escaping Borg vessels."

Martok heaved an angry sigh. "How many broke through?"

"Sixty-one," said the soldier. "Ten heading to Qo'noS, two to Gorath, and the others to targets not yet identified. Also, another wave of Borg ships has been reported in the Mempa Sector, on course for more remote parts of the Empire."

Grim stares passed between Goluk and Martok. The

general placed a hand on Martok's shoulder. "It was a glorious battle."

"Yes," Martok said. "But what will that matter if no Klingon remains to sing of it?" Nodding to the soldier, he said, "Open a channel to Qo'noS. We need to alert the home guard."

The warrior moved briskly to one of the bridge's few operational panels and tapped in a series of commands. "Channel open, Chancellor," he reported.

"On-screen," Martok said.

The gunmetal hash of electronic snow on the viewscreen gave way to a murky, unsteady signal from the High Council chamber in the Great Hall of the First City. Looking back at Martok was his political nemesis, Councillor Kopek. *"What news, Chancellor?"*

"Our fleet has fallen," Martok said. "The enemy is en route to worlds across the Empire. I trust you know where duty lies, Councillor."

Kopek nodded. *"Of course. We will defend Qo'noS, my lord."*

"Summon every ship that can reach you in time," Martok said. "The fate of our homeworld is now in your hands."

"The Borg will not come to Qo'noS and live, Chancellor. When your fleet returns home, your throne will await you."

Martok smirked. "With you sitting on it, I presume?"

With no trace of mockery, Kopek replied, *"Today is not a day for politics, Chancellor. Today is a good day to die."*

Perhaps he longs for his place in Sto-Vo-Kor *like*

the rest of us, after all, Martok thought. He didn't know whether *Fek'lhr* would permit such a vile spirit as Kopek to redeem himself with a single hour of heroism, but part of him wanted to believe that it was possible—and that every warrior deserved such a chance.

He saluted him. "*Qapla',* Kopek, son of Nargor."

"*Die with honor, Martok, son of Urthog. Qo'noS out.*"

The signal ended, and the screen went dark.

I have fought the good fight, Martok told himself, but he found no solace in the thought. With his leg broken and his ship adrift, there was nothing more for him to do but stand and wait to see if the Empire's final hour had come around at last.

"Someone bring me a drink," he said.

12

———

Erika Hernandez sat alone at a dressing table in her quarters on *Titan*. She stared at her reflection in the large oval mirror. With her hands resting in her lap, she concentrated on her hair and felt the energy demands of her catoms as she altered her coiffure to match her fickle whims.

Her wild mane of thick, curly black hair retreated toward her head and turned an intense shade of indigo. Eyeing the more conservative spill of deep blue hair over her shoulders, Hernandez frowned. "I don't think so," she muttered to herself.

It took great effort to rein it back to a compact bob and shift its color to an auburn hue that matched her memories of cinnamon, fresh from the jar in her mother's kitchen. A fleeting whimsy drove her to go blond for all of eleven seconds.

She halted her hairstyling experiments as the door signal softly disturbed her privacy. "Come in," she said.

The door opened. Captain Riker entered, followed by two other officers—a bald human man and a young Trill woman—who wore the same rank insignia that he did. The trio was barely inside the room before Hernandez had used her catoms to restore her hair to its previous state, a mass of black waves that covered her back.

"Captain," Riker said. "I hope we're not interrupting."

"Not at all," she said. She added with a teasing grin, "And thanks for knocking this time."

The Trill woman gleamed with fascination. "How do you do that with your hair?"

"Catoms," Hernandez said. "Sophisticated nanomachines made and infused into my body by the Caeliar. The catoms can direct energy and reshape matter in remarkable ways, if they have enough power. Unfortunately, this little parlor trick's about all I have left in me—and to be honest, it's tiring me out."

Folding his arms, Riker said to the other two captains, "She's being modest. When she showed up on my bridge a few hours ago, she turned Ensign Rriarr's phaser to dust with a glance."

Hernandez shook her head and gave a tired grin. "Captain Riker's giving me a bit too much credit," she explained. "When I did that, we were still in orbit of New Erigol, where I had access to the Caeliar gestalt. Without that power to draw from, I can barely curl my hair."

The Trill cracked a smile, but the older man had the stern carriage of one who had seen too many days of war. Hernandez wondered if he saw her as clearly as she saw him.

He cleared his throat and threw a look at Riker, who dipped his chin at the reproach and gestured at his colleagues.

"Captain Hernandez," Riker said, "permit me to introduce Captain Ezri Dax of the Federation *Starship Aventine* and Captain Jean-Luc Picard of the *Enterprise*."

Unable to mask her confusion, Hernandez cocked her head and eyed Picard with suspicion. "But . . . you're the one the voice calls *Locutus*," she said.

Dax's and Riker's eyes widened in horror and surprise, and Picard froze as they looked at him. His face became pale, and he looked lifeless, Gorgonized. At last, he replied in a shocked whisper, "You heard a voice . . . call me . . . *Locutus*?"

"Yes," she said, listening to the inhuman chorus of distant voices that filled every empty space in her thoughts. "Are you telling me the rest of you don't *hear* that?" She looked from one captain to another in an effort to gauge their reactions. Their obvious dismay and withdrawn body language told Hernandez that her revelation had left them ill at ease. "Great," she said. "You think I'm crazy, right? Think I'm hearing things?"

Picard stepped toward her. His voice was cautious and gentle. "Do you know what you've been hearing? Its name?"

Anticipating the direction of his questions, she replied, "Yes. Do you?"

As if he were reading her thoughts, he said under his breath, "The Collective." He looked at Riker and seemed to draw strength from the younger man's quiet fortitude. Turning back toward Hernandez, he continued, "When I hear the Borg, it sounds like a roar of voices, more like a noise than a chorus. Then the strongest voice overpowers the others. Is that what you hear?"

She shook her head. "No." She closed her eyes and let the ever-changing chaos of the Collective cascade inside her mind. "I hear all of them," she explained. "Every voice adding to the others, like a conversation. But I also hear the unifying voice, both on its own and when it speaks through the Queen."

"I hear only the many," Picard said.

"I hear what I choose to hear," Hernandez said. "I can isolate lone voices, if I try hard enough."

Riker swapped excited glances with Dax and asked Hernandez, "Can you communicate with them? Talk to them?"

"No," Hernandez said. "I can eavesdrop on their party, but I'm definitely not invited, if you know what I mean."

Picard paced slowly. "Captain, have you ever encountered the Borg before now?"

"Never even heard of them before today," she said.

"But you can hear the Collective in your thoughts," Picard said, lost in his own musings as he reversed direction and kept pacing. "Even though you've never been assimilated."

Hernandez hadn't encountered the term *assimilated* in the brief and heavily redacted file that Riker had let her read, and she wasn't certain she wanted to find out what it meant.

Captain Dax interrupted Picard's pensive perambulations. "It's probably related to the catoms the Caeliar put into her body. Somehow those nanomachines let her tap in to the Borg Collective's frequency, and—no offense, sir—with greater precision than you can." The sharp-eyed young woman focused on Hernandez. "You mentioned that you can tell one voice from another in the Collective. You also mentioned the Queen. Does that mean you can tell if the Queen's leading the attack on the Federation right now?"

"Yes," Hernandez said. "The armada's under her direct control." Closing her eyes again, she attuned herself to the thoughtwaves of the Borg monarch. "She's young, newly installed," Hernandez continued, even as she struggled to glean more details. "Full of fury. She . . . she even thinks of herself as being expendable—as long as Earth is destroyed."

Desperate, Picard asked, "Why? What's driving them?"

"I can't tell," Hernandez said. "It's all too muddled."

Riker and Dax pressed in closer, and Dax asked, "Can you tell us where the Borg Queen's ship is?"

Clearing her mind of all other questions, Hernandez sought that detail and found it. "I know where she is," she said. Then she opened her eyes and let her tears fall. "She's leading a phalanx of several dozen Borg vessels."

Riker's voice was taut with urgency. "But where *are* they?"

Hernandez palmed tears from her face. "Destroying Deneva."

13

The Queen had emerged from her chrysalis with two mandates coded into her being: Destroy Earth, and crush the Federation.

For too long, we have obsessed over Earth, she had directed her trillions of drones, attuning the Collective's will to her own. *It has lured us, tempted us, thwarted us. No longer.*

She had projected her murderous fury to the drones and adapted them to the lightning pace that she and the Collective now demanded of them. *We offered them union. Perfection. They responded with feeble attempts at genocide. Earth and its Federation are not worthy of assimilation. They would add only imperfection. Since they offer nothing and obstruct our quest for perfection, they will be exterminated.*

It was all coldly logical and mechanically precise, but none of that mattered to the drones. They would follow the will of the Collective and execute the Queen's dictates without question or hesitation. No justification had to be given to drones. The Queen, however . . . she made different demands.

She was a conduit, a voice for something that no

longer had one. Its will existed outside her, and it *was* her, all at once. It was the Collective—not a chorus of voices but one voice speaking through those bound into its service.

The drones, the cubes, the Unimatrix, and even the Queen all were nothing more than the trappings of the Collective's true nature. *It* was the authentic essence of the Borg, and *It* told the Queen that the time had come for worlds to burn.

From her attack force, she dispatched six cubes toward the next inhabited planet that lay along their course to Earth.

Leave nothing alive, she commanded her drones.

And she knew that they would obey, without question.

Captain Alex Terapane bolted from his command chair to point at his preferred target on the main screen. "All ships, fire on the flanking cube! Clear a path for the escaping transports!"

The bridge crew of the *U.S.S. Musashi* scrambled to carry out his order as the ship bucked and shuddered under a fierce barrage by the Borg. His first and second officers had both been killed in the opening minutes of the battle, and there was no turning back now. With five other Starfleet vessels—the starships *Forrestal, Ajax, Tirpitz, Potemkin,* and *Baliste*—the *Musashi* was struggling to fend off an equal number of Borg cubes. The enemy vessels had approached at such high speeds that there had been almost no time to brace for the attack.

The *Musashi* slipped through a gap in the Borg's

firing solution as the security chief, Lieutenant Commander Ideene, called out, "Torpedoes away!"

Terapane tensed to sound a victory cry. Then he watched the three transphasic torpedoes slam into the Borg cube's shields, which flared and then retracted but didn't fall. He snapped, "Hit them again!"

A thundering impact snuffed the lights and pitched the deck violently. Terapane fell and landed hard on his left hip. White jolts of pain shot through his torso. He forced his eyes to relax from their agonized squint just in time to see the *U.S.S. Tirpitz* vaporized on the main viewer. Seconds later, the *Ajax* suffered the same fate and vanished in a flash of golden fire. Then came the *Baliste*'s blaze of glory, as it followed the others into oblivion.

"Strigl," Terapane shouted to his ops officer. "Tell *Forrestal* and *Potemkin* to regroup—protect the transports!"

"Comms are jammed," Strigl replied. "All frequencies."

Pulling his brawny form back into his chair, Terapane snarled at his security chief, "Ideene! Report!"

"Targeting scanners are gone, I have to aim manually," said the square-jawed Orion woman. "Firing!"

Another volley of transphasic torpedoes soared from the *Musashi,* slammed through the nearest Borg cube, and pulverized it in a bluish-white fireball. As the burning cloud dissipated, Terapane saw another cube struck by a double volley from the *Potemkin* and the *Forrestal*. The black hexahedron erupted and disintegrated. Spontaneous whoops of celebration filled the *Musashi*'s dim, smoky bridge.

Then a scissoring crisscross of green energy blasts

from the four remaining Borg cubes slashed through the *Potemkin* and the *Forrestal* and transformed both ships into chaotic tumbles of fiery wreckage. Dozens more beams lanced through the hundreds of fleeing civilian transports, reducing them to glowing debris.

With Starfleet's defense forces shattered, the four remaining Borg cubes accelerated away from the *Musashi,* into orbit of Deneva, millions of kilometers away.

We're all that's left, Terapane realized. His ship was Deneva's last defender, and it was outnumbered and outgunned. "Arm all transphasic warheads," he said to Ideene.

"But I don't have a target," Ideene protested.

Terapane shot back, "Arm every warhead we have, right now, wherever they are—in the tubes, in the munitions bay, I don't care. Do it now." He took a deep breath. "Helm, put us smack in the middle of those cubes, best possible speed, on my mark." Throwing a look back at Ideene, he snapped, "Well?"

"Warheads armed," she replied.

On the main viewer, the four cubes were demolishing Deneva's orbital defense platforms, which had been heavily upgraded after the Dominion War. *Not upgraded enough,* Terapane brooded, as he watched the Borg turn them to scrap. Then the cubes spread apart in high orbit and turned their formidable weaponry against the planet's surface.

"Captain," Ideene said, "because of the Borg's deployment pattern, at best we might be able to take out two of them." She started to say something, but she stopped and averted her eyes toward her console. She swallowed. "Even in a best-case scenario, we can't save Deneva, sir."

"No, we can't," Terapane acknowledged. "But I won't just hand the Borg their victory. I plan on making them pay for it." He used the controls on his chair's armrest to open a shipwide comm channel. "All decks, this is the captain. All noncombat personnel, abandon ship. Medical teams, evacuate sickbay, and split up to provide support for as many manned escape pods as possible. All pods will be ejected in two minutes." He closed the comm channel. "Mister Strigl, prep the log buoy."

Terapane sat and passed the final two minutes of his life in quiet reflection while his crew readied the *Musashi* to make its futile sacrifice. He thought of his wife and sons on Rigel IV, of the countless lives being extinguished on Deneva, of the grim fate that seemed to lie in store for all of the Federation. Watching the Borg cubes bombard the world that he had been tasked to defend, he seethed. *Every second you wait, more die,* his conscience scolded. His reason countered, *They're all going to die today, anyway. Two minutes won't make any difference.*

The hull resounded with the metallic thumps of magnetic clamps opening. Lieutenant Strigl swiveled his chair around from the ops console to report, "All escape pods away, Captain."

"Release the log buoy, Mark," Terapane said.

Strigl keyed in the command. "Buoy's away," he said.

Terapane stared at the carnage on the viewscreen and saw no point in lying to himself. He wasn't about to work a miracle or save the day; nothing would be gained by what he did next. But his ship had been named for the famous samurai Miyamoto Musashi, and it seemed only right and proper, in the aftermath of such a colossal failure, to fall on his sword.

If his figurative seppuku also happened to claim the lives of a few more of his foes, so much the better.

"Helm, is the course plotted?" he asked.

"Aye, Captain," replied the young Vulcan pilot.

He looked at Ideene. "Tactical?"

"Armed and ready, sir. Just say go."

The atmosphere of preternatural calm on his bridge filled Terapane with pride in his crew. "It's been an honor, friends," Terapane said. "Helm . . . engage."

In a flash of warp-distorted light, the pinpoint of Deneva became the shallow curve of its northern pole, which sprawled beneath two Borg cubes unleashing a cataclysm of emerald fire. The *Musashi* had dropped to impulse directly between them.

In one word, Captain Alex Terapane fell on his sword.

"Go."

Ione Kitain's whole world was on fire.

Great peals of thunder overpowered the screaming that seemed to fill every corner of Lacon City. The street outside her residential tower heaved like a chest expanding with breath, and then it cracked and collapsed into itself, swallowing dozens of people who had been fleeing without direction.

Millions of people all around her, throughout Deneva's lush Summer Islands, were panicking, descending into a communal terror that assailed her keen Betazoid senses like a tsunami.

Every animal impulse in her brain told her to run, to seek shelter, but she knew there was no point. There were no hiding places to be found. So she huddled in the arched entryway of her apartment complex and focused her psionic senses through the maelstrom of fear to find her husband's mind amid the mayhem.

Sickly green pulses of energy fell from the heavens. Titanic mushroom clouds billowed skyward at multiple points around the horizon, turning the dusk to darkness. Every detonation rocked the city with the force of an earthquake.

From high overhead, Ione heard the mournful whine of a failing engine. She looked up in time to see a damaged personnel transport spiral out of control and slam into a commercial tower, several blocks from her home. Its impact shattered the entire façade of the building, and the transport exploded in a flash, followed by gouts of flame. With the tower's center all but obliterated, its upper portion swayed like a wounded giant before it plunged at an angle, crushed the lower half, and toppled into the streets. A toxic cloud of pulverized debris, atomized bodies, and glass and metal shards spread through the artificial canyons of the urban center.

Lacon City reeked of smoke, death, and sewage.

The buzz of emergency-service aircars and other antigrav vehicles ceased all at once. At first, Ione thought they had gone—and then she heard the dull thuds and crunches of hundreds of vehicles falling to Earth and caroming off buildings and the elevated pedestrian walkways above the streets. Her best guess was that an energy-dampening field had blanketed the city.

That means our shield's completely gone, Ione realized. *It won't be long now.* Fear began to cloud her thoughts and dull her telepathic senses. Then her husband's thoughts touched her own.

I am near, wife. I am at the fountain.

She bolted from the archway and sprinted through streets littered with broken, burning vehicles and mounds of smoldering debris. *I'm coming, my love,* she projected to her *Imzadi.*

Another blast, closer than all the others. A deathly silence washed over the street. Ione flattened herself against a pile of shattered asphalt and covered her head with her arms as the shockwave hit. It ripped through the upper sections of the buildings on either side of her. A delicate music of destruction lingered behind it and deluged the boulevard with a storm of broken glass. Most of it was sandlike, tiny abrasive granules, but a few substantial chunks gouged her back and thighs.

She tried to be stoic, to contain the sharp agony of her wounds rather than accost her husband's own telepathic mind with them, but her control was compromised by anguish and fear. Minuscule fragments of glass bit into her palms as she forced herself up from the ground. Then a pair of strong brown hands gripped her forearms and lifted her to her feet.

He'd found her.

"Elieth," she said, smiling sadly at her husband.

He responded with typical Vulcan stoicism. "We must move," he said, pulling her into motion beside him. He ushered her out of the street and toward the space beneath the overhang of an elevated promenade. His peace officer's uniform was ripped and stained with dust and blood. One of his ears was mauled and bloodied. She reached toward it in sympathy. "You're hurt."

"Quickly," he said, applying gentle pressure with one arm on her back, until they were sheltered under the promenade. A moment later, she understood the reason for his urgency.

Bodies began falling into the street.

The sounds were more horrible than anything Ione had ever imagined. Her stomach heaved in disgust with every wet, muffled impact, every dull slap of flesh meeting stone. Just meters from where she stood, the street became an abattoir.

When the grotesque percussion ceased, Ione realized she was weeping into Elieth's shoulder. At any other time, he would have radiated intense disapproval for such an overt exhibition of emotion. Instead, he imparted comforting thoughts.

Don't be afraid. The worst is over.

Staring out at the apocalyptic cityscape, Ione replied, *I sincerely doubt that, my love.*

Despite all the times that Elieth had argued to her that regret was a worthless emotion, Ione wished that they had been on the last transport out of Lacon City.

When the order had come from Deneva's president to evacuate the planet, however, she and Elieth had stayed behind to lend their expertise to the Civil Defense Corps. She had applied her skills as a particle physicist to improve the city's defensive shields, to buy more time for the transports to be loaded and launched. Elieth's job had been to maintain order at the launch site and make certain that the most vulnerable citizens had been given priority, especially families with young children.

The plan had been to meet back at home after the last transport was away. Looking back, she saw their apartment tower being consumed from within by a raging blaze.

"We could have left," she said, knowing it wasn't true.

"There was insufficient room on the transports," Elieth said, calm in the face of calamity. "We also did not fit the criteria for prioritized rescue."

Spite and selfishness surged inside her. "I'm a daughter of the Fourth House of Betazed, and you have a badge. We *could* have left." As soon as she'd said it, she felt ashamed.

Elieth let her remarks pass.

A deep rumbling resonated in every solid surface, and the city was bathed in a terrifying monochromatic green radiance.

Ione trembled, and her heart pounded furiously. Adrenaline coursed through her, but she had no use for it. Embracing her *Imzadi,* she opened her mind to his. *What will you miss most?*

I will not be aware of any loss after I have ceased to exist, Elieth responded. *So I will miss nothing.*

Unswayed by his resolute devotion to logic, Ione shared, *I'll miss music. And you.*

It was only a blink, a micro-expression that vanished almost as soon as it manifested, but Ione saw the crack in Elieth's façade. Beneath his carefully trained discipline, he was grieving just as deeply as she was—and perhaps far more. He made a silent confession: *If it were possible for one with no awareness to miss something . . . I would miss you most of all.*

He tightened his embrace, and Ione shed grateful tears for that one last moment of proof that Elieth, youngest son of Tuvok and T'Pel, truly loved her.

Her tears cut trails across her grime-covered face. Then the viridian glow from above brightened, and she cringed. "I didn't think it would end like this."

Nor did I.

A pulse of light and heat penetrated every atom of the city, and then there were no more tears.

The sun was sinking below the horizon and painting all of Paris with a single shade of salmon-pink light, when President Nan Bacco heard her office door open behind her.

She turned to face her lone visitor, Esperanza Piñiero. Tears ran in streaks from Piñiero's dark brown eyes. The chief of staff crossed the room to the president's desk. Agent Wexler remained outside and closed the door behind her. By the time Piñiero reached the desk, she looked too distraught to speak. She bowed her head and struggled to control her breathing.

Bacco anticipated Piñiero's news with deep anxiety. She didn't want to know the truth; she didn't want to make the disaster real by allowing its tragedies to be spoken. But what she wanted didn't really matter anymore.

"Esperanza," she said. "Tell me. In simple words."

Piñiero palmed her eyes dry and forced herself into a ragged facsimile of composure. "We've lost Deneva," she said.

A churning tide of sickness and a destabilizing feeling of emptiness struck Bacco at the same time. Overwhelmed, she sank into her chair, faltering like an invalid. There had been no surprise in Piñiero's report, but it was still devastating to confront it as a hard truth. Billions more dead. *Billions.*

"What's coming next?" Bacco said.

"Regulus is under siege now, and an attack on Qo'noS is imminent," Piñiero said. "Martok's fleet is gone. All he has left is a rear guard at the Klingon homeworld."

Even if it would amount to merely going through the motions, Bacco was determined to serve a purpose until the bitter end. "Do we have any forces close enough to help them?"

"Admiral Jellico redeployed the *Tempest* and its battle group from Ajilon to Qo'noS six hours ago. Admiral Akaar can't guarantee they'll get there in time to make a difference."

Bacco felt like a chess player who knew she had already been checkmated but was obliged to continue until the endgame. "Which worlds are getting hit next?"

"Elas and Troyius are both facing attacks in two hours," Piñiero said. "So are Ajilon, Archanis, Castor, and Risa."

I feel like I'm drowning. Bacco closed her eyes for a moment. "What about the core systems?"

"Borg attack groups are on course for Vulcan, Andor, Coridan, and Beta Rigel. ETA five hours."

It would be negligent of me not to ask, Bacco reminded herself. "And Earth?"

"Eight hours, Madam President." Despair loomed

over Piñiero like a black halo. "Ma'am, this might be a good time to consider moving your office into the secure bunker at Starfleet Command."

Bacco sighed. "I think it's a bit late for *that*." She reached forward and activated the comm to signal her assistant. "Sivak, round up the cabinet members and the senior staff, and have them meet me in the Roth Dining Room in one hour."

"Certainly, Madam President. Should your guests inquire, shall I tell them that formal dress is demanded or optional?"

"They can show up naked for all I care. And tell the chefs I want to see the best of everything they've got. If they've been waiting for a chance to impress me, this is it."

"Yes, Madam President. I'm sure the kitchen staff will find your enthusiasm for their work deeply inspiring."

"And have them set a place for you as well, Sivak."

She savored the moment of stunned silence that followed. It was rare that Sivak spoke without sarcasm or a subtle jab of wit, so hearing him reply with courtesy was a rare delight. *"Thank you, Madam President,"* he said. *"The dining room will be ready to receive you and your guests in one hour."*

"Thanks, Sivak," Bacco said, and she closed the channel.

Piñiero planted one hand on her hip and gesticulated with the other. "Ma'am, what was *that* about?"

"Dinner," Bacco said. "If you have a special request, I suggest you send it to the kitchen sooner rather than later."

The chief of staff blinked. She looked as if Bacco had just swatted her in the back of the head with a baseball bat. "Do you really think an impromptu state dinner is what we need right now? We're eight hours away from seeing Earth get turned into a glowing ball of molten glass."

"Exactly," Bacco replied. "It's an old Earth tradition. The condemned get to enjoy a final meal, so they can savor what it means to be alive one last time before they die." She stood and circled around her desk to join Piñiero. "This might be our last supper, Esperanza—so let's dine with style."

A bittersweet smile broke through Piñiero's veil of gloom. "I like the way you think, ma'am."

Bacco shrugged and said with a wry grin, "It's my job."

4527 B.C.E.

14

Pembleton and the other human survivors pushed into the middle of their shelter, closer to the pile of fire-heated rocks, and listened with unease and suspicion as Lerxst answered their questions about the Caeliar's bizarre proposal.

"Help me understand," Graylock said, holding out his empty palms. "You want to use us as batteries?"

Lerxst replied, "Engines would be a better analogy. Even that falls short of the mark, however. What we are suggesting is a fusion of our strengths, for our mutual survival."

Thayer narrowed her eyes at Lerxst. "But you did say that you'd be using our bodies as a source of power."

"In the short term, yes," Lerxst said.

Steinhauer, who kept his hands busy threading fibers into the loop of a snowshoe, looked up and said, "Why not use one of those creatures that killed our man Niccolo?"

"It is not merely biochemical reactions that we require," Lerxst said. "The interaction of our catoms is similar in many respects to the synapses of your brains. To sustain ourselves and maintain the integrity of our consciousness, we would need to bond with a sentient being, one with enough neuroelectric activity to power our catoms. Mere animals will not suffice."

Pembleton said, "So we've established why you need us. Why do we need you?"

The Caeliar lifted his arm and made a sweeping gesture at the confines of the shelter. "Your current situation appears to speak for itself," he said. Directing their attention to the ailing Crichlow, he added, "Our catoms could enhance your immune systems and enable you to adapt to this world's aggressive pathogens." He pointed at Thayer's mechanically augmented foot. "They would also speed your recovery from injuries and prolong your ability to survive a famine."

"I presume that's a best-case scenario," Graylock said.

Lerxst bowed slightly to the engineer. "Yes, it is."

Graylock shook his head slowly. "Now let's hear the worst-case scenario."

"The fusion of our catoms and gestalt with your organic bodies does carry significant risks," Lerxst said. "Normally, we would not attempt anything so complex without first conducting extensive research and testing. Given the primitive nature of our surroundings and the urgency of our respective crises, we would have to attempt this bonding without such preparations."

Thayer's anger put an edge on her voice. "Get to the point. What happens if it goes wrong?"

Tense silence followed her question. Lerxst's demeanor was subdued as he replied, "An unsuccessful fusion could result in the death of the intended host, the dispersal of the Caeliar consciousness, or both. It could also inflict brain damage on the host, turning him or her into an automaton under the control of the bonded intelligence; or the bonded entity might prove incompatible with the host and would become corrupted. It is also remotely possible that your bodies' immune systems might reject the catoms as foreign tissue and treat the fusion as a form of infection. Any or all of these outcomes might occur."

"Great," Steinhauer said. "Just great."

Graylock scowled at the grousing private before saying to Lerxst, "Brain damage? Death? It sounds as if the risks of this 'fusion' far outweigh the benefits."

"The alternative is death," Lerxst said.

"For you, maybe," Pembleton replied. "As soon as we have enough snowshoes to go around, we're going south." :

"Or north," Graylock said. "Whichever way the equator is."

The Caeliar turned his inscrutable visage toward Pembleton. "How far do you think you'll get? Shall I draw you a map of what lies ahead?" Lerxst hadn't raised his voice, but there was something smug and angry in his manner. "This is an *island,* Gage, more than a hundred kilometers from the nearest major continent. You and your friends can no more flee from your predicament than we can from ours."

Pembleton looked at Graylock. "Your call, sir."

The lieutenant's brow tensed, and a V-shaped wrinkle formed between his thick eyebrows. He pinched the bridge of his nose. "To hell with rank for a minute," he said. "This is all of our lives on the line. We'll put it to a vote, a show of hands. Who wants to risk becoming a Caeliar meat puppet?"

A look around the room revealed not a single raised hand.

"All right," Pembleton said. "Who votes to look for a way off this island?" He lifted his own arm, and four others reached for the drooping fabric ceiling.

Graylock nodded, and they put their arms down. "The ayes have it," he said to Lerxst. "Escape, five; meat puppets, zero."

"Please reconsider, Karl," Lerxst said. "If we don't join together now, while my people still have the strength to control the process of the fusion, we might never have another chance."

"Sorry," Graylock said. "We've made our decision."

"Then both our peoples will die," Lerxst said.

The Caeliar envoy stood and walked out of the shelter. As he exited through the overlapping flaps of the shelter's portal, a gust of subfreezing air slipped past him and momentarily cut through the pungent miasma of body odor, bad breath, and mildew.

Graylock got up, tied the flaps closed, and returned to the heated rocks with the other survivors. He reached forward, picked up the makeshift cooking pot, and poured himself a bowl of bitter bark soup. He had a worried look on his face as he confided to Pembleton, "If Lerxst is telling the truth about this being an island, we're in big trouble."

"Relax, sir," Pembleton said, pretending to be confident. "We'll be fine. After all, you're an engineer, aren't you?"

Exhausted and perplexed, Graylock replied, "What does that have to do with anything?"

Pembleton shrugged. "So there's an ocean. How hard can it be to make a raft?"

The lieutenant sipped his soup and winced. "Harder than you think, Sergeant. A lot harder."

"Didn't Thor Heyerdahl cross an ocean on a raft?"

"Yes, he did," Graylock said. "But that was the Pacific in high summer, not an arctic sea in deep winter. Also, Heyerdahl built his raft in Peru, where he had access to the right kinds of wood and fabric. At the rate we're going, we'll probably end up drifting out to sea on ice floes, like dying Inuit."

Pointing in the direction of Junk Mountain, Pembleton said, "Do you want me to go get Lerxst and bring him back? Should we just give up now and ask the Caeliar to mulch our brains and put us out of our misery?"

Graylock sighed. "No."

"Then we'd better start thinking of ways to stay warm, dry, and afloat," Pembleton said, "because the only way we'll survive until spring is if we get *off this island*."

"Let the inner edges slide over each other as you step," Steinhauer said, coaching Graylock. "And roll your foot a bit when you lift it. Exaggerate your stride a little."

Graylock did his best to turn the young MACO's directions into actions, but he continued to stumble and teeter as he trudged across the snow-covered plain by the fjord. "*Scheisse,*" he said under his breath. "I feel like I'm drunk."

"It takes some getting used to," Steinhauer said. "Of course, if you think going forward is hard, wait until it's time to learn how to turn around."

Glaring in frustration, Graylock muttered, "I can hardly wait." He took another halting step forward, supporting his weight with two walking poles. The snow settled under his feet.

"Right now, it's harder because you're breaking a trail," Steinhauer said. "It'll be easier when you're following." He watched Graylock make a few more clumsy lunges and said, "Sir, stop a second. Watch me." Graylock halted and turned his head to observe the private, who moved in gliding strides. "As you finish each step," Steinhauer said, "pause a bit before you put your full weight on the shoe. It helps smooth the snow and pack it better for the person behind you."

Nodding, Graylock said, "Okay. Noted."

"Give it a try," the MACO said.

The engineer did as Steinhauer had said, easing into each step, keeping his eyes on the terrain ahead so that he could train his muscle memory to feel when his stride was correct. After a few minutes of exhausting pushing against the wet snow, his movements became more graceful, though still tiring.

"Now you're getting it," Steinhauer said. "Hold a second. It's time to learn how to turn."

Graylock was grateful for a chance to stop, even if only for a minute. He was the only one of the survivors with no previous experience at snowshoeing, so he had committed himself to an intensive training regimen. Once he mastered the basics of the skill, the only barrier to the team's departure would be Crichlow's fever.

Steinhauer shuffle-stepped alongside Graylock. "When you have a lot of room to turn around, like we do here, the easiest thing is to walk a wide semicircle," he said. "But in a forest or on a slope or narrow trail, that might not be possible. In those situations, you'll have to do a kick turn, like so." He lifted one of his snowshoes high off the ground while keeping the other firmly planted. Then he set his lifted shoe down at a right angle to the other, and brought the second one up and set it down parallel to the first. In a few kicks, he had done an about-face. "It's hard on the hips," he said. "And it's easier with poles than without. Use them to keep yourself steady."

As Graylock emulated the MACO's athletic leg lifts and turns, he strained a muscle in his groin, stopped, and doubled over. Through gritted teeth, he said, "I hate you."

"Wait till tomorrow, when your whole body starts aching," Steinhauer said. "Then you'll *really* hate me. Breathe a minute, then we'll head back to the slope near the shelter, and I'll teach you how to use kick steps to make climbing easier."

Graylock squatted and watched his breath form white clouds while he waited for his pain and nausea to subside. He had almost recovered his equilibrium when he saw someone in the distance, standing outside the shelter and frantically beckoning him and Steinhauer to return.

Steinhauer made a few comical hop steps sideways and placed himself directly in front of Graylock. "I'll break the trail back, sir," he said. "Are you ready to move?"

"I'm fine," Graylock said, masking his lingering discomfort. "Move out. I'll be right behind you."

The MACO cut a fast path across the open snow, and Graylock did his best to keep his eyes on the man's back and his feet in the smooth rut Steinhauer's snowshoes had carved. Just as the private had said minutes earlier, following a trail was far less taxing than breaking one. Less than two minutes later, he aped the young German's sidesteps up the slope to the camp. Once they were in the cleared area around the fire pit, they unwrapped the snowshoes' crude bindings from their boots and hurried inside the weather-beaten, ice-covered shelter.

As soon as Graylock was inside, he saw Pembleton and Thayer hovering over Crichlow, who was deathly pale and breathing in short, weak gasps. Graylock freed himself from the bulky layers of fabric in which he had wrapped himself for the afternoon of outdoor training. Wiping cold sweat from his beard, he said, "Sergeant. Report."

"He's dying," Pembleton said. "We tried keeping him warm and cooling him off. Nothing works."

Graylock frowned. He'd feared the worst a few days earlier, the morning after Lerxst had left their camp. Crichlow's symptoms had been steadily worsening, and without a doctor or the hand scanners, they'd had no idea what was wrong or how to help him. They'd fallen back on the basics: keep him warm, dry, and hydrated, and let him rest. It hadn't helped.

Crichlow had always been pale, and his face had always had a gaunt and awkward quality. Now, despite the wiry scraggle of beard whiskers on his chin and upper lip, he looked almost skeletal. Lying on his back, partly mummified in his bedroll, he stared up at his comrades with dull eyes that lay deep in their sockets. His lips parted, and a weak tremor shook his jaw as air hissed from his mouth. Everyone leaned closer to hear him as he said in a hoarse whisper, "Kiona . . ."

Thayer reached out and pressed her palm to his face. "I'm here, Eric," she said.

"Sorry, love," Crichlow said.

She shook her head. "For what?"

He was looking in Thayer's direction, but his eyes didn't seem to be focusing on her, or on anything else. "For my part," he rasped. "For what . . . we did to you."

His apology made Thayer wince. She hadn't spoken to any of the MACOs since the failed attempt to commandeer the control center of Mantilis, but she had confided to Graylock her fear and her resentment of them—Pembleton in particular, since he had been the one who'd pulled the trigger and maimed her.

"Not your fault, Eric," she said. "You're the only one who *didn't* point a weapon at me."

"Still . . . sorry."

She leaned down and kissed his forehead. "No worries."

A reedy breath passed from his lips, and then he was perfectly still. For a moment, the only sound was the low cry of the wind and the snapping of loose fabric on the outside of the shelter. Steinhauer and Pembleton both touched forehead, chest, and each shoulder with their right hands. Thayer reached over and nudged Crichlow's eyelids closed.

Pembleton wasted no time on sentiment. "Steinhauer," he said, "sanitize Crichlow's gear, and parcel it out to the rest of the team. When you're done, we'll take him up by the rocks and bury him in the snow."

"That's it?" asked Graylock. "We're just going to toss his naked body in a drift?"

Steinhauer and Thayer both turned away and pretended to be busy with other tasks as Pembleton replied, "What would you prefer, Lieutenant? Should I dump him in the fjord?"

"He deserves a proper burial," Graylock said.

"I agree," Pembleton said, "but the ground is frozen solid, and we're short of food. We need to save our strength for the trip, not waste it digging a hole."

"What about a funeral pyre?" asked Graylock.

"We're low on firewood, too, remember?"

Graylock sighed and nodded. "I know. It just feels heartless to throw him aside like this."

Pembleton replied, "Heartless would be carving him up as food. But since we don't know what killed him, we can't risk it." He pulled the flap of Crichlow's bedroll over the dead man's face. "After we put him outside, we should break down everything but the main shelter and get ready to travel. We need to be on the move by daybreak tomorrow."

"So soon?" asked Graylock.

"We're losing light every day, sir," Pembleton said. "At this rate, we're looking at God only knows how many months of night, starting in just a couple of weeks. If we aren't floating to warmer climes by then . . . we're finished."

A few days later, during their journey south, the survivors passed another interminable night huddled for warmth inside a crude shelter, which they had insulated from the wind by burying it inside a snow drift.

Rows of metal poles and sheets of taut fabric lashed together kept their fresh excavation from imploding on them while they slept. It didn't keep the cold out, though. Drafts of air so frigid that they felt like razors slipped through gaps in the shelter and always seemed to find Kiona Thayer, no matter how deep in the huddle she hid herself.

Tucked in that cluster of bodies, hidden in the dark, she stayed close to Karl Graylock, her fellow officer. She relied on him not just for heat but to act as a barrier between her and the MACOs, whom she still viewed with anger and anxiety.

Though she had never been attracted to Graylock, the tickle of his beard on her shoulder was a comfort as he wrapped himself around her. She dreaded awakening each morning to another day in exile with Pembleton and Steinhauer. At night, she dreamed of the only thing she truly cared about any longer: Earth, home soil, so far away now, farther than she'd ever imagined it would be.

Memories of Earth haunted Thayer's every waking moment, so she tried to spend as much of her time as possible asleep. Growing up in Québec, she had often thought of herself as being acclimated to the cold, perhaps even impervious to it. This world's arctic circle had taught her differently. Now the bitter wind was the enemy, and sleep's gray realm was her only haven from the constant discomfort of numb fingers and toes.

Some of her dreams took her to tropical locales; others put her fireside in her father's home, outside Montréal. She often dreamed of being back aboard the *Columbia* or in training on Earth or reliving her first day on campus at Dartmouth. Sometimes she was young again, and sometimes she was her current age but revisiting a past chapter of her life, like a tourist.

The one detail that was consistent in all her dreams, however, was that her left foot was whole. And that made it all the more terrible to awaken to her scarred, mangled extremity, which now required mechanical reinforcement.

She was running through tall grass in a Vermont apple orchard with her older sister, Winona, when a hated voice shattered the moment. "Up and at 'em," Pembleton barked, his baritone voice filling the tent. "Only five hours of light today! We can't waste a second of it. Everybody up! Let's go!"

Québécois epithets flew to her lips and no further.

Breakfast barely qualified as a meal. Steinhauer lit a small fire to reheat some weak broth they had saved from their last boiled rodent of several days earlier. They also drank as much wretched bark tea as they could swallow, because Graylock had noted that Crichlow, who had made a point of spurning the foul-tasting beverage, had been the one to grow sick and die.

"No more," Steinhauer said after half a cup. "One more drop, and I swear I'll vomit."

"Drink it," the engineer said. "Quinine tastes terrible, too, but it helped people fend off malaria."

"I think you only make us drink this piss to take our minds off the cold," Thayer said between lip-pursing sips.

Graylock smiled at that. "Is it working?"

"No," she said.

Minutes later, all traces of their camp had been cleaned up, stowed away, and hefted onto their backs for the continuing march toward the equator. Steinhauer returned from checking and collecting the traps, which he put out each night in the hope of snaring a few more small rodents to sustain them another day. That morning, unfortunately, he returned emptyhanded. He packed away the traps, and Pembleton led the team onward, into a landscape concealed by dense, spinning flurries of falling snow.

The quartet moved in single file, with the three men taking turns as trail breakers, sometimes in shifts as short as five minutes. Thayer slogged along behind them, doing her best to keep up but knowing full well that she was slowing them down.

The survivors hugged the coastline rather than try to scale the rugged slopes and peaks of the barren arctic landscape. As a result, their journey often seemed to entail long periods of little to no forward progress, as they trekked parallel to their course, and occasional periods of backtracking, when the shoreline switched back around one body of water or another.

A few hours out of camp and less than two hours shy of nightfall, they found themselves circumnavigating a frozen, narrow fjord. When it was Graylock's turn to take the lead, he started breaking a trail across the ice sheet.

Pembleton shouted ahead, "Lieutenant! What the hell are you doing? Trying to get us killed?"

"It's less than a kilometer across," Graylock said. "But it's got to be at least nine kilometers long. It'll take hours to go the long way around, but if we take the shortcut, we can reach those trees and still have time to set traps before dark."

Despite the fact that Pembleton was swaddled in layers of fabric that looked like a portable tent, his contemptuous slouch was easy to detect. "That's a saltwater fjord, Lieutenant," he said. "There's no guarantee it's frozen solid all the way across or that the ice is thick enough to hold your weight. If you feel like taking a bath in water that'll shock you dead in less than thirty seconds, be my guest, sir."

Graylock reversed course with a series of kick turns and waved Pembleton ahead on the original trail around the fjord. "Lead on, Sergeant."

"Yes, sir," Pembleton replied, moving down the desolate shoreline, breaking a trail through the snow with smooth but flagging strides. On either side of the fjord, high cliffs of bare, black rock ascended into the violet sky.

From the back of the line, Steinhauer said, "I would give anything to be on Earth right now."

"Right now, it's around 4500 B.C.," Pembleton replied as he fell back behind Thayer and let Graylock take the lead again. "You'd be living in the Neolithic period."

"That'd be fine," said Steinhauer. "Someone in Sumer is inventing beer about now."

"That's right!" Graylock hollered back from the point position. "*Mein Gott,* I could use a beer."

Trying to distract herself from the acidic churning and pathetic growling of her empty stomach, Thayer asked, "What about agriculture and written language? The Sumerians are inventing those about now, too."

Her observation drew a few moments of thoughtful silence from the three men.

Then Steinhauer replied, "I'd rather have the beer."

"And some barbecue," Pembleton said.

Graylock added, "With a side of beer."

"Well," Thayer said, rolling her eyes, "I'm happy to see we at least have our priorities straight."

Lerxst had sacrificed the corporeal bonds of his body to preserve the integrity of his memory and awareness—and now those, too, were starting to slip forever from his grasp.

I'm losing myself, he shared with the gestalt.

Their communion had been winnowed to four voices. Of these, Lerxst was the strongest, with only Sedín as his close equal. Ghyllac and Denblas clung to vestiges of coherence, but their thoughts had become increasingly disjointed as they faded.

All four knew that they were dim shadows of their former selves, but the quality of their past lives now eluded them. They wandered together through lightless catacombs of twisted metal and shattered stone, always near one another, like bodies united in deep space by a weak but undeniable gravity.

This place had a name, Denblas thought, disguising his plea for information in the form of a declaration.

His query lingered in the gestalt, but none of the four minds submerged into the bond could produce the answer. Denblas repeated himself. *This place had a name.*

So did we, once, replied Ghyllac. *It's lost now, like us.*

All of them felt the depths of history yawning below them, but not one of them could recall the events that had delivered them to this gray purgatory. They were simultaneously one in the gestalt and four in the world but only to the extent that they still sensed themselves as separate beings. Lerxst tried to mask his shame as he realized that although he remembered his name, the specifics of what he had considered his identity had become fragmented and opaque in his memory.

He wondered with naked confusion, *Who are we?*

Sedín answered his question with a question: *What are we?*

We are those who are and that which is, Denblas added.

It was an evasion. The four knew that they were the same, but none could name their species. They defined themselves now in the hollow context of knowing what they weren't.

A swift current of images and sounds surged through the gestalt. Lerxst couldn't tell if they were real memories or delusions, snippets of history or the products of a deranged imagination. They all were rooted in the physical and tangible, the empire of crude matter and the illusion of solidity, and they ran like a river flowing into a canyon, like vast jets of energy sinking into the insatiable maw of a singularity.

Light and sounds, artifacts of the tangible, passed from the grasp of the gestalt and vanished into the darkness.

Then came a terrible moment of clarity, as one cluster of catoms and then another released their energy reserves to bolster the gestalt. *Our core catom groups are breaking down,* Lerxst realized. *Our memories are collapsing into entropy.*

We're really dying, Sedín replied.

Deep, flat notes of dismay droned in the gestalt, and Lerxst extended himself to call for harmony's return. Then he sensed the diminished scale of the gestalt, and he understood the cost at which his clarity had been purchased.

Denblas was gone.

Lerxst and Sedín both seemed to have been fortified by their consolidation with their lost colleague, but Ghyllac appeared to have reaped no benefit from Denblas's demise.

Worse still, Ghyllac was no longer Ghyllac.

Where the essence of Ghyllac once had blazed, there was now a dark spiral of confusion, a mind trapped in the endless discovery of the present moment, with no sense of its past and no anticipation of its future. The echo of Ghyllac would spend the rest of its existence imprisoned in a limbo of the now.

Without thought, without memory, his catoms serve no true purpose, Sedín lamented. *They are expending energy without gain.*

The implications of her statement troubled Lerxst. *Is it our right to decide when his existence no longer has meaning?*

He doesn't even have existence, Sedín argued. *Without the mind, his catoms are an empty machine. A waste of resources. If you won't take your share of their reserves, I'll take them all.*

Lerxst understood the deeper threat implicit in her

words. If she absorbed all of the residual energy from Ghyllac's catoms, it would reinforce hers to a level of stability much greater than his own. Inevitably, he would find his catoms depleted far ahead of hers, and the only logical choice would be for her to consolidate his remaining energy into herself. He could either hasten Ghyllac's premature demise or else guarantee his own.

Very well. We'll consolidate his energy reserves into our catoms. There was no masking the deep regret he felt at his decision. They weren't killing Ghyllac, whose essence had already been lost, but taking the last of his catoms' power made Lerxst feel as if he had crossed a moral line.

Were we ever friends, Sedín?

I don't remember. Why do you ask?

Lerxst hesitated to continue his inquiry. *When you and I begin to fade . . . will you consolidate me as you did Ghyllac?*

As we *did Ghyllac.*

I will concede your semantic point if you'll answer my question. Are we mere fodder to each other? Will we meet our end united or as mutual predators?

We'll improvise, Sedín said. *It's how we survive.*

But what of the moral considerations?

They need to be secondary, Sedín replied. *All that matters is that we survive until the humans return. Then we shall bond with them, for their own good. Their synaptic pathways can be easily mapped and made compatible with our needs. As soon as it becomes practical, we will facilitate their journey toward this planet's populated middle latitudes.*

You underestimate the humans' natural antipathy for enslavement, Lerxst warned.

And you overestimate the strength of their free will.

He suspected that only bitter experience would disabuse Sedín of her illusion of omnipotence. *Heed me,* he told her. *If you try to yoke them, they will fight back.*

Let them, Sedín replied. *They will lose.*

It had been hours since Karl Graylock had been able to feel his toes. For a long time, they had been painfully cold, and then for a while, he had been aware of their being numb. Now they felt like nothing at all. The harder he tried not to think about frostbite, the more he dwelled on it.

Pembleton fell back from the trail-breaker position and slipped into the line behind Graylock, who now had Steinhauer's back to focus on. One shuffling, ankle-rolling step followed another. Graylock's stride was well practiced after only five short days of snowshoeing along the island's coast. He no longer needed to look at his feet while he was slogging forward against the ice pick wind and through hypnotic veils of falling snowflakes.

He had started the journey with an appreciation for the austere beauty of the empty arctic landscape, but he had since come to think of it as the proscenium to his traveling misery show. To one side lay low hills blanketed in snow, stretching away in gentle white knolls toward the distant mountains. On the other side was a sheer drop down fearsome cliffs of black rock, to a relentless assault of surf against the sawtoothed, obsidian boulders that jabbed up from a sea as black as the night sky.

Steinhauer led the foursome up a gradual rise. He kicked with the sides of his snowshoes and made a diagonal stair in the snow. After a few minutes, he began to fall backward. Graylock caught him and heard the labored gasps of the younger man's breathing. "It's all right, Thom," he told the private. "It's my turn to break. Fall back a while." Graylock handed the man into Pembleton's grasp and then stepped forward.

Each sideways chop at the hillside buried Graylock's feet in snow, which he carefully stamped down to make solid steps for the others. It was harder than regular snowshoeing, and for much of their journey they had avoided it when possible, opting for the most level paths they could find. As they'd neared the far southern end of the island, however, they had been forced to climb several shallow inclines to avoid plunging over sheer cliffs and to detour around impassable formations of rock that cut across the beaches and extended out into the turbulent sea.

Each step brought Graylock closer to the top of the hill and revealed more of the vast seascape that lay beyond. The ocean at night was pitch dark. The jagged cliffs on his right became more gradual, and ahead of him they descended in a steep but no longer vertical drop to the water.

Then he stepped over the crest and beheld the easy slope down to the rocky beach. The snow thinned and then ended roughly sixty meters before reaching the water, revealing miles of black sand. Majestic rock formations knifed up from the sea less than a hundred meters from shore. Great swells of black water curled around the rocks like ripples in a gown.

The vista possessed a stark beauty—but it was a wasteland.

And, as Graylock had feared, there wasn't a tree in sight.

He felt light-headed. Was it from not having eaten for three days? Or was it the result of six days of forced march over snow and ice, through an unforgiving wilderness? He reasoned it was probably both, colliding inside his frostbitten body and overwhelming his already sapped will.

The rest of the team huddled close beside him. They all stared at the wind-blasted shoreline. Coal-black sand and stones were lapped by inky waves, which broke into gray rolls of foam. Then a fierce wind blasted stinging particles of sand and ice into their faces, and the survivors shuffled clumsily about-face to protect themselves from the scouring gales.

Graylock said, "We have to go back."

"We're not going back," Pembleton said. "We have to go forward, across the water, or we'll die."

With a sweep of his arm toward the beach, Graylock snapped, "What am I supposed to build a raft from, Gage? Rocks? At least when we were on the mountainside, there were trees."

Thayer snapped, "Then why didn't we build the raft there?"

"Because the goddamned fjords are frozen!" Graylock stopped himself. He took a breath and said to Pembleton, "Even if we make it back to Junk Mountain, we're stuck until spring."

Pembleton's voice started out soft and grew louder as he repeated, "No . . . no . . . No . . . NO!" Overcome by frustration, he spun away from the group, then pivoted back. "Don't you get it?" He made wild gestures with his outstretched hands. "We have to go forward! It's our only chance. We *won't make it* to spring—not here and not on the mountain."

"Not without help," Graylock said.

"Tell me you're not saying what I think you're saying," Pembleton said. "Are you suggesting we bond with the Caeliar?"

Graylock hunched his shoulders and lifted his hands in a plaintive gesture. "What choice do we have, Gage? You said it yourself, we won't make it to spring. And I'm telling you, we can't sail until the ice thaws. Remember what Lerxst said. The catoms would help us survive famine and fight off disease."

"Only if we're lucky," Thayer cut in. "If we're not, we'll either end up dead or brain-fried. Is *that* what you want, Karl?"

"Dammit, be logical about this," Graylock said. "If we don't bond with the Caeliar, we'll die for certain. If we do, we might die anyway, just differently. But there's also a chance we could live. We'd be changed, but at least we'd be *alive*. Don't you think that it's at least worth taking the risk?"

Pembleton and Thayer exchanged dubious glances, and then each gave Graylock a grudging nod of agreement. The engineer looked around for Steinhauer, to confirm his assent to the plan.

The first things Graylock saw were Steinhauer's abandoned snowshoes. His eyes followed the deep, ragged bootprints that led away from them down the slope. One discarded layer of Caeliar fabric after another lay beside Steinhauer's trail. Then he saw Steinhauer, who was halfway to the water's edge, peeling off his protective layers of clothing as he went.

"*Scheisse,*" Graylock muttered. "Steinhauer's losing it." He stumbled over his own feet in his haste to turn around, and Pembleton and Thayer did little better. By the time they began breaking their own haphazard trails down the slope, Steinhauer had almost reached the water. He had stripped to his jumpsuit and boots, and he carried his phase rifle in one hand.

"Thom, stop!" called Pembleton as he charged downhill. "Put your gear back on, Private! That's an order!"

Steinhauer ignored them and kept walking toward the sea.

The trio in pursuit kicked free of their snowshoes when the snow became too shallow to hold a trail. Graylock and Pembleton sprinted the rest of the way to catch up to Steinhauer, while Thayer limped awkwardly far behind them.

The two men were still several meters away from catching Steinhauer when the private turned and aimed his rifle at them. "Don't come any closer," he said.

Pembleton and Graylock slowed to a careful walk. "Calm down, Thom," the sergeant said. "We just—"

The phase rifle blast struck the ground at their feet with a deafening shriek. Both men recoiled and halted. Behind them, Kiona slowed her own approach and then stopped at a distance.

Standing ankle-deep in the frothing surf, Steinhauer looked like an emaciated wild animal dressed in human clothing. His face was gaunt, and his eyes, though sunken in their sockets, burned with feral desperation. Spittle had turned to ice in his ragged beard whiskers. Behind massive clouds of exhaled breath, he shivered violently, and his jaw chattered loudly. The tips of most of his fingers were black and blistered with frostbite almost to the first knuckle. Graylock was amazed the man could still hold a rifle in his condition, never mind fire it.

"I won't go back," he said, his voice breaking into a near-hysterical pitch. "I can't. Too far. Too cold." He shook his head from side to side with mounting anxiety. "Can't do it. Won't."

With slow, cautious movements, Graylock extended his open hand to Steinhauer. "Thom, please. Put down the rifle, get dressed, and come with us. We have to go back to the Caeliar. It's the only way."

"Not for me," Steinhauer said.

In a fluid motion, he flipped the barrel of his phase rifle up and back, held its muzzle inside his mouth with his right hand, and pressed down on its trigger with his left thumb.

A flash of light and heat disintegrated most of his head.

The weapon fell from his hands. His decapitated body collapsed and fell backward into the pounding surf.

Graylock and Pembleton stood in silence for a minute and watched the waves wash over Steinhauer's corpse. Then Pembleton waded out to the body, retrieved the phase rifle and a few items from the dead man's jumpsuit, and returned. "We'll collect the fabric he left behind on the way down," he said. "A few more layers might make the trip back a bit less miserable."

As he followed the sergeant back up the beach to their snowshoes, Graylock felt a pang of regret at leaving Steinhauer unburied. He interred his guilty feelings instead. With no food left and temperatures dropping daily, he and the others could no longer afford to be sentimental; death was a simple reality in the hard land of the winter.

Thayer picked up Steinhauer's cast-off snowshoes. "These'll make good firewood," she said. "Where should we make camp?"

"We should get moving," Graylock said. "Right now."

Thayer looked askance at him. "In the dark?"

"Might as well," he said. "Because if my math is right . . . for the next five months, dark is all we're going to have."

2381

15

———

Riker and Picard stood behind the desk in *Titan*'s ready room and watched Admiral Alynna Nechayev on the desktop monitor. *"We just broke through the Borg's jamming frequencies,"* she said, her lean and angular features now drawn and pale. *"It's confirmed Deneva's been wiped out. It's gone."*

Maybe I did Deanna a favor by leaving her with the Caeliar, Riker brooded. *At least she's safe from all of this.*

"How much time until the Borg reach Earth?" asked Picard.

Nechayev replied, *"About seven hours. Maybe less. Why? Have something up your sleeve, Captain?"*

"That remains to be seen," Picard said. "But Captain Dax informs us she has an idea in the works."

"Say no more," Nechayev said. *"Unless you need us to play a part, maintain operational security. You've all been given full presidential authority to do whatever it takes. I'm counting on you two and Captain Dax to make the most of it."*

Riker nodded. "Understood." His door signal

chimed softly. "If you'll excuse us, Admiral, Captain Dax has arrived."

"By all means," Nechayev said. *"Nechayev out."*

Riker turned off his desktop monitor and said, "Come."

The door sighed open. Dax entered, followed by Hernandez. The two women seemed to project an aura of excitement mixed with apprehension. They stopped in front of Riker's desk. "We have something," Dax said. "As always, it's a long shot."

"Naturally," Picard said. "What is it?"

Hernandez replied with confidence and élan, "Supersedure."

The term meant nothing to Riker. He threw a confused glance at Picard, who looked similarly befuddled, then said to Hernandez, "I'm afraid you'll have to explain that to me."

"I was telling Erika about some of the oddities of Borg social structures," Dax said. "And she immediately drew the comparison to a bees' nest."

Picard reacted with a dubious frown and said to Hernandez, "I trust Captain Dax also explained that you're not the first person to apply that flawed analogy to the Borg."

"Yes, she did," Hernandez said. "But I still think you ought to hear the details of our plan."

"Hell," Riker cut in, "I just want to find out what 'supersedure' means."

Making small gestures as she spoke, Hernandez replied, "It's a technical term for the process by which bees replace old queens with new ones."

"I got the idea when Erika mentioned her ability to hear the individual drones," Dax said. "That suggests that her link with the Borg is precise and deep. If we could give her a way to talk to the Borg, maybe we could use that ability to introduce her to the Collective as a new queen."

Picard walked out from behind the desk to face the two female captains more directly. "I'm hardly an expert on the subject of bees," he said. "But I seem to recall learning in elementary school that most beehives react to the arrival of a strange queen by killing the intruder."

"That's why I won't be presenting myself as a stranger," Hernandez said. "I'll use my catoms to impersonate the Queen's presence inside the Collective."

Riker replied, "Forgive me, but that sounds a bit vague. You said you'd never encountered the Borg before. What makes you so sure you can trick them into thinking you're their queen?"

"Her voice," Hernandez said. "It's unique within the Collective, much like the piping a queen bee uses to direct her hive. My catoms can resonate on an identical frequency and make my thought patterns a dead ringer for the Queen's."

Dax added, "There are two stumbling blocks to linking Erika to the Collective without losing her to it. First, we'll need to physically patch her into a vinculum. Second, she'll need a lot of raw power to help her drown out the Queen's voice."

Hernandez continued, "The *Aventine* has more than enough power to help me pump up the volume, so to speak."

"Once she does, she can take control of the Borg armada, or part of it, at least. Then she turns the Borg against themselves. It'd be like someone with multiple personality disorder whose personas start attacking each other."

Riker grinned. "Leave it to a joined Trill with psychiatric training to make that comparison."

Returning his smile, Dax said, "Go with your strengths—that's what my mom always said."

Picard paced past the two women, stopped, and turned back. "I admire your proposal for its audacity, Captains, but I can't endorse it." He looked Hernandez in the eye. "The technology you carry within your body is too advanced, too potent, to risk letting it be assimilated by the Borg."

The youthful woman blinked with confusion. "Assimilated?"

Captain Picard cast an accusing stare at Dax. "Didn't you tell her what the Borg do when they encounter new species and technologies?"

Dax averted her eyes and replied in a humbled tone, "I may have skipped that part of Borg 101."

Riker could see the strain on Picard's face. Clearly, in the course of trying to formulate an explanation of assimilation for Hernandez, Picard was reliving the various ordeals he had suffered at the Borg's hands. To spare his former commanding officer that effort, Riker spoke up instead.

"With organic beings, it's a physical process," he said. "A Borg drone, queen, or sometimes even one of their ships, injects its victims with nanoprobes. These nanomachines bind with the subjects' RNA and effect a number of biological changes. More important, they suppress the subjects' free will and make them extensions of the Borg Collective, which gains access to its drones' memories and experiences. On a more practical level, the Borg assimilate technologies and concepts by stealing them."

Hernandez nodded and looked somber. "In other words, the Borg take all your best toys and make you a zombie."

"Basically, yes," Dax said.

Picard's countenance was haunted by his memories. "It's far more terrible than anything you can imagine," he said, though not to anyone in particular. "Part of you remains trapped inside yourself. You become a spectator to the hijacking of your mind and body. It's like a nightmare from which there's no awakening. You see everything, and you can't even shut your eyes."

A grim silence descended on the room.

Dax coughed to clear her throat. "Well, we weren't planning on risking Erika, for whatever that's worth."

"Any time you enter a Borg ship, it's a risk," Riker said. "And unless the *Aventine* has another amazing innovation we don't know about, I'm guessing you'll need to board a Borg ship to gain access to a vinculum for Captain Hernandez."

"You're right," Dax said. "I do plan on boarding a Borg ship to use its vinculum. But first, I plan to have my people eliminate every drone on the ship and neutralize its defenses. Erika won't set foot on it till it's been secured."

With his composure recovered, Picard replied, "That's a tall order, Captains. How do you intend to carry it out?"

Nodding toward Hernandez, Dax said, "Erika has a very keen sense for where the Borg are. If we give her natural gifts a boost, she can help us pinpoint a small scout cube or some other smaller Borg vessel traveling alone."

"I'd need energy and equipment to extend my range and enhance my precision," Hernandez said. "If I could make a direct interface with *Titan*'s sensor module, it'd be a big help."

Riker nodded. "All right. I'll have my science officer help you set it up."

Picard sounded doubtful and dismissive. "Even a brief infiltration of a Borg cube is dangerous," he said to Dax. "What, may I ask, is your plan for *capturing* such a vessel?"

Dax's voice took on an aggressive edge. "We'll fight them with the same tactics the Hirogen used on us," she said. "Erika picks a target, and the *Aventine* uses its slipstream drive to catch it. We fire a few low-yield transphasic torpedoes to knock out their shields. Then our strike teams beam in with projectile weapons, chemical explosives, and energy dampeners replicated from the ones we captured. The *Aventine* emits an energy-dampening field to suppress the Borg ship's regenerative capacity and defensive systems. Then my people go deck by deck, section by section, and secure the cube. Once we eliminate all the drones and access the vinculum, we send over Erika to do her thing—and coronate a new queen for the Borg."

The grimace on Picard's face was sterner than any Riker had ever seen. Picard heaved a deep sigh. "I can't fault you for a lack of ambition," he said, "but I remain unconvinced. Your plan is beyond dangerous; it runs the risk of granting the Borg access to a staggering new level of technology. Furthermore, you grossly underestimate their speed and ferocity."

Riker thought he heard an undercurrent of fear in Picard's voice, and he wondered if perhaps the captain's recent brief reassimilation had inflicted deeper wounds than Picard let on.

Picard continued, "Put simply, Captain Dax, your plan is foolhardy."

Undaunted, Dax replied, "It's also our only chance."

From the first moment Hernandez stepped inside *Titan*'s stellar cartography lab, she was overwhelmed by a sense of déjà vu. Standing beside Molora Pazlar at the end of the widow's-walk platform, she watched the galaxy appear from the darkness and take shape in reduced form all around them.

Pazlar freed herself from her metal motor-assist armature and said with a smile, "When you're ready, just give a push to come up and join me." Then she vaulted straight up, off the platform, with the same ease that Hernandez herself had once taken for granted in Axion.

Hernandez hesitated to follow the science officer, unsure of how much freedom of movement she would have in her new clothing. At Captain Riker's request, Hernandez had exchanged her Caeliar-made attire for the current Starfleet duty uniform. The black jumpsuit with gray shoulder padding and a burgundy-colored undershirt had appeared in her quarters' replicator, complete with the rank insignia for a captain.

She took a breath, bent her knees a bit, and sprang with grace into the open space above. It felt strange, she thought, to be back in a uniform after eight centuries of wearing gossamer. She added it to the other aspects of her past—sleep and hunger—that had caught up with her since she'd fled her captivity in Axion. A lifetime of sensations had come back to her in a matter of hours.

Within moments, she was beside Pazlar, who reached out and manipulated elements of the simulation in much the same way that Inyx had plucked stars from the darkness in the Star Chamber, during the century that Hernandez had helped him seek a new homeworld for the Caeliar. *I hope he's all right,* she thought. *The Quorum must've been furious at him for letting me get away.*

"It's easy to configure," Pazlar said. She raised an open palm and extended it. As she drew her hand back, a low-opacity holographic interface appeared. "You can alter any of the simulation parameters with this. Just be careful if you start messing with the gravity." She cocked her head and gestured at the lower part of her body. "I'm a bit fragile, you see."

"Understood," Hernandez said. She reached forward and expected to find herself miming physical interaction with the projected controls. Instead, when she pushed her fingers on the various padds and slider panels, they met with the same resistance she would have expected of a physical console. Muted feedback tones followed each of her inputs. "It's very intuitive," she said.

"I know," Pazlar said. "Xin—I mean, Commander Ra-Havreii—designed the interface himself." The slender blond Elaysian averted her eyes when Hernandez glanced over at her.

"All right," Hernandez said. "I've set up a signal feed on the same frequency as my catoms. How do I activate the sensors?"

Pazlar pointed at a radiant blue panel on the interface. "Press that, and the sensor module switches into high gear. You'll be able to pull up high-resolution scans on anything within a hundred light-years."

"Then the only thing I still need is a simulated quantum field to power my catoms."

Nodding, Pazlar said, "We can't generate even a fraction of the energy that the Caeliar were making at New Erigol, but we'll give you everything we can."

"It'll be enough," Hernandez said. "Axion had to sustain itself, millions of Caeliar, and who knows what else. I just need enough to boost my catoms back to full strength. A fraction ought to do the trick, I'd think."

The science officer tapped her combadge. "Pazlar to Ra-Havreii," she said, and Hernandez noted a subtle shift in the woman's vocal inflection—it became gentler and a bit higher. "We're ready for the simulated quantum field."

"Perfect timing, Melora," Ra-Havreii replied. *"Stand by while I bring it online. . . . Charging the deflector."* The channel closed with a soft double beep a few seconds later.

Hernandez waited to feel the infusion of new strength. Several seconds passed with no change. Pazlar filled the silence by explaining, "It might take a few minutes to bring the main deflector up to full power as a quantum-field generator."

"I know," Hernandez said. "I was the one who wrote the plan for the reconfiguration."

"Right," Pazlar said, flashing an embarrassed grin.

After another awkward moment, she added, "I'm sure Commander Ra-Havreii was able to make the changes. You can count on him."

Overcoming her aversion to meddling in others' business, Hernandez said, "Commander, may I make an observation?"

"Of course," Pazlar said.

"I've noticed that you and Commander Ra-Havreii seem to have a very cordial working relationship."

Immediately, Pazlar became tense and defensive. "So?"

"Don't misunderstand," Hernandez said. "I'm not making any assumptions about your relationship with—"

"Xin and I don't *have* a relationship," Pazlar said. "We're just friends."

Unable to suppress a knowing smile, Hernandez replied, "If you say so, Commander."

Pazlar crossed her arms and spent a moment looking flustered. "All right, there was one time when he tried to kiss me, but it didn't happen, and it was all a big misunderstanding—just crossed wires, you know? It didn't mean anything."

"Forget I mentioned it," Hernandez said. "It's none of my business, anyway. Sorry I pried."

Apparently unwilling to drop the subject, Pazlar added, "I made it very clear that I don't feel that way about him."

"No doubt," Hernandez said.

A fresh silence yawned between them. Then came Ra-Havreii's voice, filtered through the overhead comm. *"Engineering to Pazlar. Quantum field stabilizing at full strength . . . now."*

Again, Hernandez opened her senses to the state of the local ambient energy potential. She was rewarded by a flood of strength and focus as her catoms pulsed with renewed vigor. Nodding to Pazlar, she said, "I'm ready."

"Sensors online and ready," Pazlar said. "The system's all yours now, Captain."

Hernandez closed her eyes and felt a rush of raw data from *Titan*'s sensors being transmitted directly to her catoms, which processed all of it and accelerated her synapses to keep pace. Then she extended the range of her senses and let herself hear the intimidating chorus of the Borg Collective.

Millions of voices some near, some distant. Clustered in groups as small as three or as large as thousands, a roar of minds yoked to the will of something that included them all and yet remained apart from them, aloof and domineering. She fought to parse their cacophony and subdivide it into manageable blocs. With effort, she began to separate them by sectors, and then by subsectors, and then by individual ships.

"I hear them," she said to Pazlar. "I see them."

Holding the snapshot of the Borg armada in her mind, she began to search it; she combed it for lone vessels, stragglers, outriders, or scouts. Her mind raced from one target to the next, flitted from sector to sector at the speed of thought.

Each time she found a promising lead, she targeted *Titan*'s sensor module on the coordinates that she heard echoing from that link in the Collective. Her first effort found a trio of small Borg vessels— ostensibly a light attack group but still too formidable for the *Aventine* to challenge alone. Several subsequent leads proved to be massive assault cubes en route to major star systems; such targets would be too heavily manned by drones for the *Aventine*'s limited strike forces to overcome.

Then she found it. The ideal target.

Zeroing in with *Titan*'s sensors, she said to Pazlar, "Have a look at this." The simulated galaxy expanded and flew away as the holographic projection enlarged a detailed sensor scan of a small Borg probe, traveling alone. "I'm not reading any major targets along their trajectory," Hernandez said. "They might be a long-range recon vessel."

Pazlar summoned a new command interface and made a quick evaluation of the ship. "Definitely a scout of some kind," she said. "Probably no more than fifty to a hundred drones onboard. What are their coordinates?"

"Bearing zero-one-three, approximately ten-point-five light-years from Devoras." She felt a profound trepidation as she added, "Inside Romulan space."

Grinning, Pazlar replied, "Good thing they're on our side in this fight."

That's right, Hernandez reminded herself, ashamed that she had succumbed so easily to old fears. *Things changed while I was gone. The Romulans aren't the biggest problem anymore.*

Pazlar tapped in more commands. "Target locked in," she said. "Sending its coordinates to the *Aventine*." A moment later, she added, "*Aventine* confirms: target acquired."

"Now all we have to do is go get them," Hernandez said, with a bit more brio than she had intended.

Throwing a cautionary look in her direction, Pazlar said, "I wouldn't be in such a hurry to meet the Borg if I were you. Finding them was easy." She eyed the image of the black ship in front of them and frowned. "What comes next won't be."

The transporter beam released Hernandez as her new surroundings took shape around her. The transition felt smoother than it had in her days aboard the *Columbia*. It helped that the process was faster, but she was certain that the confinement beam had been made less oppressive—a change for which she was grateful.

Freed from its paralyzing hold, she found herself in a transporter room aboard the *Aventine*. Several security personnel from *Titan* had beamed over with her. Lieutenant sh'Aqabaa and Senior Petty Officer Antillea flanked Hernandez, and Lieutenant Shelley Hutchinson stood behind her. The Andorian and the reptilian female, whom Hernandez had been told was of a species known as the Gnalish, stepped off the padds. Hutchinson, a trim woman with short brown hair, walked around Hernandez and followed her colleagues out of the transporter room.

Waiting to greet Hernandez were Captain Dax and a lean man with short black hair whose face was defined by parallel drooping ridges on his cheeks. "Captain Hernandez," Dax said. "Welcome aboard the *Aventine*. This is my second officer and senior science officer, Lieutenant Commander Gruhn Helkara."

"Thank you, Captain," said Hernandez, stepping down from the platform. She offered her hand to

Helkara, who shook it. "Pleasure to meet you, Mister Helkara."

"Likewise, Captain," Helkara said with a polite nod.

"Well," Dax said, "I hate to beam and run, but I need to get back to the bridge. Mister Helkara will escort you to main engineering, where you can offer Chief Engineer Leishman the benefit of your technical expertise."

Hernandez nodded. "I understand, Captain. Thank you."

Dax smiled, turned, and left the transporter room. Hernandez reflected on how much Dax reminded her of herself at that age, as a young starship captain, brimming with confidence and as-yet-unrealized potential.

Behind Hernandez, the transporter's energizer coils came alive with a deep hum. She pivoted on her heel and saw five more shapes materialize: two human men, a Vulcan woman, and a male and a female of different species that she didn't recognize. All carried imposing-looking rifles and other combat equipment.

Helkara touched Hernandez's elbow to guide her. "Captain," he said. "We should go. Lieutenant Leishman is waiting for us."

"Of course," Hernandez said. She followed him out of the transporter room into the corridor. Security personnel, attired in padded and reinforced all-black uniforms, moved past her and Helkara in groups. Most of them were armed with the same rifles that she had seen in the hands of the officers who had beamed in after her. A few carried stockier weapons with wide barrels. As she and Helkara turned a corner, they passed a squad of security personnel who were field-stripping their weapons, making modifications to them, and reassembling them.

She and Helkara stepped inside a turbolift. "Main engineering," he said as the doors closed. A high-pitched pulsing hum accompanied their descent.

"Your people look pretty confident with those rifles," she said. "But how're they going to fire them once they're inside a dampening field?"

"TR-116s fire chemical-propellant projectiles ignited by a mechanical firing pin," Helkara said. "Gas-capture recoil drives the reloader at a rate of nine hundred rounds per minute. No power needed except a pull on the trigger."

"In other words, they're primitive firearms."

"I wouldn't call them primitive. More like a modern update of a classic idea. They were designed during the Dominion War for use against the Jem'Hadar, but they didn't make it much past the testing phase until the Tezwa conflict." He caught her quizzical glance and grinned sheepishly. "None of what I'm saying means anything to you, does it?"

Hernandez grinned. "Not really, no."

"Sorry," he said. "Maybe when this mess is over, we can hook you up with some light reading to bring you up to speed."

"I'd appreciate that," she said.

The turbolift stopped, and the doors opened on the manic activity of the *Aventine*'s main engineering deck. Helkara led Hernandez into the middle of the commotion. Sparks fell from upper levels around the warp core as critical components were welded back into place, and the bulkheads were lit by infrequent flashes of acetylene light. A dozen discussions—some between people in the compartment, some over the comms—overlapped beneath the low-frequency throbbing of the antimatter reactor.

In an alcove opposite the warp core, a group of engineers were gathered around a hip-height table of control consoles. At the far end was a young, brown-haired human woman doling out assignments. "Selidok, tell your team they have ten minutes to finish adjusting the yields on the warheads," she said to an alien who wore a mist-producing apparatus in front of his nostrils. To a diminutive lieutenant who resembled an upright pill bug, she continued, "P7-Red, we need at least twenty more of those energy dampeners replicated and distributed, on the double." Turning toward a looming Vulcan man—Hernandez guessed the ensign was at least 193 centimeters tall—the chief engineer said, "Navok, what's the status of the slipstream drive?"

"All components are operating within expected parameters," Navok said. "However, we continue to have difficulty predicting the phase variances."

Hernandez blurted out, "You can control the pattern of the phase variance by projecting soliton pulses ahead of you, inside the slipstream."

Everyone at the table looked in Hernandez's direction, and Helkara said to the woman at the end of the table, "Lieutenant Leishman, allow me to introduce Captain Erika Hernandez, our new technical adviser."

Leishman's reaction was barely noticeable. "All right," she said to her team. "You have your assignments. Navok, see if you can apply Captain Hernandez's suggestion for a soliton pulse."

"Aye, sir," Navok replied.

"Meeting adjourned," Leishman said. The junior officers split up and left the compartment. The chief engineer circled around the table to greet Hernandez. "Captain. A pleasure."

"Glad to be of service, Lieutenant." Hernandez motioned toward the table of consoles. "Care to show me your biggest technical hurdles?"

"Sure," Leishman said. She turned to the console and called up several sets of schematics on adjacent displays. "We have two small problems to deal with. The first is that we need to shore up our transphasic shielding to keep the Borg from slicing us in half before we hit them with the energy dampener."

Hernandez reached forward to input some commands. She paused before touching the interface. "May I?"

"Be my guest," Leishman said.

After centuries of dissecting and trying to improve on Caeliar technology, Hernandez found it easy to analyze and reconfigure twenty-fourth-century Starfleet software and hardware, which was much simpler by comparison. She rewrote power-distribution algorithms and adaptive shield-harmonic subroutines as if by instinct. By her reckoning, she had, in a matter of seconds, advanced Starfleet defensive technology by at least a decade.

She turned to the wide-eyed chief engineer and asked, "What's your second problem?"

Neither Leishman nor Helkara responded right away. They were both mesmerized by the designs and formulas that Hernandez had crafted in front of them. After a few seconds, Leishman grinned and snorted with amusement. "Something tells me you're gonna have a bright future at Starfleet Research and Development, Captain."

"We'll see," Hernandez said. Then she prompted Leishman, "Your second 'small problem,' Lieutenant?"

"Right," Leishman said, calling up a new array of complex computations on the tabletop's assorted display screens. "We're tracking the Borg ship you located, but it's pretty far away from here." She directed Hernandez's attention to a specific equation. "The problem is one of control. Once we engage the slipstream drive, we'll catch up to the Borg in a matter of minutes. But if we come out of slipstream too soon or too late, we'll be too far away to make a sneak attack. They'll have time to raise their defenses, and we might end up the hunted instead of the hunter. Unfortunately, our sensors and conn weren't made to drop in and out of slipstream with that degree of precision."

Hernandez studied the data on the screens and considered what Leishman had said. "Yes," she replied. "I see the problem."

Leishman said, "Does that mean you can help us?"

"That depends," Hernandez said. "Do you think you can persuade Captain Dax to let me fly her ship into combat?"

The chief engineer threw a questioning look at Helkara, who smirked and replied, "I think that can be arranged."

Dax emerged from her ready room feeling charged and impatient. Captain Picard had told her to have a plan before taking her ship into action; with her plan in place, she wanted to be in motion, tearing through a quantum slipstream for a rendezvous with a Borg ship whose minutes now were numbered.

Taking her seat beside her first officer, she asked, "How much longer, Mister Bowers?"

"Ten minutes at the most, Captain," Bowers said. "We're beaming over the last of the reinforcements from *Enterprise* and *Titan* right now."

She leaned closer to him and lifted her chin toward Erika Hernandez, who was seated at the conn. In a whisper, she inquired, "How's our new pilot doing?"

"Fine, so far," came Bowers's hushed reply.

"Good," Dax said. She swiveled her chair toward the tactical station, where Lieutenant Lonnoc Kedair was working with an intense focus on her console. "Tactical, report."

The Takaran security chief snapped her head up and answered with poise and calm, "Transphasic warhead yields adjusted for shield collapse only. Our own shields have been updated to stay a few steps ahead of the Borg's weapons"—she nodded toward Hernandez—"courtesy of our guest."

Dax grinned at Hernandez. "Sounds like you've had a busy morning, Captain."

"Haven't we all?" replied Hernandez.

Looking to ops, where Ensign Svetlana Gredenko was filling in for the critically wounded Lieutenant Mirren, Dax asked, "Ops, do we still have a solid lock on the Borg scout vessel?"

"Aye, Captain," Gredenko said.

"Helm," Dax said, "is the slipstream drive online yet?"

"Affirmative, Captain," said Hernandez. "Main deflector is fully charged, and chroniton integrator is online. Ready to engage on your order."

A signal chirruped on Bowers's armrest display. He silenced it with a tap of his index finger and said to Dax, "The last of the strike-team members are aboard, sir." Something on his screen made him do a double-take. "And you have a visitor."

"A what?"

Bowers relayed the message to her command display, at the end of her chair's right armrest. He lowered his voice. "It's Commander Worf from the *Enterprise,* sir. He beamed aboard with the last squad of reinforcements, and he's waiting for you in transporter room one. Says he won't leave till he sees you."

Dax stood from her chair. "Tell him I'll be there in a minute. Until then, hold the attack."

"Understood," Bowers said.

"You have the bridge, Commander," Dax said.

She strode to the turbolift as quickly as she could without looking as if she was in a hurry. The ride to Deck Three took only a matter of seconds, and then she walk-jogged to transporter room one. The door slid open ahead of her, and she entered to see Worf standing alone in front of the transporter platform. In one hand he held his *bat'leth,* in the other his *mek'leth.* He regarded her with quiet resolve. "I request permission to join your attack on the Borg, Captain."

Dax looked at the transporter operator, an imposing male Selay whose cobralike cranial hood was marked by a colorful pattern that reminded Dax of hourglasses. "Dismissed," she said.

"Aye, Captain," the Selay replied. He put the transporter console into standby mode and made a quick exit. The door closed with a muffled hiss behind him.

Dax walked slowly toward Worf as she asked, "Does Captain Picard know you're here?"

"Yes," Worf replied. "He granted my request to volunteer for this mission."

"I find that hard to believe," Dax said. "Captain Picard doesn't think we should even *attempt* this mission. So why would he loan me his first officer?"

Bristling at the naked suspicion in her tone, Worf broke eye contact and lifted his chin in a display of defiant pride. "When it comes to fighting the Borg, I am one of the most experienced tacticians in Starfleet. Even if the captain does not approve of your plan, he wants you to have the best possible chance of success."

"Can I let you in on a little secret, Worf?" Dax smirked as he looked back at her. "The way you lifted your chin and looked away just then? That's one of your tells. Every time you do that, I know you're hiding something." The abashed look on Worf's face—and the speed with which he averted his fuming stare—told Dax she had scored a verbal direct hit. "Why don't you try telling me what you're really doing here?"

Worf sighed and set his weapons on the transporter platform behind him. "Captain Picard did ask me to try to change your mind about the attack. He considers it a foolhardy effort."

"And what do you think of it, Worf?" She tried to look into his eyes, but he turned his head to show her his stern profile.

"What I think is not important," he said.

"In other words, you agree with me, but you don't want to dishonor your captain by second-guessing his orders." His silence told her more than anything he might have said in response. "Let me ask you a question," she continued. "If we don't take the offensive in this battle, what are we supposed to do? If Captain Picard objects to my plan, what's his?"

The Klingon's prodigious eyebrows knitted together above the bridge of his nose as he frowned in irritation. "The captain has not yet presented his plan," he said.

Dax reached out and placed her hand on his arm. "Let me save us both a lot of talking, Worf. I'm sure that if you tried, you could give me a dozen good reasons not to go forward with the attack, and I could give you a dozen good reasons why I should. But in the end, it'll all come down to one simple fact: This is my command; I call the shots here. Starfleet protocol demands that I show Captain Picard deference because of his seniority, but if push comes to shove, he doesn't outrank me, Worf. I'm a captain, the same rank as him. This is my ship, and I am taking her, and her crew, into battle. And that's final."

He looked at her with both respect and pride. "That is exactly as it should be," he said. "And I will be proud to serve under your command."

"That's kind of you to say, but you're not coming with us," Dax said. "The *Enterprise* needs you more."

Worf became bellicose. "Do not be foolish, Ezri. You will need every advantage you can get against the Borg."

"I already have an advantage," she said with a broad smile. "I'm a Dax, remember?"

A proud gleaming broke through his wall of gloom. "It is at times like this that I see Jadzia in you," he said. "Are you certain you will not reconsider my petition?"

"Positive," Dax said.

He stood. "Then I wish you success and glory in the battle to come. *Qapla'*, Ezri, daughter of Yanas, House of Martok."

She got up and stood in front of him. "*Qapla'*, Worf, son of Mogh." Then she wrapped her arms around his barrel-thick torso and hugged him with all the strength she could muster. He returned her embrace for several seconds, and then they parted.

He picked up his weapons from the platform, climbed the stairs, and stepped onto a transport pad. Turning back, he said, "Victory against these odds will be almost impossible."

Dax narrowed her eyes. "I wouldn't say impossible."

Worf replied with a smirk, "I meant for the Borg."

There were a thousand potential distractions on the bridge of the *Enterprise,* but every time Captain Picard looked up from the padd in his hands, his eyes found the blackened cavity of his ready room. Engineers and mechanics carried out scorched bulkhead panels and the charred remains of his chair and a crate's worth of his personal effects, all incinerated.

He fixed his eyes once more on the padd, which felt cold in his palm. Updates from the *Aventine* confirmed that Captain Dax and her crew would be ready to launch their bold—and possibly suicidal—attack on the Borg within a matter of minutes.

It's an audacious plan, he admitted to himself. *I only wish it didn't seem so . . . futile.* Perusing its details, he feared all the ways that it could fail. *If the Borg adapt to the transphasic torpedo, the* Aventine *will be an exposed target,* he brooded. *Even if the strike teams board the probe, there's no guarantee they'll prevail. And those crude weapons are bound to produce friendly-fire casualties.* He frowned as he scrolled through a summary of the plan's later phases. *Worst of all, it could backfire beyond our worst nightmares. If the Borg assimilate Captain Hernandez, there's no telling what kind of evil we might unleash on the galaxy.*

A female voice with a vaguely British accent interrupted his pessimistic musings. "Excuse me, Captain."

He looked up to see Miranda Kadohata, the ship's second officer, standing in front of him. "Yes, Commander?"

"The final roster of personnel who've transferred to the *Aventine* is ready, sir," she said. "I routed the report to your command screen."

He nodded and started calling up the file. "Thank you." After a few moments, he realized Kadohata was still there, as if she was waiting for something. He looked up at her. "Something else, Commander?"

She raised her eyebrows as she glanced away. The gesture accentuated the normally subtle epicanthic folding around her eyes, emphasizing her mixed European-Asian human ancestry. "Starfleet Command passed along a suggestion from Seven of Nine, but I'm not sure you'd approve of it, sir."

Her apprehensiveness piqued his curiosity. "Go on."

"There is one weapon we haven't considered using on the Borg," she said, "and maybe we should."

"And that would be . . . ?"

"A thalaron projector," Kadohata said. "Like the one Shinzon had aboard the *Scimitar*."

Picard recoiled slightly. "A thalaron weapon," he muttered. "Rebuilding such a device would antagonize every power in the quadrant—an outcome your predecessor died to prevent."

"I'm aware of that, sir," Kadohata said. "However, a cascading biogenic pulse powered by thalaron radiation would, in theory, be able to destroy the Borg's organic components. Without their drones or the organic portions of their ships—"

Picard cut her off with his raised hand. "Point taken, Commander," he said. Then the port turbolift door opened, and he saw Worf step onto the bridge. "We'll continue this another time."

"Aye, sir," Kadohata said, and she turned and walked back to ops. As Kadohata settled in at her post, Worf offered a discreet nod of greeting to Lieutenant Choudhury at tactical, then sat down in his chair beside the captain.

"I talked to Captain Dax," Worf said.

"And . . . ?"

"She declined to approve my transfer," Worf said. "And she is proceeding with the attack."

Picard breathed a disappointed sigh. "Of course she is."

"You do not approve of her plan," Worf said.

"It's not up to me to approve or disapprove, Mister Worf," Picard said. "I simply lack Captain Dax's confidence in her odds of success."

Worf shifted his posture, straightening his back. "I reviewed her attack profile," he said. "It is bold, but I believe it has a reasonable chance of securing the Borg probe."

"Yes, but what then, Number One? Does pitting Captain Hernandez in mortal psychic combat with the Borg Queen strike you as a viable strategy? Or as yet another in a long line of hopeless delaying tactics?"

Undaunted by the captain's pessimism, Worf replied, "I will not know until I see how the fight ends."

"That's what I'm afraid of, Mister Worf." Picard frowned. "Are you certain you tried every argument to dissuade Captain Dax from going forward with this?"

"She did not give me the chance," Worf said. In a more diplomatic tone, he asked, "May I offer some advice, Captain?"

"By all means, Commander."

"A lesson I learned while I was married to Jadzia remains just as true today about Ezri: She is a Dax. Sometimes they do not think—they just *do*."

16

Ezri Dax took a breath and settled her thoughts. Within moments, she and her ship would plunge headlong into the chaos of battle. She was determined to take one brief moment of quiet before the storm in order to steel herself for whatever followed.

Months earlier, when Captain Dexar and Commander Tovak had been killed, Dax had stepped up to fill the void at the top of the *Aventine*'s chain of command. That moment had inaugurated her captaincy. The one that was about to unfold—an arguably insane, all-or-nothing assault on which depended the survival of everything she had ever known—would *define* her captaincy.

On the main viewer, stars stretched past, pulled taut by the photonic distortions of high-warp travel.

She wiped the sweat from her cold palms across her pant legs and set her face in a mask of resolve. It was time.

"Helm," Dax said, "engage slipstream drive on my mark."

Erika Hernandez keyed the commands into the conn and answered, "Ready, Captain."

Dax looked at Bowers. "Sam, tell the transporter rooms and strike teams to stand ready. Tactical, raise shields and arm torpedoes." She lifted her voice. "Three. Two. One. *Mark.*"

Hernandez patched in the slipstream drive.

It was like being shot through a cannon of blue and white light or a faster-than-light patch of whitewater rapids. A peculiar, quasi-musical resonance filled the ship, like the long-sustained peal of a great iron bell but without the note that started it ringing. Dax detected no real difference in the sensations vibrating the deck under her feet, but adrenaline and anxiety were enough to crush her back against her chair.

Then the rush of light became the black tableau of space, and at point-blank range in front of the *Aventine* was the Borg reconnaissance probe. As promised, Hernandez had guided them out of their slipstream jaunt with surgical precision, into a perfect ambush position against the Borg.

Dax sprang to her feet. "Fire!"

"Torpedoes away," replied tactical officer Kandel.

Three electric-blue streaks arced toward the Borg ship and flared against its shields, and a fourth sailed through with no resistance and hammered the long, dark vessel amidships.

Kandel reported, "Direct hits! Their warp field's collapsing!"

"Stay with them, helm," Dax said, before she realized that Hernandez was already compensating for the changes in the Borg ship's velocity. *Not bad for a person who learned to fly starships in a different century,* Dax mused.

Hernandez matched the Borg's course and speed

almost perfectly, then said, "We're at impulse, Captain."

"Strike teams, go," Dax said.

Gredenko relayed the order from ops to the *Aventine*'s twenty transporter sites, which included four upgraded cargo transporters and six emergency-evacuation transporters. More than two hundred Starfleet security personnel were, at that moment, being beamed inside the Borg probe. If the estimate of the ship's drone complement was accurate, her people could expect to outnumber the enemy by a ratio of four to one.

Dax hoped that it would be enough, because once they were deployed, there would be no reinforcements—and no turning back.

"Transports complete," Gredenko said.

"Helkara, activate the dampener field," Dax said.

The Zakdorn science officer keyed in the command and replied, "Field is up and stable, Captain."

She nodded. "Good work, everyone."

Bowers watched Dax as she returned to her seat. Once she had settled, he said, "Now comes the hard part: the waiting."

The single drawback to Dax's plan lay in the dampening field that the *Aventine* was projecting toward the probe. By using the Hirogen's tactics, her crew had neutralized the Borg ship's weapons, shields, communications, and ability to repair itself. However, the field also prevented contact with the strike teams inside the vessel, and it made it impossible to beam them out or to send reinforcements. Unless and until the strike teams gained control of the ship and established visual contact with the *Aventine,* there would be nothing for Dax to do but sit and wait—and keep a volley of transphasic torpedoes armed and ready to fire, in case her captaincy's defining moment turned out to be a historic blunder.

The shimmering haze of the transporter beam dissolved into the darkness of the Borg ship's interior, and Lieutenant Pava Ek'Noor sh'Aqabaa felt her antennae twitch with anticipation.

Heat and humidity washed over her. "Flares!" she ordered, bracing her rifle against her shoulder. "Arm dampeners!"

Ensign Rriarr moved half a step ahead of sh'Aqabaa and snapped off several quick shots from the flare launcher mounted beneath the barrel of his T-116 rifle. Pellets of compressed, oxygen-reactive illumination gel made glowing green streaks across the deck, bulkheads, and overhead of the Borg vessel's frighteningly uniform black interior.

Clanging footsteps echoed around the strike team of *Titan* security personnel, and the ominous footfalls grew closer. Through tiny gaps in the ship's interior machinery, sh'Aqabaa caught sight of drones advancing on their position at a quick step. Red beams from Borg ocular implants sliced through the dim and sultry haze. "Activate dampeners," sh'Aqabaa said.

She and the rest of her strike team keyed the replicated dampeners attached to their uniform equipment belts. Senior Petty Officer Antillea switched on several more of the small spheres and lobbed them down the passageways and around corners. All around them, and everywhere one of the spheres rolled, the faint lighting inside the scout ship faltered and went black, along with any powered machinery or data relays.

The intimidating thunder of converging footsteps slowed. Looking out through the vast empty space in the middle of the probe's hull, toward sections along its opposite side, sh'Aqabaa saw dozens more sites going dark. Then the entire probe shuddered, and darkness descended like a curtain drop.

"Seek and destroy," sh'Aqabaa said, advancing toward the enemy, her finger poised in front of her rifle's trigger.

Then the Borg drones quickened their pace. In the uneven light of the flare plasma, shadows both massive and misshapen crowded in her direction. As she turned the corner to her right, Antillea was at her left shoulder, while Rriarr and Hutchinson broke down the left corridor. In unison, they opened fire.

Muzzle flashes lit the passageway like strobes, and the explosive chatter of the rifles was deafening. High-velocity monotanium rounds tore through the oncoming wall of Borg drones, spraying blood across the ones advancing behind them.

Gunfire echoed from every deck of the ship.

Another rank of drones fell, holes blasted through their centers of mass, vital organs liquefied by brutal projectiles. And still the next waves never faltered, never hesitated. Not a glimmer of fear or hesitation crossed their pale, mottled faces, and sh'Aqabaa knew they would never retreat or surrender. This was a battle to the death.

Her rifle clicked empty. A push of her left thumb against a button ejected the empty magazine as her right hand plucked a fresh clip from her belt and slapped it into place.

In the fraction of a second it took her to reload, the drone in front of her charged, grabbed the barrel of her rifle with one hand, and forced it toward the overhead. His other hand shot forward, and sh'Aqabaa caught the glint of emerald light off a metallic blade. She twisted from the waist and pivoted, dodging a potentially fatal stab.

A staccato burst of gunfire flew past her and perforated the drone, who let go of her rifle as he collapsed backward.

Sh'Aqabaa nodded her appreciation to the Bolian officer who had fired the rescuing shot, then leveled her weapon and felled another rank of drones.

Lines of tracer rounds overlapped in the deep green twilight. Drowned in the buzzing clamor of the assault rifles were the distant alarums of struggle and flight from other sections of the ship. *Can't let ourselves get pinned down,* sh'Aqabaa reminded herself. *Have to keep moving.*

She shouted over the buzz-roar of her rifle. "Second Squad! Advance, cover formation, double-quick time!"

Behind her, the second six-person team that had beamed in with hers hurried down a corridor perpendicular to the one in which she and the rest of First Squad were fighting. Within seconds, the rapid clatter of weapons fire reverberated from Second Squad's new position.

Then came an agonized caterwauling from behind her. She glanced over her shoulder. Rriarr had been impaled by a drone's deactivated drill, which had penetrated the Caitian's armored combat-operations uniform by sheer force.

A scaly hand shoved her to the right. "Move, sir!"

As she slammed against the bulkhead, sh'Aqabaa saw Antillea suffer a killing jab that had been meant for sh'Aqabaa herself. A drone plunged a stationary but still razor-sharp rotary saw blade attached to the end of his arm into the Gnalish's throat. Antillea twitched and gurgled as blood sheeted from her rent carotid, but she still managed to squeeze off a final burst of weapons fire into the drone. Then the reptilian noncom and her killer fell dead at sh'Aqabaa's feet.

The Bolian ensign tried to provide sh'Aqabaa with covering fire, but she could see that he was beginning to panic.

Feeling the battle rage of her Andorian ancestry, sh'Aqabaa screamed a war cry and resumed firing, eschewing safe center-of-mass shots for single-round head shots. Each sharp crack of her rifle sent another bullet through another optical implant, terminated another drone, dropped another black-suited killing machine to the deck missing half its head. Then her rifle clicked empty again. She ejected the exhausted clip and jabbed the butt of her rifle into the face of the drone charging at her, knocking him backward. Then she fired a round of flare gel into the face of the next-closest drone.

It bought her only half a second, but that was all she needed. She slammed a fresh magazine into her weapon and unloaded in three-round bursts on the remaining drones in front of her. When her third clip was empty, so was the corridor.

"Tane, collect Antillea's belt," sh'Aqabaa told the Bolian, who nodded, despite his face being frozen in an expression of shock. Without a word, he kneeled beside the slain Gnalish, removed her equipment belt, and strapped it diagonally across his chest as if it were a bandolier.

On the other side of the intersection, Lieutenant Hutchinson was doing the same for Rriarr. Her backup, a Zaldan enlisted man, stood sentry, checking up and down the various passageways for any sign of new attackers. The probe resounded with far-off gunfire.

Loading a fresh clip into her TR-116, sh'Aqabaa stepped beside Hutchinson. "Ready?"

"Yes, sir," Hutchinson said. "Now what?"

"Reload, regroup, and go forward," said sh'Aqabaa.

Hutchinson and the others fell into step behind sh'Aqabaa, who led them back up the main passage. Second Squad was several intersections ahead of them, apparently having made quick work of whatever they'd encountered along the way. "Check all corners," sh'Aqabaa said to her team. "Take no chances."

Around the first few corners, they found only dead drones. As they got closer to Second Squad, the area looked clear. The passage was open on their left to a wide, yawning space in the middle of the probe. In its center, on an elevated structure, was the secure area where the cube's vinculum was housed.

Ahead of sh'Aqabaa and First Squad, a spark flashed off the edge of the partial left wall. She and the others pressed against the bulkhead to their right and crouched for cover.

"Stray shot?" Hutchinson speculated.

"Maybe," sh'Aqabaa said, peering into the shadows on the far side of the ship. "Be careful, and watch the flanks." She stood and led her team forward to catch up with Second Squad.

A burning sledgehammer impact in sh'Aqabaa's gut knocked her backward before she heard the crack of gunfire or saw the flash of tracer rounds slamming into her and her team.

Then she was on the deck, doubled over and struggling to hold her abdomen together. A sticky blue mess like the core of a smashed *kolu* fruit spilled between her fingers.

She heard heavy footfalls drawing closer, and she wondered if it was the Borg coming to finish them off.

I won't be assimilated, she promised herself. She fumbled with one blood-slicked hand to pry a chemical grenade from her belt. She barely had the strength to pull it free.

Dark shapes hove into view above her.

Sinking into a dark and silent haze, she decided it didn't matter anymore. *It's over,* she thought. Her strength faded, and the grenade slipped from her grasp, along with consciousness.

The oppressive monotony of the Borg probe's interior was one of the most disorienting environments Lonnoc Kedair had ever seen, and the near-total darkness enforced by the energy dampeners only made it more so. Every time her eyes began to adjust to the shadows, another blinding flash of rifle shots or another stream of tracers made her wince and turned the scene black again.

Marching footsteps echoed from a few sections ahead of her and her squad from the *Aventine*. Red targeting beams from Borg ocular implants criss-crossed erratically in the dark.

Kedair waved her squad to a halt with raised fist. At her back was T'Prel, and across from them were Englehorn and Darrow. With quick, silent hand gestures, Kedair directed Darrow and Englehorn to alternate fire with her and T'Prel. Then she looked back and signaled ch'Maras and Malaya to guard the rear flank.

She detached an energy dampener from her belt and primed it. Twenty-odd meters away, at the intersection, a platoon of Borg drones rounded the corner, spotted her and the rest of her team, and sprinted toward them, firing green pulses of charged plasma from wrist-mounted weapons.

Their flurry of bolts dissipated into sparks as it made contact with the outer edge of the squad's dampening field. Then Kedair lobbed her spare dampener at the drones, aimed her rifle, and waited for the Borg's roving ocular beams to go dark. They all went out at once, like snuffed candles.

With a tap of her finger against the trigger, a stutter-crack of semiautomatic fire dropped two drones to the deck.

T'Prel crouched beside Kedair and snapped off a fast series of single shots, and each one found its mark at a drone's throat, just above the sternum.

The rear ranks of drones hurdled over their dead, in a frenzy to reach the intruders.

Whoever said this ship would have only fifty drones was either lying or out of their mind, Kedair decided as she fired the last few rounds in her clip. There was no break in the buzz of weapons fire while she and T'Prel reloaded; Englehorn and Darrow had started firing just in time to overlap them.

Two more drones down. Four. Six. They kept getting closer.

Darrow set her weapon to full auto and strobed the corridor with a steady stream of tracers. Then her clip ran dry.

Kedair and T'Prel snapped fresh clips into place. Able to count the rear rank of drones in a glance, the Takaran security chief switched over to full automatic and mowed down the final handful of Borg in the corridor. She released the trigger as the last drone fell in a bloody, shredded heap. The tang of blood and the acrid bite of sulfur hung heavily in the sweltering darkness.

"Like clockwork," Kedair said to her team. "Nice work. Let's keep moving. Malaya, ch'Maras, on point."

The rear guard moved past Kedair and the others and advanced through the passage, occasionally peppering the overhead or the bulkheads with streaks of flare gel. As she followed them, Kedair retrieved her spare dampener from the deck, deactivated it, and put it back on her belt.

At the end of a long corridor, they arrived at a T-shaped intersection. The perpendicular passage was open on one side into the great empty space that surrounded the vinculum, which was housed in an hourglass-shaped structure at the probe's center. Kedair stared out at the other sections of the ship. From the highest deck to the lowest, the interior of the probe was almost as dark as space, except where weapons fire flashed white, explosions blossomed in crimson, or flares bathed their surroundings in lime green. The constant, echoing rattles of rifle fire reminded Kedair of the sound of construction work.

Movement caught her eye from the opposite side of the ship. A group of black shapes moved in quick steps through the murky shadows, heading straight toward a Starfleet strike team that had its back turned to the ambush. Out of force of habit, Kedair reached toward her combadge before she remembered that the energy dampeners had cut off all communications. She considered shouting a warning to the other strike team, but then she thought better of advertising her squad's position, and she doubted that her voice would carry all that distance with enough volume to pierce the din of the ongoing battle.

There's more than one way to get someone's attention, she realized, and she lifted her rifle, put her eye to the scope, and targeted a bulkhead support beam near the Starfleet team. Her single shot pinged off the metal beam, startling the other Starfleet team, whose sharpshooter immediately turned his weapon toward her. Kedair looked up from behind her scope and pointed emphatically in the direction of the coming ambush.

The sharpshooter and his fellows dropped into covered positions and took aim at the approaching pack of drones. From a distance, all Kedair saw was a blaze of tracers and the violent, twitching dance of the mortally wounded. Then the Starfleet squad's commander was up and shouting, but Kedair couldn't hear what the man was saying. The shooting came to an abrupt stop, and the squad fired some flare rounds down the passageway.

As soon as the corridor brightened, Kedair saw what she'd done. A bullet-riddled Starfleet strike team lay on the deck in a spreading pool of its own blood. Four of her brothers and sisters in arms had been shot down on her command.

Kedair wanted to scream as if she had been the one who was shot. Denial and guilt collided in her thoughts while she stared wide-eyed at the carnage she'd carelessly provoked.

"Sir," T'Prel said, "we need to keep moving and clear this deck." The Vulcan woman's flat, uninflected manner of speaking conveyed no sympathy or pity for Kedair's tragic mistake, and that suited Kedair perfectly.

"All right," Kedair said. "Take point with Englehorn."

T'Prel and the human man stepped away and continued the sweep through the Borg probe. Kedair turned her back on the bloody consequence of a moment's error, already knowing she would bear its memory with shame until the day she died.

Enterprise security officers Randolph Giudice, Peter Davila, Kirsten Cruzen, and Bryan Regnis stood guard beside an opening that led to the probe's center. Two of their shipmates—an acerbic Vulcan woman named T'Sona, and Jarata Beyn, a hulking Bajoran man whom Giudice had nicknamed "Moose"—used compressed-gas tools to sink self-sealing anchor bolts into a bulk-head opposite the gap.

Giudice winced at the series of sharp pneumatic hisses and reverberating *thunk*s of metal piercing metal. "Hurry up," he said, impatient to be on the move again.

He tried not to think about the fact that Dr. Crusher had told him he shouldn't be moving around at all for a few more days; it had been less than ten hours since she and the rest of the *Enterprise*'s medical staff had spliced him, Davila, and Regnis back together after their harrowing fight with the Hirogen boarding party.

Hiss-thunk. Hiss-thunk. "Anchors secure," T'Sona said.

Jarata threaded four thin but resilient cables through the eyes of the anchor bolts, then affixed the cables to grapples cocked in the barrels of four hand-held launchers. "Ready to go," he said to Giudice.

"Nice work, Moose," Giudice replied. He slung his TR-116 across his back and picked up one of the grapple guns. Davila, Regnis, and Cruzen did like-wise. "Time to go to work," he said, bracing the de-vice against his shoulder. He shut one eye and peered with the other through the launcher's targeting scope. "On count of three. One . . . two . . . *three*."

Four grappling hooks soared away through the bulkhead gap, down toward the hourglass-shaped vinculum tower at the heart of the Borg ship. Each grappling hook penetrated the black tower's chaotic twists of exterior machinery and stuck fast, directly above an entrance passage whose access walkway had been retracted into the tower's foundation.

Working quickly, Giudice and his team took up the slack from the cables and secured them as tightly as they were able. "Moose, T'Sona, watch our backs. We're going in." He locked a handheld pulley over his cable and then attached himself to it with a safety line that was looped through a carabiner on his belt. In a few seconds, the other three humans had also hooked up their pulleys and safety loops to their zip lines.

"Now the fun part," Giudice said with a smirk. Gripping his pulley with both hands, he pulled himself up onto the ledge of the barrier that stood between him and the great emptiness on the other side. He waited until Davila, Cruzen, and Regnis were perched beside him atop the barrier. "Three . . . two . . . one."

They tucked their knees toward their chests and let gravity do the rest. The incline was fairly shallow, less than fifteen degrees, but within seconds, they were hurtling through open air at an exhilarating speed. Deep aches and sharp pangs—aggravated by his sudden, extreme exertion—reminded Giudice of the impaling wound he'd suffered hours earlier.

He stole a glance at Davila and saw that the older man, who had been slashed across his chest, was also in considerable pain. *I guess even Starfleet medicine has its limits,* Giudice mused. Only Regnis had recovered fully from the Hirogen attack, despite having been garroted nearly to death. Giudice scowled. *Some guys have all the luck.*

The vinculum tower loomed ahead of them. Giudice clutched the braking clamp on his pulley and slowed his descent. On either side of him, the rest of his team decelerated. Moments later, their feet made contact with the tower, and they braked to a halt as they bent at the knees to absorb the impact. With practiced ease, they detached their safety lines and dropped down onto the platform in front of its recessed entrance.

Davila nodded at the bulkhead which had sealed the tower's entrance. "Looks like they were expecting us."

"I guess we'll have to knock," Giudice said. "Cruzen, want to do the honors?"

While her comrades took cover around the corners from the entrance alcove, Cruzen moved forward. The petite, innocent-looking brunette removed her backpack, opened it, and retrieved a peculiar demolition charge. It was a malleable chemical explosive with a binary chemical detonator. Though less powerful than Starfleet's most advanced photonic charges, it would suffice to open the passage—and it had the advantage of being able to function despite the energy-dampening fields being generated by the *Aventine* and its strike teams.

Cruzen primed the detonator and fixed the charge in place against the barricade. She made a final tap of adjustment and then sprinted back toward Giudice and the others. "Fire in the hole!"

She ducked around the corner with Giudice half a second before a massive explosion spouted orange fire out of the alcove and rocked the entire Borg probe. The cloud of fire and oily, dark smoke persisted for several seconds. Aftershocks trembled the vinculum tower as the blast effects dissipated.

"Hell of a boom, Cruzen," Giudice said. "I hope the vinculum's still in one piece."

"Should be," she said. "I used a shaped charge."

She peeked around the corner. "Looks okay from here."

He heard the heavy percussion of approaching footsteps. "And what about the drones guarding it?"

"They're fine, too," she said.

"Great." He unslung his rifle and thumbed off the safety. In a smooth pivot step, he rounded the corner and fired several controlled bursts directly into the advancing company of Borg. There were so many, in so dense a formation, that he didn't need to aim. All he had to worry about was running dry on ammo. Glaring left and right at his teammates, he snapped, "What're you waiting for? Invitations?"

As if suddenly remembering why they'd come, Davila, Regnis, and Cruzen stepped out on either side of Giudice and formed a skirmish line. Davila and Cruzen fired while Giudice reloaded, and Regnis held his fire until he and Giudice could cover for the others. Working together, they cut down rank after rank of drones. For a moment, Giudice almost felt guilty about it, as if he and the others were shooting defenseless foes. Then he remembered what any one of those drones would do if it laid hands on him or any member of his team, and he resumed firing.

Regnis said to Giudice between blazing salvos, "Lieutenant? You know we're all down to our last two clips, right?"

Giudice shouted back, "Yes, Bryan, I see that."

"Well, I still see a lot of drones coming, sir."

"I see that, too, Bryan. Everyone, aim for effect!"

The team's shots became more precise, but the attacking drones drew inexorably closer. Then, all at once, there seemed to be only a half-dozen of them left standing. Unfortunately, that was when all four of the team's rifles clicked empty.

The drones prowled forward, pale revenants of malice.

"Crap," Giudice muttered.

Davila said, "We were close, too."

"Too bad the Borg don't give mulligans," Regnis said.

Reaching toward her belt, Cruzen asked, "Grenades?"

"No," Giudice said. "It might damage the vinculum."

The six Borg were only a few meters away. Giudice and his team had retreated to the edge of the platform and had nowhere left to go. Giudice wished he could just shimmy back up the zip line. He glanced upward and had an idea. "Everybody down!"

He used his weapon's gel-flare attachment to paint all six advancing drones with radiant green splatters, and then he hit the deck beside his team.

Less than two seconds later, an overpowering barrage of sniper fire from the distant sides of the probe tore through the six drones. As Giudice had guessed, sharpshooters from other strike teams had wanted to help him take the vinculum—they just hadn't been able to identify their targets in the dark.

"That's what I'm talking about," Giudice said as he and the others stood and eyed the captured vinculum. "Teamwork."

Erika Hernandez manned the *Aventine*'s conn and eyed the black, oblong vessel on the main viewer with dread and enmity.

Her hatred was fueled by what the probe and the other Borg vessels had done at the Azure Nebula. She was beginning to understand the threat that the Borg Collective posed to Earth and its Federation. She could only hope that her wrath would be strong enough to overcome her fear when the time came to add her voice to the Collective's dissonant chorus, in an effort to bring at least part of it under her control.

At the aft stations of the bridge, Captain Dax and her first officer, Bowers, conferred in muted tones with the *Aventine*'s science officer, Helkara. They and the other officers on the bridge all presented calm appearances, but there remained a palpable undercurrent of tension. No one wanted to speculate about what might be happening inside the Borg ship. *We're all hoping for the best and expecting the worst,* Hernandez brooded.

An alert beeped on the ops console. Ensign Gredenko silenced it with a feather touch and said, "The Borg ship just vented a small amount of plasma."

Dax and Bowers hurried back to the center of the bridge. "Magnify," Dax said.

The image on the viewscreen snapped to a close-up view of a small exhaust portal low on the Borg ship's aft surface. Another brief jet of rapidly dissipating plasma appeared. Moments later, two short plumes occurred in quick succession. "The delay between ventings has been exactly five seconds," Gredenko reported. The bridge crew watched with anticipation. Then came three rapid spurts of plasma. "Five-second delay," Gredenko repeated. "Counting down to next venting. Three . . . two . . . one." Right on cue, a series of five fast plasma ejections sprayed from the port. "Fibonacci pattern and timing confirmed."

"All right," Bowers said. "Mister Helkara, lower the dampening field. Kandel, keep the shields up and the weapons on standby, just in case it's a trap."

Helkara tapped at his console and replied, "Dampening field is down, sir."

Immediately, Hernandez heard a few lonely Borg voices from aboard the probe. They had been cut off from the roar of the Collective, and they sounded disoriented and afraid. She stole nervous glances at the rest of the bridge crew and quickly realized she was the only one who heard the panicked drones.

"Lieutenant Kedair is hailing us from the Borg ship," Kandel reported.

"On speakers," Dax said.

Kandel replied, "Channel open."

"Lieutenant," Dax said, speaking up toward the comm, "this is *Aventine*. Go ahead."

"The Borg probe is ours, Captain," Kedair replied. *"The vinculum is intact, and we've taken it offline while we make our modifications for Captain Hernandez."*

Dax nodded. "Good work. Is it safe for her to beam over?"

"Not yet," Kedair said. *"There are still a few drones kicking around in here, but we have them cornered. Once we finish them off, we'll be ready to proceed to phase two."*

"Well done," Dax said. "Keep us posted. *Aventine* out."

The channel closed with a barely audible click from the overhead speaker. Hernandez's thoughts drifted as she tuned out the bridge's muffled ambience of urgent business. Her mind reached out as if to the Caeliar gestalt, the way it had in Axion when she'd eavesdropped on her captors. Now, however, she was listening to the Borg drones on the probe ship.

A bond was formed, a communion of sorts . . . and then she was seeing through the drone's eyes.

It was wounded and immobilized, lying on a deck inside the Borg ship. To her eyes, the interior of the probe vessel looked more like an automated factory than a starship. A celadon glow suffused its vast, deceptively open-looking architecture.

She felt the drone's labored breathing, the dull pain throbbing in its abdomen, the quickened beating of its heart. Its thoughts were chaotic and wordless, little more than surges of emotion and confusion. Then it reacted to the presence of Hernandez's mind with a desperate attempt to merge. It reminded her of the way a hungry infant might reach for its mother.

Its vulnerability and fear took hold of her, and she felt a deep swell of compassion for the mortally wounded drone. *Don't be afraid,* she assured the drone, acting on a reflexive desire to provide comfort. The drone relaxed; its pulse slowed. As its breaths became deep and long, it began to feel to Hernandez like a psychic mirror that reflected her will and desires.

Then a pair of Starfleet personnel turned the corner a few meters away. They had weapons braced at their shoulders as they advanced on the fallen drone.

Hernandez lost sight of the difference between herself and the drone. Its fear became hers as it stared into the barrels of two rifles, pointed at its face from point-blank range.

A shocked half-whisper passed her lips, and she felt the drone speaking with her, as if they shared a voice: "No . . ."

The bond was broken in a crack of gunfire.

Slammed back into the solitude of her own consciousness, Hernandez recoiled with a violent shudder. She gripped the sides of the console to steady herself. Her eyes glistened with tears of anguish and fury, as if she had just witnessed the slaughter of her own flesh and blood. She knew that the Borg were still the enemy of humanity and its allies and that the Collective had to be stopped, but now she was also convinced that there was more to this implacable foe than she had been told—and perhaps more than Starfleet and its allies realized.

A brown hand settled gently on her shoulder. Bowers leaned down and asked quietly, "Are you all right, Captain?"

For a second, she considered telling him about her vision of the drone, but then she thought better of it. *These people are terrified of the Borg,* she realized. *If they think I'm bonding with the enemy or sympathizing with them, there's no telling what they might do to me.*

"I'm fine," she lied. "Just nerves, I guess."

Bowers nodded. "It'll be a while before they're ready for you on the Borg ship," he said. "Maybe you should go back to your quarters and rest a bit before we start phase two."

Hernandez forced herself to muster a grateful smile. "Sounds like a good idea," she said. She got up and walked to the turbolift as Bowers summoned a relief officer to the conn.

Before she stepped inside the lift, Dax intercepted her. "I just wanted to thank you for all your help today," Dax said. "I doubt we'd have succeeded without you at the conn."

"You're welcome, Captain," Hernandez said. "Could I ask a favor in return?"

Dax's eyebrows peaked with curiosity. "Depends. What'd you have in mind?"

"Seeing as you mean for me to pose as the Borg Queen in an hour or two, it would help if I knew as much about the Borg as possible," Hernandez said. "Can you give me clearance to review all your files about them? Including the classified ones?"

"Consider it done," Dax said. "But be warned—there's a lot of it. I doubt you'll get through it all in an hour."

That drew a genuine smirk of amusement from Hernandez.

"Don't worry," she said. "I'm a fast reader."

Lonnoc Kedair's first order after the *Aventine* deactivated its dampening field had been to have wounded personnel beamed back to the ship for emergency medical treatment.

Her second order had been to make sure every drone on the probe vessel was "one-hundred-percent dead."

"As opposed to mostly dead?" T'Prel had inquired with her trademark arid sarcasm. Kedair had responded with a withering glare that made it clear she was in no mood for witty repartee.

She stood in front of the vinculum, which a team

from the *Enterprise* had captured and taken offline. The vertical shaft was capped at its top and bottom by diamond-shaped, emerald-hued polyhedrons. An intricate cage of protective black metal surrounded each major component, and the core shaft was surrounded by several rows of horizontal bands. It vaguely reminded Kedair of a warp core on a Federation starship.

Irregular impacts echoed in the cavernous space outside the vinculum's tower. Kedair looked down the passage and through the blasted-open entrance to see her people clearing the corpses of Borg drones from the tower by tossing them over the edge of the entrance's exterior platform, into the belly of the ship, which was a random-looking pit of snaking pipes and jutting machinery.

Kedair fought the urge to contact sickbay on the *Aventine* and pester Dr. Tarses for an update on the wounded personnel. *Just let the medics work,* she told herself. She dreaded going back to the ship. Sooner or later, she would have to write and submit her after-action report for this mission, and she was torn over whether to describe her blunder as the result of incompetence or of negligence. All that really mattered to her was that the officers who had obeyed her order to fire not face a court-martial; as far as Kedair was concerned, they were as much victims as the people they'd shot.

"All squad leaders have checked in, Lieutenant," T'Prel said, interrupting Kedair's guilty ruminations. "All drones have been neutralized, and all decks have been secured."

"Good," Kedair said. She stepped away and tapped

her combadge. "Kedair to *Aventine*. We're ready for the engineers."

"Acknowledged," Commander Bowers replied over the comm. *"They're beaming in now."*

There was a faintly electric tingle in the air before the first sparkle of a transporter beam appeared in the darkness. Then six figures took shape in a flurry of particles and a euphonic wash of sound. The effect brightened the entire vinculum chamber for several seconds. When it faded, Lieutenant Leishman and five of her engineers stood before the mysterious Borg device, holding toolkits and eyeing their surroundings with equal parts apprehension and professional curiosity.

"This ought to be interesting," Leishman said, smirking at the vinculum. "Assuming *Voyager*'s technical specs are accurate."

Unable to stomach Leishman's good mood, Kedair extinguished it with a glower as she said, "Whatever you're gonna do, Mikaela, do it fast. It's time to give the Borg a new queen."

17

A flash of movement and a snap of jaws, the sting of fangs breaking flesh, a rush of terror—

Deanna Troi awoke with a shudder and pulled her arms up and in, striking a defensive pose. Her hands and feet were stiff and cold, and a tingling of chilled gooseflesh traveled up her legs. Exhaled breaths became white clouds above her. Shaking off her disorientation, she realized she was no longer in her quarters.

The room was narrow, but its ceiling was far above, at a dizzying height. A clamshell-shaped skylight was directly over Troi, who tucked her chin to her chest and examined her own situation. She was lying on a dull metal slab and surrounded by bizarre machines, which pulsed with violet light and whose purposes she couldn't begin to divine. An especially large and fearsome-looking contraption hovered near the ceiling, above a point several meters past the foot of what Troi surmised was an operating platform. Along the top of one wall, in the only area uncluttered by machines and unobstructed by crisscrosses of drooping cables, was a broad observation window.

Inyx stood behind a transparent barrier to her right. He appeared to be engrossed in a complex task and did not yet seem to be aware that Troi had regained consciousness.

She reached slowly toward her chest and gingerly touched where Ree had bitten her. Searching with her fingertips, she found the rips in her uniform but no corresponding wounds in her flesh. Though the air in the laboratory felt cold to her, she wasn't in any real discomfort. Closing her eyes, she focused on the sensations from within her body, in an effort to assess her own condition. *No pain,* she realized. *That's good . . . I hope.*

Troi opened her eyes to find Inyx looming over her.

"You're awake," he said in his mellow baritone. "Good."

Inyx, like the other Caeliar, projected no emotional aura that Troi's empathy could detect. If his intentions were sinister or duplicitous, she had no way of knowing beforehand. She propped herself up on her elbows and asked, "Where are we?"

"In my lab," Inyx said. "It was the only sterile facility in Axion that was properly equipped to assist you."

She tried to swallow, but her mouth felt too dry. "The last thing I remember, Ree attacked me."

"A misunderstanding, apparently," Inyx replied. "He used his species' natural venom to place you temporarily in a suspended state. It was a crude solution to your dilemma, but it did briefly stave off the immediate crisis."

Panic quickened her pulse. "Venom?"

"There is no danger, Deanna," Inyx said. "I've purged the toxins from your system and stabilized you—for the moment. I didn't wish to take any further steps without your informed consent, however. That's why I've revived you."

Pondering the degree to which Inyx must have examined her to be able to cleanse her system of Pahkwa-thanh venom, Troi surmised that he had likely become privy to all of her extant medical issues. "You know that I'm pregnant . . . don't you?"

"Yes, Deanna."

After days of running from the heartbreaking truth of her situation, confessing it almost felt like a relief. "Do you also know that it's not going well?"

"That much was clear when I saw that its mutation had threatened your life," Inyx said. "I would like to help you."

Tears rolled from her eyes and blazed fiery trails across her cold cheeks and over the edge of her jaw. "The captain of *Titan* is my husband and the father of my child," she said. "I want to go back to my ship and be with him."

"I'm sorry, Deanna, that won't be possible." Before Troi could protest, Inyx added, "*Titan* escaped orbit and returned to your Federation approximately ten hours ago."

The news cut through her like a blade. Shock dominated her thoughts. *My* Imzadi *left me? He's gone?* Denial took hold. "How could *Titan* be back in the Federation already?"

"It repurposed a subspace passage that we had created for reconnaissance purposes," Inyx said. "With assistance from Erika Hernandez, *Titan*'s crew enlarged the subspace aperture and used it to make a near-instantaneous journey home. As I'm sure you can imagine, the Quorum is feeling rather vexed."

Troi lay back on the slab and covered her face with her hands. "I can't believe he left me," she muttered.

The part of her that was an officer understood Riker's actions perfectly. No doubt, he'd been forced to choose between saving the ship and the majority of its crew or risking their freedom for the sake of the already captured away team. Viewed in that light, Troi knew that her captain's decision had been logical. But the part of her that was a wife shrank beneath the crushing emotional blow of Will's abandonment.

Inyx said, "Deanna, we really can't afford to wait any longer. I am ready to assist you medically, but I require your permission to proceed."

She lowered her hands and folded them protectively across her abdomen. "Dr. Ree wanted to do this days ago," she said. "I wouldn't let him. I don't know why not. Maybe I was hoping for a miracle." A surge of emotion constricted her throat. It took her a few tries before she could continue. "But I guess it's time to accept that maybe some things weren't meant to be."

"I don't understand," Inyx said.

Troi replied, "I'm giving you permission to proceed. To terminate my pregnancy."

The imposing Caeliar scientist recoiled from her, as if in horror. "Deanna, I think you've mistaken my intentions." He recovered a small measure of his composure and continued, "As I've explained to you before, the Caeliar abhor violence and will not terminate sentient life for any reason. Likewise, for us to abandon a life in peril that could be saved is also anathema." Resuming his proud bearing, he finished, "I was not asking to end your pregnancy, Deanna, but to repair it."

"You could do that?" she asked, amazed at the very idea.

"And more," Inyx said. "I have spent a considerable fraction of the past several centuries learning about humanoid biology, mostly for Erika's benefit. However, I am certain that I possess the knowledge and expertise to restore the proper, natural genetic pattern of your fetus and to repair the damage in the unfertilized ova of your uterus. While I won't impose my cures on you or your child without consent, I am not too proud to beg you to accept my help." He transformed the waggling cilia at the end of one of his arms into a semblance of a long, bony humanoid hand, and he extended it in invitation toward Troi.

"Grant me your permission, Deanna," he said, "and I will heal you—and your child."

The passage through the catacombs of Axion grew narrower with every step Keru and Torvig took. "Where are we going, Vig?"

"Just a bit farther, Ranul," Torvig said. "If my senses are accurate, there should be an opening twenty-two meters ahead."

Their voices and scuffling steps echoed and carried in the pitch-dark tunnel. "I wish you'd told me we were going spelunking," he said to the Choblik engineer, his voice echoing off the close walls. "I'd have brought one of the palm beacons."

"Not necessary," Torvig said. "There is an increase in the ambient light ahead, at the tunnel's terminus."

Keru's eyes saw nothing but the same pools of darkness broken by occasional patches of deep shadow. "I'll take your word for it, Vig." He looked back over his shoulder and found the path back just as dark as the path forward. "I wonder which one of our Caeliar observers is trailing us right now."

"You could simply ask them," Torvig said.

"I don't really care that much," Keru replied.

They continued walking without speaking for thirty seconds, the two of them shades barely visible to Keru's eyes, and then Torvig said, "The passage slopes downward here. Mind your step."

Keru slowed his pace just enough to adjust his stride to the new descending grade. He noticed the sharpness of Torvig's silhouette in front of him, and he realized that he, too, could now see the growing illumination ahead. The air was getting warmer as they advanced toward the pale blue flicker.

"Vig, how'd you even find this passage?" he asked.

"I would rather not answer with too much specificity, since we are being monitored," Torvig said. "Let it suffice to say that the senses I was granted by the grace of the Great Builders enabled me to perceive a shift in Axion's quantum field. I attuned my senses to its particular properties and traced the field to its source point. Which is six-point-two meters ahead."

The ensign's explanation drew a smile from Keru. It hadn't occurred to the Trill security chief until that moment that though the Caeliar had destroyed the away team's tricorders, Torvig's bionic enhancements—including his cybernetic eyes and his assortment of advanced computing and sensory devices—made him an ideal, self-mobile substitute for the lost equipment. Only a few months earlier, Torvig had put his implanted systems to good use saving *Titan* after an ill-fated encounter at Orisha with the Eye of Erykron. *After a feat like that,* Keru mused, *filling in for a tricorder must seem like child's play.*

The duo reached the bottom of the sloped passage and made a hard switchback turn. Then they moved from the shadows into twilight and into the heart of a blue sun in a few short steps.

Keru lifted his arm to shield his eyes. The duo stood on a ledge overlooking a vast, hollow sphere of a chamber. Hovering at its center was a huge, brilliant orb of electric-blue fire. Its deafening roar, like an endless thunder of crashing waves and the angry buzz of a hundred billion bees, overpowered him.

Averting his gaze, Keru looked at Torvig, whose metallic eyes blazed with reflections of majestic azure lightning. "Vig!" Keru shouted over the sonic assault of the hidden sun. "What is that thing? Is it the Caeliar's power source?"

"I believe so, Ranul," Torvig said, his normally quiet voice cybernetically amplified and frequency-shifted to cut through the noise. "Its output exceeds my ability to measure."

Another squinting look around convinced Keru that sabotage was out of the question. The distance from their ledge to the burning orb was at least a hundred meters, and if the scorching tingle on his skin was any kind of warning, he was certain he didn't want to get any closer to the object than he already was. There appeared to be no other vulnerable points or exposed systems inside the polished silver-gray chamber. He also suspected that whatever the orb proved to be, destroying it would no doubt prove to be a death sentence for every living thing on New Erigol, starting with himself and Torvig.

He patted Torvig on the back and nodded for the ensign to follow him. They returned the way they had come, and after gazing into such intense light, the darkness seemed much deeper to Keru's eyes. "I don't get it," Keru said, his ears still ringing from exposure to the bone-shaking wall of sound. "If the Caeliar have that much power at their command, why go to the trouble of harnessing a sun and a planet?"

Torvig replied, "I suspect that the planet and the star were shelled in order to mask this source, sir. If it were possible to study the link between the two shells, I might hypothesize that the harnessed star provides the energy to support the shell around the planet, whose purpose is to contain the emissions of this exotic-particle generator."

"Exotic particles?" echoed Keru. "What kind of particles?"

"I have not yet identified them," Torvig said. "They are more energetic than anything I have observed before now."

Keru wished that he and Torvig had access to *Titan*'s main computer and sensor module. He asked, "If the planet wasn't covered up, how detectable would those particles be?"

"To anyone with the ability to scan that frequency, they would be the brightest energy source in the galaxy."

It took a moment for Keru to process Torvig's

report, and when he did, he began chuckling at the irony of it.

The engineer seemed perturbed by Keru's reaction. "I was not aware that I had committed a faux pas or spoken in jest."

Regaining control of himself, Keru stifled his chortling and said, "I'm not laughing at you, Vig. I'm laughing at the Caeliar." He imagined his friend's bemused reaction concealed by the darkness. "I just think it's funny that a species that puts such a premium on going incognito uses a power source that can be seen from across the universe."

18

———•———

Beverly Crusher stepped inside the holodeck and found herself surrounded by green leaves, blue sky . . . and mud.

The portal closed behind her with a deep, soft rumble of servomotors and a muffled thud of contact. Then all she heard was blissful quiet. A mild breeze susurrated through the thick walls of leaves and grapes and rippled the shallow puddles in the muddy lanes between the vineyard's rows. The rich aroma of turned earth mingled with the sweet scent of country air after a night of spring rain. Tattered clouds sped by, high overhead.

Verdant hills rolled one beyond another, along the horizon, past the far end of the straight lane between looming stands of grapevines. The only signs of technology in the otherwise pastoral landscape of La Barre, France, were a handful of metallic towers linked to Earth's weather-control grid.

She turned in the other direction, toward the closer end of the row. Her small, pivoting steps squished and slipped in the slick, peaty muck. As far as Crusher could see, she was alone in the vineyard. There was no sign of workers, and no robotic tenders or harvesters were in use. The vineyard looked deserted.

But she knew better.

Walking slowly and taking care to plant her steps on tiny islands of dry ground scattered along the path, she skulked down the dirt lane until she spied Jean-Luc, two rows over, through a tiny gap in the leafy vines. Her vantage point came and went from view as the breeze rustled the greenery, by turns momentarily revealing him and concealing him with foliage.

Crusher tried to keep her voice down as she said, "Computer, modify program. Give me a temporary passage through the vines, to the row where Captain Picard is standing."

A two-meter-wide path appeared without a sound through the two rows of vines that separated her from her husband. She moved in gingerly steps through the passage. As soon as she reached her desired row, the holodeck closed the route behind her, silently knitting shut the walls of branches.

The suction of mud on her boots made it impossible for Crusher to sneak up on Jean-Luc, so she didn't try. Still, she approached him slowly, with caution, to gauge his reaction. When she was a few meters away, he turned his head and acknowledged her with a melancholy look. "Beverly."

"What are you doing here?" she asked, stepping beside him.

He gazed into the foliage. "I needed a place to think."

She rested her left hand against his lower back and took a few seconds to look around at the bucolic simulation of his childhood home. "Why here, Jean-Luc? Why now?"

"Because it might soon be gone forever," he said.

"Not without a fight," she said. "The war's not over yet."

Jean-Luc inhaled sharply and stepped away from her. "Are you certain of that?" He walked slowly along the muddy trail, his hands brushing through the leaves and vines, his fingertips lingering delicately over the fragile Pinot Noir grapes. "Why should I believe that Captain Dax's plan will amount to anything more than another postponement of the inevitable?" He stopped and pulled a small bunch of grapes toward him. "At this point, I suspect it's all a matter of too little, too late." Pinching one tiny, violet fruit between his thumb and forefinger, he continued, "No one heeded my warnings when it might have made a difference. Not the admiralty, not the president, not the council. I told them this day would come, but no one listened." He crushed the grape into skin and juice, and dropped it on the ground. Then he looked away, past the end of the row. "Now all of this . . . history . . . will be lost. Trampled underfoot."

He resumed walking, moving in quick strides. Beverly stayed close beside him, refusing to let him leave her behind. "So, is that it?" she asked. "You've already lost, so why finish the battle? What happened to the man who demanded we draw a line in the sand and say 'no further'? Is this all that's left of him?"

Near the end of the lane, Jean-Luc stopped and frowned as he gazed toward the distant hills. Avoiding eye contact with Crusher, he reached over and pulled toward him a length of the vine that was thick with leaves and heavy with fruit. Rolling its rough skin between his fingers, he sighed. "A vine is like a person, Beverly," he said, his voice somber. "Some of its nature is the product of heritage, but its personality also reflects its experiences. A gentle season can give it a mellow quality, and adversity can add depth to its character"—he looked up at her—"but only up to a point. There's a limit to how much damage and pain one vine can absorb before it turns bitter and brittle . . . and before it withers and dies."

He let the vine snap back into the embrace of its mother plant and continued walking, though much more slowly this time. Beverly was certain now that the dark mood that traveled with Jean-Luc was more than just anxiety about the apparent unstoppability of the Borg invasion. Her suspicion was confirmed as they emerged from the narrowed field of vision enforced by the vineyard row, to behold the sight on the nearest hill.

Where she had expected to see Château Picard, there stood only the scorched ruin of a house, a pile of charred timbers toppled at oblique angles over the pit of a black and broken foundation. Its interior was nothing but mounds of ash and rubble, cinders and shattered stone—exactly as it had been nearly ten years ago, the morning after the fire that had killed Jean-Luc's older brother, Robert, and his young nephew, René.

She took his arm. "You shouldn't do this to yourself."

There were tears in his eyes, and his face looked stricken as he placed his hand over hers. "I'm all that's left."

"No," she said sternly, commanding his attention. "*We're* all that's left." She touched her belly, where their son grew. "*Us,* Jean-Luc. *Us.*"

He shut his eyes as tightly as he could to stanch the flow of his tears, and he clenched his jaw to hold back the flood of bitter grief and fear that Beverly knew raged inside him.

She pulled him to her and forced him to turn away from the grim vision of his sundered home. He embraced her as he buried his face between her neck and shoulder, but Beverly still felt as if she were standing outside the wall of his despair, making futile efforts to peek inside.

There wasn't a millimeter of space between them, but it felt to her as if the man she loved were light-years away—and growing more distant by the day. And the Borg were to blame.

"I won't let them take you from us," she said.

"Neither will I," he said.

It wasn't what he'd said but how he'd said it that made Beverly tremble and fear that the worst was yet to come.

Worf pressed the door signal outside Jasminder Choudhury's quarters and waited patiently. Seconds later, he heard her invitation, shaken by grief's vibrato: "Come in."

He stepped forward, and the door opened. Jasminder stood in front of the sloped windows of her quarters, one arm across her chest, the other hand half hiding her face. Worf took slow, cautious steps toward her. Behind him, the door sighed closed.

Exorcising all edge and aggression from his voice, he asked, "Are you all right?"

"Yes," she said. "Why do you ask?"

"It is unlike you to leave your post, even with permission," he said. "I was concerned."

She brushed a tear from her cheek and looked at him. "What about you? I thought you had the bridge?"

"I gave the seat to Kadohata," he said.

Turning back toward the windows and the nebula beyond, she said, "I just needed a few moments. No telling when we'll get another lull, right?"

"True," he said. He stepped closer to her as she folded her arms together in front of her and lowered her head. On the coffee table in front of her, a small hologram projector displayed a miniature, ghostly image of a majestic, multilimbed oak tree in front of a quaint rural home. Settling in beside Jasminder, Worf noticed that she was staring at the hologram.

He didn't need to ask where the image had been recorded. It was easy enough to guess. "It is possible your family escaped Deneva before the attack," he said.

"Possible," she said, choking back a hacking sob. "Not likely." Her eyes were red from crying. "But that's not what's killing me." She nodded at the hologram. "It's the tree."

"I do not understand," he said.

Her jaw trembled, and she covered her mouth with her hand for a moment until she was steady enough to talk. "Thirty-two years ago, my father and I planted that tree in front of our house. My mother used to have a picture from that day in our family album—my dad with his shirt off and a shovel in his hand, me holding up the new tree while he filled in the dirt. Dad used to joke that he couldn't remember which was skinnier that day, me or the sapling." Her face brightened behind a bittersweet burst of laughter. "I don't remember, either. It was barely a tree, not even as thick as my arm." Sorrow overtook her face again. "See those two figures under the tree in the hologram? That's me and my dad, last year, when I was home on leave. Look how big that tree is: almost sixteen meters tall, nearly two and a half meters around at the base. It's just amazing . . . or it was. Now it's gone, and I'll never see it again."

Fresh tears rolled from her eyes, but the emotion flowing behind them was anger. "I just feel so damned stupid," she said. "I should be crying for my mother or my father or my sisters, all my cousins, my nieces and nephews . . . and what am I crying over? A tree. I'm going to pieces over a *tree*."

She was shaking, and Worf saw then that Jasminder's aura of serene detachment and dispassionate resolve had been shattered. The sudden loss of her home and family and the violent rending of every tangible connection to her past were pains he knew well. The murders of Jadzia and K'Ehleyr were old wounds for him, but the pain they brought him had never diminished.

"You do not mourn the tree," he said.

She shot a defensive glare at him. "Then why am I crying?"

"You weep for what it represents."

Jasminder regarded him with a stunned look for a few seconds, then turned her searching gaze at the hologram. "Myself?" she wondered aloud, and shook her head. "My home?"

"I see many trees on your family's property," Worf said.

"But this is the one I . . ." Her voice trailed off as she followed his leading question to her own understanding. "It's my father," she whispered, her eyes fixed on the spectral image. "A symbol of our bond, our relationship."

Worf nodded. "For a Klingon warrior, there are few things more important than one's father and how one honors him."

She turned toward him, and he saw the dawning of a terrible understanding in her eyes. "My father's gone, Worf."

The outpouring of her grief was incremental for a few seconds, and then it cascaded out of her, like an avalanche exploding without warning from a fractured mountainside.

He pulled her toward him as she howled with rage and sorrow. Her guttural wails made him think of the Klingon warriors who were storming the fields of *Sto-Vo-Kor* that day.

Her cries subsided, but still she lingered in his embrace, as deathly still as someone in deep shock. In a voice hoarse and raw, she said, "I just can't believe it, Worf. Everything I ever called home is gone." She looked up at him with tearstained eyes. "Do you have any idea what that's like? To have your whole world blown away? Your whole family taken from you?"

His early childhood came back to him in bitter flashes. Memories of fire and fear on Khitomer. Bodies and blood.

"Yes," he said in a sympathetic whisper. "I do."

19

───◆───

Dr. Simon Tarses felt his feet slip-slide for the third time in a minute while he struggled to close Lieutenant sh'Aqabaa's shredded torso. He shouted over his shoulder, "Somebody mop up this blood before I break my neck over here!"

Turning back toward Nurse Maria Takagi, who was assisting him, he snapped, "Clamp the aorta, dammit!"

His temper was flaring, but he couldn't afford to waste precious seconds reining it in. There were five different colors of blood pooling on the deck between the biobeds, and the air was filled with pained cries, delirious groans, and panicked screams. Then the main doors gasped open, and a troop of medics carried in four more security personnel who were broken and saturated with their own blood.

A triage team led by the *Aventine*'s assistant chief medical officer, Dr. Lena Glau, descended on the new arrivals. They worked in rapid whispers and grim, meaningful glances. At the end of several seconds' review, Glau pushed a lock of her sweat-stringy dark hair from her face and called out directions to her gathering flock of nurses and medical technicians. "Move the chest wound to the O.R., stage the bleeders in pre-op, and call the time on the head wound."

Sealing off a major tear in sh'Aqabaa's vena cava while dark blue ichor oozed over his gloved fingers, Tarses called over to Glau, "Lena, what've you got?"

"More friendly-fire victims," she said, following her patient with the chest wound as he was moved on his antigrav stretcher toward the O.R. "I have two minutes to save this guy."

"Let me know if you need a hand," Tarses said, and then he gritted his teeth while he struggled to work around the tattered remains of his Andorian patient's traumatized pericardium.

Glau replied, "Looks like you've already got your hands full, but thanks, anyway." She, her patient, and her surgical-support team vanished inside the O.R.

He grimaced at the critically wounded Andorian *shen* on the biobed between himself and Takagi. Ideally, he'd have performed her operation in the *Aventine*'s main surgical suite, but sh'Aqabaa's vitals had crashed too quickly. There hadn't been time to move her to O.R. before the need to operate had become imperative. He didn't know who was to blame for the shortage of surgical arches, but as Tarses rebuilt sh'Aqabaa's chest cavity by hand, he promised himself that someone at Starfleet Medical would get an earful about this.

Assuming Starfleet Medical still exists tomorrow, he reminded himself. *Or, for that matter, assuming we still exist tomorrow.*

The other three members of sh'Aqabaa's squad were in the hands of the *Aventine*'s chief resident physician, Dr. Ilar Prem, and its surgical fellow, Dr. Nexa Ko Tor. Dr. Ilar was a Bajoran man with a slight build, finely molded features, and dark eyes capable of snaring one with a sudden, shockingly direct stare. Dr. Nexa was a female Triexian with ruddy skin and deep-set eyes that seemed custom-made for keeping secrets. Her most impressive quality as a surgeon was the ability to use her three arms to operate on two patients with equal efficacy at once.

Prem's patient was a human woman, and Nexa was working on two men, a Zaldan and a Bolian. Even from across the room, Tarses could tell that none of the three surgeries was going well. The vital-signs displays above the biobeds fluctuated wildly, and then they began to go flat.

"Cortical failure!" called Ilar's nurse.

A medical technician who was assisting Nexa with the Bolian patient scrambled for resuscitation gear as he declared, "Cardiac arrest!" Meanwhile, Dr. Nexa and Nurse L'Kem were turning all their attention to the Zaldan, whose body was twisted by a series of gruesome convulsions while he gagged on an overflowing mouthful of maroon blood.

Tarses wanted to sprint across the room to intervene, to take charge, to try to save three lives at once, but he knew there wasn't anything he could do for those patients that his fellow physicians weren't already doing. Instead, he kept his eyes trained on the bits of shattered bone, the ragged flaps of rent skin, and the semiliquefied jumble of damaged organs that he and Takagi were racing to reassemble inside sh'Aqabaa.

Minutes passed while he blocked out the tense,

barked orders and the rising tide of desperation that
surrounded him. Then the sharp clanging of a medical instrument ricocheting off the bulkhead and the
clatter of it bouncing across the deck made him look
up. Dr. Ilar tore the bloody gloves from his hands and
hurled them to the floor, cursing under his breath. He
stormed out of the main sickbay and into the triage
center.

Dr. Nexa accepted her forced surrender to the inevitable with a greater modicum of grace. She looked
at Nurse L'Kem and said, pointing to the human, the
Bolian, and then the Zaldan, "Time of death for Lieutenant Hutchinson, 1307 hours; for Lieutenant Tane,
1309 hours; and for Crewman Doron, 1311 hours."
L'Kem noted the times in the charts and gave the
padd to Nexa, who reviewed it, signed it, and handed
it back to the Vulcan nurse.

Tarses had just finished stabilizing sh'Aqabaa and
was making some temporary closures to the incisions
as a precaution before moving the Andorian lieutenant to the O.R. He looked up as Dr. Nexa sidled up to
the biobed beside Nurse Takagi and asked, "Is there
anything I can do to help, Doctor?"

"No," Tarses said, surprised at how cold and un-
feeling his own voice sounded. "She's stable. Go help
Ilar with those two bleeders who came in."

The slender Triexian nodded and ambled silently away. It still amazed Tarses that for a person
with three legs, Nexa made so little sound when she
walked.

"Okay," he said to Takagi. "She's ready. Have the
medtechs come move her to the O.R., and tell them to
find me another surgical arch, stat."

"Yes, Doctor," Takagi said, stepping away to summon help.

He stood beside the biobed as he peeled the gloves off his hands, and he thought of Ilar's outburst minutes earlier. *A stickler for regulations would put Prem on report for that,* Tarses thought. He looked down at sh'Aqabaa and brooded on how hard he'd already fought to save her; then he pondered how he might react if she didn't make it out of surgery.

If she dies, I'll probably start throwing things, too.

Tuning her mind to the frequency of the Borg Collective was proving more difficult than Erika Hernandez had expected. She felt she was close to being able to link with it, as she had with the Caeliar gestalt centuries earlier, but the closer she got, the more elusive the Borg's voice became.

She stared at her access to the vinculum and asked engineer Mikaela Leishman, "Are you sure this thing is set up correctly?"

"Positive," Leishman said. "It's responding to your own biofeedback, just like you asked."

Beside the *Aventine*'s chief engineer was its second officer and science department head, Gruhn Helkara. The Zakdorn clenched his jaw, pushing up his facial ridges. "If you don't feel up to this, we should scrub the mission now."

"I'm fine," Hernandez said. "Just let me concentrate."

She closed her eyes and focused on aligning her brainwaves with those of the Collective. She blocked out the muggy climate inside the Borg ship, the discomfort of her semi-invasive neural interface with the vinculum, and her own fear.

Two oscillating tones, slightly mismatched, served as her guide. Hers was the shorter, faster wave of sound; the more she relaxed, the closer her alpha-wave tone matched that of the Borg.

Perfectly measured, crisp footfalls approached. She knew before she heard the voice that it was Lonnoc Kedair, the security chief. "The transphasic mine is armed," she said to Leishman and Helkara. "How's our royal infiltrator doing?"

"She's working on it," Leishman said.

Hernandez was very close to bringing her psionic frequency into synch with the Collective's when Helkara's combadge beeped and broke her concentration. Dax's comm-filtered voice sliced through the low thrumming and anxiety-filled silence inside the vinculum. *"Commander Helkara, report,"* she said.

Opening her eyes to glare at Dax's three officers, Hernandez noted the abashed look on Helkara's face.

"We're almost there, Captain," he said.

"Well, get there faster," Dax said. *"The Borg are minutes away from hitting five major targets, including Andor, Vulcan, and Qo'noS. If this plan's gonna work, it has to happen now."*

Leishman and Helkara traded glances of dismay. Kedair stared intently at the pair, awaiting their reaction. Helkara replied to Dax, "We need a few more minutes, Captain."

"We're out of time," Dax said. *"What do you have now?"*

Hernandez beckoned to Leishman. "I have an idea."

The engineer arched her eyebrows. "I'm listening."

"I'll be able to adjust my modulation faster if you remove the feedback buffer from my interface," Hernandez said.

Helkara dismissed the suggestion with the energetic waving of both hands. "Absolutely not," he said. "Without that, you'll run the risk of a counterattack by the Borg."

"I'm a big girl, I can handle it," Hernandez said. "Look, the buffer is most of what's slowing me down. If I don't get inside the Collective's head right now, billions of people are going to die. Risking my life to save all of theirs makes sense, at least to me." She raised her voice. "Captain Dax, I'm asking permission to remove the buffer and face the Borg head-on."

"Granted," Dax said. *"Gruhn, Mikaela, get it done."*

"Aye, Captain," Helkara said, acquiescing with reluctance.

"Aventine out," Dax said, closing the channel.

The wiry Zakdorn frowned and ran a hand through his thatch of black hair. He pointed at the interface jury-rigged to the vinculum and said to Leishman, "Remove the buffer, Lieutenant."

Leishman stepped forward, tapped a few buttons on the control panel, and reached under the console to pull free a sheet of isolinear circuits, from which dangled a bundle of optronic cables. Holding the deactivated component in one hand and leaning on the other, Leishman shook her head at Hernandez. "I hope you know what you're doing, Captain," she said.

"So do I, Lieutenant," Hernandez said.

Then she turned her thoughts to fusing with the Borg.

A crowd of frazzled bodies and fearful faces had gathered in the combat operations center in the secure bunker below Starfleet Command.

Towering screens high on every wall showed images from orbital platforms above five different worlds, and a sixth hard-line feed showed President Bacco and her cabinet gathered in the Monet Room at the Palais de la Concorde in Paris.

Admiral Edward Jellico leaned against the room's enormous central strategy table, flanked by his colleagues, Admiral Alynna Nechayev and Admiral Tujiro Nakamura. Together, they watched the majestic displays that surrounded them and awaited a catastrophe. An undercurrent of comm chatter and muted voices droned beneath the pall of fear that filled the room. For the junior officers working in the command center, there was still work to be done, something to focus on, tasks to distract them from the terror of speculating about what would happen next.

For Jellico and the other admirals assembled in the command center, there was nothing left to do but wait. They had drafted their plans and moved thousands of starships and hundreds of thousands of people like pieces on a chessboard—all in what felt to Jellico like an increasingly pointless effort to escape what they all knew was really checkmate.

Quietly, he said to Nechayev, "We've done all we could."

"Yes, Ed, we did." She smiled sadly in his direction and then, with tremendous subtlety and discretion, placed her hand on top of his. It was a small gesture of friendship and comfort, but in the pressure of the moment, it touched Jellico profoundly.

And for just a few seconds, he almost smiled, too.

Then a masculine voice boomed from the overhead comm, *"Borg attack fleets are within two minutes of Vulcan, Andor, Coridan, Rigel, and Qo'noS."* The subspace feeds switched to show nearly identical images, of five groups of eight to ten Borg cubes. An electric prickling raised every hair on Jellico's body, and fear washed through him like a surge of ice water in his veins.

"Order all ships to intercept and engage," he said.

History will say we tried, he brooded, as his order was relayed to the fleets above five distant worlds. *Assuming that history remembers us at all after the Borg get done with us.*

The coming battles all were light-years away, but watching them unfold on the desktop monitor in his ready room on *Titan,* William Riker felt as if he were in the thick of the melee.

Less than a few light-minutes from four Federation member worlds, fleets of allied ships rallied in formation and raced to meet the enemy. Riker watched them speed toward the Borg cubes and was both grateful and enraged that he and his ship weren't there to do their part.

I should be watching this on the bridge, he told himself. He got up from his chair, took a few steps toward the door, and stopped. *What if the battle goes against us? Morale's bad enough as it is. Do I really want to make my crew watch the end of Vulcan or Andor?*

Then he imagined what Troi would say: *They're strong, Will. They can handle it. Trust them—and let them see your trust.*

He forced himself back into motion and out the door, onto the bridge. Lieutenant Commander Fo Hachesa vacated the center seat as Riker approached. "Repairs are continuing on schedule, Captain," said the Kobliad acting XO.

"Very good," Riker said, taking his seat. "Patch in the feed from Starfleet Command on the main viewer."

Hachesa pulled his hands to his chest as a nervous frown creased his brow. "The battle in the core systems, sir?"

"Yes, Commander," Riker said. Noting the man's discomfort, he continued, "Is there a problem with that?"

Spreading his hands, Hachesa said, "Lieutenant T'Kel suggested that earlier, but I disagreed."

Riker glanced toward the tactical console, where T'Kel was directing an icy stare at Hachesa. Looking back at Hachesa, Riker asked him, "On what grounds?"

"I did not want to jinx it," Hachesa said.

It took a few seconds for Riker to be certain that Hachesa was, in fact, utterly serious. "Overruled," Riker said. "This isn't like quantum mechanics, Fo. We won't affect the outcome by observing it." He nodded to T'Kel. "Put it on-screen."

While the Vulcan woman carried out the order, Hachesa confided to Riker, "I also feared it might be bad for morale."

"Thousands of Starfleet personnel are about to put

their lives on the line," Riker said, loudly enough for all on the bridge to hear. "Many of them are about to make the ultimate sacrifice. Since we can't be there to fight beside them, we owe it to them to bear witness— and to remember their courage."

Images of the five battles appeared on *Titan*'s multi-section main viewer.

That was when Riker realized that maybe Hachesa's instincts had been right after all.

Picard stood at the center of the *Enterprise*'s bridge, his posture erect, his bearing proud, and his soul mired in despair.

On the main viewer, enormous Borg cubes moved in clusters. The sheer mass of each attack group was more daunting than Picard had ever dared to imagine.

The sight of even a single cube was enough to set his pulse racing and fill his stomach with acid. Instantly, he was back in the hands of the Collective, being absorbed, erased, violated, and entombed inside himself. He was lording over the slaughter of Wolf 359. He was hearing the voices whispering below the fray at the Battle of Sector 001. He was alone.

Lieutenant Choudhury's voice pulled him back into the moment. "Klingon and allied forces have engaged the Borg at Qo'noS and Beta Rigel," she said. "Allied battle groups moving into attack formations at Andor, Vulcan, and Coridan."

Worf stepped forward to stand on Picard's right side. Out of the corner of his eye, Picard saw that his first officer was emulating his stance, in a show of solidarity and dignity. It was to Worf's credit, Picard thought, that he saw no need to sully the moment with words, and Picard showed Worf the same stoic courtesy in return.

The images of battles far removed blazed with the cold fire of transphasic torpedoes.

Picard wanted to believe that Starfleet was ready for this fight. He wanted to believe that the Federation would endure this crisis, as it had so many others before it.

Then the torpedoes found their marks . . . and he knew that the only truth left to believe was the one promised by the Borg.

Resistance is futile.

"Torpedoes are away," announced the tactical officer of the *U.S.S. Atlas,* and Captain Morgan Bateson clenched the armrests of his chair as he watched the missiles on the main viewer spiral toward their targets.

"Reload and keep firing, Reese," Bateson said. "Don't give them time to regroup." He stole a quick look at his fleet's deployment pattern on his command monitor. "Kedam, tell the ships on our port flank to spread out. They're too close."

The Antican operations officer replied, "Yes, sir," as he relayed the order to the other ship's commanding officers.

"Five seconds to impact," said Lieutenant Reese.

Bateson's hands were coated in cold sweat. He'd fought at the Battle of Sector 001, which had taught him a costly lesson about how devastating a single

Borg cube could be in battle. Now he was leading an attack against ten cubes.

We outnumber them four to one, he reminded himself as the transphasic torpedoes detonated against the Borg ships with a blinding flash. *Please, God, let it be enough.*

He didn't expect more than a handful of the cubes to emerge intact from the blistering blue firestorm that engulfed them. Then a black corner pierced the dissipating fog, followed by another . . . and then by six more.

"Two cubes destroyed," reported Lieutenant Kedam. "The remaining eight cubes are still on course for Vulcan."

Commander Sophie Fawkes, the *Atlas*'s first officer, said, "Helm, attack pattern Foxtrot Blue!"

"Second salvo's away," Reese declared from tactical.

Fearing the worst, Bateson said, "Ready another."

On the main viewer, he saw the fleet's second barrage of transphasic warheads flare like a blue sun . . .

. . . and all eight cubes burst from its flames unscathed.

Dear God. "All ships, break off!" Bateson ordered. "Fall back to Vulcan orbit and regroup!"

"Sir," Kedam said. "The *Billings* is leading the reserve wing on a collision course with the Borg ships."

Bateson looked to his XO. "Fawkes, hail them! Tell them to break off!" She tried to do as he asked, but Bateson knew it was too late. He watched in horror as the *U.S.S. Billings* and more than a dozen Federation starships were blasted into scrap and vapor by the Borg cubes, which rammed their way through the spreading cloud of smoldering debris.

Reese cried out, "The Borg are locking weapons!"

"Helm, evasive!" Fawkes shouted.

The young Andorian *chan* at the conn struggled to guide the *Sovereign*-class vessel through a series of rapid and seemingly random changes in speed and direction, but the hull rang under a succession of crushing blows from the passing Borg cubes. A brutal impact sent the *Atlas* spinning and rolling and plunged its bridge into darkness for several seconds.

When the overhead lights and bridge systems came back on, Bateson was crestfallen as he confronted the grim scene on the main viewer. Only a handful of ships from his attack fleet were intact, and even fewer appeared to be operational.

"Kedam, open a channel," Bateson said, fuming mad at his failure to halt the Borg's genocidal march. "Warn the Vulcans: The Borg will reach orbit in one minute."

President Bacco, her cabinet, and her advisers stood and traded nervous whispers around the conference table in the Monet Room, sequestered below the Palais de la Concorde. Esperanza Piñiero positioned herself to monopolize access to the president.

"We still have time to get you to safety, ma'am," she said, her tone more insistent than it had been the last three times she had made this suggestion. "There's a high-warp transport standing by. We can have you halfway to Rhaandar by the time the Borg reach Earth."

"Enough," Bacco said. "One more word about this, and I'll have Agent Wexler put *you* on that transport by yourself."

Piñiero scowled. "You say that like you think it'd be a punishment, ma'am."

"Hush," Bacco said. "There's nowhere to retreat to, anyway. We're making our stand here, Esperanza. Besides, if the Federation falls, I don't want to live to see it. Now, step aside. You're blocking my view."

She didn't really want to see any more of the developing calamity, but it was as good an excuse as any to end their conversation. The room's multiple display screens all showed similar images, telling the same story. Starfleet vessels were broken and burning or scattering in confused retreat. A Klingon fleet was making one valiant sacrifice after another to defend Qo'noS. Borg cubes advanced all but unopposed on the strongholds of the Federation and its allies. And volley after volley of transphasic torpedoes made not one blessed bit of difference.

The Borg were winning the war.

Off to one side, Admirals Akaar and Batanides conferred with Seven of Nine, who had joined them to review the latest dispatches from Starfleet Command. The admirals' faces were easy to read: naked fear. Seven, as usual, maintained an inscrutable mien as she whispered to the two flag officers. The statuesque former Borg drone turned, took a few steps toward the table, and faced Bacco. "Madam President," she said, snaring everyone's attention. "The Borg have adapted to the transphasic torpedo."

The admirals joined Seven, and Akaar said, "We've confirmed it, Madam President. As of this moment, the Federation no longer has a defense against the Borg."

Energy and signals from the Borg Collective coursed through the catoms that infused Erika Hernandez's body and mind. A surge of raw power flooded her senses, giving flavor to colors and sounds to the cold touch of wires against her flesh. It was narcotic and addictive, and the ocean of tiny voices that was swept up in the psychic wave of the Collective's imperial will was both suffocating and awe-inspiring.

She had expected it to be more like the gestalt, but its similarity was only superficial. Many voices had been fused into a single consciousness, but not willingly. Unlike the Caeliar, who had united their minds for the elevation of their society as a whole, the Borg Collective subjugated sentient minds and then yoked their hijacked bodies to serve its own aims.

The deeper she delved into the Collective, the more she realized that it was nothing like the gestalt. It was darker, almost primordial in its aggression, brutally authoritarian, and utterly domineering. She hadn't realized how much she had taken for granted the benign nature of the Caeliar gestalt; where it had linked individuals with a warm bond of common purpose that respected its individuals' right to free will, the Collective hammered disparate entities together with cold force, like a blacksmith crafting a sword in a forge of ice.

Hernandez wanted to flee from its casual cruelty, free herself from its oppressive embrace, but there was too much at stake. *I have to keep going,* she told herself. Pushing her mind into deeper levels of connection with the Collective, she felt her thoughts taking on its primal hues. *I have to surrender myself to the Collective and experience it the way the drones do. I need to hear the Queen and know what she sounds like.*

Surrendering to the gestalt had been like returning to the womb and becoming a fluid in an endless stream of consciousness. Submitting to the Collective felt more like being swallowed in a tar pit, enclosed in oily darkness, smothered, and silenced.

Then, alone in the dark, Hernandez heard it.

The voice of the Borg Queen.

Harsh and autocratic, it was a psychic whip of fire on the backs of the drones. Even the cube-shaped ships answered to its unswerving command. Hernandez let herself see what the Queen wanted her to see: fleets of Starfleet and Klingon starships being crushed without mercy or regret, orbital defense platforms above five worlds being obliterated with ease, and the cubes' preparations for surface bombardments that would turn those worlds into lifeless slag.

Vulcan. Andor. Coridan. Beta Rigel. Qo'noS.

In moments, they would all be gone.

Erika Hernandez directed her catoms to vibrate in harmony with the essential frequency of the Borg Queen and steeled herself to speak to the Collective.

Only then did she realize she had no idea what to say.

Charivretha zh'Thane watched green bolts fall from the sky above Therin Park on Andor. As the matron of her clan, she had refused to abandon her home. It would have served no purpose, she'd decided. There was nowhere safe to go, and her *chei,* Thirishar, and his bondmates and their offspring all were long gone from Andor. There was nothing left here for her to protect.

She'd still hoped it wouldn't end like this, that Starfleet would devise some brilliant tactic to repel or thwart the Borg's latest incursion. During her years as Andor's representative on the Federation Council, she had often been amazed by Starfleet's seemingly endless resourcefulness.

Not endless after all, she admitted, as a viridescent fireball descended toward the park. Strikes beyond the city's perimeter trembled the ground under her feet.

Too jaded to mourn the loss of her own life, zh'Thane felt a profound sorrow for the doomed beauty that surrounded her and the several thousand other Andorians who had chosen to await their end in Therin Park. Cloistered in the heart of the capital city, it was a place of great natural beauty. Its aquatecture filled the air with the gentle burbling of flowing water, and its sprawling gardens and terraced waterfalls were designed to create secluded enclosures. Exotic, colorful fish in its ponds nipped and leaped at floating transparent spheres that housed dancing flames. Though portions of the park had been damaged by terrorist bombings years earlier, it had been rebuilt into something even more beautiful than what had been lost.

Vretha doubted that would be the case this time.

She drew her last breath of cool, floral-scented night air.

Then she and the park, along with the fish and the flowers and the soft music of flowing water, were gone.

All that remained was fire.

The skies of Vulcan wore many colors. At daybreak, brilliant shades of pink and vermillion ruled the lower degrees of the heavens. At midday, faded hues of amber and cinnamon set the tone. Come sunset, gold and crimson owned the horizon.

At every longitude of Vulcan, the red and bronze dome of the sky was split by jade-colored thunderbolts from orbit.

T'Lana had ventured alone into the vast wasteland of the Forge in search of solitude and healing. Her judgment as a counselor and as a Starfleet officer had been compromised by her ego and by her own surety that she'd known better than everyone around her, about everything. It had taken a failed—and, in retrospect, disastrously misguided—mutiny against her commanding officer to make clear to her just how skewed her reasoning had become. Faced with the inexcusable nature of her actions, she had done the only logical thing: She had transferred off the *Enterprise,* requested an indefinite leave of absence, and returned to Vulcan to place herself in the care of experts who could guide her back to the path of selfless reason and logic.

She saw the death stroke falling and wondered, *Did I play some part in this tragedy? Were my actions part of a series of errors that led the Federation to this moment?*

Logic suggested that she was succumbing to egotism again. In any reasonable evaluation of the matter, her own role would likely prove to be so small as to be inconsequential. *Only a rank egotist would seek to accept solitary blame for an event of such epic proportions,* she assured herself.

Her inner eyelids blinked shut as the blast of burning emerald plasma slammed down into the heart of ShiKahr and turned the city to slag, vapor, and rubble. The shockfront from the detonation raced from the vanished metropolis as a kilometers-tall mushroom cloud reached into the soot-blackened sky.

T'Lana watched the tsunami of pyroclastic ash, displaced sand, and toxic fallout surge across the flatlands, toward the rocky peaks and canyons of the Forge. *At its current rate of speed, the blast wave will reach me in six-point-two seconds,* she deduced. *I will not reach sufficient cover in time.*

She had come home to complete the *Kolinahr* and purge herself of emotions and prejudice. It therefore struck her as ironic that her final musings were so deeply emotional. She was filled with regrets for her life's unrealized possibilities.

I can never make amends for betraying Captain Picard.

I can never apologize for insulting Ambassador Spock.

A blast of heat kicked up the sand and seared her skin, a stinging harbinger of the lethal onslaught to come.

I will never be able to tell Worf how I desired him.

The roar of the explosion struck with stunning

force. T'Lana shut her eyes . . . and accepted what she could not change.

Erika Hernandez gave orders without speaking, in a voice that wasn't hers, to an army that had no choice but to obey.

Cease-fire.

It was like opening the clamshell skylight in Inyx's lab. She pictured an event, an outcome that she desired, and the Collective turned itself to fashioning her wishes into reality.

The barrages against the planets stopped. She was anguished to see how much damage had already been wrought. Great glowing scars on the surfaces of five worlds spread horrid, ash-packed clouds through their atmospheres.

The symptom addressed, Hernandez looked to the cause.

The cubes. The hostile drones. The Queen.

Destroy them, she commanded, and throughout the Collective, her legions of followers complied without question, oblivious of the fact that they were the targets in their own crosshairs.

Firefights erupted inside Borg ships throughout known space. Drones cut one another down, pummeled one another with ruthless efficiency, slashed and shattered and impaled one another with mindless abandon. The cubes turned their awesome batteries against one another and blasted themselves to pieces.

Borg attack fleets in deep space dropped from warp as they hammered one another with weapons fire.

The Collective stood divided, every cube a battlefield in an instant civil war.

Aftershocks rocked the Collective. So many drones being extinguished at once was an excruciating jolt, and Hernandez felt her mind recoil and shrink from the horror of it. Without the feedback buffer, she was forced to experience every Borg drone's death, every violent end, every lonely submersion into darkness. With each passing second, a thousand more voices cried out in the night, and her guilt felt like knives in her heart.

Then one voice rose above the carnage, that of a presence unlike any other Hernandez had encountered.

It was indomitable. Amoral.

Seductive and insidious.

The Queen answered Hernandez's challenge.

In a blinding flash of agony, Hernandez understood the true nature of the Borg . . . and for the first time in more than eight centuries, she was afraid.

A second queen. In all its millennia of expansion, assimilation, and steady progress toward perfection, the Collective had never before found itself torn between two monarchs.

Even when the Borg Queen had been forced in times past to manifest in multiple bodies at once, all of her avatars had represented the same will, the same mind, the same purpose. The guiding voice had always been unique and inimitable.

Now, on the cusp of the Collective's latest triumph, an impostor had risen. Harmony became discord; unity turned to conflict. Perfection had been tainted.

The Borg Queen quelled the millions of confused plaints and imposed order.

Sleep, she decreed. *Regenerate.*

These were the most basic directives the drones knew. They were among the first to be written, the building blocks for all that had come afterward. Willed by the Queen, they were irresistible fiats that overrode all other directives.

Throughout the enemy's territory, her drones halted their self-destructive struggles and sought out alcoves in which to replenish themselves and aid the restoration of their vessels. As the drones dropped out of the Collective, the Queen searched the still-waking minds for her rival.

Cube after cube went dark, slowed, and stopped in space, as the drones hibernated. The Queen pushed the blank spots in the Collective from her mind and raced among the swiftly dwindling points of consciousness. Then there was but one besides herself.

Not human, not Borg. Something familiar but still alien.

Designation is irrelevant, the Queen decided. *The intruder must be removed.* She searched the isolated scout vessel for any remaining drones to serve her, but she found none. There were many humanoid interlopers on the ship, however. She decided they would suffice as replacements.

The ship awakened slowly to the Queen's will. It had not been engineered to play such a singular role, but it had been designed to support and create new drones—and to destroy all that opposed it, within and without.

More important, as with all creations of the Borg, it had been made to do one thing above all else: adapt.

Everyone in the combat operations center was talking at once, and Admiral Jellico could barely hear what Admiral Nechayev was saying from across the room. "Speak up, dammit!" he shouted.

"It's confirmed, sir," Nechayev hollered back. "The Borg cubes fired on each other, and now they've all stopped, dead in space." She turned away as a harried-looking Arcturian captain thrust his padd into her hands. Turning back toward Jellico, Nechayev lifted her voice to add, "All the Borg cubes are showing heavy damage—most of their cores are exposed."

We might never get another chance, Jellico realized. "All ships, reengage! Press the attack while we can!"

His legion of officers snapped into action, rallying the fleet and directing an immediate counterattack. Watching the massive screens full of tactical diagrams shift to represent the recommitted battle forces, Jellico dared to hope.

If we're fast enough, we might just survive this.

"Fawkes, we need to strike now!" Captain Bateson bellowed, as the *Atlas* accelerated on an attack heading. "Who's left?"

His first officer studied her tactical monitor and frowned. "*Exeter, Prometheus,* and *Kearsarge.*"

"Well, tell *Prometheus* to do its three-way-split trick. We need to hit as many of those cubes over Vulcan as fast as we can." Too energized to stay seated, he sprang to his feet and prowled forward. "Helm, attack pattern Theta-Red. Weapons, hit the Borg with everything we've got: transphasic torpedoes, phasers, bad grammar—whatever it takes!"

The reddish orb of Vulcan grew swiftly larger in the frame of the *Atlas*'s main viewscreen, and within seconds, the mangled and immobilized Borg cubes lingering in orbit became visible.

At tactical, Lieutenant Reese's youthful and delicately feminine features hardened with resolve. "Targets locked, sir."

Lieutenant Kedam at ops added, "*Kearsarge* and *Exeter* have their targets, and *Prometheus* has initiated multivector assault mode." A signal beeped on Kedam's console. He eyed the display and glanced back at Bateson with a crooked grin. "New orders from Starfleet Command, sir: Reengage the Borg."

"Typical brass," Bateson said, rolling his eyes.

"*Prometheus* has its targets, sir," Kedam said.

Bateson decided that if ever a moment had called for the invocation of Shakespeare, this was it. "Once more unto the breach, dear friends, once more! *Fire at will!*"

His blood was hot in his veins and his pulse heavy in his temples, almost to the point of vertigo, as he gazed in awe at the staggering volume of sheer firepower that the *Atlas* and its allies loosed upon the Borg cubes. Great clusters of blazing warheads and brilliant slashes of phaser energy lanced through the black monstrosities in orbit of Vulcan and pummeled them into wreckage and dust. Any piece large enough to be detected by a scanner was targeted and shot again, until every hunk of bulkhead and every vacuum-exiled drone had been disintegrated.

"All targets eliminated," reported Lieutenant Reese.

"Secure from Red Alert," Bateson said, cracking his first smile in weeks. He gleamed with satisfaction at his first officer. "Thank Starfleet Command for their permission to engage—and tell them the attack on Vulcan is over."

Erika Hernandez gasped for breath and couldn't fill her lungs. Her mind was empty of thoughts but filled with white agony. All at once, dozens of cubes and countless thousands of drones had been annihilated, and their savagely curtailed suffering was too much for her to shut out or shunt aside.

Then came the real pain.

Psionic attacks pierced her memories like spears of fire, searing her to the core of her soul. Every engram jolted into action was transformed, bastardized, tainted into a memory of torment and violation.

She was a child again, screaming for rescue as her family's home went up in flames, and blistering licks of orange heat consumed her beloved stuffed-animal companions . . .

No, our house never burned . . .

A dank basement, a dust-revealed shaft of dull gray light through a narrow window, her uncle sitting beside her on a sofa with torn upholstery and old stains, his hand resting somewhere that it shouldn't have been . . .

He never did that! It's a lie!

She was sixteen and on her back in the snow, on a slope in the Rocky Mountains. Kevin, the boy she'd adored since eighth grade, was on top of her—with his hands at her throat and a narcotic haze clouding his crazed countenance. Her flailing and kicking and twisting bought her no freedom, not even one more tiny breath. She scratched at his wrists but couldn't reach his face. He was exerting himself, and clouds of exhaled breath lingered around his head, which was backlit by a full moon, giving him an undeserved halo as he throttled her.

That's not what happened! He was my first love!

None of her protests mattered. Each stab into her psyche twisted another cherished moment of her life into something sick and shameful. Every milestone of achievement, every fleeting moment of tenderness and connection, was trampled. It was the psionic warfare equivalent of a scorched-earth policy. Her foe intended to leave her no safe haven, no place to retreat, nowhere she could go to ground.

Hernandez didn't know how to fight something like this. It was too powerful, too ancient, too cruel. It had no mercy, and it possessed aeons of experience with shattering minds and devouring souls. A destroyer of worlds, an omen of the end of history, it was not merely the Borg Queen—it was the singular entity beyond the Queen, the very essence of the Collective.

A cold darkness enveloped her, and she felt her fear being leached from her, along with joy and sorrow, pride and shame. *This is assimilation,* she realized. *It's even worse than Jean-Luc said. All you can do is surrender.*

Physical sensations returned with an excruciating spasm.

Hernandez's back arched off the deck, and fiery needles shot through her arms and along her spine. A scream caught in her constricted throat, behind her clenched jaw. Sickly green light was all she saw in the dark blur that surrounded her.

Helkara shouted, "Pull the rest of the leads! Now!"

"Not yet!" Leishman said. "Too much residual charge!"

Hands pulled at cables that snaked under Hernandez's skin, and she heard the hiss and felt the tingle of a hypospray at her throat. "We're losing her," Helkara fumed. "Somebody get a medic! Chief, get that first-aid kit over here!"

The convulsions ceased, and Hernandez let her body relax on the deck. Her vision started to clear and sharpen, but she felt utterly drained, and she began shivering intensely.

"Bring blankets," Leishman said to someone running past.

Hernandez reached out and took Leishman's forearm in a weak grasp. "Queen," she croaked, surprised at how difficult it was for her to form words. When she tried to speak again, all that issued from her lips were reedy gasps.

Helkara leaned in and asked Leishman, "What'd she say?"

"She said, 'Queen.' I guess the Borg Queen shook her up."

"No kidding," the Zakdorn science officer said.

Vexed by their obtuseness and quickly losing consciousness, Hernández let go of Leishman's arm and grabbed Helkara's collar. She yanked his face down to her own and stammered in a brittle whisper, "The Qu . . . Queen . . ."

Helkara pried her hand from his uniform and straightened his posture. "Is on her way to Earth—we know, Captain," he said, placing her weakening hand on her chest and patting it in a patronizing manner. "We'll deal with her next. Right now, you need to rest. Just hang tight till the medics get here."

The sedatives they had given her were kicking in, and the edges of her world were growing soft and fading away.

Morons! she raged, imprisoned inside her tranquilized body. She wanted to warn them, but then she sank into the smothering arms of dark bliss, unable to convey a simple report:

The Queen is here.

The news was almost too good for Nan Bacco to believe it. She kept waiting for the correction, the retraction, the nuanced clarification that would negate what she and her people had just witnessed on the subspace-feed monitors in the Monet Room.

A hushed conference between Seven of Nine and Admirals Bàtanides and Akaar ended, and Akaar strode to the head of the conference table. He lifted his large hands and silenced the nervous chatter that had filled the room.

"We've just received confirmation from Starfleet Command," he said, lifting his chin and letting his long gray hair frame his squarish features. "The Borg attack fleets at Vulcan, Andor, Coridan, Beta Rigel, and Qo'noS have been routed."

He had more to say but was cut off by the room's thunderous applause and whooping cheers of jubilant relief. Bacco permitted herself only a tight, grateful smile, for fear of tempting the Fates with premature celebration. She caught sight of a deep frown on Piñiero's face, and then she noticed that similarly grave expressions were worn by Batanides, Akaar, and Seven.

Akaar lifted his palms again and hushed the assembled cabinet members and advisers. "There were reports of infighting among several other Borg battle groups, but those have now ceased—and all remaining Borg attack fleets are once again on the move." He met Bacco's questioning look and added, "Including the one on its way to Earth."

4527 B.C.E.

20

⎯•⎯

Karl Graylock, Kiona Thayer, and Gage Pembleton were desperate and dazed with hunger after eight days of exhausting snowshoeing in a brutal deep freeze. Walking on unraveling snowshoes, they trudged through the endless night, up the side of Junk Mountain, their every step resisted by frigid knives of screaming wind and pelting sleet.

Less than two hundred meters up the slope of Junk Mountain, Graylock's snowshoes finally came apart beneath him. First his left foot plunged through the sagged webbing, and then his right foot tore free of its rotted binding. "*Scheisse,*" he cursed under his breath, fearful of triggering an avalanche.

Pembleton poked at the snow with his walking stick. "It's pretty hard-packed," he gasped in the thin air. "You didn't sink much past your ankles." He tapped the side of his snowshoe with the stick. "We probably don't need these anymore."

"Probably not," Graylock said. Thayer and Pembleton pulled off their snowshoes. Graylock gathered up the broken pieces of his footwear and stuffed the fragments into folds and under flaps on his backpack;

they'd make decent kindling once they dried. Looking up the slope, directly into the path of the gale-driven sleet, he winced and said, "Let's keep going."

Graylock remembered the way to the Caeliar's redoubt as well as Pembleton did, so he took the lead as they ascended into the lashing gusts of the storm. It was up to Pembleton to keep watch for the local predator that had slain Mazzetti weeks earlier. All Thayer had to do was keep herself upright while hiking uphill over ice and snow with her braced foot.

From a distance, the three survivors would have looked all but identical. Mummified in multiple layers of the now-sullied silver-gray Caeliar fabric, only their heights distinguished them; Pembleton was the tallest, followed by Graylock, and then Thayer. It occurred to Graylock that they had not seen one another's face in more than a week. As the temperatures had plummeted, they had resisted removing any but the tiniest strips of their swaddling, and then only for absolute necessities.

In the mad swirls of sleet that surrounded him, his view of the path ahead was limited to its next few meters. Fighting gravity to push his weakened body up the mountainside left his head spinning. The next thing he knew, he was on his hands and knees, dry-heaving through his face wrappings.

Hands closed tentatively around his arms. Thayer and Pembleton labored to pull Graylock back to his feet.

"Don't quit on us now, you Austrian clod," Thayer said.

He wobbled as he found his footing. "Well, since

you asked so nicely," he mumbled to her. "Gage, can you . . . ?"

"Take point? Sure." Pembleton stepped past Graylock and led the trio up the slope, past icicle-draped rock formations. Towering snowdrifts had formed against the windward side of the huge black crags that jutted from the pristine slope.

Concealed beneath a deep blanket of snow, the shape of the terrain had become unfamiliar to Graylock's eyes. He hoped that Pembleton's wilderness combat training would enable him to find the entrance to the Caeliar's buried laboratory.

The effort and the exhaustion, the hunger and the pain . . . they all blurred together as Graylock forced his aching muscles to go through the motions: taking one step and then another, walking where Pembleton had walked, never looking back.

His eyes felt leaden, and an overpowering desire for rest sapped his will to continue. *So cold I can't even feel it anymore,* he mused, poised on the edge of a hallucination. He was all but ready to collapse face-first into the snow when a mitten-wrapped hand yanked him forward.

"I found it," Pembleton said. "The tunnel's pretty slick, but I think we can make it down. Come on!"

The three survivors doffed their backpacks and huddled around a cave in the snow. It looked like an enlarged version of a trapdoor spider's lair. The sides of the opening were sheathed in ice and dusted with clinging snow that had gathered in a long, shallow slope at the bottom. Graylock peered cautiously over the edge and down the icy incline. "It's mostly clear," he said. "But how—"

A quick push sent him headfirst over the edge. He put out his hands by reflex. They slipped over the ice and did nothing to slow him down as he caromed off the sides, but the snow piled at the end broke his fall, and he was able to use his arms to guide himself down the slope on his chest. Then he slid to a stop in the pitch-dark corridor that led to the shielded lab.

He got up, dusted himself off, and walked back to the opening. When he glared up at his two comrades, Kiona said, "Sorry. Impulse."

"I'm fine, thanks for asking," he said, projecting wrathful sarcasm. "Get down here."

Graylock stepped back and waited. Seconds later, Thayer slid feet-first onto the snow and glided on her buttocks into the corridor. He helped her up, and she called back up to Pembleton, "Clear!" Next, the trio's backpacks were dropped, and Thayer helped Graylock recover them and move them to one side. After the third one, Thayer again yelled back, "Clear!"

Then Pembleton joined them, landing and sliding as Thayer had. Graylock and Thayer pulled him to his feet. He brushed the snow off the backs of his legs as he asked, "Where do you think the Caeliar would be?"

"Probably near whatever energy-storage system they were living from," Graylock said. "We should probably start looking in the lab." The engineer opened his pack and removed the fire-making kit. They quickly fashioned small torches from their remaining thick branches of firewood and some strips of their old uniforms soaked in salvaged machine oil. Pembleton lit two torches with a flint and steel, passed them to Thayer and Graylock, then lit his own.

Weak firelight and massive shadows danced on the metallic walls.

Graylock started down the corridor, and the others followed him. It felt strange to him to be back inside an artificial structure again. Their footsteps were loud and crisp on the hard floors, and they reverberated in the empty passages. The wind sang mournful songs in the dead city's empty spaces.

Away from the ice chute and the brunt of the wind, Graylock peeled off the layers of fabric wrapped around his head. The final layers felt glued to the front of his face, and he teased the fabric loose with gingerly tugs. As it came free, he saw why it had held fast. It was crusted with dried blood. Exposed for two weeks to extreme cold and aridity, his sinuses and lips had cracked like salt flats in the desert.

Thayer and Pembleton coaxed off their own bandages, revealing the same kind of cold-weather damage to their faces. What alarmed Graylock, however, wasn't the blood but the bones. Their cheekbones looked as if they might pierce their skin at any moment. Touching his own face, Graylock realized with horror how gaunt they all had become. *We look like walking corpses.*

They turned a corner, entered the lab, and found the cavernous space deserted. Every corridor and chamber they had explored had deepened Graylock's profound unease; as they wandered through the open space, he felt as if he were lurking in a crypt. "I think we're too late," he said. "They're gone."

"Maybe if you tried calling for them," Thayer said. "What was the name of the one you knew?"

"Lerxst," Graylock said. He looked to Pembleton

for an opinion. The man shrugged as if to say, *Why not?* Raising his voice, Graylock called out for the Caeliar scientist. "Lerxst?"

There was no answer but the keening of the wind.

He tried again: "Lerxst?"

His voice echoed several times.

Then a sepulchral groan shook the ruined city.

"Maybe we should leave," Pembleton said, turning a wary eye toward the ceiling, while Thayer threw frightened glances in every other direction.

"Not the worst plan I've ever heard," Graylock said.

They turned to retreat from the lab—and saw a specter looking back at them. It was barely there at all, a ghostly approximation of a Caeliar's shape, as if made of steam.

Unable to mask the fear choking his voice, Graylock squeaked out, "Lerxst?"

An electric jolt spiked through Graylock's mind and rooted him to the floor. Thayer and Pembleton stood shaking beside him. Then a voice—at once feminine, malevolent, and invincible—whispered inside his thoughts as a chill like death crusted the trio's bodies and faces with a delicate layer of frost.

Sedín.

Pinpricks of cold fire became unbearable stabs of pain across every square centimeter of Graylock's body. He wanted to scream and run, but he couldn't move. There was nowhere for his agony to go, so it rebounded on itself, creating a feedback loop of suffering that drowned out every other sensation. He kept expecting to pass out, to implode under the strain, but Sedín wouldn't let his mind shut down.

She wouldn't let him escape; she just hammered and hammered.

No! he raged. *I won't be . . . won't become . . . a . . . cy—*

—borg.

The hunger had found new strength. Three drones, easily controlled. Two males, one female. Properly replenished, they would serve. But these were nearly depleted. *The female must be preserved to produce more vessels,* decided the hunger. *One of the males must be consolidated for the collective good.*

It read the chemical engrams of the males' minds. One was a warrior, the other an engineer. *The engineer's knowledge is more valuable,* the hunger concluded.

The drones' tools were crude and clumsy, but they would suffice. Organic nourishment, though inefficient, also would have to do until a more efficacious means of sustenance and maintenance could be devised. Until then, adjustments to these beings' simple genetic code would maximize their longevity and facilitate needed energy-saving biological processes.

Operating the drones as though they were limbs, the hunger used the female and the engineer to terminate the warrior. Its loss was regrettable but necessary. With care and precision, its body was cut apart, meat and fat separated from bone, the edible from the inedible. When all of the warrior's digestible fuels had been isolated, the hunger recharged her two remaining drones with the resources liberated from the third.

When warmer weather returned, the search could begin for a new source of energy. Until then, these vessels of the hunger had to be protected and their energy conserved.

Survival would depend on patience.

Sleep, the hunger bade its drones. *Sleep.*

Icy seawater crashed over the gunwales of the launch as it neared the shore. Sedath, the second-in-command of the private icebreaker *Demial,* took the brunt of the chilling spray but turned his head and shut his eyes until the stinging mist abated. He opened his eyes and saw the rowers smirking at him.

"Pick up the pace, men," he said, his voice as level and professional as ever. He didn't begrudge his men a bit of amusement at his expense, but discipline had to be maintained.

At the rear of the launch sat Jestem, the *Demial*'s athletic and weathered commanding officer, and Karai, a nervous and evasive young executive from the consortium that owned the icebreaker and employed its officers and crew. Both men were eager to be ashore, though for different reasons. Jestem was a glory seeker, always on the lookout for another chance to grab a measure of fame and acclaim. Karai's ambition was more prosaic: He was in it for the money.

Sedath looked up at the pale sky. The sun had just peeked over the horizon, casting a golden glow on the arctic mountains. The landing party would have barely enough time to climb the slope to the lowest edge of the astounding scar that *something* had gouged into the primeval rock.

The scar fascinated Sedath. He had studied dozens of old topographical maps and surveyors' drawings of this peak on the *Demial*'s months-long sea journey, and he was certain that the multitude of jagged, semi-vertical rock formations that dotted the lower slope had not been there just a few decades earlier.

It's a meteorite, he surmised. *Has to be. The distribution of the debris on the slope suggests an oblique impact from above.* Although the *Demial*'s principal mission was to search the seabed for carbon fuel deposits, Sedath had always viewed his work aboard the arctic explorer as an opportunity to conduct scientific research far away from the meddling of the company's sponsored labs or the ideologically extreme halls of academia.

Let the commander have the glory, he mused. *Karai can keep the money. I just want to run some tests on those meteorites.*

The hollow scrape of aluminum over pebbles and sand told Sedath that the launch had reached the shore of the fjord. Malfomn, the ship's graying, square-jawed gendarme, got up from his seat next to Sedath and vaulted over the side of the launch. The older man landed with a splash in the frigid, knee-deep water, grabbed the prow of the launch, and towed it farther onto the shore. Sedath stood, laid a plank from the front benchboard to the bow, walked across it, and made a short hop to dry land.

Jestem and Karai were the next out of the launch, followed in short order by the rowers and the ship's surgeon, Dr. Marasa. To the same degree that Karai, Jestem, and Sedath himself were overcome with enthusiasm for the consortium-ordered fact-finding mission, Marasa had wanted no part of it. The weary-looking physician shivered as he took in his sur-roundings. "Okay, we've seen it," he grumped. "Can we go back now?"

"Quit complaining, Doctor," Jestem said. "We're heading up the slope for a closer look at whatever hit this mountain."

Marasa narrowed his eyes. "I bet it was a rock."

Jestem replied, "Just put your snowshoes on, Doctor."

Malfomn, Karai, Sedath, Jestem, and Marasa set down their backpacks, unstrapped their snowshoes, and started putting them on. Jestem was the first to finish securing his bindings. He began slide-stepping away, heading for the incline. "Come on," he called back. "We're losing the light, gentlemen!"

The rest of the group was about to set out after him when Malfomn called out, "Hold up! Everybody, stop!" All eyes turned toward the gendarme, who pointed at a nearby rocky outcropping. "What's that, between the rocks?"

It was difficult at first for Sedath to see what Mal-fomn was talking about. Then he began to discern ar-tificial-looking shapes and angles lurking beneath the deep, driven snow. "Malfomn, come with me, we'll check it out."

Sedath and Malfomn split away from the group and sidestepped up a gradual hillside to the rock for-mation. As they got closer to it, he saw pieces of metal jutting up out of the snow and catching the morning sunlight. As soon as he was close enough, Sedath reached out with one gloved hand and tugged on the narrow beam. It shifted a bit in the snow. "Help me pull this up," he said to the gendarme.

Together they took hold of the metal bar and pulled it free of the snow. It was half again as long as Sedath was tall, and its edges were twisted and jagged, as if from shearing stress.

"Do you recognize this alloy?" he asked Malfomn.

The older man shook his head. "Never seen anything like it." Nodding at the snow where they'd found it, he added, "Maybe we ought to do a little digging here, see what we find."

"Good idea," Sedath said. They retrieved their entrenching tools from the back of their packs and started shoveling away the snow and ice. Within a few minutes, beneath only a thin layer of the snow cover, they had exposed more metal pieces and a large patch of tattered, metallic-looking fabric. Lifting it and eyeing it in the sunlight, Sedath speculated, "Part of a shelter, you think?"

"Maybe," Malfomn said. "But I don't know anybody anywhere who makes shelters with materials like this—do you?"

Sedath bunched the shredded fabric and stuffed it into his pocket. "No, I don't," he said. He cast an apprehensive look up the mountainside at the raw wound in the stone and turned back to Malfomn. "We should get back to the others," he said. "Jestem wants to climb that slope and make it back to the *Demial* before sundown." Stepping closer to the gendarme, Sedath added in a confidential tone of voice, "Have the rowers come up here and finish digging this out while we're gone. Whatever they find, I want it wrapped in a tarp and stowed in the launch."

"Yes, sir," Malfomn said. "It'll be good for them to have work to do while we're up on the mountain."

"My thoughts, exactly," Sedath said.

The two men kick-stepped back down the hillside. Back on level ground, they split up; Sedath cut across the plain to rejoin the commander, and Malfomn detoured to the shore and relayed Sedath's orders to the rowers before regrouping with the climbing expedition at the base of the mountain.

"What'd you find?" Jestem asked Sedath.

"I'm not sure yet," Sedath said, and it was an honest, if evasive, answer. "Some metal and some fabric."

Jestem frowned inside his fur-lined parka hood. "Metal and fabric? Like you might find in a hastily concealed base camp?"

"Possibly," Sedath said, not refuting the commander's hypothesis, even though he had a more exotic idea of his own.

Karai shot a worried glance at Jestem. "Commander, the consortium has to defend its rights to all claims in this territory, mineral or chemical, or else we'll lose them."

"I know that," Jestem said.

"If another landing party has arrived ahead of us, we can't let them seize any materials or stake any—"

Jestem cut in, "I get it!" He nodded to Malfomn. "Keep your weapon handy, Mal. Seems like we might not be alone up here." To the rest of the group, he declared, "Let's go! Follow me."

As the climb began, Sedath pulled a corner of the fabric from his pocket and stole another look at it. It was lightweight but substantial enough that no light penetrated its weave; it slipped easily between his gloved fingertips, like gear oil. Its metallic threads reflected a rainbow of colors as they caught the light. He truly had never seen anything like it before, and he had no idea how it had been made. But if his hypothesis about its origin proved to be correct, then Sedath was about to make a great discovery for science.

Of course, if we actually find an alien spaceship, he admitted to himself, *the commander will be the one who gets famous, and Karai'll probably end up the world's richest man. The best I can hope for is to get the first look at the thing before it gets shut away in some company lab.*

He grinned beneath his balaclava. *I can live with that.*

"Over here!" Jestem was far ahead of the rest of the group, standing near an ice fissure at the bottom of a steep cliff patched with snow. Sedath and the others hurried their pace, but only with difficulty. None of them had snowshoed in a long time, and the hike up the slope had proved exhausting for everyone—except the commander, apparently.

Malfomn and Sedath reached the fissure, where Jestem stood at the mouth of a narrow ice cave, staring into its depths. Sedath looked back and admired the view of the fjord. At its far end, near the channel, the *Demial* lay at anchor, silhouetted on quiet waters that reflected the dusky afternoon sky. A whistling gale sparkled the air with a dusting of ice crystals lifted from the slope around the landing party.

Karai and Marasa arrived looking wilted and sounding out of breath. The doctor said, "I promise to rig a clean drug test for anyone willing to carry me back down."

Before anyone could take Marasa up on his offer, Jestem turned and said to Sedath, "Give me your palmlight, will you?"

Sedath undid the loop that held his portable light on his belt and handed the device to Jestem—who, as a privilege of his rank, usually traveled light and expected everyone else to come prepared with whatever he might need. The commander switched on the palmlight and aimed its narrow beam down the ice shaft. He squinted and said, "Sedath, do you see that surface down there?"

Peering into the foggy gloom, Sedath replied, "I think so."

"What does that look like to you?"

He watched the way the light reflected off a bare patch of the cave's floor, and he nodded. "Metal," he said.

Jestem turned off the light, tucked it into his own belt, and said, "We're going down there. Secure some safety lines in the cliff face, and relay our coordinates to the *Demial*."

"Yes, sir," Sedath said. He nodded to Malfomn, who set himself to work hammering spikes into the stone cliff face and securing sturdy ropes to them. Sedath removed his pack and dug out the radio. He turned it on, set it to the ship's frequency, and pressed the transmit button. "Landing party to *Demial*, acknowledge."

The watch officer's voice squawked and crackled over the barely reliable portable transceiver, "*Demial here. Go ahead.*"

"Our coordinates are grid *teskol* seventeen, azimuth three-fifty-six-point-two, elevation one thousand three hundred nine."

"Noted," said the watch officer. *"Any details for the log?"*

"We've found an opening in a cliff wall," Sedath said, and then he paused as Jestem snapped around and glared at him, as if to say, *Not another word—not yet.* Composing himself, Sedath continued, "We're going underground to see where it leads, so we'll be out of touch for a bit."

"Got it. Watch your step down there."

"Count on it. Landing party out." He switched off the radio and tucked it back inside his pack. He walked back to the others and saw that Malfomn had finished securing two safety lines and was hurling their coils of slack down the ice shaft. Sedath sidled up to Jestem, who was still gazing down into the subterranean darkness. "Sir," Sedath said, "maybe I should go first, just this once."

"Nonsense," Jestem said, slipping back into his practiced persona of nonchalant bravery. "I was just getting my bearings, that's all. Let's get down there before we lose the light."

There was no time for Sedath to protest. Jestem locked his jacket's climbing loop around the safety line and started down the shaft, his boots slipping clumsily across the snow-dusted ice as he worked his way down the rope, using his hands as a brake. Half a minute later, the commander was at the bottom, shining his borrowed palmlight down the tunnel.

Sedath directed and supervised the descents, and he was the last person down. After a few strides away from the ice, his footsteps echoed against metal, much as they did aboard the *Demial.* He halted in mid-step as Jestem, Karai, and Malfomn spun around and shushed him. As soon as he stopped, they turned away and seemed to be listening intently, so Sedath did the same.

Faint sounds reechoed in the darkness, so softly that they almost became lost in the melancholy moaning of the wind through the passages. Then the sounds became closer and clearer: a soft scrape and several light footfalls.

"Lights," Jestem said, switching on his palmlight. Karai, Malfomn, and Marasa did the same. Empty-handed, all that Sedath could do was stand to one side and try to gaze past the crisscrossed beams to see what might emerge from the darkness.

Two shapes shuffled into the penumbra of the palmlights. At first, all Sedath could see were their dark outlines, but even from those, he was certain that he was looking at a man and a woman. They were emaciated and garbed in tattered, loose-hanging bits of fabric, which fluttered in the chilly breeze that never seemed to cease. The beams from the palmlights were reflected in the pair's eyes, which even from a distance had a disconcerting emptiness that sent a shiver of fear down Sedath's spine.

"Identify yourselves," Jestem called out.

Karai said with venomous anger, "We know who they are—corporate spies." Sneering at the disheveled figures limping and walking stiffly out of the darkness, he added, "Looks like they already got what they deserve, too."

Then the mysterious duo stepped fully into the harsh glare of the palmlights. They were definitely a male and a female, but Sedath was certain they weren't Kindir. For one thing, their hands each had only a single opposable thumb instead of the normal two. Even more shocking to him were their pallid, mottled-gray complexions. Kindir skin varied in pigmentation from golden brown to ebony, and no one in the history of the world had ever had eyes the color of the sky—but this woman did.

The landing party was still and silent, dumbfounded by the significance of this encounter: They were face-to-face with living, intelligent beings not of their world.

The alien woman spoke in a monotonal voice. Her words didn't sound like any of the dozens of major languages on Arehaz. She repeated herself as she and her companion advanced on the landing party.

Jestem muttered to Sedath, "Any idea what she said?"

"No clue," Sedath said.

The aliens stopped at arm's length from the landing party. The woman spoke again, repeating her monotonal declaration. Then she and the man each extended one hand to the landing party.

"I think it's some kind of greeting," Sedath said.

He stepped forward to take the man's hand, but Jestem grabbed his shoulder and stopped him. "Looks like she does the talking around here. Let me handle this." Jestem took half a step forward and offered his hand to the woman. "I am Salaz Jestem of the icebreaker *Demial*," he said. "On behalf of Kindir around the world, welcome to Arehaz."

The woman grasped the commander's extended hand. Slender metallic tubules broke through the skin between her knuckles and leaped like serpents into the fleshy part of Jestem's wrist. He convulsed and then became rigid. The light left his eyes.

Sedath and Malfomn sprang to Jestem's aid. The male alien's hand struck in a blur, locked around Sedath's throat, and lifted him off the ground. The female let go of Jestem and snared Malfomn's arm before he could land his punch.

The two men struggled in vain to free themselves. Despite the aliens' gaunt appearances, they were amazingly strong. Out of the corner of his eye, Sedath saw Dr. Marasa spring to catch Jestem, who had staggered away from the melee in a daze.

Marasa shook Jestem by his shoulders. "Commander? Are you all right? Are you hurt?"

Jestem looked up at Marasa—and then he lifted one hand to the doctor's throat and skewered it with two silver tubules from his own knuckles. Marasa twitched in Jestem's clutches, and next to Sedath, Malfomn was quaking and wearing a glazed look as the female alien withdrew her tubules from his wrist.

Then Sedath felt a bite on his own neck, like a pair of tiny fangs piercing his carotid. A dark, muffling curtain of terror descended on his thoughts as the female spoke again. This time, hearing her inside his mind, he understood her perfectly.

You will be assimilated.

2381

21

Gredenko looked back from ops and said, "Starfleet Command is confirming all reports, Captain."

Dax smiled and heaved a deep, relieved sigh. Applause and cheering filled the *Aventine*'s bridge, and even Bowers let down his guard for a moment to pump his fist and shout, "Yes!"

It really worked. Dax could barely believe it. Assaulting the Borg probe ship had been a terrible risk and the wildest of long shots, but they had done it—and played a decisive role in saving five allied worlds from annihilation.

As the applause tapered off, Dax joined Lieutenant Kandel at tactical and asked, "How long before Captain Hernandez can tap into the Borg vinculum again?"

The Deltan woman replied, "We don't know yet, Captain. The last report from Lieutenant Kedair said that Captain Hernandez had to be disconnected from the vinculum for her own good."

"Has the captain regained consciousness?"

"Yes, a few moments ago," Kandel said.

"Then I want her patched back into the vinc—" A thunderclap and a jarring impact knocked the bridge into a confused jumble of bodies falling and tumbling in the dark.

Bowers shouted, "Shields! Tactical, report!"

Several more blasts shook the *Aventine* in rapid succession. "Taking fire from the Borg ship," Kandel called back over the din of explosions.

"Return fire!" Dax said. "Target their weapons!"

"Firing," Kandel said. On the main viewer, blue streams of phaser energy skewered the Borg scout's hull, vaporizing its primary and secondary armaments. Dax hoped she wasn't inflicting more friendly-fire casualties on her boarding teams.

The lights flickered back to full strength as Bowers said, "Helm, evasive pattern sigma. Give tactical a clear shot at the other side of the Borg ship."

"Aye, sir," replied Lieutenant Tharp. The Bolian guided the ship through a series of rolling maneuvers that dodged the Borg's next barrage. Then a fresh wave of phaser and torpedo hits from the *Aventine* halted the Borg's attack.

"Cease-fire," Bowers ordered. "Gredenko, damage report."

The ops officer's hands moved lightly and quickly over her console as she compiled data flooding in from several decks and departments. "Weapons grid overload," she said. "Shields offline. Direct hit to the main deflector—minor damage, but we've lost the ability to generate a dampening field."

"I'll bet that was the Borg's intention," Dax said.

Gredenko added, "There's more, Captain. We've also lost our long-range comms. Complete system failure."

"Sam, start beaming our people back," Dax said. "I

want them off that ship, on the double. Then I want it fragged."

"Aye, Captain," said Bowers, relaying the order to Kandel with an urgent nod.

A moment later, Kandel looked up from the tactical station and said, "Scattering fields are going up in the core of the Borg ship—and the boarding parties report they're under attack!"

Bowers snapped, "By whom?"

Kandel's reply confirmed Dax's fear: "By the ship, sir."

The walls were alive, and the floors couldn't be trusted. Hungry maws filled with shining cables writhing in viscous black fluids had started to appear in the middle of bulkheads and corridors, as if invisible knives were slashing wounds into the ship's metal flesh and revealing its biomechanoid innards.

Helkara looked around the transforming vinculum tower in shock. Over the deafening screeches of wrenching metal, he shouted, "What the hell is going on?"

"The ship's adapting," Kedair said, looking around in terror at the collapsing catwalks and wildly undulating wires that whipped like angry serpents in the space around the ship's hollow core. "That means it's about to start either killing us or assimilating us. Either way, I'd rather not stick around to find out." A booming groan from the ship seemed to answer her.

Leishman and a Mizarian paramedic named Ravosus strained to lift Erika Hernandez to her feet. "C'mon, Captain," Leishman said, grimacing under the effort of lifting the semiconscious woman. "We have to get you out of here."

As they carried her toward the exit, Hernandez's eyes snapped open, and her hand lashed out and snared Kedair's sleeve. "The Queen," she said. "She's here. On this ship."

Kedair tapped her combadge, intending to order the rest of the boarding teams to evacuate the Borg ship. Her metallic insignia returned a dysfunctional-sounding chirp that signaled an error. "Must be a scrambling field," she said, thinking out loud. She pried Hernandez's fingers off her arm, then pointed across the narrow causeway that had been extended to link the vinculum tower to the interior structure of the Borg vessel. "You three, get Hernandez to a beam-out point. Go!"

Helkara blocked the exit and protested, "What about you?"

"I have to set the detonator on the transphasic mine," she said. Then she added a lie: "I'll be right behind you. Go!" A hard slap on the Zakdorn's back impelled him into motion. Leishman and the medic hurried along behind him, supporting the dazed but now weakly ambulatory Hernandez between them.

One minute for them to cross the bridge, Kedair calculated, *two minutes to the nearest enhanced transport site. Add a minute for insurance.* She turned back and faced the dark heart at the center of the Borg vessel. The inside of the vinculum tower was now a horror show of biomechanical viscera spreading like a cancer, metastasizing into every open space. To reach the transphasic mine and set its detonator, she would have to fight her way through that snaking mass of lethal, merciless pseudo-flesh and hold her ground for at least four minutes.

There was no point sending anyone else to do it; she was the only one likely to have a chance of success . . . and she decided that she'd gotten enough of her people killed for one day.

From a sheath on the back of one of her slain comrades, she drew a sword with a monomolecular edge. Alone and resolved, she gazed into the yawning cavity of steel teeth, slithering sinew, and oily black death. It taunted her with evil whispers, as if daring her to rush in where all others feared to tread.

She lifted her blade and charged.

Every turn seemed to lead to a dead end. Dark chords of panic rang out from all directions, echoing and vanishing into the shadowy recesses. The inside of the Borg probe was a maze of snaking conduits and sliding walls. Great slabs of machinery moved of their own volition behind the façades, traveling with deep rumbles and ear-splitting screeches.

Erika Hernandez had recovered most of her strength and was sprinting behind Leishman and Helkara, with Ravosus close behind her. She wished they could run faster. In theory, Helkara was leading them out of the industrial-style labyrinth, back to one of many secured platforms where a quartet of transporter-pattern enhancers had been set up to facilitate a rapid evacuation of the ship. In practice, he was steering them down passages to nowhere.

They rounded a corner, and Helkara slammed into a solid wall of layered metal plating and overlapping conduits. Leishman ran into him, and Ravosus collided with Hernandez and then awkwardly backed away, into the corridor from which they'd come.

Helkara stumbled backward and squinted in pained confusion at the barrier. "What the . . . ?" Staring in dismay at his tricorder screen, he said, "There should be a passage here."

"We were warned about this," Leishman said, pulling Helkara back the way they'd come, past Hernandez, around the corner. "The ship's reshaping itself, corralling us." As soon as she had turned the corner, she stopped, looked around, and asked with obvious alarm, "Where's Ravosus?"

Hernandez opened her catom senses to the energies that dwelled inside the Borg vessel's vast machinery, all of it guided by a sophisticated inorganic intelligence. She saw the patterns in its alterations of form, and she felt it focusing itself to strike. Behind all of it, she heard the voice of the Queen.

"He's gone," Hernandez said. "Follow me."

She led her two remaining comrades down a narrow pass between two bulkheads. It was barely wide enough for Leishman to pass; her shoulders scraped the sides, and Helkara had to shuffle-step at an angle to follow. Several meters away, at the end of the sliver-thin passage, the sickly green glow of the ship's energy-transfer systems lit the way.

Leishman called out in alarm, "I'm snagged on something!"

Hernandez stopped and looked back. Black tendrils squirmed up through holes in the waffle-grid deck plates and snaked around Leishman's ankles and up her legs. Hurrying back to the trapped engineer, Hernandez saw Helkara reaching for his phaser. "Stop," she said, holding out one hand. "You could hit Mikaela!"

Helkara stared past her, and his jaw went slack as a shadow fell over him. "I think we have bigger problems," he said.

Her catom senses had already told her what was happening, but she needed to see it for herself.

She looked over her shoulder.

The path ahead went black. The passage was closing on them.

Resistance is futile, hissed the Queen, invading the sanctum of Hernandez's thoughts.

We'll see about that, Hernandez projected in reply.

"Take my hand, Mikaela!" she shouted. "Gruhn—you, too!"

The two officers reached out for Hernandez's outstretched hands. She grasped their wrists.

The walls pressed inward and reached for the trio with eager tentacles. The deck fell away beneath them.

And another took its place.

She had found the royal frequency and made it her own.

For every trap the Borg Queen triggered, Hernandez improvised a defense. Rebuilding the lost deck behind her, she pulled Leishman and Helkara with her as she fought for each step. Prehensile twists of tubing as thick as her arms wrapped around her throat, Leishman's waist, Helkara's legs. Hernandez answered each attack with a focused mental image of its opposite. The physical reality of the Borg ship, for aeons the solitary domain of the Borg Queen, now bowed to her imagination. Tentacles withdrew or broke apart. Vanished decks rebuilt themselves. The lethal pressure of closing bulkheads became the freedom of open space. Then her back struck the final barrier, and at her command, it turned to coal-black dust.

The trio collapsed onto the secured platform, which had been partitioned from the rest of the Borg ship by directional dampening field projectors. Arranged in a large square formation were four transport-pattern enhancers, all blinking in their ready standby mode.

Hernandez dropped Leishman and Helkara into the middle of the enhancers, tapped the combadge on Helkara's chest, and said, "Boarding party to *Aventine*. Two for emergency beam-out!"

"Acknowledged," said a voice made small by being filtered through the combadge. *"Stand by for transport."*

Leishman and Helkara were still staggering weakly to their feet as Hernandez bounded away, clear of the pattern enhancers, and landed with preternatural grace atop a centimeters-thin railing. Perched on it, she felt the same rush of power that she'd had in Axion. Having attuned the catoms in her body to the Borg's unique wavelength, she had usurped their strength.

The images in Hernandez's mind were absolutely clear.

She saw Kedair being smothered inside the vinculum tower, her life fading, her mission to trigger the transphasic mine on the verge of failure. There was no direct route to the transport-shielded tower, no way for anyone to come to Kedair's aid . . . no one except Hernandez.

She coiled and tensed to leap off the railing into the moving parts of the Borg ship, already visualizing herself negotiating its grinding gears with impunity.

The whine of a transporter beam began to fill the air.

"Where are you going?" Leishman asked over the eerie wails and mechanical clankings of the ship's infernal works.

Hernandez looked over her shoulder. "To save Kedair."

Helkara and Leishman became pillars of swirling particles as the transporter beam took hold, and Hernandez leaped off the railing and fell willingly into the belly of the beast.

Lonnoc Kedair knew that she was close to the detonator controls for the transphasic mine, but she couldn't see it. Entombed in the squirming black tangle that surrounded the Borg vinculum, all she saw was darkness, as if she'd drowned in tar.

There was no air to breathe, nowhere to move, no way to get any leverage for a counterattack. Her feet had been pulled from under her, and stinger-tipped tentacles began impaling her from the front and from behind.

Horrendous grinding sensations filled her torso as the Borg ship's mechanical limbs pierced her body in several places at once. Almost as quickly as the wounds were inflicted, her body fought to heal them, but it was a losing battle. Several centimeters thick, the tentacles battered her with blunt force, snapping her bones, rending her skin, and pummeling her last hoarded breaths from her lungs.

She cried out in agony and felt her scream buried in the smothering, oily lubricant of the Borg machine. The foul liquid seeped into her nostrils and poured into her mouth. Reflex and instinct told her to spit it out, but she had no more breath left to push with.

Needling jabs pricked her skin with sharp, icy twinges. *Assimilation nanoprobes,* she realized. For a moment, she regretted the aggressive combination of antiassimilation implants and injections she and the other boarders had received. Although the Borg's nanoprobes had faced and overcome some of these prophylactic measures in the past, they had never encountered this precise amalgam of genetic and neurological blockades. *Lucky me,* Kedair realized. *Since I can't be assimilated, I get to spend more time being chewed up. Great.*

Tentacles at either end of her torso pulled in opposite directions, and she realized only then that it meant to rip her in half. Then the shearing tension began, and excruciating pain expelled everything from her mind except agony.

No amount of rapid-healing possessed by any Takaran could keep pace with what was being done to her; the Borg ship was breaking down her resilient body by degrees. Kedair's mouth contorted as the pressure intensified, and the dark, metallic-smelling fluid found its way inside her ears. Then, fully submerged inside the horror, she heard it.

Beneath the frantic pounding of her pulse, a malevolent whisper lurked in the suffocating fluid of this dark womb. Its message penetrated her thoughts, and she knew that it couldn't be debated or bargained with. *Strength is irrelevant,* it told her. *You are small, and we are endless. You are one, and we are legion. You will become as we are. You will become part of us.*

Kedair was ready to surrender to the darkness.

Then there was light.

The vile tentacles pulled out of her flesh and retreated into the walls. The crushing press of machines and needles and saws fell away, and some of the contraptions that turned humanoids into drones fell to pieces and scattered across the deck. Kedair's body fell free, and she landed in a twisted, mutilated heap on the floor. Through the cloudy stains in her vision, she saw that her left arm was partially severed and dangled by a tendon just below the elbow. Everything had a flat, distorted quality, and when she tried to blink away the slime, she realized she had only one working eye. The other had been gouged out to make way for some monstrous implant.

She heard footsteps approaching.

Turning her head, she saw Erika Hernandez striding back into the vinculum tower, heading directly toward her. The woman's uniform had become stained and tattered, but Hernandez herself looked none the worse for whatever she'd endured. She asked Kedair, "Can you walk?"

Kedair sputtered through a mouthful of filth, "Both my legs are broken." She jerked her head toward the transphasic mine, which had been securely affixed to the Borg ship's central plexus—essentially, its nerve center. "Set the detonator. We—" She paused to hack up a mouthful of viscous black oil and spat several times to clear her mouth. "We have to frag this ship."

Hernandez walked toward the mine. "Tell me what to do."

"It's already armed," Kedair said, wincing as her back and chest muscles began pulling shattered bones back into place before mending them. "Enter a delay in seconds using the touchpad, then press 'Enable' to start the countdown."

Standing at the detonator, Hernandez keyed in the data. She hurried back to Kedair. "It's running," she said, kneeling beside Kedair's mangled body.

Kedair asked, "How long?"

"Seventy-five seconds," Hernandez said.

"Are you crazy?" Kedair snapped. "That's not—"

A three-clawed biomechanoid tentacle lunged at Hernandez from behind. Kedair meant to shout or point or give a warning—then, without seeming to notice or care, Hernandez lifted a hand in a dismissive gesture, and the tentacle shredded into scrap metal. Hernandez straightened Kedair's mauled limbs and prompted her, "You were saying?"

It took Kedair a second to recover her wits. "It's not enough time to reach a transport site," she said.

"Yes, it is," Hernandez replied. She slid her hands under Kedair, who at first felt no contact—and then she realized that she was floating a few centimeters above the deck. She was in Hernandez's arms and being lifted gently over the woman's shoulder. "Hang on," added Hernandez. "This part won't be fun."

Kedair's full weight rested on Hernandez's shoulder, and the youthful woman carried Kedair out of the vinculum tower at a brisk pace. The bobbing cadence of Hernandez's stride and the pressure on Kedair's abdomen made the Takaran cough up more of the bitter, toxic black fluid she'd inhaled while snared in the Borg ship's grasp.

Between hacking coughs, she saw more serpentine appendages lash out at Hernandez, who deflected each attack with the slightest motions of her fingers, like a sorcerer cowing demons. Passages and exits closed themselves with piping and components that spread like black metallic ivy, but the hastily risen barriers retreated ahead of Hernandez, who parted them with broad waves of her hand.

They passed through the last portal and reached the platform outside the tower. The bridge back to the ship's outer superstructure had been retracted. The space above them, which only minutes earlier had been empty, now was alive with moving metal and blue black clouds of some primordial matter that flashed with static electricity.

"Are you afraid of heights?" Hernandez asked.

"No," Kedair said.

Hernandez grinned. "Good."

She stretched one hand toward the distant top of the ship's interior, and then they were aloft, rising away from the platform and accelerating toward the shadowy maelstrom overhead.

Kedair, still draped over Hernandez's shoulder, watched the vinculum tower shrink beneath them. "How in the name of Yaltakh are you doing this?"

"Easy," Hernandez said. "I imagine I've already done it."

They arrowed through the center of the ship's brewing thunderhead, and an eye of calm swirled around them as they passed. Then they were near the top deck of the ship, and a dampener-secured platform equipped with transporter-pattern enhancers hove into view.

"Ten seconds," Kedair said. "No pressure."

Hernandez alighted on the platform, leaned forward, and shrugged Kedair off her shoulder. Catching the wounded woman with one arm, she tapped her combadge with her free hand. "Hernandez to *Aventine*! Two to beam up!"

"Energizing," replied a transporter chief over the comm.

Kedair clasped Hernandez's arm and grinned. "In case we don't make it," she said, "nice try."

The paralyzing embrace of the transporter's annular confinement beam found them, and the Stygian steelscape of the Borg ship began to fade behind a glittering veil—then a flash turned everything white.

The Borg scout ship vanished from the *Aventine*'s main viewer in a fiery blue detonation.

Dax paced in quick steps behind Lieutenant Kandel, manic with anxiety. "Tell me we got them," she said, pestering the tactical officer for the third time in fifteen seconds.

From the other side of the console, Bowers tossed a sidelong frown in Dax's direction. "And you wonder why I don't let you go on away missions."

Pressing herself against the tactical panel beside Kandel, Dax said to Kandel, "Report, Lieutenant."

The Deltan woman finished reviewing the data on her screen in a calm, unhurried manner, looked up at Dax, and said, "Transporter room two confirms

Captain Hernandez and Lieutenant Kedair are aboard. The lieutenant is being rushed to sickbay."

"Where's Captain Hernandez now?"

Kandel nodded at her companel. "In the transporter room."

"Patch me through to her," Dax said. She waited for Kandel to confirm that she had opened a channel, and then she said, "Captain Hernandez, this is Captain Dax. Are you all right?"

"I'm fine, but I need to meet with you, alone, right now."

Bowers glanced at Dax, as if she needed reminding of the damage her ship had just taken and the dire need for repairs and a new plan. "Can this wait an hour, Captain? We have a lot—"

"Right. Now. In my quarters."

The vehemence of Hernandez's demand left Dax taken aback. She twitched her eyebrows at Bowers, who shrugged in return.

"All right, then," Dax said. "I'm on my way."

The door to the VIP guest quarters opened at Dax's approach, and she entered unannounced. A few paces into the compartment, she saw Hernandez leaning against the bulkhead.

Hernandez regarded Dax with a dour frown. "You're the second captain to barge into my quarters without knocking today," she said. "Doesn't Starfleet teach courtesy anymore?"

"My ship, my rules," Dax said. "Besides, you made it pretty clear—on an open channel—that you were in a hurry to see me." Spreading her arms in a sarcastic pantomime of openness, she added, "Well, here I am. Talk." She folded her arms across her chest while she waited for the other woman's reply.

As she meandered toward Dax, Hernandez wore a troubled look. "Bear with me, Captain," she said, her voice quieter than it had been. Her shredded uniform hung loosely on her slender frame. "What I need to tell you is vital, but it's hard for me to come at a problem straight. After eight hundred years with the Caeliar, keeping secrets becomes a virtue."

"I understand," Dax said. Hernandez stopped a mere arm's length in front of her. Looking more closely at her, Dax saw that despite the youthful appearance of her face and physique, Hernandez's eyes possessed an ancient light. It was a curious trait Dax had seen in joined Trills with very old symbionts.

Rubbing her palms slowly against each other, Hernandez said, "I read everything in your files about the Borg before I went to that ship. I thought I was ready for whatever I'd find. I was wrong."

"If you're blaming yourself over what happened during the counterattack, don't," Dax said. "As far as I'm concerned, you deserve a medal for saving three of my officers—especially going back for Kedair like you did."

Hernandez averted her eyes and stepped away from Dax, toward the windows that looked out on the deceptively placid starfield. "I'm not talking about what the Borg do," she said. "I'm talking about what they *are*. I wasn't ready to believe it." Her voice fell to a hush, and Dax inched closer behind her to listen as she continued. "I was expecting a group mind, but that's not really what the Borg is. It's *one* mind, one tyrant consciousness enslaving all the others. What it does to individuals is beyond cruel—it's sadistic, barbaric. And it's so . . . empty. It's a hunger void of form, a frozen pit that can never be filled, no matter how much it eats—and the larger it gets, the more it wants."

She looked at Dax. "It was like a melody I'd heard before, but now it was changed—darker, more dissonant. Instead of uniting the minds, the way a conductor guides the musicians in a symphony, it buries them, makes them into mute spectators, while it uses their bodies as tools. It's like a prison of lost souls, with trillions of beings chained to the will of something that doesn't even know what the hell it wants."

"Sounds like a bad Joining," Dax said. Noting Hernandez's uncomprehending head shake, she added, "Sometimes, when a Trill symbiont is incompatible with its new host, it creates a persona so terrible that the only proper response is forced separation."

"That about sums it up," Hernandez said. Sorrow darkened her expression. "The worst part is how familiar it felt."

Suspicion percolated in Dax's gut. "Familiar?"

Stepping away, perhaps hoping to insulate herself from Dax with a bit of distance, Hernandez said, "I first noticed it a few hours ago, after the boarding teams contacted us. When we lowered the dampening field, I was able to sense one of the dying drones on the Borg ship in the same way that I used to be able to sense the Caeliar. And when I was inside the Borg ship and it regained full power, it was like I was back in Axion."

Dax kept a wary eye on Hernandez. "Is that all?"

"It's just the beginning," Hernandez said, stopping at her quarters' wall-mounted companel. She activated the screen with a gentle tap. It was crowded with multiple side-by-side windows of information—starmaps, ships' logs, and more.

"Records from *Voyager* and the *Enterprise*-D both suggest the origin of the Borg is somewhere deep in the Delta Quadrant," Hernandez said. Swapping one starmap for another, she continued, "When the Caeliar homeworld was destroyed, the event created a number of passages through subspace—the tunnels you and your people were trying to shut down. Those were the stable ones."

A diagram of a subspace passage took on a distorted twist. Hernandez explained, "Some of the tunnels cut through time as well as space; that made them unstable, and they collapsed shortly after the Erigol cataclysm, from which only three Caeliar city-ships escaped." She drew bright, straight-line paths across the starmap with her fingertip. "One of those passages tossed the city of Axion deep into the Beta Quadrant, about eight hundred and sixty-odd years ago. A second one threw the city of Kintana into another galaxy at the dawn of time."

"And the third city . . . ?"

"Mantilis," Hernandez said, inscribing another line across the map, from the Azure Nebula to the Delta Quadrant. "Several members of my landing party were trapped in that city when it vanished. Until now, the Caeliar believed that Mantilis was lost or destroyed in some distant past. Now, based on my analysis of Borg nanoprobes and my own experiences with the Collective, I have a new theory. Through some kind of botched version of the process that made me what I am . . . they became the Borg."

Dax approached the companel to study the data up close. She imagined the horrified reaction it would provoke in Captains Riker and Picard—and likely in any human who was made aware of it. The origin of the Borg was a tragic confluence of long-past human actions and errors. "Are you sure about this?"

"Positive," Hernandez said with a satisfied smirk.

Shaking her head as a frown creased her brow, Dax said, "According to Captain Riker, we wouldn't stand a chance against the Caeliar, so why are you acting like this is good news?"

"Because now I know which of the Borg's weaknesses we can exploit," Hernandez said. "And if Caeliar technology made the Borg, maybe it can *un*-make them, too."

22

———

Riker was waiting for the punch line. Still grappling with disbelief, he said, "The Caeliar created the Borg?"

"I don't think it was intentional," Hernandez said. She stood, attired in a new Starfleet duty uniform, in front of the companel in the *Enterprise*'s observation lounge and faced Riker, Dax, and Picard. Nodding at the side-by-side images displayed on the screen behind her, she said, "The similarities between Borg nanoprobes and Caeliar catoms are too profound to be coincidence. But they're not obvious, because their exterior configurations are completely different, and inside, in their cores, the nanoprobes have been badly corrupted."

Picard sat at the head of the curved table on Riker's left, his countenance stern as he listened to Hernandez. "Your evidence is compelling, Captain," he said. "But how does this knowledge help us or the Federation in the time we have left?"

Across the table from Riker, Dax folded her hands on the table in front of her and said, "We have a plan."

"You had a plan several hours ago," Picard replied. "It nearly cost Captain Hernandez her life."

Dax bristled. "It also saved five planets and cut the Borg invasion force in half."

"But if the Borg had assimilated her Caeliar technology—"

Riker interrupted, "They didn't, and there's no point arguing about something that *didn't* go wrong. We need to plan our next move, not dissect our last one." Realizing that he had only added to Dax's smug air, he looked at her and continued, "But the limited success of one reckless plan doesn't mean we should embrace another." With the room's tensions balanced, he added, "That said, we should at least hear what they have in mind."

"Very well," Picard said. He looked at Dax and waited.

Dax volleyed the expectant look toward Hernandez and said, "It was your idea."

"It's simple," Hernandez said to Picard and Riker. "We need to prevent the Borg from attacking any more planets and put them in a position where we can deal with all of them at once. I'm proposing that we end their invasion by luring them all back here to us, in deep space."

Picard telegraphed his skepticism with one arched eyebrow. "And how, precisely, do you propose that we do so?"

Dax interjected, "By tempting them with the one kind of bait they can't resist: the Omega Molecule."

Riker asked, "How are we supposed to create one without any boronite? Replicators can't make it, and the nearest source is over two hundred light-years away."

Hernandez said, "We're not going to make Omega

Molecules, we're going to bring them to us. More precisely, we're going to make the Caeliar bring them to us, by persuading them to move their city-ship here from New Erigol." She reached over to the companel and keyed in some new commands. An image of an Omega Molecule appeared on the screen. "After I came back from the Borg ship, I remembered reading in your files that the Borg worship 'Particle 010' as a symbol of perfection. I knew there was something familiar about it, so I bypassed your security protocols and accessed your data on the molecule. When I did, I knew where I'd seen it before, and it all made sense.

"The Caeliar power their city with an Omega Molecule generator," Hernandez continued. "All the energy they harness from the shells around their planet and its star is used to mask the OMG's emissions. If I can get them to bring Axion here, free of that shielding, it'll be like a beacon for the Borg. They won't be able to resist it."

Grim-faced, Picard replied, "And once the Borg armada converges on us . . . what then?"

"We let the Caeliar deal with them," Hernandez said.

Picard got up from the table and paced away, visibly agitated. "Your last plan was reckless," he said to Dax. "This one is insane. Have you considered the risks? Never mind the damage the Borg could do if they assimilate Caeliar catoms. What if they gain control of an Omega Molecule generator? They'd have unlimited power to wreak havoc throughout the galaxy—and beyond. And if they were to lose control of the generator, an Omega Molecule explosion of that magnitude would destroy subspace for millions of light-years in every direction. Warp flight as we know it would cease to exist in this galaxy and several others."

Dax replied, "Yes, it's dangerous. We know that. But it's not like we have any better options. It's the best chance we have of stopping the Borg while there's still something left of the Federation to save."

"There are other options," Picard said. "We haven't tried using thalaron weapons against the Borg, and there's every reason to think thalaron radiation will affect the drones the same way it affects all other organic matter. If Commander La Forge can rig our deflector to emit a large enough thalaron pulse, we could wipe out the entire Borg armada."

Riker shot a dubious look at his former captain. "That's what Starfleet said about the transphasic torpedo, and the Borg have already adapted to that Hell, for all we know, the Borg already have a defense against thalaron radiation."

"Perhaps," Picard said. "But we have to try, and it might buy us the time we need to organize and fight back."

"It's too late for that," Hernandez retorted. "We're long past settling for half-measures and stopgaps. We need to *end* the war with the Borg, Captain—and we need to end it now."

Leaning forward, Riker said, "I'm not convinced thalaron weapons are the best choice. Once that technology's unleashed, it'll be impossible to contain ever again." Looking at Dax and Hernandez, he continued, "But I also think we're forgetting one important fact about the Caeliar. First and foremost, they're isolationists, and just as important, they're pacifists. Not only will they not use force against the Borg, they might prevent us from defending ourselves."

Hernandez shook her head. "No, you're misreading them. They may be pacifists, but they're not suicidal. They won't let the Borg assimilate them or hijack their technology."

"What makes you so certain they could stop them?" asked Picard, his voice rich with cynicism. "I read the report you gave to Captain Riker. A squad of MACOs from your ship got the better of the Caeliar in 2168 and destroyed one of their cities. I guarantee you, the Borg will pose a far deadlier threat than your ship's military company."

"The MACOs took the Caeliar by surprise," Hernandez said, a deep bitterness infusing her words. "The Borg won't."

With sharp suspicion, Picard said, "What if they sympathize with the Borg?"

"I think that's unlikely," Hernandez said.

"But not impossible," Picard countered. "You said yourself that Caeliar technology was the likely foundation of the Borg's nanoprobes. What if the Caeliar see the Borg as a kindred race?"

"Actually," Dax said, "we're counting on it."

Riker and Picard exchanged befuddled stares. Then Riker said to Dax, "Come again?"

"No offense, Captains," Dax said, "but we—and Starfleet—have been pursuing the wrong strategy against the Borg. We've tried to match strength with strength, violence with violence. We keep getting suckered into battles of attrition we can't win."

Hernandez added, "The key to securing the Caeliar's help is to change our mission. Instead of destroying the Collective, we should liberate it. The Borg don't need to be wiped out, they need to be saved. The Caeliar can help us do that."

"Are you mad?" Picard said. "The Borg are laying waste to worlds, and we need to *save* them?"

"I'm disappointed," Hernandez said. "You of all people should know this. You were assimilated and came back; you know from experience what it's like to be smothered in that nightmare. Now imagine trillions of beings like yourself, all trapped in that hell. They're *slaves,* Jean-Luc, and we might have the power to release them."

Dax added, "I think that as Starfleet officers—as *sentient beings*—we owe it to them, and to ourselves, to at least try."

Picard turned away and stared out a window at the stars. "As you pointed out so eloquently, Captain Dax, we hold the same rank. I can't compel you not to pursue this course of action." He looked over his shoulder at her and Hernandez. "You ignored my advice before, and I expect you'll do so again. So be it."

"If only it were that simple," Dax said. "Unfortunately, this time, I actually need your consent."

Picard turned back to face the other captains. "Why?"

"Because we need your help," Dax said. "The *Aventine*'s subspace transmitter got fried when the Borg hit us with our shields down, and *Titan*'s transmitter is too badly damaged to be repaired in time." She traded dismayed looks with Hernandez and added, "Our only hope of contacting the Caeliar is to reconfigure the *Enterprise*'s transmitter to create a subspace microtunnel, through which Erika can link with their gestalt."

Frowning, Picard returned to the table and rested his hands on the top of his chair. "So . . . if I refuse, this plan cannot proceed?" Dax and Hernandez nodded. "Then consider it vetoed."

The two women looked dejected, and Riker knew how they felt. He was certain something was wrong with Picard. In as diplomatic a tone as he could muster, he said "Captain Dax, Captain Hernandez, would you give us the room, please?"

Dax got up from her chair as Hernandez switched the companel screen back to its standby mode. The two women left the observation lounge. After the door hushed closed behind them, Riker reclined his chair a bit and let the silence weigh on himself and Picard, to see if his old friend and former commander had any desire to elaborate.

Finally, Picard said, "I take it you disagree with my decision, Will."

"Frankly, yes," Riker said.

Picard pulled back his chair and settled into it. "We can't take that kind of risk with the Borg," he said. "This is bigger than the Federation. If we give the Borg a chance to acquire the kind of technology the Caeliar possess, we might condemn the entire galaxy to suffer our fate—and maybe others, as well."

"If we don't stop the Borg now, that's all pretty much guaranteed," Riker said. "Besides, you're talking like the Federation's already gone. If the Caeliar can help unmake the Borg, we can end this without more bloodshed *and* save the Federation. Isn't that what we ought to be aiming for?"

Hatred hardened Picard's frown. "I'm not sure the Borg deserve such mercy," he said.

"Maybe not," Riker said. "But what about the individuals trapped inside the Collective? Do they deserve it?"

Swiveling his chair away from Riker, Picard mumbled, "Perhaps. I don't know."

"Captain Hernandez seems to think they do. And given a choice, I'd rather try to save lives than destroy them."

"It's not so simple a calculus," Picard said. "How can I commit myself to aiding the enemy when my people are poised on the brink of destruction?" He turned and looked Riker in the eye. "Maybe *you* can explain that to me."

An unspoken accusation seemed to lurk in Picard's words, and it struck an uneasy chord in Riker. "What's really bothering you, Jean-Luc?"

"Aside from Borg invasion fleets marauding through Federation space?"

Riker replied, "Yes, besides that. You sounded as if you were blaming me for something. More than that, you don't sound like yourself—not like the man I served with for fifteen years. Where's *that* Jean-Luc Picard?"

"*Et tu?*" Picard breathed a heavy, defeated sigh. "First Beverly, now you. Who was this other man you all claim to have known? I thought it was me, but I keep hearing otherwise."

"The man I know isn't afraid to risk taking the high road," Riker said. "He wouldn't let fear make him choose certain defeat instead of a shot at victory, just because success might mean mercy for an enemy that had hurt him."

"Is that what you think this is about? A vendetta? Or some simple phobia? I wonder, then, whether you ever knew me at all."

"You keep pushing me away," Riker said. "Did I do something to offend you? Was it something I said?"

Picard shook his head. "Of course not."

"But there is something that's bothering you, isn't there?"

"It's not my place to interfere," Picard said.

"It's not interference if your advice is invited."

Wound up with tension, Picard turned his chair away from Riker, stood, and paced along the bulkhead opposite the windows. He folded his hands together in front of him as he walked the length of the observation lounge, turned back, and retraced his steps. He stopped in front of the companel. "I don't really have advice, Will. Just confusion."

"About what?"

"How could you abandon Deanna?" Picard fixed Riker with a forlorn stare. "You left her behind, Will, and your away team."

"I did what I had to do," Riker said, pushing back against the rising tide of his guilt.

Picard moved in slow steps toward the windows. "Had I been in your place," he said pensively, "I'm not sure I could have chosen duty over Beverly so easily."

"I never said it was easy," Riker replied. "But I've seen you make decisions like that before. With Nella Daren, for one."

Holding up one hand, Picard replied, "That was different. For one thing, I wasn't married to Nella." He folded his arms. "For another, Nella wasn't pregnant. Beverly is."

A surge of grief and anger clenched Riker's jaw. All the feelings he had suppressed since Deanna left *Titan* rushed back in force, crowding his thoughts. He pressed his fist to his mouth as he fought to master his bitter, desperate emotions.

Picard took note of Riker's reaction and froze, his face a mask of embarrassment and sympathy. "What have I said, Will?"

The last thing Riker had wanted was to make this conversation about him. He inhaled sharply and set his still-clenched fist on the tabletop. "Deanna and I . . . ," he began, before his voice trailed off, swallowed up in his sorrow. He composed himself and continued in a clipped, strained voice. "We—we've been trying to start a family. It was hard. Hormone injections. Fertility treatments. Gene therapy." Finding a dispassionate frame of mind from which to continue was difficult. "We thought we'd done it," he said. "About half a year ago. But it . . . Deanna . . . we had a miscarriage."

"*Mon dieu,*" Picard whispered, and he seemed to deflate as he let go of a deep breath. He looked stricken by the news as he settled back into his chair. "I'm so sorry, Will."

"It's been a wedge, forcing us apart," Riker confessed. "After she recovered, we tried again. We thought this time it would all be okay, but it wasn't. The new embryo was deformed, and it'll miscarry, too—it's only a matter of time. But Deanna won't terminate the pregnancy, even though this one could kill her. And I think it's my fault."

"How is *any* of that your fault?" asked Picard.

"I was supposed to be the voice of reason," Riker

said. "After the first miscarriage, I should have said enough and put an end to the whole thing. But the empathic bond between me and Deanna makes it hard to say no to her. I don't even remember anymore which one of us wanted a family. All I know is that I'm supposed to protect her." He slammed his fist on the table. "And when she needed me most, I left her behind! Alone, on the other side of the goddamn galaxy!" He finally unclenched his hand, but only so he could use it to cover his closed eyes.

Sotto voce, Picard asked, "Have you tried talking with anyone about this?"

"Yeah," Riker said. "I talked to Chris. What a mistake."

"Not an easy subject for a captain to discuss with a member of his crew," Picard said, acknowledging Riker's dilemma. "Not even with a trusted first officer."

Lowering his hand, Riker opened his eyes and nodded at Picard. "Exactly," he said. "Until now, I didn't really get how vital it is to keep some things from my crew—how valuable personal privacy is."

"I understand," Picard said. "Believe me."

"So, now you know what's eating me alive," Riker said. "Are you ready to tell me what's bothering *you*?"

Picard grimaced and drummed his fingertips on the table for a few seconds. "Our problems are similar but not the same," he said. "What they have in common . . . is fatherhood." He turned himself a few degrees closer to facing Riker and spoke in a measured hush. "For a long time, I told myself that I didn't want a family, that I didn't need one. Certainly, there were fleeting moments, days when I'd wonder, 'What if . . . ?' But I never took them seriously. Not until Robert and René died."

Riker recalled the day when Picard had received the news that his brother and nephew had perished in a fire on Earth. He saw in his friend's eyes that the pain of that tragedy still lingered in Picard's psyche, an open emotional wound.

"I even told myself I didn't need love," Picard continued. "Part of me actually believed it. Then I met Anij . . ," Mentioning the Bak'u woman's name brought a wistful, fleeting smile to Picard's face. "She showed me what I had given up and how much I really needed it. But I was still afraid. I should have just reached out to Beverly right then and made up for lost time, but I hesitated—and I almost lost her. That's what it took for me to see what she really meant to me." Powerful emotions threatened to crack Picard's stoic façade, and Riker grasped how traumatic this discussion had to be for him. Picard's eyes gleamed with the threat of tears. "So I let her into my life. And it's been a wonder and a joy, Will. I curse myself daily for not having invited her in sooner. But when she suggested we have a child together, I panicked. The idea terrified me."

With gentle curiosity, Riker asked, "Why?"

"I concocted so many arbitrary reasons that you'd laugh if I told you half of them," Picard said. "But the truth is, I was afraid it would be like tempting fate." A haunted expression settled on him like a mask. "After all these years and excuses, for me to start a family . . . it seemed like a portent of doom. And no sooner did Beverly and I conceive our son than the Borg began their invasion." He shook his head and permitted himself a bitter chuckle. "I feel like Coleridge's Ancient Mariner, after he shot the albatross. I indulged myself with one selfish act, and in the process, I've condemned countless others to suffer and die for my mistake."

Shaking his head in denial, Riker replied, "You can't be serious. You don't really believe the Borg invaded because you and Beverly conceived a child?"

"No, of course not," Picard said, his tone sharp with frustration. "It's not about logic, or reason, or causality. It's about creating new life and then being afraid you'll have to watch it die." He lifted his hands and covered his face for several seconds while he slowed and deepened his breathing. Then he lowered his hands and said, "It took me so long to let something real into my life, and now all I can think about is the Borg taking it away. Even if we stop this invasion, what then? What of the next one, Will? Must my family, must *my son,* live in the shadow of this menace every day of his life?" The anger left Picard's voice; in its place was nothing but quiet desperation. "When will it end?"

"It will end when we end it." Riker leaned forward and stared at Picard until his old friend looked back at him. "I've seen what the Caeliar can do, Jean-Luc, and I think Hernandez is right. If anyone can stand up to the Borg, they can. I also agree with Dax. If we can end this war *and* save the people assimilated by the Collective, we have a duty as Starfleet officers to try."

Picard frowned. "And if Dax and Hernandez are wrong, we'll unleash the greatest horror the galaxy has ever seen."

"So, we hasten the inevitable," Riker said, fed up

with Picard's impenetrable pessimism. "The Borg are less than two hours from Earth. Could our plan backfire? Yes, but we can't let that paralyze us. It's time for a leap of faith."

The older man shook his head dismissively and said, "You're talking about hope."

"Yes, I am."

"We'll need more than hope to fight the Borg."

"True," Riker said. "But without it, we might as well just give up." He got up and walked to the door, which hissed open ahead of him. Standing in the doorway, he looked back at Picard. "We can fight for hope, or we can give in to despair. The choice is yours, Jean-Luc. Let me know what you decide."

23

Deanna Troi felt as light as air and more fully alive than she had in months. She stood on the center of the silver disk, behind Inyx, who guided it through the breathtaking vertical spaces between Axion's grandiose platinum towers. A firm breeze whipped her hair behind her. Tossing her head back and basking in the soothing warmth of New Erigol's artificial sun, it was all she could do to contain herself and not laugh out loud.

The disk neared the tower where the away team had been housed. As she and Inyx began their gentle descent toward the penthouse's open terrace, she saw someone approaching from the main room. A familiar psionic presence brushed against her mind, and she knew with her empathic senses before she saw with her eyes that it was Tuvok. He looked up and saw her, and then he called back inside the suite to summon the others.

By the time she and Inyx touched down on the terrace, the entire away team had gathered to meet her. Vale, Keru, and Tuvok were at the front of the group, and Ree was close behind them. Dennisar and Sortollo flanked the doctor, and Torvig, as usual, lingered at the rear of the group, curious but also cautious.

"Hello, everyone," Troi said with a beaming smile.

Keru stepped forward and bear-hugged her. "To hell with protocol," he said. "I'm so glad you're all right."

It was as if he'd opened a floodgate. Within moments, Troi found herself in the center of a group embrace with the broad-shouldered Trill, Vale, and the two security guards. Torvig kept his distance, however, and Tuvok remained aloof, as usual.

Ree sidled over to Inyx. "What is her current condition?"

"She is in perfect health, Doctor," Inyx said.

The Pahkwa-thanh physician replied, "I'd be grateful if you could show me her internal scans and serum profile."

Inyx looked at Troi, who was extricating herself from her friends' arms. She nodded to the Caeliar. "It's okay."

"Very well," Inyx said. He gestured with an outstretched arm toward the far end of the terrace. "Doctor, if you'll join me over here, I'll brief you in full." The scientist and the surgeon stepped away to confer.

"How long was I gone?" Troi asked.

Vale shrugged. "About thirteen hours."

Tuvok added, "And twenty-one minutes."

"Nice to know I was missed," Troi said. "What have you been doing since I left?"

"Keru and Torvig went sightseeing," Vale said. "The good doctor's been working on his tan, Dennisar and Sortollo played about three hundred games of checkers, and I've been catching up on my reading."

Troi smirked. "Anything good?"

"Believe it or not, a former 'guest' of the Caeliar wrote a bunch of new Captain Proton novels," Vale said. She chortled softly. "I feel like I found a latinum mine."

"I'll bet," Troi said. She looked up as Inyx and Ree returned to the group. "Everything all right, Doctor?"

Ree tasted the air with a flick of his tongue and said, "To my amazement, everything appears to be perfect."

Vale discreetly rested her hand on Troi's shoulder and gave it a congratulatory squeeze. "Finally, some good news."

Inyx made a rattling rasp of a sound and commanded the team's attention. "I apologize in advance for ruining your jubilant mood," he said, "but now that Deanna's medical crisis is resolved, I think it might be time to share news of a less celebratory nature."

Keru asked, "About what?"

"About your home, the Federation," Inyx said. He conjured an oval surface of liquid metal that immediately came alive with sharp, clear images of distant worlds being assaulted by Borg cubes. "It appears that an enemy is waging a successful attack on your nation. Many of your worlds have been destroyed, including some known as Regulus, Lorillia, and Deneva."

At the mention of Deneva, Troi felt a pang of psionic alarm from Tuvok. It was acute enough to pierce the veil of the group's shared anxiety as they watched the images of destruction unfold on the hovering screen before them. The scene shifted to a starship graveyard in a blue-gas nebula. Hundreds of smashed, blackened vessels tumbled erratically on the screen.

"I thought you should know," Inyx continued, "that this information was what compelled your captain to take his ship home and leave you in our custody. In the past, the Quorum has restricted our guests' access to this kind of information. However, I found that Erika placed a great deal of importance on staying informed about events affecting her home, and I thought you might share her interest in such matters."

Vale stepped forward and interposed herself between the away team and the oval screen. "All right, that's enough. Everyone, fall out, find something else to do. Commander Troi and I will brief you all later." The others looked at her and were reluctant to leave. "That's an order. *Dismissed.*"

Torvig turned and gamboled off at a quick step, while Dennisar and Sortollo glowered and slunk away from the terrace. Ree, Keru, and Tuvok made grudging exits, leaving Vale and Troi alone with Inyx. Vale sighed and said to him, "It's not that I don't appreciate the gesture, but that kind of news can be bad for morale. It would be better if the counselor and I could discuss it with you and ascertain what the facts are before we decide what to share with the rest of the team."

"As you wish," Inyx said. "I didn't mean to upset you." He looked at the images flashing across the screen. "I should have realized how distressing this would be."

Troi noted a melancholy undertone in his voice. "Are you also concerned by this news?"

"Yes, a great deal," he said.

Touching Inyx's arm in what she hoped would be construed as a gesture of compassion, Troi said, "You're worried about Captain Hernandez."

"I am. That far from Axion, Erika's vulnerable." Inyx's voice resonated with sadness. "She could be harmed . . . or killed." He looked away from the screen, at Troi and Vale. "It would be such a waste. Erika was the most vital, vibrant being I'd met in dozens of millennia."

A knowing look passed between Vale and Troi, and the first officer sounded surprised as she asked, "Inyx, are you *in love* with Captain Hernandez?"

The looming alien bowed at the waist and half turned away, as if to conceal his ever-dour visage. "I don't know if our species experience love the same way," he said. "All I can say is that for me, she made eternity worth contemplating."

Vale threw a wry look at Troi and said, "That's about as good a definition of love as I've ever heard. Counselor?"

"Yes," Troi said with a grin. "I'd have to agree."

———

Nanietta Bacco's office was dark except for the pale light of a waning gibbous moon and the amber glow of Paris at midnight.

Bacco stood at the far western end of the spacious, crescent-shaped room and leaned her shoulder into the nook between the wall and the floor-to-ceiling window.

The cityscape looked serene, partly because the night sky was unusually empty of air traffic. Most of the people who had some other place to go were there already.

The last report from Secretary of Transportation Iliop had indicated that nearly six hundred million people had fled Earth in the past six days. Some of the planet's smaller cities reportedly had taken on the airs of ghost towns. Paris was no exception, and neither were London, New York, Tokyo, and Mumbai.

On Bacco's order, most of the Federation Council had been ferried offworld, along with the majority of her cabinet, as part of the official continuity-of-government plan. Scattered to dozens of remote sites throughout—and, in a few cases, just beyond—Federation territory, dozens of elected and appointed officials awaited the final signal from Earth that would begin the process of presidential and legislative succession.

The interoffice comm on her desk buzzed. Bacco sighed, plodded back to the desk, and opened the channel with a poke of her index finger. "What is it, Sivak?"

"Admiral Akaar and Ms. Piñiero are here, Madam President," replied her elderly Vulcan executive assistant. *"They insist on presenting your midnight briefing."*

"Fine," Bacco said. "It might be the last one they ever make, so we might as well get it over with. Show them in."

She jabbed at the switch and closed the comm. A moment later, the east door of her office slid open. Agent Wexler stepped in ahead of Fleet Admiral Akaar and Esperanza Piñiero, and the door closed behind them.

"Computer," Bacco said. "Lights, one-third." The

recessed light fixtures in the room slowly brightened to a lower-than-normal level, allowing her to see her guests with a bit more clarity and without having to squint like a blind woman.

As soon as her eyes adjusted, she got a good look at Akaar and couldn't suppress a resentful frown. She gestured at his crisp, perfect-looking uniform and salon-perfect mane of pale gray hair. "How do you do it?"

"Madam President?"

"You've been awake the past two days, just like the rest of us," Bacco said. She nodded at Piñiero. "But Esperanza and I look like we've been chasing a fart through a bag of nails, and you look like you just stepped out of a replicator. What gives?"

Akaar shrugged. "Good genes?"

"You're not endearing yourself to me, Leonard."

"My apologies, Madam President."

Circling behind her desk, Bacco replied, "Bring me some good news, and maybe we'll call it even."

"We have some," he said, "but not much. Thirty-six minutes ago, the Imperial Romulan *Warbird Verithrax* sacrificed itself to halt the Borg attack on Ardana. Casualties on the surface are still disastrously high, but if not for the heroism of the *Verithrax*'s crew, our losses there would have been total."

"Which Romulan fleet was the *Verithrax* loyal to?"

"Donatra's," Piñiero said.

Bacco nodded, as if it were all perfectly normal, but she knew that it was nothing shy of extraordinary. If the Federation and the Imperial Romulan State both survived this war with the Borg, there would be no denying that Donatra and those loyal to her had committed fully to an alliance, in both word and deed. "Has there been any reaction from the Romulan Star Empire?"

"No," Piñiero said. "Praetor Tal'Aura probably hasn't heard the news yet. For that matter, Donatra might not even know."

"Then make sure we're the ones who tell her," Bacco said. "Send an official expression of gratitude on behalf of myself and the Federation to Empress Donatra."

Piñiero nodded and made a note on a small data padd she kept handy in her jacket pocket.

Looking back at Akaar, Bacco asked, "Anything else?"

He blinked once, slowly, and cocked his head at a slight angle. "We have received a credible if not entirely corroborated report that the planet Troyius was spared from a Borg attack, thanks to an intervention by the Corps of Engineers."

Bacco's eyes widened; her curiosity was piqued. "How?"

"According to preliminary reports," Akaar said, "the *U.S.S. da Vinci* made the planet disappear."

"Forgive me for repeating myself," Bacco said. "*How?*"

A perplexed glance was volleyed between Akaar and Piñiero, and then Bacco's chief of staff replied, "No one knows, ma'am. But as soon as Captain Gomez and her crew bring the planet back, we'll be sure to ask her."

"Unfortunately, that is the end of the good news, Madam President," Akaar said. "A Borg attack fleet is eighty-four minutes from Earth, and our perimeter defense groups have been unable to slow its approach. As we feared earlier, the Borg have completely adapted to the transphasic torpedo. And whatever had them shooting at one another has stopped."

An imaginary but still unbearable weight pressed down on Bacco's shoulders, and she sank into her chair. "Admiral, is there any reasonable possibility that Starfleet can halt the incoming Borg fleet?"

The question left Akaar's face reddened with shame. "No."

"Then order all remaining vessels in Sector 001 to break off and disperse," Bacco said. "Stop wasting ships and lives. Redeploy your forces to protect refugees and outlying systems."

Akaar clenched his jaw, and Bacco suspected the hulking flag officer was struggling not to protest a direct order. A few seconds passed. He relaxed with a deep breath, and then he answered, "Yes, Madam President."

Bacco sighed. "Esperanza, do the people of Earth, Luna, and Mars know what's happening right now?"

"Yes, ma'am," Piñiero said.

Propping her elbows on the desk and steepling her fingers, Bacco asked, "How are they coping with it? Panic? Riots?"

A soft huff of amusement brought a bittersweet smile to Piñiero's face. "Nope, not a one. There are silent, candlelight vigils on the Champs-Élysées, in Aldrin Park on Luna, and at the Settlers' Monument in Cydonia on Mars. Some people are gathering in the wilderness parks or attending impromptu concerts." Her voice broke, and she looked hastily at the floor. "Families are having reunions," she continued, her voice unsteadied by grief and fear. "Outgoing data traffic is spiking as people send farewell messages to friends and family offworld." She sniffled loudly, and then she looked up and wiped the side of her hand under her nose. Her eyes shone with tears. "I guess the world is ending with a bang *and* a whimper."

Shaking her head, Bacco said, "Not a whimper, Esperanza, with dignity."

Feeling her own emotions rising, Bacco swiveled her chair around to look out upon Paris. She stared through her ghostly reflection into the night. An entire world stretched out before her, facing its imminent annihilation and displaying more grace under pressure than she could ever have imagined possible.

In that moment, she was as proud as she had ever been to call herself a citizen of the Federation.

Akaar broke the silence. "I should excuse myself and relay your orders to Starfleet Command, Madam President."

"Of course, Admiral," said Bacco. "Thank you."

He turned on his heel and made a quick exit. Agent Wexler, lurking in the shadows as always, opened the door ahead of Akaar and closed it behind him. Then the compact protection specialist faded back into the dim spaces along the periphery of the room.

Piñiero palmed her tear-stained eyes dry and stiffened her posture. "We still have eighty minutes before the Borg arrive, ma'am," she said. "Would you like to make a final address to Earth or the Federation?"

Bacco admired the nightscape outside her office window and found at last a place of serenity within herself. "No," she said with a sad grin. "Why ruin a perfectly good apocalypse?"

24

———

Picard stood in the open doorway of his ready room, with his back to the bridge. The interior of his office had been gutted to the bare bulkheads and deck plates. All traces of the fire had been meticulously scoured away, leaving the antiseptic shell of the compartment harshly lit by new, uncovered lighting fixtures. It was utterly devoid of any trace of the mementos he'd stored there before the blaze. New carpeting and furniture were scheduled to be installed in a day's time, after the ship's engineers and technicians had attended to mission-critical repairs elsewhere throughout the *Enterprise*.

His thoughts remained fixated on Captain Hernandez's revelation of the Borg's true origin. Learning of humanity's complicity in the Collective's creation only made it harder for him to accept the staggering devastation the Borg had wrought throughout the galaxy.

He remembered succumbing to the hive mind when it had made him into Locutus. His secret shame in all the years since then had been how easy it had felt to give himself over to it. He had thought it was proof of some vile defect in his character, some classically tragic flaw. Now he understood why it had been so easy, why it had felt so familiar: The heart of the Collective was just the dark side of humanity itself. Even then, his subconscious mind had understood what he had been too ashamed to admit: Despite its pitiless, remorseless drive to crush and possess and devour, the Collective had a human soul.

He heard the soft tread of footfalls on carpeting behind him. Turning his head just a bit, he saw, on the edge of his vision, Worf approaching with a padd in his hand. "Yes, Worf?"

Worf stopped a respectful distance from Picard and said, "La Forge and Kadohata are completing their modifications to the subspace transmitter and the main deflector."

"How much longer?"

Worf said, "Both systems will be online in two minutes."

"Excellent," Picard said. He looked at the indentation in the ready room's bulkhead where a replicator once had been. The sight of the empty space made him want a cup of Earl Grey tea.

Refocusing his mind on work, he asked, "Have we heard from *Titan* or the *Aventine*?"

"*Titan* has locked in the coordinates of the Caeliar's home system," Worf said. "The *Aventine* has given us the software to generate and maintain a subspace microtunnel stable enough for a high-complexity signal."

Turning away from the hollowed memory of his ready room to face Worf, Picard asked, "Is Captain Hernandez ready?"

"Almost," Worf said. "Lieutenant Chen will help

Lieutenant Commander Pazlar monitor the link to the Caeliar from *Titan*. When they signal ready, we can initiate the soliton pulse."

Picard nodded and walked to his chair. Worf followed, always close at his shoulder. They settled into their chairs, and Picard regarded the battle-scarred hull of the *Aventine*; every scorch and breach was rendered with perfect clarity on the main viewscreen. "Any news from Starfleet Command?"

"No change," Worf said. "The Borg attack fleet is thirty minutes from Earth and Mars." He took a cautious look around the bridge, where everyone was working with quiet determination. Lowering his voice, he continued, "I have a question, sir."

In the same confidential tone, Picard replied, "About?"

"Admiral Jellico's orders."

"How did you . . . ?" It took Picard a moment to reason it out. "Captain Dax told you."

"Yes, sir," Worf said. "A few minutes ago."

Picard frowned and nodded. "I take it you don't approve."

The semirhetorical statement provoked a scowl from Worf. "Running away would *not* be my first choice."

"We're long past first choices, Worf," Picard said. "The idea of surrender doesn't sit well with me, either, but the admiral may be right this time. When Earth falls, the war's over." Sensing Worf's protest, he held up a hand and continued, "Naturally, there's a plan for the continuity of government, but once the core worlds are gone, there'll be little holding the Federation together. Betazed and Trill will try, as will

Bajor, but only until the Borg reach them, a few days from now."

Worf looked away from Picard and directed his intense stare at the forward viewscreen. "And what will become of us?"

"You mean the *Enterprise*?"

"And the *Aventine* and *Titan*," Worf replied.

"That's a very good question," Picard said. "To be truthful, I haven't really thought that far ahead."

Grim anticipation mingled with dark amusement in Worf's expression. "Then it might interest you to know that we are surrounded." He pointed at the tactical display on the armrest of Picard's command chair. "The Borg armada dispersed in a radial deployment from the Azure Nebula. At present, all sectors adjacent to this one are under Borg control."

Seeing the situation rendered as a simple graphic made Worf's point clear to Picard. "We have nowhere to run."

"Precisely," Worf replied. "Neither can we remain here. The Borg will seek us out. So . . . if we cannot flee, and we cannot hide, logic dictates that we should attack."

Picard smirked at his XO. "Channeling Spock again, are we?"

"I am merely stating the facts," Worf said.

Tugging his tunic smooth, Picard replied, "Be that as it may, we won't be doing any of those things just yet—not until we see the results of our current undertaking."

A muted tone beeped from the ops console. Commander Kadohata silenced it and swiveled her chair around to report to Worf and Picard, "Commander La

Forge confirms the subspace transmitter and the deflector are online and ready to go, sir."

"Very good," Picard said. He looked left, toward Choudhury at tactical. "Lieutenant, hail Captain Hernandez on the *Titan*. See if she's ready to proceed."

"Aye, sir," Choudhury replied. She keyed the message into her station's companel, and a few moments later she was answered by a bright synthetic tone. "Captain Hernandez and Lieutenant Commander Pazlar both confirm they're ready to go."

Standing up, Picard said, "Then it's time. Commander Kadohata, power up the transmitter and the main deflector. Lieutenant Elfiki, prepare to generate the soliton pulse. Lieutenant Choudhury, signal the *Aventine* and *Titan,* and give them the countdown."

As his officers snapped into hushed, efficient action around the bridge, Picard noticed that Worf, as usual, had followed his lead and risen from his chair to stand at Picard's right shoulder. "Captain," said Worf, "I have another question."

"Speak freely, Commander."

"It is my understanding that we are not, in fact, sending a message through the subspace microtunnel."

Picard nodded. "Correct."

Worf went on, "However, the mission profile requires us to provide Captain Hernandez with a high-bandwidth channel, on a frequency very much like the one used by the Borg."

"Also correct," Picard said, his manner dry and matter-of-fact. "What's your question?"

"What, exactly, are we doing?"

A wry, crooked grin pulled at Picard's mouth. *I've*

asked myself the same question a hundred times in the last hour. He threw a sidelong look at Worf. "We're making a leap of faith."

Melora Pazlar moved in slow, graceful turns through the zero-gravity sanctuary of *Titan*'s stellar cartography hololab. She reconfigured the lab's holographic interfaces on the fly, to take direct control of the subspace transmitter hardware on the *Enterprise* while regulating an influx of beamed power from the *Aventine*. At the same time, she had to coordinate with several officers on all three vessels to maintain a real-time FTL datalink, in order to multiply their shared computing power.

A few meters away, between her and the microgravity catwalk that led to the corridor portal, Captain Erika Hernandez and Lieutenant T'Ryssa Chen floated in the weightless space. Chen, a cultural-contact specialist from the *Enterprise,* was supposed to be helping Hernandez set up her own interface with the hololab, but the half-human, half-Vulcan young woman seemed more focused on floating upside-down while talking Hernandez into a stupor.

"Eight hundred sixty years," Chen gushed, staring wide-eyed at Hernandez. "Wow! You must've learned so much about the Caeliar living among them for so long."

"Sometimes I think I've barely scratched the surface," Hernandez said. The youthful-looking octocentarian shot a pleading glance at Pazlar. "Commander, are we ready to send the soliton pulse yet?"

Pazlar gave an apologetic shrug. "A few more

minutes, Captain. Sorry—we're working as fast as we can." In an effort to keep Chen distracted, Pazlar added, "Lieutenant, have you calibrated the alpha-wave receiver to the captain's brainwave frequency yet?"

"Yup, did it," Chen replied, before turning her intense focus back toward Hernandez. "I read a sanitized report of your time with the Caeliar, and I really need to ask, if their bodies are composed of programmable matter—"

"Catoms," Hernandez interrupted.

"Right, catoms—but they told you they made replicas of their old organic bodies and that they perceive the physical world the same way *after* their transition to synthetic bodies as they did before—but is that really possible? I mean, okay, they can defy gravity and become noncorporeal, and that's cool—but could they do that before?"

An exasperated reaction fleeted across Hernandez's face. "I don't know," she said.

"But what does it feel like, to be able to do that?"

Hernandez sighed. "Slipping free of gravity is like being one with the wind," she said. "I don't know a better way to explain it. As for their little trick of actually *becoming* one with the wind, I have no idea what that's like. I can't do that."

Before Chen could ask a follow-up question, Pazlar cut in, "Lieutenant, synchronize the delta-wave receiver frequency with the operating frequency of the captain's catoms."

"Already done," Chen said, doing an inverted zero-g pirouette, and then she continued to Hernandez, "If the Caeliar have a steady stream of—no, wait, that's

not what I mean. If they have a . . . an unbroken—
a *continuity* of memory dating back to their organic
selves, but their bodies are completely synthetic now,
how did they keep their memories? Was each memory
engram individually copied and replaced? Did the old
Caeliar brain even *use* engrams to record memories,
like most humanoid brains, or did it use a . . . um . . .
a cranial-fluid medium, like the Sogstalabians? Or
something else, like a crystalline matrix?"

"Honestly, Lieutenant, it never came up."

"Never?"

"Well, I was only with them for about eight centuries."

Chen frowned for just a moment at the derailment
of that line of inquiry, but then she soldiered on with
her enthusiasm undiminished. "What about making
little Caeliar? After they became synthetic, did they
stop having kids, or did they find a way to simulate
that, too? If their population is zero-growth, is it by
choice, or was it a trade-off for going synthetic? Do
they still have sex for pleasure?" At Hernandez's
pointed stare, Chen added, "Not that you'd have any
reason to know."

"I'll answer that," said Hernandez, "except for the
last few parts—on one condition."

"Name it," Chen said, floating perpendicular to
Hernandez.

"That you won't ask me any more questions about
the Caeliar until after I'm finished in here."

The perky young human-Vulcan hybrid nodded.
"Deal."

Pazlar caught Hernandez's eye and nodded at the
interface controls while holding up an index finger to

convey the idea *We'll be ready in a minute*. Hernandez noted the signal with an almost imperceptible glance and then said to Chen, "I asked my Caeliar friend Inyx about this, after the city of Axion went into exile. I wanted to know how long he thought it would take his people to repopulate. He said they wouldn't, that the fifty-two million Caeliar in Axion were all that was left. They'd stopped reproducing after making the shift to synthetic bodies. As you guessed, it was a side effect of the Change. Since they weren't really worried about dying, they'd figured a population of about a billion people could keep their civilization going indefinitely. But when the cataclysm destroyed Erigol, ninety-eight percent of their species was killed."

Chen blinked a few times, as if doing so would erase her stunned reaction. "Wow," she said. "Would you happen to know what their peak population was prior to—"

"We had a deal, Lieutenant," Hernandez said.

Hanging her head, Chen replied, "Right, sorry."

Pazlar finished the last of her modifications to the hololab's systems. Twisting and turning in a balletic inversion of her body relative to her guests, she locked in the power feed from the *Aventine* and confirmed that its computers were in synch with its counterparts on *Titan* and the *Enterprise*. "We're ready," she declared. "Captain, would you care to test your connection to the interface?"

Hernandez nodded, closed her eyes, and became very still. Then, as if moving of their own accord, multiple elements of the lab's holographic interface reorganized their layout; some faded out and were replaced by others, and some became flurried with data.

After a few seconds, all of the changes reversed themselves, and the interfaces returned to Pazlar's final configuration. Hernandez opened her eyes. "Feels good."

"All right," Pazlar said. "I'm signaling the *Enterprise* and letting them know we're ready to do this thing."

Chen grinned at Hernandez, held up a hand to show her entwined index and middle digits, and said, "Fingers crossed."

"Do you make a special effort to confound expectations about your Vulcan heritage?" Hernandez asked.

"Yes, actually," Chen said.

"Don't try so hard."

Suppressing a grin at Chen's expense, Pazlar said, "Stand by, Captain. *Enterprise* is generating the soliton pulse now."

The semitransparent gauges around Pazlar peaked with massive surges of energy and torrents of data. The Elaysian science officer marveled at the complexity and sheer power of the signal the three vessels had united to create—chiefly because the most robust part of the outgoing stream was flowing directly through the mind of Captain Erika Hernandez.

Reaching across darkness and distance, Erika Hernandez felt the transmission systems of *Titan* and the *Enterprise* harmonizing with her catoms, vibrating in sympathy, reacting to her will like old limbs finally set free to move.

Safe in the redoubt of her own psyche, she opened her psionic senses. The gestalt was barely audible to her. A tremolo infused its every nuance and lent it a quality of dread. Though she was tempted to renew her contact with the Caeliar's shared mindspace, she regretted the need to surrender control again. Accepting the Change had meant letting go of her autonomy. At the time, she had felt broken, defeated, and diminished. Only with the benefit of centuries of hindsight did she appreciate the riches with which she'd been blessed in return, out of all proportion to her sacrifice. All the same, having once more tasted freedom, she savored it and was loath to give it up.

She guided her consciousness past the elaborate defenses of the gestalt and heard its voices. They were in disarray, a tumult of anger and anxiety. It felt to Hernandez like a surreal nightmare, as if she were one of the victims at the mythical sundering of the Tower of Babel, one of thousands milling about in confusion, each unable to understand any of the others.

Then the Caeliar sensed her mental presence among them, and the pandemonium was silenced. Their minds pulled away from hers as if by reflex, like a layer of grease on dishwater retreating from a drop of detergent.

Surges of shock and bitterness came in waves from the Caeliar. Bright anger emanated from Ordemo Nordal, their *tanwa-seynorral,* or "first among equals." Counterpointing his dudgeon was Inyx's conflicted mix of emotions—his resentment at her deception, his relief to be back in contact with her, and his amused pride at the true scope of her abilities.

Hernandez's thoughts took shape in the gestalt with the clarity of spoken words. "As long as I have your attention," she projected with obvious disdain, "let me apologize for my fly-by-night exit. I would have left a note, but there wasn't time."

Ordemo replied, "Your sarcasm remains as blunt as ever. No matter. Even if you had been sincere, mere words would hardly repair the damage you've inflicted."

"Still exaggerating for effect, I see," she shot back.

"For once, Ordemo has understated the matter," Inyx answered. "The feedback pulse you and *Titan*'s crew created caused significant harm to much of the apparatus we use for the Great Work. However, I suspect he and the majority of the Quorum are more aggrieved by your irreparable violation of our privacy." Though his words were chastising her, the aura of his emotions betrayed his lack of animosity.

The rest of the Quorum, however, blazed with indignation, and they were the ones she would have to persuade if humanity was to be saved from annihilation. "I won't pretend to seek your forgiveness," she said, addressing the whole of the gestalt. "That's not why I've come. I'm contacting you to ask for your help—and to tell you why you should give it."

"You're referring to the hostilities that currently threaten your homeworld, we presume," Ordemo responded.

"That's part of it."

The *tanwa-seynorral* channeled the Quorum's chilly reproof. "Then you're wasting your time and ours, Erika. We don't meddle in the affairs of others—you know that."

"Yes, I do," Hernandez said. "But I'm not asking you to help Earth—not directly. I'm asking you to help the Borg."

She started sharing images with the gestalt, aeons of memories she'd obtained from her union with the Borg Collective. Worlds plundered, technologies taken by force, all homogenized without mercy. Entire species and cultures violently adapted to service the Borg's single-minded pursuit of perfection, which its guiding intelligence defined as unfettered power.

Her plea was met with silent rejection. The gestalt recoiled en masse from her request. Even Inyx sounded perplexed by her entreaty. "Erika, the Borg are a brutal, rapacious culture. Why would you ask us to aid them?"

"Because you created them," she said. "And in a way, so did we. Look closer." She painted a mental image of the Borg's nanoprobe technology, and then she pushed past its cluttered outer shell to reveal its core components. "Their Collective operates on a frequency that is so close to the gestalt that I heard it from light-years away. It's not as sophisticated as your little psychic commune, but it's a lot more powerful."

She presented them with visions of sentient beings being assimilated. "Watch how that technology alters organic beings. Does that look familiar? It should. That was one of the outcomes Inyx warned me about before he Changed me—the suppression of higher brain functions, a mindless existence as an automaton. But the worst part of it is that they aren't really mindless. All those individual minds are still in there, each one a prisoner."

A pall of horror swept through the gestalt, and Hernandez realized with grim satisfaction that the Caeliar finally understood the truth.

"Mantilis," Inyx said, his telepathic voice muted

by shock. "It must have survived its journey through the temporal disruption."

"With both human and Caeliar survivors aboard," Hernandez said, completing her mentor's thought. "Something happened that drove them to try to unite for survival, but instead of fusing their strengths, it amplified the ugliest parts of both species, made them into a diseased reflection of us. Your paranoia and fanatical desire for conformity got tangled up with human barbarism and aggression. It was a recipe for disaster."

Inyx replied with dark melancholy, "No, Erika, it's nothing less than a complete abomination."

"Call it what you want," she said. "The Borg Collective has abducted trillions of sentient beings over the past several thousand years and laid waste to vast swaths of the galaxy. But I can guarantee you, the drones aren't to blame. Every last one of them is a slave, living in perpetual suffering. The *real* culprit is whatever's controlling the Collective and speaking through its Queen. That's the root of the problem, and to deal with it, I'm going to need your help."

Ordemo's stubborn refusal to accede to her request held the Quorum's reaction in abeyance. "Though it seems likely that an unfortunate accident created this atrocity you call the Borg, that doesn't compel us to interfere. The timeline is as it was; if the Borg were meant to exist, then the natural order of events must be respected."

"Let me tell you two things you ought to consider," she said. "First, think about the threat the Borg will pose to you and your Great Work if they assimilate my catoms and my memories of your technology.

Second, I'm not asking you to tamper with the timeline. As you might say, what's done is done. We can't change the past, but we still have a chance to shape the future."

Hernandez felt the mood of the gestalt shifting into alignment with her, but the *tanwa-seynorral* continued to resist her arguments. He said, "What, precisely, would you ask of us?"

"Bring Axion here, to my coordinates in Federation space, and I'll explain everything in person."

"And if we refuse?"

"Then you can stay hidden and afraid, until the Collective finds you. And mark my words, Ordemo, it *will* find you."

25

"The Borg attack fleet has passed Jupiter," said Fleet Admiral Akaar, his sonorous voice filling the cold, anxious silence in the Monet Room. "Four minutes to Earth."

President Bacco sat at the end of the conference table. She stared down its length at the faces of the few members of her cabinet and staff who had stayed behind to face the end with her. Jas Abrik, her top security adviser, occupied the chair to her left. Clockwise around the table from Abrik, with several empty chairs between each guest, were transportation secretary Iliop, press liaison Kant Jorel, special security adviser Seven of Nine, and Esperanza Piñiero, who was close at Bacco's right.

Sivak lingered a few paces behind Bacco's shoulder, and Agents Wexler and Kistler remained nearby, along the wall, trying without much success to be inconspicuous.

Bacco stared at the famous Impressionist painting on the room's north wall. *Bridge over a Pool of Water Lilies* was one of Claude Monet's masterpieces, a gently arcing bridge of spare blue beams over a pond crowded with pastel splashes of floral colors. The artist had painted the scene late in his career, when he had gone almost completely blind. Its complex but gentle beauty fascinated Bacco, and she lamented that it would soon pass into oblivion, with almost every other significant artifact of Earth's rich, troubled history.

"Why do you think Zife left that painting in here?" Bacco asked, startling the room's other occupants out of their own melancholy reflections.

Piñiero looked at the painting and then back at Bacco. "Are you serious, ma'am? Earth is three minutes away from being blown to bits, and you want to critique Min Zife's interior-decorating choices? With all respect, I don't think now is the best time."

"Relax, it's only a question," Bacco said. "This used to be just another meeting room before the Dominion War. Then Zife came along and had it rebuilt with every fancy gizmo he could find. The whole room got a makeover, top to bottom, but he left that painting right there. I'm just curious why."

Everyone in the room fixated on the painting— all except Seven of Nine, who afforded it a fleeting glance and no more. Bacco noticed the former Borg drone staring at the tabletop, her face a grim cipher, as usual.

"Seven?" Bacco prodded. "Any opinion on the matter?"

Looking up with stern formality, Seven replied, "The rationale for its continued display seems quite apparent."

"Really? Would you mind letting the rest of us in on it?"

The statuesque woman sighed. "Its placement opposite the chair of the president suggests that it was retained for his benefit. I suspect he found its muted palette and soft details helpful as a point of focus when attempting to concentrate."

Her answer provoked a frown from Admiral Akaar. Bacco noted his reaction and said, "You disagree, Admiral?"

"I served under President Zife, and I know exactly why it's there," Akaar said. "He loved that painting, and he wanted it displayed in this room as a reminder to himself, and the rest of us, that this is what's at stake if we fail—art, history, beauty, and everything we think of as our legacy." Lowering his gaze, he added, "It was one of his first decrees as president, at a time when everyone else in this building was obsessed with numbers and strategies and casualty reports. Our job was, and still is, to decide how to fight our enemies. But he left that painting there so we wouldn't forget *why* we fight."

Bacco regarded the nineteenth-century painting with a new, deeper appreciation. Though she had never been impressed with Zife as a president, she felt a pang of sympathy for him. Clearly, he had been more than the popular caricatures of his faults. After succeeding him in the presidency, she had learned the truth of how Zife had been removed from office, in a coup abetted by Admiral William Ross. Speaking privately with Bacco, Ross had implicated himself in the ouster of Zife, chief of staff Koll Azernal, and the Federation's secretary of military intelligence, Nelino Quafina, there in the Monet Room.

How fitting, she brooded. *Zife's presidency ended*

here, and so will mine. There's a certain perverse symmetry in that.

A rapid series of changes flickered across a wall of screens, updating the Palais de la Concorde on Starfleet's current status. Admiral Akaar reviewed the new information with a cursory look and then turned to face Bacco.

"Ninety seconds until the Borg fleet is within firing distance of Earth, Madam President," Akaar said. "The attack force is beginning to split into two groups, with one adjusting course and accelerating toward Mars."

Clammy sweat coated Bacco's hands. She dried them against the tops of her thighs. Her pulse quickened, throbbed in her temples, and left her dizzy and overheated. It was a battle to comport herself with the dignity befitting her office when an event of such unutterable gravity was imminent. For a moment, she regretted not having chosen to flee Earth when her advisers had suggested it, but then she resolved herself. *This is what I chose. No turning back now. Besides, if Earth falls, I wouldn't want to live past today, anyway—because whoever takes this job next is gonna have a lousy first press conference.*

Another fast shift in the tactical situation cascaded across the west wall's bank of situation monitors. Akaar studied them. Then he made a stunned double-take and froze.

Unable to imagine how the news could get any worse, Bacco called to Akaar, "What's happening, Admiral?"

He looked over his shoulder with his mouth agape and eyes wide with shock. "We're not sure, Madam

President. All Borg ships in this system have stopped, and we're getting reports that all Borg vessels we've been tracking have halted as well."

She asked, "Well, do we—" A shrill alert on the tactical console stole Akaar's attention from her, and she let her unfinished query trail off as the admiral raced to assemble a deluge of tactical information and situation maps into a concise report.

Then she heard him mumble, "I don't believe it."

"Admiral, I don't mean to be pushy, but I'd really like to know what the hell is happening, if you don't mind."

Akaar straightened his posture and walked back to the conference table. His voice was pitched with surprise. "Madam President . . . our scans at this time indicate that all ships in the Borg armada have reversed course and are heading at maximum speed toward the Azure Nebula."

Only one obsession held greater sway over the Borg Collective than its perverse fixation on Earth. Nothing less than the promise of perfection could eclipse the impulse to eradicate an enemy that had hobbled the Collective's quest too many times.

Now that exquisite lure blazed in the cold void between the stars. Its siren call was unmistakable. For ages the Collective had listened for it, patiently forded millennia of silence, tuned out the random noise of the universe's abandoned creations, anticipated the call of something whose power and beauty beckoned from across space and time.

It was tantalizingly close. In centuries past, the

detection of even a single molecule of Particle 010 would have been enough to divert any and all cubes to its acquisition and assimilation. No matter how many permutations of adaptation the Collective endured, that essential fact of its nature had never changed. The devotion to one cause above all remained inviolate.

Reports from thousands of cubes dispersed throughout local space all relayed the same urgent message to the Borg Queen. A harnessed source of the revered particles had been pinpointed, its mass estimated at several million times greater than the largest previously known sample of Particle 010. A source of almost incalculable power, its potential output dwarfed that of the entire Borg Collective by several orders of magnitude.

The end of the Federation would have to be postponed.

Converge on the energy source, the Borg Queen commanded. *All other priorities and directives are rescinded.* She felt the far-flung vessels and drones snap into obedient action. *Assimilate Particle 010 at any cost.*

The heavens had twisted open in front of the *Enterprise,* and a storm of light had burst forth and enveloped the ship, whiting out the main viewer and momentarily blinding Picard. He'd raised his hand to block the glare, and he'd lowered it a few seconds later, as the prismatic eruption withdrew into the spiraling-shut aperture of the massive subspace tunnel.

The bridge crew was quiet as the majestic city-ship hovered in space, dwarfing the *Sovereign*-class starship and its two companion vessels. Picard found it difficult to estimate its size, because it more than filled the viewscreen. All he saw was a narrow slice of its middle, which was packed with shining metallic towers blessed with a graceful, fluid architectural style. Delicate walkways linked many of them, and the façades of the metropolis reflected the jet black of the void and the crisp, steady light of the stars with equal and perfect clarity.

Worf eyed the alien megalopolis with alarmed suspicion. "Should we raise shields, Captain?"

"No, Mister Worf," Picard said, still somewhat awestruck by the spectacle of the great city, which had traversed thousands of light-years with apparent ease. "They've come at our invitation. I think we owe them a measure of hospitality." He looked left toward Choudhury. "Hail them, Lieutenant."

"Aye, sir," Choudhury said.

Picard admired the aesthetic sophistication of the Caeliar city, and he found himself wondering whether Riker might be right, whether the Caeliar might, in fact, be able to stand firm in a confrontation with the Borg. He stepped forward and stood behind Kadohata at ops. "Commander," he said to her, "are we picking up any . . . *unusual* energy readings from the city-ship?"

"Affirmative," Kadohata said, working with haste to keep pace with the information appearing on her console. "Massive readings, of a kind the computer can't identify."

"All scans of the Caeliar ship are to be treated as classified information," Picard said, "to be reviewed only on my authority. Understood?"

"Yes, sir," Kadohata said, entering the appropriate command-level encryptions, which, once engaged, even she would be unable to deactivate.

So far, so good, he concluded. He had taken the precaution of bypassing the main computer's automatic Omega Directive protocol, which normally would have frozen command systems and duty stations throughout the ship the moment the Omega Molecule was detected by the sensors. It was a heavy-handed safeguard against anyone other than the ship's commanding officer having access to the potentially calamitous knowledge of the dangerous and notoriously unstable high-energy particle. In this case, such a measure would have drawn unnecessary attention— and since the presence of the Omega Molecule was integral to Captain Hernandez's plan to halt the Borg assault, being saddled with the Omega Directive was a distraction Picard wished to avoid.

Choudhury looked up from her station. "Sir, the Caeliar have acknowledged our hail but are refusing audible or visual contact. They've asked Captain Hernandez to return to the city."

"Dare I ask how she responded?"

"She agreed—on the condition that the Caeliar release *Titan*'s away team. They've accepted her terms."

He nodded. "Understood. Keep me informed of any developments in the situation."

"Aye, sir."

Worf took a small step to stand closer to Picard, and he dropped his voice to a confidential level. "Once the Caeliar have Captain Hernandez back in their custody, they might go back where they came from—and abandon us to the Borg."

"Possibly," Picard said. "Though the departure of the Caeliar is hardly the worst outcome in this scenario. I'm more concerned about the risk of the Borg assimilating the Caeliar's technology, which appears to be formidable."

A muted tone from the tactical console signaled an incoming transmission. Choudhury silenced the alert with a brush of her fingertip and said, "New reports from Starfleet Command, sir. The entire Borg armada has reversed course."

"In other words," Worf said, "they are converging on us."

"Correct," Choudhury said, her tone dry but droll.

Picard asked, "How long until they reach us?"

"Fourteen hours," the security chief said.

The captain frowned. As powerful as the Caeliar appeared to be, Picard was unable to let go of his doubt that anything could truly stop the Borg. Worse, if the Caeliar either refused or proved unable to help, fourteen hours didn't leave him or his crew much time to formulate a backup plan.

He saw only one remaining alternative: to build a thalaron projector. The biogenic weapon might prove futile, but he doubted he would ever again be in a position to strike so many Borg cubes at the same time. He judged the risk worthwhile.

If it failed, then he, his crew, and the rest of the Federation were already as good as dead, anyway.

And if it worked . . . all it would cost him was his soul.

26

The shuttlecraft *Mance* ascended from Axion and passed through the city-ship's protective force field with hardly a bump.

Christine Vale sat at the aft end of the shuttlecraft's passenger cabin, across from Deanna Troi. Chief Dennisar and Lieutenant Sortollo from security sat at the forward end, and Dr. Ree and Ensign Torvig stood and awkwardly filled the space in the compartment's center. In the cockpit, Tuvok was at the controls, and Ranul Keru occupied the mission commander's seat.

Inyx had delivered the news of the away team's release from Axion with as little preamble as when, days earlier, he'd told them of their incarceration. One moment, they had thought of themselves as prisoners, and the next, their shuttlecraft was hovering beside their terrace, its boarding ramp extended.

At the urging of the Caeliar, they'd remained inside the *Mance* and had kept it landed inside Axion's shield perimeter while the city had risen from the surface of New Erigol. The sky had opened above them. At first, it had looked like a mere dark sliver, and then it had widened. The complex details of its inner mechanisms had become visible. Within moments, Axion had climbed into orbit, and then space-time itself had been torn asunder and sent pinwheeling into a blinding vortex.

The twist of light and color that had raged around Axion was unlike anything else Vale had ever seen. The vortex had exhibited a fluid quality, but it also had shimmered and pulsed. Before her eyes had been given an opportunity to adjust, Axion had sped free of the passage, back into normal space-time.

Waiting there, brilliant and still against the backdrop of stars, had been *Titan*, accompanied by two other vessels. The first was a *Sovereign*-class starship that Vale had recognized as her previous billet, the *Enterprise*-E; the other was a new *Vesta*-class explorer, a ship class she'd heard about but until that moment hadn't actually seen with her own eyes.

Via the shuttlecraft's comm, Inyx had delivered his terse valediction: *"You may go now."* Tuvok had wasted no time accepting the invitation. As soon as the channel had clicked off, the *Mance* had been airborne and on its way home.

Seeing *Titan* growing larger and sharper in front of the shuttlecraft brought a smile of relief to Vale's face. "I don't know how Will did it, but I'm glad he didn't make a liar out of me," she said to Troi. "I knew he wouldn't give up on us."

"So did I," Troi said, through her own bittersweet smile.

Vale leaned forward to keep their conversation discreet. "Are you sure you're okay?"

"Yes, Chris," Troi said, matching Vale's posture. "Better than okay."

"Good," Vale said, sincere in her concern. "You had us all pretty worried there—especially Will."

"I know," Troi said, lowering her eyes for a moment. "It's been hard on all of us. And I made it even worse for him. But it'll be all right now. I'm sure of it. I can hear him in my thoughts, and I know he's waiting for me to come home."

Unable to bury her envy, Vale blinked and looked away aft. She felt Troi's inquiring stare. Turning back to face her, she said, "Sorry. I'm happy for you, really. It's just hard for me to hear about your amazing bond with Will when I . . ." She hesitated, at a loss for words. "When I'm . . ."

"When you're still mourning Jaza?"

Vale's emotional barrier faltered enough for a single tear to escape from her eye. She palmed it away and laughed once, softly, because the alternative was to weep like a child. "Right to the heart of it, as always," she said. "Brava, Deanna."

"It's kind of my job," Troi said. "I know you've been under a lot of stress since we lost Jaza. The troubles Will and I have been going through left him . . ." She rolled her eyes toward the overhead, apparently searching for the most diplomatic word. "Not at his best," she finished. "And that left you to pick up the slack, for a lot longer than you should have. You had to do most of his job as well as your own. I'm sorry for that."

Shaking her head, Vale replied, "Not your fault."

"In a way, it was," Troi said. "I sensed what you were going through, but I was so caught up in my own pain and problems that I didn't get you the help that I should have."

"Apology completely unnecessary but accepted all

the same," Vale said. A recent memory nipped at the edge of her thoughts: the moment, a few days earlier, when she had tried to comfort the distraught Will Riker in his ready room, only to come within millimeters (and a momentary lapse of reason) of kissing him. She balked at the idea of confessing her near-miss indiscretion to Troi. Then she considered the possible consequences if she tried to hide it and it came out in a less candid manner—or, even worse, if at some point she did something as monumentally stupid as to make out with her married commanding officer.

"Deanna," Vale said, "there's something I should probably get off my chest. It was nothing, really, but I feel kind of strange about it, and even stranger about feeling like I should hide it, and I—"

"You mean when you almost kissed Will a few days ago," Troi said, as if it were some mundane detail of ship's business.

"Um, well, yeah." It took a moment to push through the shock and realize how transparent she must seem to the half-Betazoid counselor. "How did you know?"

A broad grin lit up Deanna's face. "I haven't felt Will panic like that since he met my mother."

Troi laughed, and Vale found her friend's mirth contagious. Their self-conscious chortles drew curious stares from the rest of the away team and a disapproving arch of one eyebrow from Tuvok. The muscles in Vale's face hurt from the effort of reining in her laughter. "So, you're not angry with me?"

"Of course not. You were still missing Jaza, and I'd been pushing Will away for months. It's an almost textbook example of transference, with a touch of displacement."

Vale nodded and flashed an abashed smile. "I'm glad to hear you say that. I have to admit, I was worried there for a while."

"Don't worry about it," Troi said. "It's all in the past." Then she narrowed her eyes and added in a joking caricature of a threat, "But if you ever make a pass at him again, I will have to kill you. Nothing personal."

Answering Troi's stare with a knowing smirk, Vale felt an almost sisterly bond with her. "Understood," she said.

Geordi La Forge stopped at the door to Captain Picard's quarters. He looked at the padd in his hand. He'd been driven by a righteous indignation to come this far, but standing on the precipice of action, he considered turning back, surrendering in silence, and chalking it up to the cruel compromises of war.

Not this time. He pressed the visitor signal by the door.

A moment later, he heard Picard's voice call out from behind the door, "Come."

The portal sighed open, and La Forge stepped inside the captain's quarters. Everything was clean and well ordered, as usual. Picard stood in front of a set of shelves. He was holding his Ressikan flute; its burnished metal surfaces caught the light as it shifted slightly in his grasp. The captain looked up from the instrument in his hands and seemed pleasantly surprised to see La Forge. "Geordi," he said. "What can I do for you?"

La Forge took a few steps farther inside, and the door hushed closed behind him. "We need to talk," he said.

"Of course," Picard said, setting down the flute

inside its protective felt-and-foam-lined box. He gestured toward the sofa and some chairs. "Please, come in, sit down."

Picard took a step toward the sofa before La Forge stopped him by saying in a firm tone, "I'd rather stand, sir."

Sensing the grave nature of La Forge's visit, Picard put on a wary mien. "Is something wrong, Mister La Forge?"

"Yes, sir," La Forge said. He held up the padd in his hand. "These orders you sent me a few minutes ago."

The captain hardened his countenance. "What of them?"

"You ordered me to turn the main deflector into a thalaron radiation projector, like the one Shinzon had on the *Scimitar*."

"I know what I told you to do, Commander."

Frustration made La Forge clench his jaw and his fist as he fought to find words for his outrage. "How could you give me an order like that? How can you possibly expect me to obey it?"

Picard slammed the lid of the flute box shut with an earsplitting crack. "I am not in the custom of explaining my orders, Mister La Forge! And I expect you to obey them because you're a Starfleet officer."

La Forge shook his head. "Sorry, Captain. Not good enough. Not for this." He tossed the padd at Picard's feet. "I won't insult you by pretending I have any standing to question your order. I'll just say it to your face: I refuse to obey it."

With quiet menace, Picard replied, "You're treading on dangerous ground here, Mister La Forge."

"You want to talk about dangerous? Unleashing

a metagenic superweapon—*that's* dangerous." The captain glared at La Forge, who continued, "Consider this. We're developing shields against thalaron radiation, and it's a good bet the Borg can, too. And the moment they do, this weapon becomes useless."

"But not until then," Picard snapped. "And when their armada surrounds us, we'll be able to eradicate them."

The thought of such a tactic horrified La Forge. "You're talking about mass murder."

Picard bellowed, "I'm talking about survival, Geordi! You can't negotiate with the Borg. You can't bargain with them, or seek a truce, or a cease-fire. There's no other way."

"I refuse to believe that," La Forge said. "After all we've done and all we've seen, if I've learned anything, it's that there are always alternatives to killing." He felt the captain's silent resistance and knew that he would never get him to concede the point, so he moved on. "Say you're right, and we wipe out the Borg with a thalaron weapon. What then? You know you can't put that genie back in the bottle. Once the Klingons and the Romulans find out about it, we'll be back at war."

Walking past La Forge on his way to the replicator, Picard replied, "That's a problem for the diplomats and the politicians."

"I'd say the politicians *are* the problem. Access to a weapon like that would give them ideas. Power corrupts, and a thalaron weapon that can fry a planet is a *lot* of power."

The captain seemed to ignore La Forge's remark as he stood in front of the replicator and said, "Tea, Earl Grey, hot." His drink appeared from a singsong flurry

LOST SOULS

of particles, and he picked it up and took a sip. He carried the cup to a table and set it down. "Your concerns and objections are noted for the log, Mister La Forge, but we don't have time to debate this. I need that weapon operational immediately."

"Maybe I didn't make myself clear, Captain. I didn't come up here just to register a complaint so I could work with a clean conscience. When I say I won't do it, I mean it."

Incensed, Picard shot back, "The Federation is a democracy, Mister La Forge, but this starship is not. I gave you a direct order, and I'll repeat it for the last time: Turn the main deflector into a thalaron projector before the Borg arrive."

"No," La Forge said. "Repeat it as many times as you want, it won't make any difference. I will not resurrect that . . . that *abomination*. I won't be party to whatever atrocities it winds up being used for." He stepped closer to the captain and gestured emphatically as he continued, "When Shinzon had one, you were ready to die to stop it. Data gave his life to destroy it. For me to rebuild it now would be an insult to his memory and a betrayal of his sacrifice. I can't do that. I won't.

"You want to put me in the brig? Fine. I'll walk down there and turn myself in. But I absolutely will not follow that order. It's immoral. It's illegal—and since no illegal order is valid, it's my *duty* to refuse to obey it. And yes, I know that you'll just get someone else to do it, someone who won't put up a fuss, who won't question orders, who'll just get it done.

"But it won't be me."

La Forge didn't wait for the captain's response. He turned and walked out, and he kept walking, down the corridor and into the turbolift, which he directed to main engineering. Reflecting on his outburst toward the captain, he half expected to find armed security personnel waiting there to take him into custody.

Assuming we live till tomorrow, I may have just ended my career, he realized. He was surprised to find the thought didn't scare him as much as he had thought it would. *If that's how it has to go,* he decided, *so be it.*

Then his bravado faded, and he felt an overpowering desire to hide someplace dark and have a drink . . . or two . . . or six.

"Computer, halt turbolift," he said. "New destination: the Riding Club, on the double."

Riker was about to walk into Erika Hernandez's guest quarters unannounced, until he remembered his earlier faux pas and stopped at the private comm panel. He pressed the visitor signal and waited until Hernandez responded from inside, "Come in."

The door shushed open, and he walked in to find Hernandez sitting on the floor behind her living area's coffee table, whose top was covered from edge to edge with nearly a dozen plates of food and several beverages both hot and cold.

He grinned at the sight of her one-woman feast. "I'm glad to see *someone* likes the food on this ship."

She returned his jovial look and said, "It took a while, but I found a few things your replicator actually makes well. Since the Caeliar won't make any of these in Axion, I figured I'd better enjoy them while I can." She speared a hearty chunk of light-colored meat dressed with rich brown gravy. "Care for a bite of the milk-braised pork loin? The sauce is fantastic."

"No, thanks," he said, watching her devour the forkful and then swoon with gustatory ecstasy. "I'm saving my appetite for dinner with Deanna." Lifting his chin toward her expansive repast, he added, "Do you want to take some of that to go?"

She swallowed and said, "I guess that means your away team is on its way back?"

Riker nodded. "Commander Hachesa just confirmed the *Mance* is on its final approach."

"Then I'd better get ready to go," Hernandez said. She grabbed a glass with a wide, shallow body atop a narrow stem and downed half its pale chartreuse contents in a long draught. She smacked her lips and let out a satisfied gasp. "It's not quite right with synthehol, but it's still the best margarita I've had in eight hundred years." She set down the glass and stood up.

"Before you go, I want to thank you," Riker said. "I don't know what you told the Caeliar or what you promised them, but however you did it, thank you for helping free my people."

She looked embarrassed by his gratitude. "It was the least I could do," she said. "It's what I wished someone could have done for my crew." Turning her gaze toward the floor, she added, "But what's done is done, I guess."

He empathized with her sense of loss and her guilt, and his gut impulse was to change the topic. "Will you be coming back?"

"I don't know," she said, stepping out from behind the coffee table to join him in the middle of the room. "There's a lot to do once I get back to Axion. Convincing them to come out of hiding was only the first step.

Now that they're here, they might not like what I have to say."

The apprehension in her voice stoked his concern for her. "Is it safe for you to go back?"

"Of course," she said. "They won't hurt me."

"But will they take you prisoner again? If you go back, will they ever let you leave?"

A shadow of melancholy settled upon her. "I don't know," she said. "But to be honest, that's the least of our worries."

"True," Riker said. "Can you even guess at what the Caeliar will say about helping us stop the Borg?"

"No, I can't. I know they won't help the Borg hurt us, but beyond that, it gets complicated. The Caeliar prefer to stay out of other people's business, but now that I've shown them their own link to this mess, they might take responsibility for it. Or they might not. For all I know, they might hear me out and choose to stay neutral."

Riker frowned. "In which case, we're all pretty much dead."

"Pretty much, yeah."

A few meters behind Hernandez, there was a rippling effect in the air, like heat distortion. It blurred the image of the bedroom behind it, and within seconds, it was like looking at something through a deep pool of water. The shimmer took on a metallic quality, like a hovering, vertical puddle of mercury. Then the effect stabilized, and Riker saw himself and Hernandez reflected on its serene, silvery surface.

Hernandez looked over her shoulder as if she were being called by a voice that only she could hear. She sighed and looked back at Riker. "Time for me to go," she said, favoring him with a coy grin. She turned and walked toward the liquid-metal oval that hovered a few centimeters above the deck, and she stopped in front of it and looked back. "Before I leave, I ought to thank you, too," she said. "Fifteen hours ago, you didn't know me, and you had no reason to trust me. But you did. Because of you, I got to be free again, even if just for a moment. Thank you for taking a chance on me."

He smiled with sincere admiration and affection. "You're welcome," he said.

She lingered a moment, and then she turned and stepped forward, passing through the quicksilver membrane without so much as a ripple. As soon as she had vanished into it, the liquid portal faded into vapor.

Riker stood and stared at the empty space in front of him, and he was startled as Commander Hachesa's voice crackled over the comm, *"Bridge to Captain Riker."*

"Go ahead."

"The deck officer in shuttlebay one reports the Mance *is aboard, and all away team personnel are safe and accounted for."*

"Acknowledged," Riker said, jogging toward the door to the corridor. "Riker out!" He was through the door, and as soon as he was in the corridor, he broke into a full-out sprint for the turbolift. Enlisted crewmembers and junior officers froze in his path ahead of him, caught by surprise. "Make a hole!" he shouted, and everyone reacted by reflex, pressing their backs to the bulkheads as he tore down the middle of the passageway.

He knew that it was unseemly for him to be seen running like this, to be so loud and so frantic in front of his crew, but he didn't care. His *Imzadi* was home, and she was safe—he could feel it.

Decorum be damned, he thought with a joyful grin.

La Forge stood in front of the forward-facing windows in the *Enterprise*'s crew lounge, which Will Riker had named the Happy Bottom Riding Club before he left to take command of *Titan*. Riker had said he'd chosen the name as an homage to a famous social club for aviators and early Earth astronauts, but La Forge suspected his real intention had been to annoy Worf.

The vodka tonic in La Forge's hand had become diluted as its ice cubes melted, but it hardly mattered, since the beverage had been made with synthehol.

He'd taken only a few sips from it in the half hour since he'd come from the captain's quarters, because his attention had been fixed on the massive Caeliar city-ship looming in space before the *Enterprise,* the *Aventine,* and *Titan*. The alien metropolis was kilometers wide and breathtaking in its elegance. It was packed with slender towers, sloping and curved structures that evoked waves and aquatic themes, and sky bridges that, from a distance, looked like gossamer filaments.

Behind him, the Riding Club was much less busy than usual. Most of the ship's crew was on duty or on a much-needed rest cycle, as repairs overlapped with preparations for the imminent confrontation with the Borg armada. Tensions were high. La Forge knew that he ought to be in main engineering, supervising the dozens of major projects currently under way, but he was confident that Taurik had matters well in hand.

The scent of fresh prune juice and the thump of deliberate footfalls alerted him to Worf's approach, and he looked for the Klingon first officer's reflection in the window. Worf had approached from directly behind La Forge and had revealed himself only with his last few steps. La Forge continued to face forward as Worf settled to a halt on his left.

"I guess you've spoken to the captain," La Forge said.

"I have." Worf sipped his prune juice.

La Forge looked at his drink. "Am I under arrest?"

"No," Worf said. "You are not."

He didn't elaborate, which worried La Forge.

"So what happens next?"

"The captain has rescinded his order."

That caught La Forge off-guard. He turned and looked at Worf. "Rescinded? Because of what I said?"

"Yes," Worf said, staring straight ahead into space.

"And he sent you down here to tell me that?"

"No. I came of my own accord. To thank you."

Recoiling in mild surprise, La Forge asked, "For what?"

"For saying what I should have said," Worf replied. "I feel as you do. Making such a weapon is a risk, and it would be an insult to Data's sacrifice." He clenched his jaw and huffed angrily. "I did not wish to confront the captain. But I should have." He turned his head and met La Forge's stare. "It takes courage to challenge authority on a matter of principle. What you did—for yourself and Data—was an act of great honor."

La Forge bowed his head and said, "Thank you." He looked up and out at the Caeliar city-ship. "Amazing, isn't it?"

"It is . . . large," Worf said.

"When I first saw it, I'd thought about asking the

captain permission for a visit," La Forge said. "Just to see what makes it tick, y'know? And then I wondered what Data would think of it . . . and suddenly, I didn't want to go anymore. Not because the city wasn't interesting, but because I knew that every time I saw something new, I'd want to turn and tell Data about it—and then I'd have to remember he's gone."

Worf regarded the Caeliar metropolis with a somber look. "I understand," he said. "I, too, often wish that Data were still alive. Usually in the morning, when Spot wishes to be fed."

La Forge chuckled, recalling Worf's pained expression when he'd learned that Data's last will and testament had named the Klingon as the guardian of his pet. "How's the cat doing?"

"Spot is well—and his claws are sharp," Worf said with a prideful smirk. Then he softened his expression and clasped La Forge's shoulder in a friendly grip. "Data is gone, and it is not wrong for us to mourn him. But we must not cling too tightly to the past. We are still alive, Geordi, and we have each other. Perhaps that will be enough."

Nodding, La Forge said, "It's everything, Worf. Thanks."

Worf dipped his chin and removed his hand from La Forge's shoulder. The silence between them was calm and comfortable, and La Forge felt no need to disturb it. It was enough to stand next to his old friend, watching the stars and waiting to see what the future would bring.

27

One scan after another yielded nothing but good news.

"It's truly remarkable, Captain," Dr. Ree said to Riker, who stood with him in *Titan*'s sickbay, on the other side of the biobed, holding Troi's hand. Gesturing toward the vital-signs monitor above her head, the reptilian physician continued, "All of Deanna's readings are optimal, across the board. There's no sign of damage in the uterine wall and no abnormalities in the fetus."

Troi reclined on the biobed, her face beaming with joy as she looked at Riker. "She's okay, Will," Troi said. "Our daughter is okay." Tears rolled from her eyes.

Riker, still reeling from the revelation of his wife's recovery, asked Ree, "This is the Caeliar's work?"

"Yes, sir. And I've only told you part of the good news." He called up a new screen of information on the overhead display. "In addition to healing Deanna and her child, the Caeliar saw fit to restore all of her unreleased ova as well. Which means that if the two of you so desire, there's no reason you couldn't have more than one child."

Riker asked, "What about the risk of miscarriage?"

"I'm happy to report that's no longer an issue," Ree said. "Your complications were genetic in nature, and the Caeliar have amended that—quite ably, I might add. They've also rejuvenated much of Deanna's internal physiology."

It was Troi's turn to react with surprise. She sat up quickly as she said, "Rejuvenated?"

"Yes, my dear counselor," Ree said. "Inyx reversed much of the age-related deterioration in your tissues and organs. If one were to judge your age based solely on an internal scan, you would register as a woman of thirty, in the prime of your life."

A giddy smile brightened her face as she looked at Riker and said, "I guess that explains why I feel so amazing."

"Guess so," Riker said, mirroring her happiness. He looked at Ree and asked with intense interest, "How did they do it? Genetic therapy? Nanosurgery?"

Ree cocked his head sideways and tasted the air with a flick of his tongue. "I have absolutely no idea," he said. "Deanna's treatment was performed in secret. If I seem impressed by Inyx's amazing results, I'm positively stunned by the fact that he left no discernible trace of how he did it." He switched off the biobed, and the overhead screen went dark. "If you want, I can keep running tests to see if I can uncover his methods, but I doubt I'll find anything."

"Don't bother," Riker said, helping Troi to a sitting position on the edge of the bed. "We've had enough tests."

"I quite agree," Ree said, empathizing with the suffering Riker and Troi had endured over the past several months, from the invasive rigors of fertility therapy to the heartbreak of a miscarriage and the close call of a second failed pregnancy. "My prescription for the two of you is simply this: Go spend some time alone, and assuming the universe doesn't come to a fiery end tomorrow, come back next month for a routine prenatal exam—with an emphasis on *routine*."

"Thank you, Doctor," Troi said, wrapping her arm around Riker's waist. "For everything—including biting me."

"You're welcome," Ree said.

Riker did a double-take. "He *bit* you?"

"Let's go," Troi said, cajoling Riker gently as she pulled him out of sickbay. "I'll tell you all about it . . . in private."

Will Riker's relief was so profound, the burden that had been lifted so ponderous, that he felt breathless, as if he'd gone from the pit of the sea to the peak of a mountaintop.

His *Imzadi* was home and healed.

Their child was safe.

The future was theirs again, something to look forward to instead of fear. They'd stepped to the precipice, faced the fathomless darkness, and come back whole.

He and Deanna stood in the main room of their quarters on *Titan* and held each other. The fragrance of her hair, the warmth of her body, and her empathic radiance of well-being combined in his senses to mean one thing: *home*.

She hugged him with greater vigor and pressed her face to his chest. "You don't need to say it," she said, reacting to his unspoken, still-forming thoughts and confirming for him that their telepathic bond was as strong as it had ever been.

"Yes, I do," he said. "You know I do." He kissed the top of her head. "I'm so sorry I left you. I didn't want to."

"I know," she said, reaching up to stroke his cheek.

"Please forgive me," he said.

Deanna pressed her palms softly on his cheeks and pulled his face to hers. She planted a delicate kiss on his lips and another on the tip of his nose. "I forgive you," she said. "It was a terrible choice. I'm sorry you had to make it."

Clasping her hands in his own, he felt the sincerity of her forgiveness and the intensity of her elation. Lost in a giddy haze, he asked, "Are you hungry?"

"Not at all," she said, shaking her head and smiling.

"Neither am I," he said, and they laughed for a moment. It was goofy laughter, like an unmotivated overflow of joy.

In a blink, Deanna's mood turned bittersweet, and tears welled in her eyes. "Thank you," she said.

"For . . . ?"

"For supporting me when we argued with Dr. Ree a few days ago. I know you disagreed with my decision, for all the right reasons, but in sickbay, you always took my side. You trusted me."

"I *believed* in you," he said, looking with wonder at the amazing woman who had deigned to spend her life with him. "And, as always, my faith in you has been richly rewarded."

She relaxed back into his arms, and he was glad to support her weight. It had been months since they'd felt this close, this in tune with each other, and he found it deeply gratifying to feel wanted—and *needed*—again.

"After everything," Deanna said, "I still can't believe it's finally happening for us. A family, Will. Children. We can even have more than one if we want."

"If I didn't know it was thanks to science, I'd call it a miracle," he replied with a grin.

Deanna reacted with a sigh and a look of concerned dismay. "Now all we have to fear is the Borg," she said. Riker tried to think of some way to defuse her anxiety, but he was at a loss, because he knew she was right. She continued, "We're so close, Will. So close to living the life we've always wanted, and now we're hours away from the biggest confrontation with the Borg we've ever seen. We've fought so hard for this child, for us, for a second chance. I can't stand the thought of seeing it taken away." She implored him as much with her gaze as with her words, "Please tell me we have a plan, Will. *Please*."

"I know Captain Hernandez does," he said. "And Jean-Luc might be cooking up one of his own. So, yes, there is a plan."

"Okay, so *they* have plans," she said. "What about *us*? What are *we* going to do?"

Riker shrugged, glib humor his defense of last resort. "The same thing we always do," he said. "The impossible."

Ranul Keru found Torvig—with guidance from *Titan*'s main computer—in a remote, hard-to-reach forward compartment located just above the main deflector dish. The young Choblik engineer stood on a narrow catwalk and gazed through a broad sliver of a viewport. He turned his ovine head in Keru's direction as the tall, brawny Trill approached him. Light from the surrounding machinery glinted off Torvig's metallic eyes and cybernetic enhancements. For once, the normally loquacious young ensign remained silent and resumed staring out into space.

The security chief stepped carefully across the grid-grated catwalk, mindful of its low guardrails and the precipitous drop into the workings of the deflector dish. Shuffling along for the last few steps, he sidled up to Torvig and asked, "Hiding?"

"I desired an isolated place in which to think."

"Your quarters aren't private?"

"I've not yet earned enough seniority to receive private accommodations," Torvig said. "Since my return, Ensign Worvan has asked me one hundred thirty-four questions about what I observed during our incarceration in Axion. He's been most *persistent* in his efforts."

Keru tilted his head and smirked. "Gallamites are like that." He looked out the narrow gap to see the majestic lines and mass of Axion, shining against the sprawl of the cosmos. "Is something bothering you, Vig? You seem . . . out of sorts."

"I'm unaware of any direct irritation to my person."

"No, I mean, are you experiencing anxiety about something?"

Torvig shifted his weight back and forth, from one foot to the other, and his mechanical hands clenched the railing in front of him. "Is it true that the Borg armada has reversed course and is on its way here?"

"Yes," Keru said.

"Then my answer is yes. I'm feeling anxiety."

"It could be worse," Keru said, heaving a disappointed sigh. "While we were in Axion, a lot of people from here and the *Enterprise* and the *Aventine* boarded a Borg scout ship and fought in close-quarters combat. We lost Rriarr, Hutchinson, Tane, Doron, and about half a dozen other really good people. And sh'Aqabaa might live through surgery, or she might not." It was a bitter sting for Keru that he had been denied the chance to fight the Borg face-to-face. Even after so many years, he would have found such violence deeply cathartic for his beloved's death at their hands. Now, facing much less forgiving odds, he doubted he would have such an opportunity again.

He looked at Torvig and realized the squat, short ensign was quaking. "Calm down, Vig," he said. "Officers don't shiver."

"I apologize, Ranul," Torvig said. "I'm having trouble remaining objective about our circumstances. Until now, I'd considered the Borg as a phenomenon, or as an abstraction of accessories and behavioral subroutines for a holodeck program. Now that I'm about to face them, I realize that I'm not ready."

Keru squatted next to Torvig and patted the Choblik's armored back. "You'll be fine, Vig. Nothing to be scared of."

"At the risk of sounding insubordinate, I disagree," Torvig said. "Do you recall my tests of the crew? The ones I used to verify a link between my crewmates' anxious behaviors toward me and their feelings about the Borg?"

Rolling his eyes, Keru said, "How could I forget?"

"I now have a greater understanding of one part

of that equation," Torvig said. "Now I'm afraid of the Borg, too. It was a mistake for me to compare their cybernetics with those of the Choblik. The Great Builders' technology was a boon to my people—it gave us individuality and sentience. The Borg's technology takes away those things. It debases its members." He let go of the railing and lifted his bionic hands in front of his face, flexing them open and shut. "I imagine my mechanical elements betraying me, and it frightens me. That's what it would be to become one of the Borg." Looking plaintively at Keru, he added, "Don't let them do that to me, Ranul."

Keru reached out and clutched Torvig's bionic hand, thumb to thumb, flesh to metal, and he looked his friend in the eye. "I won't let it happen, Vig. To either of us. You have my word."

Most of the beds in the *Aventine*'s sickbay were still full when Captain Dax walked in, and Dr. Tarses and his medical staff looked wrung out by a day of gruesome surgeries. She caught his eye with a wave and waited while he walked over to her.

"Thanks for coming," he said.

Up close to Tarses, Dax saw that the young doctor's hair was matted with sweat, and his eyes were red from exhaustion. She nodded and said, "Where is she?"

Tarses took a few steps and motioned with a tilt of his head for Dax to follow him. She walked with him past one row of biobeds, and then past a triage center, into a recovery ward. All of the beds in this compartment were occupied as well. Near the far end of the ward was the person Dax had come to talk to. She reached out to Tarses and tugged his sleeve. "I'll take it from here," she said, and he acknowledged the dismissal with a polite nod and let her continue past him.

Dax approached the problem patient without hesitation and placed herself at the foot of the bed. "What's this I hear about you not wanting to return to duty?"

Lonnoc Kedair stirred from her torpid, dead-eyed languor to meet Dax's accusing stare. "It's not about what I want," the Takaran woman said. "It's about what I deserve."

"If I could, I'd give you a month's liberty," Dax said. "I read Simon's report. You got mangled pretty bad on that Borg ship. Unfortunately, we have about four thousand more of them on their way here, and I need my security chief back at her post." She frowned as Kedair turned her head and averted her eyes. "In case I wasn't clear, I'm talking about you."

"You were clear," Kedair said. "I wasn't. I'm not saying I deserve time off. I'm saying I deserve to be in the brig."

Just what I didn't need, Dax brooded behind a blank expression. *Something to make my day a little more interesting.* "Care to elaborate, Lieutenant?"

Kedair seemed unable to look Dax in the eye. The security chief shut her eyes, massaged her green, scaly forehead, and combed her fingers through her wiry black hair. "On the Borg ship," she began, and then she paused. After a grim sigh, she continued, "I made a mistake, Captain."

"Stay here. I'll convene a firing squad," Dax quipped.

"Curious choice of words," Kedair said. "Because

that's basically what I did." Looking up, she added, "I caused at least three friendly-fire deaths during the attack, sir. Maybe more."

Dax stepped to the side of Kedair's bed and moved closer to her, so that they could speak more discreetly. "What happened, Lonnoc? Specifically, I mean."

"I was looking out across that big empty space in the middle of the ship," Kedair said, her eyes turned away while she searched her memory for details. "I thought I saw an ambush closing in on one of our teams. It was so dark, and everybody was wearing black, and with TR-116s in their hands, at a distance, they looked like Borg with arm attachments." Dax nodded for her to go on. "With the dampeners, we didn't have any comms, so I fired a warning shot at the team that was—that I *thought* was being ambushed. I signaled them to turn and intercept." Kedair closed her eyes, and her jaw tensed.

Wary of pushing too hard, Dax asked, "What happened next?"

"The first team took cover and waited for their targets to close to optimal firing distance. Then they—they lit 'em up." She shook her head. "A few seconds later, the squad leader called cease-fire, and they popped off a few gel flares. That was when I saw what had happened." She bowed her head into her hands for a few seconds, then she straightened and added, "Lieutenant sh'Aqabaa's still in critical condition. The rest of her squad from *Titan* is dead."

The rest of Kedair's actions on the Borg scout ship after the boarding op were starting to make sense to Dax. "Is that why you volunteered to stay behind when the Borg Queen attacked? To try and make up for your mistake?"

"I did that because it was my duty, and because it was the right tactical choice," Kedair said defensively. "Please don't psychoanalyze me, Captain. I can always go see Counselor Hyatt if I'm in the mood for that."

"I think Susan might echo my diagnosis," Dax said. "But you're right, it's not my job to give you therapy. It's my job to give you some perspective and put you back at your post."

"You ought to put me out an airlock," Kedair grumped.

Sharpening her tone, Dax said, "That's *enough*, Lieutenant. Listen to what I'm telling you. You did not pull the trigger on Lieutenant sh'Aqabaa and her team. It's not your fault."

"How can you say that? I flagged my own people as a target. I gave the order to fire. How can it possibly *not* be my fault?"

"It's called the 'fog of war,' " Dax said. "You go into sensory overload. Everything happens so fast, you can't process it. Mistakes happen." She sighed as she confronted painful memories from her years on the *Destiny* and on Deep Space 9. "I saw it a lot during the Dominion War. It had nothing to do with how well trained someone was or the quality of their character. In combat, you have no time to think. Information gets scrambled. You're surrounded by chaos, and you try to do the best you can—but no one's perfect."

Kedair's eyes narrowed. "Sounds like an excuse," she said. "And not a very good one, either. I don't want to make excuses, Captain. I should have verified the target before I told my people to fire."

"I've read a lot of reports from squad leaders who were on that ship," Dax said. "I doubt you really had the time to check every target. No one did. Under the circumstances, I'd say your actions were entirely reasonable."

Angrier, Kedair replied, "I was sloppy. I lost track of where my people were. It was my job to know."

Vexed by Kedair's toxic brew of self-pity and self-loathing, Dax leaned forward and took hold of the security chief's collar. "I'm trying to be patient, Lonnoc, but you're not making this easy. Stop feeling sorry for yourself. This is war. It gets bloody. People die. Deal with it." With a shove, she released Kedair and continued, "The team on the other level could have fired gel flares first, just to see who they were shooting, but they didn't. That was their call, not yours.

"Add up the facts. You had no communications, in the dark, in hostile territory, while under attack, and you made an honest mistake. You want to blame yourself? Go ahead. Wail and gnash your teeth and cry yourself to sleep at night—I don't give a damn. There was no criminal negligence here and no criminal intent—in other words, absolutely no basis for a court-martial.

"So I'm giving you a direct order, Lieutenant: Get your ass out of that bed, and report to your post on the bridge. We're less than ten hours from facing off with a quarter-billion Borg drones in more than four thousand cubes, and I don't plan on letting you goldbrick your way through it. Understood?"

Kedair stared at Dax in shock, her eyes wide, her jaw slack, her back pressed as deeply into her pillows as she had been able to retreat in the face of Dax's harangue. The Takaran woman blinked, composed herself, and sat up. She swung her legs over the side of the bed and stood up, facing Dax.

In a level, dignified voice, she said, "It's a damned good thing you switched to the command track, Captain. Because if this was you as a counselor, you suck at it."

"*That* is called insubordination, Lieutenant. And if you keep it up, it *will* get you a court-martial."

The security chief smirked. "Good to know. Now, at least I have something to shoot for."

Axion was windless and silent beneath the endless night of deep space. Erika Hernandez drifted alone through the motionless air that surrounded the city-ship inside its invisible force field.

Darkness and starlight were reflected to perfection on the brilliant façades of the metropolis, which gleamed with its own inner light. Hernandez felt the awareness of the millions of Caeliar who dwelled in the city. Now conscious of her bond with the gestalt, they shied from her in subtle ways. They would never deny another mind in their communion, but many of them radiated discomfort at the discovery that it now included a non-Caeliar.

As meticulous as the Caeliar kept their city, to Hernandez, it still felt less antiseptic than either of the Starfleet vessels she'd visited in the past several hours. Inside the sheltering embrace of the city, she caught the fragrance of green plants—grass and trees, bushes, flowers—and the rich scent of fertile earth. Water still danced in the fountains.

None of that distracted her from her search.

Inyx had left the Quorum hall before she'd finished her proposal to the *tanwa-seynorral*. As soon as he'd gone, he'd started masking his thoughts from the gestalt, withdrawing from contact. *Apparently, the Caeliar appreciate privacy on a personal level as well as a cultural one,* Hernandez realized. Nonetheless, she suspected that she knew where he would be.

She was correct.

She descended without a sound, her posture relaxed, legs crossed at the ankles, arms at her sides. Air displaced by her passage tousled her mane of dark hair and fluttered the fabric of her Starfleet uniform. For the sake of nostalgia, she alighted on the glossy black water of the reflecting pool by the petrified tree. Inyx stood beneath the tree's bare boughs, in whose ragged shadows he seemed to have partially vanished.

Without causing so much as a ripple, Hernandez walked calmly across the pool to the tree's small island at the far end. She bounded onto the isle with her last step and landed with balletic grace in front of Inyx.

Feigning boredom, he said, "I wondered how long it would take you to master that trick."

"Not long," she said. "Less than eight hundred years." She cocked a teasing eyebrow. "Told you I was a fast learner."

"About some things," he said.

She ambled past him and made a slow circle of the tree, letting her hand play across its glassy, obsidian surface. "I've never seen you in such a hurry to leave the Quorum hall," she said. "Did my proposal bother you that much?"

"I made my objections to the gestalt," he said, and then he added, with an extra degree of sarcasm, "But of course, you know that, since you are, apparently, completely attuned to the gestalt and can share in it whenever you please."

She took his rebuke in stride, because she had already sensed his pride in her accomplishment. "I'm sorry I lied to you, Inyx," she said. "But your people aren't the only ones who value privacy."

He made a derogatory huffing noise inside his air sacs, which puffed up around his shoulders. "There is a difference, Erika, between privacy and secrets—and between secrets and deceptions." His ire dissipated. "What's done is past. I'm more concerned about your next potentially fatal mistake."

"I know it's a risk, but I think it's worth taking," she said. "And the Quorum agrees with me."

"By a narrow margin," Inyx replied.

"I'm certain it will work," she said.

"Certainty is not the same thing as infallibility," he said. "If you're wrong, or if you've underestimated the Borg's capacity for adaptation, you might be condemning this galaxy and many others to aeons of oppression."

"If I'm wrong—if I fail—I'm counting on you to persuade the Quorum to honor the spirit of our agreement and protect the galaxy from the Borg."

He said with grim regret, "I can't promise that, Erika."

"Promise me that you'll try," she said.

With a small bow from his waist, he said, "You have my solemn pledge. I *will* try." Melancholy seeped into his voice. "I wish it didn't have to be you taking this risk."

"Well, it's not like anyone else is in a position to do it," she said. "You sure can't, and neither can those starship crews." She shook her head. "Believe me, if there was another way, I'd take it."

"If you do not wish to make such a sacrifice, why go?"

"Because my people need me, Inyx. They need me to step up and do something no one else can. And all those people trapped in the Collective need me even more than the Federation does. I failed a lot of people when I let the Romulans get the drop on me and destroy my convoy. I led my crew into captivity, and then I failed to control them, and millions of *your* people died. All these centuries, I've been living with those failures, with no way to atone for any of them. Now, I might have that chance."

Inyx passed a long moment in somber reflection.

"The consequences of failure seem clear enough," he said. "But what would be the price of success? If your plan goes as intended, what will become of *you*, Erika? Will you ever come back to Axion? Will I ever see you again?"

Unable to hold back the tears welling in her eyes, she replied, "I don't know."

"Then perhaps you've finally received your wish," he said, with a tenor of defeat. "You'll finally be free of Axion . . . forever."

She placed herself directly in front of him. "Maybe," she said. "But that doesn't mean I'm happy about it."

With both hands, she reached up and gently pulled Inyx's ever-frowning visage down to hers. "I probably won't get a chance to do this later."

She kissed his high, leathery forehead with tender affection. "Good-bye, Inyx."

28

"Whatever Captain Hernandez is planning, it involves the Borg, and that means it has the potential to go horribly wrong."

Picard stood at the head of the table in the *Enterprise*'s observation lounge and watched the seated Captains Riker and Dax nod at what he had just said. At his invitation, they had beamed over to meet with him in private aboard the *Enterprise,* so that they could confer without risking the interception of their conversation by the Borg—or by the Caeliar.

Exasperated, Dax replied, "You want a contingency plan for what to do *after* we're surrounded by more than four thousand Borg cubes?"

"Better than not having one," Riker said, scratching pensively at his salt-and-pepper-bearded chin.

Dax blinked, conceding the point, and replied, "For that matter, we'll need one even if she succeeds. I mean, have we even thought about how we're supposed to repatriate a quarter-billion ex-Borg from across the galaxy?"

"We're getting ahead of ourselves," Picard said. "Frankly, as powerful as the Caeliar seem to be, I doubt they—or any other entity, short of the single-letter variety who shall not be named—can effect such a change by force."

"There's another scenario to consider," Riker said. "What if they succeed but only temporarily? The Borg Collective is based on adaptation. Even if she frees all the drones from the Collective's control, who's to say it'll be a permanent shift?"

Nodding, Picard said, "Those are all valid concerns. In success or in failure, Captain Hernandez's proposal—what little we know of it—will present us with staggering logistical and tactical crises. In just over eight hours, the first wave of the Borg armada will reach us. Whatever backup plan we intend to prepare, it needs to be ready by then."

Riker leaned forward and folded his hands together. "If this turns into a shooting match, I think the Caeliar can take care of themselves," he said.

"Against these odds?" asked Dax.

"That I don't know," Riker said. "But if the fight turns against them, the Caeliar can open a subspace tunnel and slip away. Which doesn't help us but would keep the Omega Molecule generator out of the Borg's hands."

Dax frowned. "Captain Picard made a good point the last time we talked with Captain Hernandez. A team of twenty-second-century MACOs outflanked the Caeliar and destroyed one of their cities. That gives me the impression that strategy and tactics aren't the Caeliar's forte. What if the Borg get the better of them? What if they can't escape to safe ground?"

"Then we have a problem," Riker said.

"More than a problem, Will," Picard said. "A disaster." Resting his hands on the headrest of his chair, he continued, "If Hernandez fails to disband the Collective, our top priority must be to prevent the Borg from assimilating anything of the Caeliar. If that means abetting their escape, so be it. But if the only way to keep their city-ship from the Borg is to destroy it, then we need to be prepared to take that step."

Dax keyed in some commands on the tabletop interface at her seat. She called up a map of Axion on the wall companel behind Riker. "This is based on scans and observations made by Captain Riker's away team while they were in Axion," she said. "It shows the approximate position of the Omega Molecule generator. That's what powers the Caeliar's civilization, and it's probably our best chance of destroying them if we have to. If we can destabilize the generator when the armada's on top of us, we could vaporize them instantly."

"Along with the rest of the galaxy," Riker said. "We'd also end warp flight in most of the local group. Not exactly what I'd call a plan for victory."

Arms out, palms up, Dax said, "If you know another way to destroy Axion and the Borg at the same time, let's hear it."

He rolled his eyes and shrugged. "Well, we know the Caeliar can modify their subspace passages for time travel."

"Tell me you're not serious," Dax said. "What do you plan to do? Go back in time, find the origin of the Borg, and wipe them out before they ever existed?"

"Why not?" Riker said. "They tried to do it to us."

"And look what that got them," Dax said.

Picard raised his voice. "Captains, *please*." He

waited for Dax and Riker to calm down and acknowledge him. "We need to consider every alternative at this stage, no matter what the ethical or broader tactical consid—"

"Bridge to Captain Picard," Worf said over the comm.

"Go ahead, Commander."

"We are detecting extreme levels of local subspace disruption," Worf said. *"And we are being hailed by Axion."*

"Red Alert, Mister Worf. I'm on my way. Picard out." As the channel clicked off, he added to Dax and Riker, "Captains, will you join me on the bridge, please?" Picard was already stepping through the door to the bridge by the time Dax and Riker had risen from their seats. He had no idea what fresh calamity was unfolding, but he had a sinking feeling that, as with so many events of late, it would be one for which he had no plan.

Riker hurried onto the bridge of the *Enterprise* several seconds behind Captain Picard, who was met at the trio of command chairs by Commander Worf. Picard and Worf conferred in tense whispers as Riker and Dax moved past them, down to the center of the bridge. Then came Picard's authoritative baritone: "Commander Kadohata, put Captain Hernandez on-screen."

Kadohata tapped a sequence of commands into the ops console, and the main viewer blinked from an image of Axion to the youthful beauty of Erika Hernandez.

Beside her was an alien with a bony, skeletal body and an enormous, bulbous head fronted by a stretched, frowning visage. Riker looked at the be-ing's pearlescent sea-green eyes, its skin of mottled purple and gray, and the tentacle-shaped ribbed air sacs draped over its shoulders, and he realized that its head reminded him vaguely of an octopus.

"Hello, Captains," Hernandez said. *"I'm glad I found you together, as this concerns all of you."*

Picard stepped forward, passing between Dax and Riker to place himself at the forefront of the conversa-tion. "Captain Hernandez," he said, "have the Caeliar agreed to help us?"

"Yes," she said. *"After a fashion."*

Suspicious, questioning looks passed between the captains on the *Enterprise* bridge. Turning back to-ward the main viewer, Picard asked, "Would you care to be more precise, Captain?"

"First, I should apologize to all of you and your crews for misleading you, but I give you my word that I believed it was in everyone's best interest for me to do so."

Holding up one hand, Picard cut in, *"Misleading* us? About what, Captain?"

"It would take too long to explain," she said. *"Be-sides, you'll see for yourselves soon enough. All I can say is that old habits die hard, if at all, and if I learned anything living with the Caeliar, it was how to play my cards close."* She looked at Riker and then at Dax as she continued, *"Will, Ezri, thanks for treat-ing me like part of your crews. It was nice to feel like I was home again, back in Starfleet. I knew I'd missed it, but until today, I hadn't realized just how much."*

"Captain," Picard said, "what's going to happen?"

"I honestly don't know for certain," Hernandez

said. *"No matter how this plays out, you and I prob-ably won't see each other again. If I and the Caeliar fail, then we're all about to have·a very bad day. And if we succeed, then something new awaits us—all of us."* She smiled. *"Wish us luck."*

Riker eyed Picard's profile. The elder captain was standing slackjawed and at a loss for words as he watched Hernandez close her eyes and lift one hand in front of her, fingers spread wide, as if she were reaching for some unseen object.

Just as Riker was about to ask Picard what was wrong, Inyx spoke and snared everyone's attention with his mellifluous baritone. *"Captains, for your own safety, I recommend you move your vessels to within one kilometer of Axion—immediately."*

Picard still seemed frozen, so from the aft deck of the bridge, Worf called out, "Helm, put us alongside Axion, distance eight hundred fifty meters. Com-mander Kadohata, relay those orders to *Titan* and the *Aventine*."

Kadohata and Lieutenant Weinrib gave overlapping replies of "Aye, sir" as they carried out Worf's orders.

On the main viewer, Hernandez's raised hand began to glow. A nimbus of light formed around it, growing so bright that it shone through her fingers, making them blaze red like hot coals. Her face was the very portrait of serenity. She opened her eyes, which burned with an inner fire, and she said, *"It's time."*

A hush fell over the bridge.

Captain Picard tensed with a sharp intake of breath.

Proximity alerts shrilled from multiple consoles.

"Massive energy surge from the Caeliar city," called out Lieutenant Choudhury at tactical.

"Subspace tunnels," added Lieutenant Dina Elfiki, who was racing to keep up with the rush of data on her console. "Thousands of them, opening in a spherical distribution around Axion." The attractive, chestnut-haired science officer added, "The city is definitely controlling them, Captain."

"Incoming vessels," Choudhury announced.

Worf replied, "Shields up!"

Riker wished that he was on the bridge of his own ship at that moment, but he was also grateful that his crew at least had Vale, Tuvok, and Keru back aboard to lead them in his absence. On the viewscreen, Erika Hernandez maintained a steady countenance.

Choudhury looked at Worf. "Borg cubes are emerging from the subspace tunnels, sir—thousands of them. The entire armada."

"Split screen," Worf said. Kadohata adjusted the main viewer to show two images: Hernandez and Inyx on the right and, on the left, the arriving Borg armada surrounding Axion and blotting out the stars with their sheer numbers.

Dax sounded as if she simply couldn't believe what she was seeing. "The Caeliar brought the Borg here sooner? Why?"

Riker shrugged, equally dumbfounded.

Then he looked at Picard, who nodded slowly, as if with a dawning comprehension. Riker sensed that something unspoken was transpiring between Picard and Hernandez.

Finally, Picard said to Hernandez, "You're not disbanding the Collective . . . are you, Captain?"

"No," Hernandez said. *"We're assimilating them."*

A two-meter-tall oval of mirror-perfect quicksilver

took shape behind Hernandez, who turned and stepped through it without so much as a ripple. Then the oval faded into vapor, sublimated into nonexistence, leaving only Inyx on the screen.

Riker snapped, "What's going on? Where'd she go?"

"To the source," Picard muttered.

Glaring at Inyx, Riker said, "Show me where she is!"

"*As you wish,*" Inyx said.

The Caeliar's image dissolved to that of a view from deep inside a massive Borg vessel. A haphazard, slapdash collage of metal, tubes, wires, ducts, and random machinery filled the screen, all of it illuminated through its narrow gaps by a sickly viridian light. The point of view roved through the dark, industrial-looking labyrinth until it found open space and arrowed down toward the vessel's core. Passing like a phantom through solid matter, the image speared its way into the central plexus, to the most elaborate Borg vinculum Riker had ever seen.

In the bowels of that biomechanoid horror, Erika Hernandez walked without fear toward an advancing phalanx of Borg drones. Behind them, atop a dais festooned with regeneration pods and a plethora of bizarre devices, stood the Borg Queen, commanding her foot soldiers forward to intercept her rival.

"No!" Riker shouted. "You have to stop her! She doesn't know what she's doing!"

Inyx replied, "*I assure you, Captain, Erika knows exactly what she is doing. And I would have stopped her if I could.*"

Riker watched, horrified, as the drones set upon Hernandez in a savage pack—and impaled her with assimilation tubules.

29

———

Hernandez fell into the arms of the drones and gave herself up, surrendering to their violations. Viselike hands seized her arms and ripped every loose fold of her clothing. Assimilation tubules extended from the drones' knuckles and pierced Hernandez's flesh, each puncture as sharp as a serpent's bite.

A cold pain coursed through her, surged in her blood, and clouded her thoughts. There was no fury in the drones as they smothered her, only the brutal, simple efficiency of machines subjugating flesh and bone.

Beyond the one-sided melee, the Borg Queen stood on her dais and regarded Hernandez's fall with haughty dispassion.

The voice of the Collective flooded Hernandez's mind like seawater pouring into a sinking ship, and her thoughts drowned in the aggressive swell of psionic noise. Panic bubbled up from her subconscious. For a moment, she wished she had prevented the drones from injecting her. It would have been within her power to turn them back, to wrest them from the will of the Borg Queen, but instead she had let them strike unopposed—because that was the plan and had been from the start.

A black fog of oblivion enfolded her.

This is the only way, she told herself. *The only path.*

None of the Caeliar could do this for her. Hernandez knew that only she could serve as the gestalt's bridge to the Borg. The Caeliar, with their bodies of catoms, were immune to assimilation; the Borg's nanoscopic organelles needed at least some trace amounts of organic matter to invade and transform as part of the assimilation process. In the body of a Caeliar, the organelles would find only other nanomachines—all of which would be far more advanced and powerful than the organelles and utterly impervious to them.

It would have been equally futile for any member of the Starfleet crews to volunteer for Hernandez's mission. Without the Caeliar catoms that infused her body, and which had altered her genetic structure, another organic being would be unable to survive the assimilation process while acting as a conduit for the focused energies of the gestalt.

Only I can do this, Hernandez reminded herself. *I have to hang on. Can't give up . . . not yet.*

The icewater in her veins turned to fire as assimilation organelles and Caeliar catoms waged war for possession of her body. Needles of pain stabbed through her eyes, and a burning sensation pricked its way down her back.

Every inch of her was consumed with excruciating torments. Two deafening voices raged inside her head: the soulless roar of the Collective and the hauntingly beautiful chorus of the gestalt.

As the Collective became more aware of the gestalt through its bond with Hernandez, the singular intelligence behind the Borg launched a mind-breaking assault on her psyche. Unlike the first time the Borg had assailed her, however, Hernandez wasn't alone. Reinforced by the shared consciousness of the Caeliar, she dispelled the Borg's demoralizing revisions of her memories. Its lies broke like waves against an unyielding seawall.

She felt the Caeliar gestalt reassert its primacy in her mind and body, and then it landed its own first blow against the Collective, dredging up fragments of an ancient memory—bitter cold and empty darkness, loneliness and despair, fading strength and dwindling numbers. And, above all, *hunger.*

Paroxysms of rage shook the Collective, and Hernandez knew, intuitively, that the Borg armada was firing en masse at Axion, unleashing every bit of destructive power it could marshal. All of the Collective's hatred and aggression was erupting, and the Caeliar had become its sole focus. As the bombardment hammered Axion's shields, however, there wasn't a glimmer of distress or even concern in the gestalt. At best, the Caeliar reacted to the fusillade with equal parts curiosity and pity.

So much sorrow and anger, opined the gestalt. *Such a desperate yearning . . . but it doesn't know what it seeks, so it consumes everything and is never satisfied.*

A surge of strength and comfort from the gestalt flowed through Hernandez, and the chaos of its struggle with the Borg gave way to a sudden peace and clarity.

Then the Caeliar projected their will through her fragile form and usurped control of the Borg Collective.

The Caeliar gestalt beheld its savage reflection.

The Collective looked back, hostile and bewildered, like a wild thing that had never seen a mirror nor caught sight of itself in still waters.

Inyx perceived the shape of the Collective and was shocked at how it could be both so familiar and so alien. Two great minds, the Collective and the gestalt, had shared a past until their paths had diverged. The Borg had been forced down a road of deprivation and darkness, while the Caeliar, despite being wounded, had been afforded the luxury of a more benign destiny. Now their journeys, separated by time and space, had converged.

A roar of voices spoke the will of the Borg.

You will be assimilated. Your diversity and technology will be adapted to service us. Resistance is futile.

The gestalt was overwhelmed with pity for the primitive and autocratic posturing of the Collective. Like a child that had never been disciplined, it laid claim to all it surveyed, seized everything within reach in rapacious flurries of action, and never once questioned if it had the right to do so.

Brute force was the Collective's tactic. The drones that surrounded Axion outnumbered the Caeliar population five to one. Across the galaxy, there were trillions of drones, in tens of thousands of star systems, on innumerable cubes and vessels. Had the Collective's conflict with the Caeliar been one of simple numbers, there would have been no contest.

How tragic, Inyx mused openly in the gestalt. *It doesn't understand at all.*

Ordemo Nordal replied, *All it sees is power to be taken.*

Edrin, the architect, asked, *Do we know who it is?*

It's time we found out, said Ordemo.

The *tanwa-seynorral* focused the gestalt's attention on breaking through the noise of the Collective, penetrating to the true essence of the Borg, exposing its prime mover, revealing the mind at its foundation and the voice behind its Queen.

Wrapping herself in the shelter of a hundred million hijacked minds, the Borg Queen sought refuge from the scalpel-like inquisition of the Caeliar. With patience and precision, the gestalt evaded the crude latticework of enslaved minds and found the Queen lurking in the dark heart of it all. Then it pushed past even her, in search of the truth.

Cut off from the Collective's core essence, the Borg Queen stumbled in confusion—deposed, disoriented, directionless.

Locked in the core of every Borg nanoprobe was the key to the Borg's ethereal shared consciousness, an invisible medium that spanned great swaths of the galaxy. Unseen, it was never heard directly except through the Queen. Its presence was always felt by every drone, and every sentient mind it pressed into service amplified its power.

At first, it seemed less a personality than a collection of appetites. It was fear and hatred and hunger, and beneath even those primal urges lurked a deeper wound, the impetus for its insatiable appetites: an inconsolable loneliness.

It had no memories of its own, no name beyond *Borg*, but as the gestalt took its full measure, it was recognized by one and all for what and who it truly was.

Sedín, said Inyx, baring his grief for what had become of his confidante and beloved companion of several aeons. Sedín had been brilliant, imaginative, and ambitious. To see her debased into a violent scavenger was both horrifying and heartbreaking. Even worse was contemplating the atrocities she had wrought on other sentient beings. Those were crimes beyond atonement.

Once, she had been a Caeliar scientist and poet. All that remained of her now was a tormented fragment of consciousness, a suffering with no name and no connection to its own greatness. Inyx imagined that Sedín, in a moment of weakness, had been unable to let herself disincorporate. She had clung too fiercely to life, lingering even after her faculties of reason had faded, rendering her little more than a sophisticated machine bent on feeding its own ravenous energy needs and perpetuating its own existence.

Taking the initiative, Inyx projected comforting impulses to Sedín, quieting her rage. Then he counseled her, *It's time to let go, Sedín. Let yourself rest. Let the light fade.*

She fought. Rage and fury pulsed through the Collective. Driven by fear and habit, Sedín lashed out, to no effect.

Inyx calmed Sedín's psychic rampage with a dulcet tone, a harmonizing thoughtwave of love. The Collective fell silent.

He reached out across space and found Erika, teetering on the edge between resistance and surrender, and bolstered her with the will of the gestalt. *Balance has been achieved,* he told her. *The next step is yours.*

Hernandez's mind was clear as she got up from the deck inside the vinculum. The pack of drones that surrounded her retreated in confusion as she looked past them and met the panicked gaze of the Borg Queen, and they parted before her as she walked forward to speak to Sedín through the deposed monarch.

"Can't you see what you've done here, Sedín?" she said. The drones all were watching her, and through her bond with the gestalt—and the gestalt's new link to the Collective—Hernandez realized that everything she did and said here would be known by every Borg drone throughout the Milky Way.

Ascending the steps of the Queen's dais, she continued, "Did you forget everything you stood for? Nonviolence, pacifism, the Great Work . . . did they all lose their meaning for you?" As she reached the top of the dais, the Borg Queen stumbled backward and collapsed before her. Hernandez felt the Queen's dismay and discerned its cause: She was unable to make sense of what was happening. The nature of the Caelar had caught the Collective by surprise; despite having believed they could assimilate nigh-omnipotent beings, the Borg had met their betters.

Standing over the fallen Queen, Hernandez understood that the Borg's figurehead was powerless now; she had become little more than another, glorified drone.

Hernandez turned away from her, shut her eyes, and extended her senses within the Borg vessel, throughout its armada, and then, with the power of the Caeliar gestalt, across the entirety of the Collective—all of which was one mind, one damaged sentience craving peace but not knowing how to find it. She lifted her hand, fingers parted wide, as a somatic cue to focus and direct the power of the Caeliar.

"Sedín, have mercy on all these souls you've stolen. You've held them all long enough, and you've done enough damage—to them, to the galaxy, and to yourself. This has to end." She quelled Sedín's fear and let the gestalt begin to place the wounded Caeliar sentience fully under control. "We have to lift this cruel veil from your victims' eyes," she continued. As the gestalt wrested the last vestiges of control from Sedín, the Collective dissolved, leaving behind trillions of minds still bound to one another by a shred of shared awareness.

She spoke now to the drones. "Awaken . . . and know yourselves."

Across the galaxy, a trillion drones reeled at the sudden absence of the Collective, as if an invisible hand had released its throttling grip on their throats and let them all breathe for the first time in six thousand years.

In unison, they inhaled and tasted freedom. Their numerical designations were stripped away, leaving some with nothing—and giving others back their names.

Clarity brought awareness . . . and then came bitter

memories. Staggering multitudes of liberated psyches remained inextricably linked, their thoughts exposed and crowded in on one another, and the result was pandemonium.

A billion minds panicked without the Collective's guidance, and a billion more laughed in triumph at the fall of their oppressor. Tens of billions emotionally imploded and filled the shared mindspace with their plangent wails of grief. Searing tides of rage swelled and swept like a force of nature through the emancipated drones. What one felt, all felt, all at once.

The entire Borg civilization was in chaos. In the span of a single breath, it had descended into madness.

Hernandez couldn't breathe. She was only one woman, one mind, one spark of consciousness trying to stand against a tsunami of sorrow and terror.

She could hear the psychic voice of every drone calling out for succor, the doleful cries of those who had awakened to find their lives shattered beyond recognition, the misdirected fury of those who had tasted revenge and hungered for more.

A flood-crush of feelings and memories pummeled the gates of her mind. Souls masculine, feminine, neuter, and wholly alien to her all turned toward the light, the radiance of the Caeliar and their Omega Molecule generator, and they all saw Hernandez as the conduit to those long-sought perfections.

I can't finish this without your help, she told the gestalt. *We've come this far. Take the final step.*

The gestalt struggled to cope with the onslaught of

negative emotions from the freed Borg drones. Such cacophony offended their precious harmony of mind, and all that Hernandez could do was hope that they would rise to the challenge it presented. Then came Inyx's reply. *We're ready, Erika.*

Strength surged in her chest like a river breaking through a dam. She felt Axion's generator increase its output by orders of magnitude, and suddenly the overmatched gestalt had assumed control. Its energy flowed within her and empowered her, and through her it found the Borg.

Hernandez gave the power a purpose. She shaped it, molded it, directed it. She spread it across the galaxy, to every last drone, on every cube, in every complex, on every assimilated world. In every corner of the galaxy that had been darkened by the scourge of the Borg, Hernandez opened the way.

Her body rose from the deck and ascended quickly toward the high ceiling above the vinculum. *Freedom,* she thought, and the core of the Borg cube obeyed her. The massive supports and exterior structures of the vinculum peeled away and opened like a steel flower in bloom, revealing the great hollow core of the Borg Queen's domain. Her catoms burning brightly with the light of the Caeliar, Hernandez soared into the great emptiness above.

Open your eyes, she told her new brothers and sisters in the gestalt. *See the future. It's here. Its time has come.*

Jean-Luc Picard had never broken down like this. Not when Robert and René had died, not when he'd gone home after being liberated from the Borg for the first time, not when Gul Madred had nearly shattered him beyond recovery.

He collapsed onto his knees, unable to stand against the storm of emotions that raged against him. All thoughts of pride were forgotten now. He had no sense of the other people on the bridge of the *Enterprise*. In the final moments before he had been felled by the psionic barrage, Riker and Worf had moved to his sides to shield him from the crew's sight.

It doesn't matter, he realized, submerging into the ocean of his hopelessness. *The center didn't hold. It's all falling apart. There's nothing we can do.*

Doubts and fears dragged him deeper into his own bottomless despair. How could he ever have hoped to fight the Borg? He was only one man, mortal and weak, and the Borg were a force of nature. He'd failed to challenge them in System J-25, when he first encountered them. He'd underestimated them a second time and had ended up facilitating the slaughter of his own people at Wolf 359. If not for Data, he'd have been beaten by the Borg Queen. Arrogant enough to think he could fool them long enough to infiltrate one of their ships, he had tried to impersonate Locutus, only to succumb to assimilation *again*.

I'm a failure, he berated himself. *I might have lived out my life in peace, but I had to tempt fate by starting a family. I've doomed us all.*

Heavy sobs wracked his chest. He cried into his palms until his ribs hurt and his eyes burned and mucus filled his sinuses.

And across the galaxy, a trillion drones wept with Locutus.

A quarter-billion voices were screaming at Deanna Troi.

She pitched forward to the deck of *Titan*'s bridge, and Christine Vale was at her side in an instant. "What's wrong, Deanna?" Vale asked. Troi wanted to reply, but she could barely breathe through the avalanche of wild emotion smothering her.

Vale snapped out orders. "Tuvok, she needs you! Rager, we need a medic. Keru, tell Ree to check on all psi-sensitive personnel immediately."

The world around Troi seemed to fade behind a wall of anguished keening and wordless, angry roars of noise. It was all coming from the Borg, but they had none of the focused malice or icy detachment that had marked their previous encounters with the Federation. There was only tragic lamentation and sullen fury, emotional aftershocks of a shattered culture of slavery.

Then a comforting thought broke through the bedlam, and Troi became aware of warm fingertips against her temple and cheek. *My mind to your mind,* Tuvok projected, easily surmounting her crumbled psychic barriers. *My strength becomes your strength. My calm becomes your calm. Our thoughts are fusing. Our memories are merging. We are united. We are one.*

She opened her eyes and saw *Titan*'s bridge clearly. Everyone, it seemed, was watching her and Tuvok, who hovered on the edge of her vision, though he was foremost in her thoughts. Troi still sensed the mental turbulence of the millions of distressed souls in the Borg armada who were crying out for help, but the mind-meld with Tuvok had given her the strength to restore her telepathic barriers and recover her composure. She saw in Tuvok's mind that the meld had proved fortuitous for him as well; his own control also had faltered from the shock.

Inside the meld, he asked, *Are you all right, Counselor?*

Yes, Tuvok. Thank you.

The crew's attention was pulled away from Troi and Tuvok as Keru pointed at the main viewer and shouted, "Look!"

On the center screen, the Caeliar metropolis of Axion began to shine with an unearthly glow. It grew brighter in a rapid flash, like a star building up to a supernova, yet Troi found something about its penetrating white radiance comforting.

What she saw next was more than just a turning point in history. It was the end of an era and the dawn of another.

It was a moment too incredible to be coincidence.

It was a moment of destiny.

A trillion pairs of eyes bore witness.

It was a vision, a phantasm sprung fully formed from the void, a revelation of what had been and what was to come. The former Queen was no more, laid low, made common, deposed. In her place had risen a hue and cry of inconsolable sorrow.

A billion mothers awoke from the Collective's iron bondage to find their children riven from them. Billions of children opened their eyes to find their parents gone forever, along with worlds they could barely remember. Spouses, lovers, friends, and comrades sought one another through the gestalt and found few of their numbers still living. Billions of souls were alone.

There were no rich or poor. No one was famous, powerful, or privileged. There were simply those who had awakened. Liberated from the cold grip of the machine, they searched for the keys to their lost identities. Then they found them, and the gestalt sang with a trillion names reclaimed from the fog, revealed by the blaze of light piercing the gloom.

Every mind touched by the gestalt looked to the source.

Where once a dark tyrant had reigned, a bright and dazzling queen now rose like the dawn, bringing illumination and comfort. Unfettered by the bonds of gravity, she soared freely, bursting with light, a splendor among shadows, exorcising six thousand years of night in a single moment of ineffable beauty.

The harsh chord of the Collective yielded to the harmony of the gestalt. Then there was no more pain, no more rancor, and no more sorrow, for those things had passed away, leaving only the possibilities of the present and the promises of the future.

A living death was conquered, and for a trillion souls who had dwelled in night, it would never again hold dominion.

We are the Caeliar.

Riker kneeled beside Captain Picard and kept one hand on his friend's back and the other in a firm but gentle grip on his arm. Captain Dax was on the other side of the *Enterprise*'s captain, in a pose that mirrored Riker's. It was Riker's suspicion that Dax was just as uncertain as he was about how to react to Captain Picard's inconsolable emotional collapse.

Picard was on all fours, doubled over, face almost touching the carpeting of the bridge, hyperventilating and sobbing. Then he stopped with a sharp intake of air, and he clawed at the deck for several seconds before bunching his hands into fists under his chin. His body quaked as if he'd just come in from the cold.

As desperately as Riker wanted to defend Picard's pride by concealing this display from the rest of the bridge crew, he knew that it would be even more damaging for them to see their captain carried off the bridge. In any event, this wasn't Riker's ship, and it wasn't his call to make, it was Worf's. Until the XO said otherwise, Picard would remain where he was.

Choudhury looked up from the tactical console and pointed at the main viewer as she shouted, "Something's happening!"

Axion had flared like a supernova, flooding the screen with light and all but bleaching the solid spherical formation of Borg hulls of their details. Then the armada of Borg ships—every cube, probe, and sphere—cracked open and bled light. Intense white radiance poured from every fractured vessel. In a flash, the *Enterprise* went from being huddled in a pit of starless metal darkness to dwelling in a heart of pure light.

As Riker, Dax, and the bridge crew watched, the multitude of imposing black ships imploded. Vast sections of every ship were sucked inward, and delicate spines of brilliant, gleaming metal jutted out from their cores, reaching in every direction. Within seconds, the Borg vessels had all become incandescent spheres surrounded by dense formations of long spikes. Squinting against the ships' blinding glare, Riker mused that they looked like massive sea urchins cast from flawless silver.

Picard's breathing steadied, and he looked up through tearstained eyes, first at Dax and then at Riker. In a knowing whisper, he said, "Everything's changed."

Then he turned his gaze to the image on the main screen. He stared in wonder, taking it all in . . . and then, ever so slowly and by infinitely cautious degrees, Picard cracked a smile.

"Everything's changed," he repeated.

And then he laughed. Not like someone amused by a joke or given over to the mirth of madness; he let out the triumphant, joyous gales of a man tasting freedom after living in chains.

Riker threw an amused, wary look at Dax.

She shrugged. "As long as he's happy," she said.

Of the fifty million Caeliar bonded through the gestalt, only Inyx was willing to do the unthinkable. He dissolved the last of Sedín's corrupted essence, condemning the last of her residual charge into the gestalt at large and returning her, in a poetic and somewhat entropic fashion, to the home she had unknowingly sought for six millennia, with trillions of innocent beings yoked to her unconscious purpose.

It is finished, Inyx declared, overcome with shame

for his deed, sorrow for his friend, and relief for the end of her pain.

The gestalt empathically echoed his agonies, and from Ordemo Nordal, he felt the blessing of absolution. *There was no other way,* Ordemo said. *It was too late to save her.*

Then it was time to open themselves to the sentient minds they had set free, which they welcomed into the gestalt. It was a decision motivated partly by mercy; after all that Sedín's victims had endured, in light of all they had lost, the Quorum concurred that the gestalt had an obligation to alleviate their suffering and offer them a safe haven, a new beginning.

A more honest accounting of the situation demanded that the Caeliar admit the truth, however: They needed the emancipated drones as much as the drones needed them.

Hernandez had persuaded the gestalt to aid her by appealing to its own sense of self-interest. Standing before them only a short time earlier, she had argued her point with passion.

"Your obsession with privacy is killing you," she'd said. "You made these catom bodies of yours, and you figured you'd live forever in your invulnerable cities, in your invisible planet. You never thought about what would happen if you had to procreate. It never occurred to you that your whole world could get shot out from under you and take ninety-eight percent of your people with it. Well, it did. And the law of averges says this won't be the last time something bad happens to you.

"How many more losses can you take and still be a civilization? What if another accident happens? Or a new, stronger enemy finds you? The Cataclysm nearly *exterminated* you. Haven't you ever stopped to consider that all your efforts on the Great Work will be lost if you die out?

"If you want to explore the universe, you'll need strength, and the best place to find that is in numbers. I don't know if there's any way for you to get back the ability to reproduce, but it's not too late for you to learn how to share. You need to bring non-Caeliar into the gestalt. You need to teach others about the Great Work—before it's too late."

Her proclamation had provoked a schism in the Quorum and sent shockwaves of indignation through the gestalt. The debate had been swift and bitter, but in the end, it had fallen to Ordemo Nordal to persuade the majority that Hernandez was right. It was time to expand the gestalt or accept that it was doomed only to diminish from this moment forward. The Quorum and the gestalt had to choose between evolution and extinction.

In the end, it proved not so difficult a choice, after all.

As the gestalt embraced the freed and bewildered drones in its protection, Inyx appreciated at last how right Hernandez had been. The Caeliar had granted to the Borg all it had sought for millennia: nearly unlimited power, a step closer to perfection, and the secrets of Particle 010. In return, the legions of drones who flocked into the warm sanctuary of the gestalt had given the Caeliar what they had most desperately needed: strength, adaptability, and diversity. In one grand gesture, the Caeliar had become a polyglot society with an immense capacity for incorporating new ideas, new technologies, and new species.

For the Borg, it was the end of aeons of futile searching.

For the Caeliar, it was the end of an age of stagnation.

The lost children had come home. The gestalt felt whole.

Now the Great Work can continue, Inyx announced, initiating the newest members of Caeliar society to its ongoing mission. *More important,* he added, *now the Great Work can evolve.*

Jean-Luc Picard was on his feet again. He felt taller than he had in ages. So many emotions were whirling in his mind that he couldn't name them all. Relief and joy were at the forefront of his thoughts, with wonder and gratitude close behind.

The aft turbolift door opened, and Beverly stepped out. She hurried straight to his side. "Worf called me," she said.

She reached up, as if to touch his arm in a gesture of polite and dignified comfort.

Too full of life to settle for that, he embraced her, pulled her close, and pressed his face into the tender space between her neck and shoulder. He reveled in the sweet scent of her hair, the pliant warmth of her body, the gift of her every breath, the miracle of their child—their *son*—growing within her.

At first, she seemed caught by surprise, and he understood why. Picard had never been one for public displays of affection, especially not in front of his crew. He no longer cared about that. She was his love, the one he had waited for, the one he had almost let slip away because he had been too timid to follow his heart, too cautious to indulge in hope.

He was done being careful. More than fifty years earlier, it had taken a Nausicaan's blade through his heart to teach him that lesson the first time. It had taken a trip to the edge of annihilation to remind him that life was not only far too short, but also far too beautiful and far too precious to enjoy alone.

"I'm all right, Beverly," he whispered. "We all are." He pulled back just far enough to kiss her forehead and then her vibrant red lips. Parting from her, he looked around the bridge and saw a dozen faces bright with mildly embarrassed smiles. He brightened his countenance to match and said, "Carry on."

Riker and Dax stepped forward to pat his shoulders. Just as Riker was about to say something, he was interrupted by Lieutenant Choudhury. "Captain," she said to Picard. "Incoming hail, sir. It's Captain Hernandez."

"On-screen," Picard said, stepping forward behind the center of the conjoined conn and operations consoles.

Erika Hernandez's girlish features and enormous, unruly mane of sable hair appeared on the main viewer. *"Will, Ezri, Jean-Luc, I just wanted to speak to you one last time before we go, to tell you that I'm okay—and to say good-bye."*

"Before 'we' go?" Picard said, echoing her. "You mean you and the Caeliar?"

A sly grin tugged at Hernandez's mouth. *"You don't need to speak of us as separate entities anymore,"* she said. *"I am one of the Caeliar now. In fact, I have been for a long time; I just hadn't been able to really accept it until now."*

Riker stepped forward on Picard's left and asked, "Erika, what's happened to the Borg?"

"There are no more Borg," Hernandez said. *"Not here, or in the Delta Quadrant, or anywhere else, for that matter. There are only Caeliar."* Her wan smirk became a broad smile. *"And if you'll excuse us, we have a new mission to begin."*

Dax edged forward and said, "What mission?"

"To find and protect cultures of peace and nonviolence—so that perhaps someday in the distant future, the meek really can *inherit the universe."*

"Good luck," Riker said.

"You, too," Hernandez said, and then the signal ended.

The screen switched back to the view of magnificently glowing, urchin-like Caeliar vessels huddled around the miniature star of Axion. Then, though Picard wouldn't have thought it possible, all of the ships and the Caeliar metropolis flared even more brightly, scrambling the main viewer image into a distorted crackle of white noise. Less than a second later, the light had vanished—and so had Axion and its brilliant new armada.

On the screen, tiny and alone in the cold majesty of the cosmos, were *Titan* and the *Aventine*. The rest was silence.

Worf relaxed his shoulders a bit and said to Choudhury, "Cancel Red Alert."

Whoops of jubilation erupted from the other officers around the bridge. Picard and Riker clasped each other's forearm and slapped each other's shoulders. "We did it," Riker said.

"No," Picard said. "Erika did it. We just lived

through it." He smiled. "And that's good enough for me."

He and Riker let each other go, and Riker turned to help Dax coax Worf into joining the celebration. Picard fell back into Crusher's arms and treasured the moment. There was a lightness in his spirit, an exuberance and an optimism he hadn't felt since the earliest days of his command of the *Enterprise*-D.

It took him a moment to put a name to this sublime feeling.

I'm free, he realized. *I'm free.*

Admirals Akaar and Batanides were pressed against the situation monitors in the Monet Room and surrounded by a clutch of junior officers, all of whom were scrambling to confirm the latest reports from the *Enterprise, Titan,* and the *Aventine.*

If the subspace messages from the three starships were true, it would be nothing less than a miracle. It would be one of the most stunning reversals in the history of the Federation.

President Bacco knew she ought to be waiting on the admirals' report with undivided attention, but she was focused on a different spectacle. She and the other civilians in the room had gathered in a tight huddle in front of the painting *Bridge over a Pool of Water Lilies.*

Tucked in a fetal curl on the floor beneath the painting was Seven of Nine.

The statuesque blonde was normally so intimidating—Jas Abrik had described her with the less forgiving adjective "castrating"—that it shocked Bacco to see her like this.

Only minutes earlier, Seven had been conferring with the admirals and analyzing the reaction of the Borg armada to its sudden dislocation across vast reaches of space. Then, before anyone had realized anything was wrong, Seven had staggered away from the situation consoles, dazed and trembling. Seconds later, she had collapsed to the floor and folded in on herself.

Most of the people in the room had reacted by backing away from Seven, as if she might be transforming back into a drone bent on assimilating or assassinating them all.

Bacco had dashed from her chair toward the fallen woman, only to be forcibly intercepted by her senior protection agent.

"Ma'am, you should stay back," Wexler had said.

"Stay close, Steve, but get your hands off me."

Wexler let go of Bacco's arms and backed off. "Sorry, Madam President." She'd continued past him to Seven's side, and he had fallen in right behind her. His presence had seemed to reassure the others, who had slowly regrouped in a clutch around Seven.

Now Seven lay on her left side, with her arms wrapped around her head, unable or unwilling to respond to the gentle queries from Bacco and the others.

Piñiero asked Seven, "Can you hear us?"

No answer.

"I think she's hyperventilating," Abrik said.

Secretary Iliop said, "Maybe she's having a seizure."

Agent Kistler joined the huddle. "A doctor's coming."

Press liaison Kant Jorel asked, "Should we take her pulse?"

Piñiero threw a glare at him. "Are *you* a doctor now?"

Abrik cut in, "I wouldn't touch her if I were you. Last time we checked, those Borg implants of hers still work."

"Oh, for crying out loud," Bacco grumbled. "Move." She reached a hand toward Seven but paused as Akaar called to her.

"Madam President," the gray-haired admiral said, his voice loud and bright with the promise of good news. "The all-clear signals have been verified, and Captain Picard has confirmed that the Borg threat is over."

Piñiero asked with naked cynicism, "For how long?"

"Forever," Akaar said. "Captain Picard reports that the Borg . . . no longer exist."

Wide-eyed, Abrik stammered, "H—how?"

"The captain assures me it is 'a long story,' which he will explain fully in his report."

"He damned well better," Bacco said. "Because that's a story I want to hear." The sound of the secured door opening prompted her to look over her shoulder. One of the Palais's on-call doctors and a pair of medical technicians hurried inside, and Agent Kistler waved them over toward Seven.

"All right, everyone," said Agent Wexler. "Move back, please. Let the medical team through. Thank you."

Even as the others retreated to make room for the medics, Bacco stayed by Seven's side. The stricken woman was whimpering and sobbing into her shirt-sleeves.

The doctor, a young Efrosian man who sported a haircut and a goatee that were trimmed much shorter than was customary in his culture, kneeled beside Bacco. "Madam President, we can take it from here," he said, opening his satchel of surgical tools.

"Just give me a moment," Bacco said. She reached out and placed her hand lightly on Seven's shoulder. Leaning down, she whispered in as soft and soothing a voice as she could muster, "Seven, it's Nan. Are you all right? Can you hear me, Seven?"

Bacco waited, her hand resting with a feather touch on Seven's shoulder. Then she felt a stirring, a hint of motion.

Seven's breathing slowed but remained erratic. In gradual motions, she lowered her arms, pushed herself from the floor, and rolled onto her back. As her face and left hand came into view, Bacco gasped.

The Borg implants were gone. A tiny mass of fine, silvery powder lay on the floor where Seven had rested her head, and a glittering residue clung to her left hand and temple.

"Seven," Bacco said, stunned. "Are you all right?"

With her beauty no longer blemished by the biomechanical scars of the Borg, Seven looked up at Nanietta Bacco with the tear-streaked face of an innocent.

"My name is Annika."

30

Rubble and dust crunched under Martok's boots and cane as he struggled to the summit of a great mound of shattered stone and steel, which only that morning had been the Great Hall.

He ignored the bolts of pain shooting up his broken leg. It had been crudely set and splinted with long, inflexible strips of metal salvaged from a ruptured bulkhead on the *Sword of Kahless*. His flagship's sickbay and all of its medical personnel had been killed during the calamitous battle against the Borg hours earlier. Without any of the advanced surgical tools that could repair his fractured femur, he had been forced to settle for a more old-fashioned treatment of his wound.

At the peak of the smoldering mound of debris, he steadied himself and kept his weight on his good leg. Pivoting in a slow circle, he drank in the devastation around him. The First City was a husk of its former self. Only the scorched, denuded skeletons of a few prominent architectural landmarks were still recognizable. Where once the city's main boulevard, the *wo'leng*, had cut like a scar from the Great Hall to the smooth-flowing waters of the *qIJbIQ*, its second great river, significant portions of the broad thoroughfare had been erased by chaotic smears of smoking wreckage and crashed transport vessels.

Thick clouds of charcoal gray and deep crimson blanketed the sky. A sharp, acrid bite of toxic smoke was heavy in the air, and the profusion of airborne dust left the inside of Martok's mouth dry and tasting of chalk. It reminded him of historical accounts of Qo'noS in the years immediately following the Praxis disaster, which had pushed the Klingon homeworld to the brink of environmental collapse. This was a catastrophe almost on par with that one. Seven major cities on Qo'noS had been destroyed before the Borg cubes had, inexplicably, withdrawn on reciprocal courses, back toward the Azure Nebula.

Councillors Kopek, Qulka, and Tovoj had died with the home guard fleet and a force of their allies defending Qo'noS. Councillors Grevaq, Krozek, and Korvog had died with Martok's fleet. Most of the other members of the High Council were at that moment missing in action, and Martok had no idea which of them would turn up alive or dead.

For the moment, Martok alone was the High Council, and the temptation to wield unitary power was taxing his will; the call of ambition was powerful, and it was all he could do to remind himself that succumbing to it was what had fatally undermined his predecessor, Chancellor Gowron.

I will not make that mistake, he vowed. *I will not be that man. That will not be my legacy.*

He limped across the ruins to stand with General Goluk.

"Do we have casualty reports yet, General?"

"Only preliminary numbers, my lord," Goluk said, poking at the portable computer in his hand.

Martok scowled to mask a sharp jolt of pain from his leg. "Tell me," he rasped.

"Sixteen million dead in the First City. Another seven million in Quin'lat, eleven million in Tolar'tu. Based on rough estimates from Krennla, An'quat, T'chariv, and Novat, we believe their combined death tolls will exceed forty-three million."

A dour grunt concealed Martok's dismay. "So, seventy-seven million worldwide?"

"Yes, my lord. Though, as I said, that's just an estimate."

Nodding, Martok looked away and let his eyes roam across the vista of death and destruction. Despite the solemnity and tragedy of the moment, he permitted himself a sardonic grin.

Goluk asked, "Is something amusing, Chancellor?"

"This is the second time since I became chancellor that the Great Hall's been leveled," Martok said. "I could be wrong, but I think I might be the only chancellor who can make that claim." He stabbed the rubble with his cane, and bitter laughter welled up from his throat. Shaking his head, he continued, "Do you know what irritates me most?" He glanced at Goluk and then looked at the shattered stone under their feet. "I'd finally learned my way around this maze, and now I have to start over again."

Both men laughed, though Martok knew neither of them had any mirth in his heart. Though the Borg had been routed, to call this a victory would at best be an exaggeration.

The day was theirs, but no songs would be sung.

———•———

President Nanietta Bacco closed her eyes and drew a long breath to calm her frazzled nerves and steady her shaking hands. She waited until the pounding of her heart slowed by even the slightest degree, and she nodded to her press liaison, Kant Jorel, and her chief of staff, Esperanza Piñiero. "I'm ready."

Piñiero said to Agents Wexler and Kistler, "Let's go."

The two presidential bodyguards stepped forward and were the first ones through the door at the end of the hallway. A deep susurrus of echoing conversations filled the air. Bacco walked with her shoulders back and her chin up, leading her entourage into the main chamber of the Federation Council, which occupied the entire first floor of the Palais de la Concorde.

Her eyes adjusted to the dimmer lighting in the chamber and to the glare of the spotlight pointed at the lectern on the podium along the south wall. Every seat in every row on both the east and west sides of the chamber was filled, including those in the supplemental rows. The visitors' gallery was packed to capacity, and a row of security personnel held back a standing-room-only crowd of Palais staff and VIP guests along the north side of the speakers' floor.

Bacco wondered if the intensity of interest demonstrated by the staff, diplomats, councillors, and guests was any indicator of the public's interest in the address she had come to deliver. *I guess I'm about to find out,* she decided.

She moved to the lectern at the front of the podium and waited while the Council's leaders called for quiet. A constellation of small red lights snapped on in the shadows on the opposite side of the room, informing her that live subspace feeds of her address were being transmitted throughout known space.

From her right, Piñiero gave her the ready signal.

Speaking to the half-shadowed faces in the gallery and the focused stares of the councillors, Bacco intoned in her most stately voice, "Members of the Federation Council, foreign ambassadors, honored guests, and citizens of the Federation . . . this day has been a long time in coming."

As the glowing text of her speech crawled up a holographic prompter situated just off-center in front of the lectern, Bacco continued almost from memory, delivering the first address in decades that she'd composed without the aid of her chief speechwriter, Fred MacDougan, and his staff, who were all still light-years away from Earth, caught up in postevacuation chaos.

"It is my pleasure and my honor to be able to bring you good news," she said. "The Borg threat is over.

"The officers and enlisted crews of three starships have done what so much of our marshaled might could not. A joint effort by the *Starships Enterprise, Titan,* and *Aventine* has turned the tide this day, bringing an end not just to the Borg invasion of our space but to the tyranny and oppression of the Borg throughout the galaxy."

Spontaneous, powerful applause and cheering erupted from the gallery and the councillors' tiers. Bacco basked in the roar of approval for a few seconds, and then she motioned for silence. Gradually, the room settled, and she continued.

"In keeping with the finest traditions of Starfleet, these three crews accomplished this not through violence, not through some brute force of arms, but with compassion. This war has been brought to an end not by bloodshed but by an act of mercy.

"They took a chance on the better angels of their natures, reached out to a new ally, and transformed the Borg Collective into something benign, perhaps even noble. I am informed that across the Milky Way, trillions of drones have been liberated, their free will restored."

As quickly as she had earned the room's praise, now she felt its condemnation. Bitter whispers traveled among the councillors, and disapproving noises hissed in the gallery.

"This outcome might feel inadequate to those among us who want revenge on the Borg. I understand, I assure you. There is no minimizing the scope of the tragedy we have endured. According to even our most conservative estimates, more than sixty-three billion citizens of the Federation, the Klingon Empire, the Romulan Star Empire, and the Imperial Romulan State were slaughtered by the Borg during this invasion."

She paused to compose herself, and she swallowed to relieve the dryness in her mouth and throat. "Sixty-three billion lives cut short," she said. "The mind boggles at the scope of it. Such a horrific crime against life seems to demand payback, in the form of a proportional response. But we must move beyond hatred and vengeance. The Borg Collective no longer exists, and we must remember that those who carried out its atrocities were victims themselves, slaves taken from their own worlds and their own families. Now the force that controlled them has been disbanded, and its emancipated drones have vanished to points unknown. There is, quite simply, no one left to blame."

A deep and thoughtful silence hung over the chamber, and Bacco took it as a positive sign as she pressed on.

"Let us instead remember those whose actions have earned our trust and our gratitude. Our staunch allies, the Klingons, stood with us in our hour of need and inspired us with their fearlessness. We witnessed great acts of gallant bravery and sacrifice by starship crews from the Imperial Romulan State and the Talarian Republic. The *Warbird Verithrax* sacrificed itself in the defense of Ardana, and the Talarian third fleet was all but destroyed holding the line at Aldebaran, halting the Borg's advance in that sector. These heroic gestures must never be forgotten." Murmurs of concurrence filled the room.

Bacco found it difficult to read the next portion of her address, but she had no choice. The truth had to be faced.

"It is unfortunate," she continued, "that at a time when we should be rejoicing in our victory, we must mourn losses so tragic. It's natural, at a time such as this, for us to think of ourselves. We had not yet completely recovered from the Dominion War, and now dozens of worlds—including Deneva, Coridan, Risa, Regulus, Korvat, and Ramatis—lay in ruins. Dozens more, including Qo'noS, Vulcan, Andor, and Tellar, suffered devastating attacks. And we must remember that the Borg did not discriminate between us and our unaligned neighbors. They inflicted widespread damage on Nausicaa, Yridia, and Barolia. It is all but impossible to quantify the true scope of this calamity, to calculate the unestimated sum of sentient pain.

"In the aftermath of such a monumental catastrophe, the prospect of rebuilding appears daunting. Some might say it's impossible to recover from such a disaster. I say it is not only possible, it is *essential*. We will rise anew. We will rebuild these worlds, and we will heal these wounds. We will reach out not only to our own wounded people but to those of our allies and our neighbors and even to those who have called themselves our rivals and our enemies."

Polite applause interrupted her, and she accepted it with a humble nod of thanks and acknowledgment. Then she lifted her voice and declared, "We will not shrink from the challenge of raising back up what the Borg have knocked down. We will honor the sacrifices of all those who fought and died to defend us, by committing ourselves to repairing the damage that's been done and creating a future that they would have been proud of.

"We will also rebuild Starfleet, to guarantee that all we have gained, with so much suffering and sacrifice, shall be preserved and defended."

This time, the clapping and cheering from the gallery were thunderous. Emboldened, she spoke more strongly, punching her words through the clamor.

"More important, though Starfleet is needed for recovery and reconstruction and to render aid, we will renew our commitment to its mission of peaceful exploration, diplomatic outreach, and open scientific inquiry. The *Luna*-class starships will continue—and, in *Titan*'s case, resume—their missions far beyond our borders: seeking out new worlds, new civilizations, and new life-forms and offering, to those that are ready, our hand in friendship.

"There are those who might doubt our ability to do all of these things at once. To them, I would say, don't underestimate the United Federation of Planets. Just because we have suffered the brunt of the injuries in this conflict, do not assume that we are weak or vulnerable. Don't mistake optimism for foolishness or compassion for weakness.

"With patience and courage, this can become a time of hope. As long as we remain united, we will emerge from these dark and hideous days into a brighter tomorrow, and we will do so stronger, wiser, and safer than we were before. Together, we can become the future that we seek and build the galaxy we want to live in. It will not come about quickly or easily. But until it does, never flinch, never weary, and never despair.

"Thank you, and good night."

Bacco stepped back from the lectern as the chamber shook with deafening applause. Shading her eyes with one hand, she saw that the councillors and the visitors in the gallery all were standing as they delivered their roaring ovation. She waved to both tiers of councillors, then to the far end of the room, before Piñiero and Wexler coaxed her to leave the podium and follow them out of the Council Chamber.

Her entourage, including security adviser Jas Abrik, fell into step around her as they moved to the exit and quick-stepped into the hallway beyond.

Only once they were through the door did Bacco realize that the corridor was now lined with members of the press. Questions were shouted at her from both sides, the words overlapping into a muddy wash of sound. Jorel and Piñiero repeatedly hollered back, "No comment! No questions, please!"

At the far end of the hallway, Wexler and Kistler ushered Bacco and her senior advisers into a secure turbolift, then stepped in after them, placing themselves directly in front of the doors as they closed, muffling and then erasing the hubbub of pestering press run amok.

Bacco sighed heavily. "Thank God that's over."

Kant Jorel replied, "It went well, Madam President."

"Yes, Jorel, I know. I was there."

Rebuked, he bowed his chin. "Yes, ma'am."

"It was a wonderful speech, ma'am," Piñiero said.

"It was all right," Bacco replied. "If Fred and his people had been here to polish it, it would've been great." She threw a pointed look at Abrik. "Whose idea was it to put them *all* on the transport to Tyberius? Was it Iliop? I'll throttle him."

He replied, "No idea, ma'am, but I thought the Churchill homage at the end was a nice touch."

"Absolutely," Piñiero agreed. "It's what people needed to hear."

Frowning, Bacco replied, "It's what *I* needed to hear." The pressure of the past month, far from being lifted, only seemed to weigh heavier on her shoulders. "The Borg are gone, but now everything else is up for grabs."

Abrik tilted his head sideways. "There's certainly the potential for a period of instability."

She looked at the middle-aged Trill as if all his spots had just fallen off. "Instability? When there's a water shortage on Draylax, that's cause for instability. We've got a dead zone for a hundred light-years in every direction around the Azure Nebula. More than forty percent of Starfleet's been *destroyed*. Sixty-three billion people are *dead*. Deneva's been wiped out, and our economy's about to implode. We're long past unstable. When the shock of all this wears off, I think we'll look back on the last sixteen years with longing and envy."

The turbolift doors opened onto the top floor, and the group stepped from the lift into the lobby outside Bacco's office. Wexler and Kistler entered the presidential office first. They stepped clear of the doorway to let Bacco, Abrik, Jorel, and Piñiero file in, and then the two agents faded into the woodwork, as always.

Bacco stepped behind her desk and looked out the panoramic window at the nighttime cityscape of Paris. She was filled with a sense of foreboding, a feeling that there was always some new evil lurking in the darkness. "It's a whole new ball game," she said. "But we have no idea who's playing—or what the rules are."

Piñiero grinned and replied with a shrug, "That's what keeps the job interesting, ma'am."

EPILOGUE

———◆———

Mourners moved in slow packs, their steps leaving crisp prints in the fine-ground regolith of pulverized stone and flesh. Tuvok noticed that the graphite-colored powder stuck to everything—his boots, his pants, his wife's shoes, the hem of her jacket, the tips of her close-cropped hair.

He had seen Deneva's lush Summer Islands years earlier, when they had boasted pristine white beaches, dazzling cities, and a thriving culture of visual arts and live music. It had been a vibrant, stimulating, and prosperous place.

When his youngest son, Elieth, had told him and T'Pel of his intention to take up residence there, it had seemed an unlikely locale for such a serious young Vulcan man. Then, after Elieth had moved, he had revealed his ulterior motive: He had gone to Deneva to persuade Ione Kitain, a daughter of the Fourth House of Betazed, to become his bride. At the time, T'Pel had decried Elieth's actions as "illogical." Tuvok suspected that his wife had used the term as a euphemism for "disappointing."

Elieth and Ione had wed while Tuvok was presumed

lost with the rest of *Voyager*'s crew, and over the next few years, T'Pel had learned to accept her new, non-Vulcan daughter-in-law. Ione's sophisticated telepathic skills had helped matters along, but what had finally earned T'Pel's respect and acceptance was the great contentment and peace of mind Ione seemed to bring to Elieth, whose logic had long felt troubled during his youth.

Squatting low to the ground, Tuvok scooped up a palmful of gray-brown dust, which had the consistency of greasy flour. It clung to his skin even as he tried to clap it off.

T'Pel looked away, past the distant clusters of roving kith and kin to the dead. "Why did we come here, husband? Starfleet told us nothing survived in the Summer Islands and that there would be no remains or relics to recover."

"I wished to see this for myself," he said, rubbing his hands clean on the front of his trousers. He stood straight. In every direction, the Summer Islands lay like flat smears barely raised from the ocean, which now was stained brown and black.

Mastering the turmoil of his thoughts had become taxing for Tuvok. Despite the psionic therapy he had done with Counselor Troi to fortify his psychic control and telepathic defenses, which had been compromised by years of neurological trauma, he felt overwhelmed. Primitive emotions threatened to crack his dispassionate veneer. Rage and grief, despair and denial—they were black clouds blotting out the light of reason.

Resolved not to embarrass himself or T'Pel or to disgrace the memory of his slain youngest son, Tuvok stood firm against the darkest tides of his *katra,* even as he feared drowning in them, submerging into madness and never surfacing again.

"We should return to *Titan* now," T'Pel said.

"No," Tuvok said. "I am not ready yet."

T'Pel was confounded by his reply. "There is nothing else for us to find or do here. Staying longer serves no purpose."

"I do not wish to explain myself, T'Pel. I will remain here while I reflect on what has happened. I would prefer that you stay with me, but if you wish to depart, I will not stop you."

In pairs and trios or in small groups, people both young and old, male and female, and pilgrims of all species milled in stunned shock across the level stretch of total desolation. Tuvok watched them all seek in vain for something that was no longer to be found, for tangible artifacts of loved ones now gone.

An empty hush of wind off the sea roared in Tuvok's ears, and the breeze kicked up clouds of foul-smelling, choking dust.

When it died down and the heavy cloud started to settle, T'Pel said, "If you are pondering the details of our son's death, I would urge you to consider that most likely, it was swift and entailed only fleeting pain."

"The specifics of his demise are not important," Tuvok said. "I question his decision not to escape with Ione when it might still have been possible."

"Elieth was committed to law enforcement and to the service of others," T'Pel said, as if she were telling Tuvok something that he didn't already know. "If he and Ione stayed behind after the final transports left, he must have thought their choice to be the one that was most logical."

Tuvok's sea of troubled emotions swelled and threatened to swallow him whole. He grappled with a surge of irrational fury provoked by T'Pel's remark. His fists clenched white-knuckle tight, and his face hardened with bitter anger.

"I can see no logic in this, T'Pel. My son is dead."

Dark clouds were pulled taut across the leaden skies of Deneva. The ash-covered peaks of the Sibiran Range were obscured by tin-dull mists, and a diffuse light cast a dim gray pall over the desolate hills and plains that spread south from the mountains.

Worf tried not to inhale too deeply. The entire planet had a dusty, smoky odor, like a lingering tang of burnt hair. During his approach from orbit, via shuttle with Jasminder Choudhury, he had seen no traces of green on the planet's surface. Until they had pierced the bottom of the cloud cover, in fact, they had barely seen the surface at all. All but the most extreme polar latitudes of Deneva were encircled by rings of ash, dust, and smoke—the airborne residue of its vaporized cities.

He stood on the scorched plain and watched myr iad shuttles and small ships descend from the death polluted sky and seek out remote places to set down Hundreds of thousands of people had come to Deneva in the past few days, since the travel interdiction had been lifted. The Federation had quarantined it surface until Starfleet had verified that visitors and returning denizens would face no lingering threats either from the Borg or from radiation and other toxins. According to a message he had received that morning from his son, Alexander, conditions were much the same on Qo'noS and many worlds of the Klingon Empire.

A few meters away from him, Jasminder kneeled and scanned a patch of soil with her tricorder. She switched off the device. "Close enough," she said, standing up as a gust of warm air pelted them both with sand.

Worf squinted against the stinging breeze. "Are you sure?"

"The whole planet's a cinder," she said. "One patch of dirt will serve as well as another. We should get started."

They walked together to the back of their borrowed shuttle from the *Enterprise* and opened its rear hatch. Most of the passenger compartment had been filled with tools, supplies, and their one piece of precious cargo. Jasminder grabbed two shovels and handed one to Worf. "Thank you for coming with me."

"I am honored . . . and moved . . . that you invited me."

She favored him with a small, bittersweet smile, and then they stepped out of the shuttle and returned to the spot she'd selected. This, she'd told him during the flight down, was where her family home had stood, before the Borg had erased it from existence. They circled the spot she'd marked until they stood on either side of it, facing each other.

"Ready?" she asked.

"Yes."

Shovel tips were pressed into the dry, blackened

soil and driven deep with pushes from their heels. The parched skin of the planet cracked and broke as Worf and Jasminder pulled on the shovels' handles. The two officers lifted thick clumps of dirt and heaved them to one side. They dug at the hard ground for a few minutes, until they had excavated a pit three-quarters of a meter deep and half a meter wide.

Setting aside the shovels, they returned to the shuttle and retrieved more supplies. Jasminder brought a large, clumsy-heavy pouch of chemicals, and Worf hefted a small drum of water onto his shoulder. They methodically emptied both into the hole.

Worf waited behind while she returned to the shuttle for the last and most crucial element.

She returned carrying in one hand a diminutive twig—Worf thought it hardly deserved to be called even a sapling, let alone a tree. He waited while she lowered it into the soaked and fertilized hole they'd prepared, and he held it upright and steady while she shoveled the dirt back in around its linen-wrapped roots. She tamped down the dirt with her boots, and then she piled more on top, until at last she had crafted a gently sloping round island around the skinny oak's wrist-thick trunk.

By the time Jasminder had finished, tears were flowing from her eyes, but she herself was quiet. She took a few backward steps, setting herself at a remove to survey her handiwork.

Worf stood beside her and said nothing. Across the blood-hallowed ground, the wind whispered its benedictions.

Jasminder wiped the tears from her face with the

back of her hand, without once taking her eyes off the tree.

"It's so . . ." Grief robbed her of words. He reached out and rested his arm across her shoulders. She huddled beside him, under his embrace, and then she started over. "It's so *tiny.*"

With a firm yet gentle clasp of her shoulder, he pulled her close and said, "It is a beginning."

Xin Ra-Havreii stood at the forefront of a throng gathered at the broad, starboard-facing windows in *Titan*'s arboretum. Much of the ship's crew had departed two weeks earlier for extended shore leave; after it had limped home to the Utopia Planitia yards above Mars for repairs and upgrades—all to be made under Ra-Havreii's expert supervision.

The Efrosian chief engineer stroked one long droop of his ivory-white mustache and speculated that his absent shipmates would regret not having been aboard to see that day's event with their own eyes.

Sometimes videos do history no justice, he mused.

A majority of the personnel who had packed into the high-ceilinged compartment to take advantage of its unobstructed view were not regular *Titan* personnel but technicians, mechanics, and engineers assigned to the Utopia Planitia facility. Among them, Ra-Havreii recognized many former friends and colleagues of his, from his days working there as a project director and starship designer. He hadn't spoken to many of them since the accident years earlier aboard the *Luna,* and he felt no desire to do so now. For their part, they seemed content to ignore him as well.

A whiff of delicate perfume stood out from the scents of flowers and green plants, and it turned Ra-Havreii's head. Standing behind his left shoulder was Lieutenant Commander Melora Pazlar, once more outfitted in her powered armature. Ra-Havreii smiled at her. "Good morning, Melora," he said.

"Good morning, Xin. Room for one more up front?"

The young Catullan man standing on Ra-Havreii's left glanced at Pazlar and then at the chief engineer, who furrowed his snowy brows and growled, "Make a hole, Crewman."

"Aye, sir," said the Catullan, as he nudged the rest of the line down a few steps to free up room for Pazlar.

She inched forward and pressed in close beside Ra-Havreii. "Thanks, Xin."

"My pleasure," he said. Looking around at the crush of spectators, he added, "I thought you hated crowds."

"I do," she said. "But I hate missing out even more."

Over the soft murmuring of the crowd, someone at the aft end of the compartment shouted, "Here they come!" Everyone leaned toward the windows and craned their necks, straining to see past everyone else, to bear witness to history.

Pazlar and Ra-Havreii shifted their weight and stood at matching angles while staring out at the stars, awaiting the main attraction. Facing aft, the blond Elaysian woman had her back to Ra-Havreii, who savored the fragrance of her hair.

"It's too bad they had to shut down my holopresence network while making repairs," she said over her shoulder, making eye contact as she noticed how close their faces were.

He nodded. "Yes, it's a shame. But the interruption is only temporary. Oh! Did I tell you about the new asymmetric interaction mode I created for it?"

"No, I don't think you did."

"You're going to love it," he said with unabashed pride in his work. "It lets your holographic avatar inflict amplified physical damage on real opponents while preventing any harmful effects from being transmitted back to you. It could prove very useful if *Titan* ever gets boarded again."

She smiled at him. "I have a theory about the holopresence system, you know."

"Really?" His eyebrows climbed up his forehead. "Do tell."

"I think it's proof you're in love with me."

Affecting a nonchalant air, he replied, "Ridiculous." Noting the amused glimmer in her gaze, he added with some hesitation, "I mean . . . love is, um, such a strong word, and we hardly—that is, we . . ."

"Simmer down, Commander," Pazlar said. "It's not the least appealing idea I've heard lately. And some of your past conquests have assured me that you know how to be gentle." Another teasing grin. "Which is important for a gal like me."

"Well, obviously," he said. Tamping down his surging excitement, he decided to handle the matter with delicacy. "I find your invitation almost irresistible," he began.

She sounded insulted. "Almost?"

"Nigh irresistible," he corrected himself. "But before I surrender to my passions—and yours—it's absolutely vital that I be completely honest with you."

"About what?"

"Well, about me," he said. "I am deeply attracted to you, Melora, and in ways that I haven't felt about someone in a long time. But I'm afraid it's simply not in my nature to be, well, *monogamous*."

She snickered, and then she laughed. "Who's asking?" Shaking her head, she turned aft and added softly, "Let's just see how our first date goes, okay?"

The more he learned about her, the more he adored her.

"Okay," he said. "Sounds like a plan."

Shining brighter than the stars, a white point grew larger as it neared the Utopia Planitia orbital shipyard. Edges resolved into forms and then into two distinct shapes linked by a glowing beam. At the forefront, a *Sabre*-class starship. Towed behind it, and held together by who knew what kind of high-tech legerdemain, was a twenty-second-century *NX*-class starship, its hull and nacelles scarred but still together.

An announcement over the intraship comm echoed from the overhead speakers. *"Attention, all* Titan *personnel,"* said Commander Vale. *"Muster starboard for passing honors."*

Outside, the *Sabre*-class vessel adjusted its course to glide past overhead, giving Ra-Havreii and the other spectators a perfect view of the registry on the ventral side of its primary hull: *U.S.S. da Vinci* NCC 81623. With precision and grace, its tractor beam guided its ward, the *Columbia* NX-02, past *Titan* to safety inside a docking slip.

Ra-Havreii didn't feel foolish or embarrassed to

have tears brimming in his eyes while he watched the *Columbia*'s long-overdue homecoming, because everyone else in the arboretum did, too. With a solemn nod of salute to the old vessel, he whispered, "Welcome home, old girl."

The personal transport pod had barely settled to the ground near Vicenzo Farrenga's home in Lakeside on Cestus III when his five-year-old daughter, Aoki, was out the pod's side hatch and sprinting for the front door of their house.

He called after her, "Sweetie, wait for Daddy!"

The sable-haired little girl stopped on the snaking path of organically shaped paving stones that led away from the landing area. Vicenzo and his cousin, Frederico—more commonly known as Fred—pulled themselves out of the vehicle with the stiffness of men tasting their first years of early middle age.

"If you want to take the twins, I'll grab your bags," Fred said, using his handheld control to open the rear hatch.

"That'd be great, thanks," Vicenzo said.

He released the magnetic locks that held in place the horizontal bar of his infants' tandem safety seat. Then he lifted them out one at a time—Colin first and then Sylvana—and guided them into a double-pouch baby sling that enabled him to carry both children at once, one against his chest and the other on his back, while keeping his hands free.

As he straightened under the weight of his heavier-by-the-day scions, he saw that Fred had finished unloading the luggage and apparently was pondering which pieces to take inside first. "Don't hurt yourself," he said to his cousin. "Start with Aoki's bags—she mostly has pajamas and stuffed animals."

"Right," said Fred, who stacked Aoki's smaller flowered bags on top of a large one with wheels, extended the bottom bag's towing handle, and pulled it behind him as he followed Vicenzo toward the broad, immaculate A-frame cedar house.

Vicenzo breathed in the cool early morning air and admired the view of Pike's Lake surrounded by mostly undisturbed forest. Sunlight sparkled on the water, and a breeze brought him scents of wood smoke and pine.

His was one of few homes that had been built around the lake. One of the most attractive features of this piece of property, in his opinion, was that none of the houses around the lake had a view of another. Each was sequestered in a nook of the shoreline and sheltered by the forest.

He checked and confirmed that his two canoes and one rowboat were still tied to the small dock behind his house. The lawn furniture didn't appear to have been pilfered during his absence, and that much more was once again right in his world. He'd just spent seventeen days making an arduous, impromptu round-trip journey with his children, who had pestered him with an endless barrage of questions. There had been no way to tell them that they had, in fact, been running for their lives from the Borg, because Mommy had said to leave Federation space.

Even after President Bacco's startling address, when it had become clear that the Borg threat was over, getting home hadn't been easy. By then, he and the children had reached Pacifica, along with several million other hastily displaced refugees. It had taken six days to get there, then five days to book passage on another transport back to Cestus III. And, as he'd feared, he'd been deprived of communications every step of the way, up to and including the moment he and the kids had landed.

Fortunately, Fred had never even considered being evacuated from Cestus III and had been home with nothing better to do, as usual. After a gentle browbeating, he had agreed to come pick up Vicenzo and his brood from the starport in Johnson City.

Trudging up the walk to the house, Vicenzo winced as both twins began crying at once. In front of him, Aoki hopped with manic energy after barely plodding along behind him for two weeks. She cut the air with a shrill plea: "Faster, Daddy!"

"Hold your horses, Pumpkin," he said.

It's good to be back at the house, he thought with relief. *It'll be nice to sleep in my own bed. And eat my own cooking.*

As he approached the front door, it swung open ahead of him, and he stopped in midstride.

His breath caught with hope and surprise.

Aoki spun around toward the house and shrieked, "Mommy!" She ran at a full gallop into Miranda Kalohata's wide and waiting arms. Miranda scooped the girl off her feet, kissed her, and spun her around and around as they laughed with glee.

Vicenzo desperately wanted to sprint to his wife, but he didn't want to risk shaking the twins, so he trotted in a funny way that minimized the bouncing of his hurried steps.

Miranda turned, perched Aoki on her sundress-clad hip, and held the girl steady with her right arm; she used her left to embrace Vicenzo and the babies. She felt amazing in his arms, and she smelled even better. He had missed every inch of her.

"Welcome back, love," she said, her eyes gleaming with grateful tears. She kissed the top of Colin's head, and then she touched her fingertips to Sylvana's sparsely covered scalp and massaged it, in a peculiar flexing gesture that Vicenzo had nicknamed the hand spider. Within moments, both twins had stopped crying. She smiled at Vicenzo. "It's good to be home."

He kissed her again. "It is now."

"A toast," Picard said, standing up from the table and raising his champagne glass. He waited for his dining companions to lift their own flutes, and he continued, "May our friendships, like fine wine, only improve with time's advance, and may we always be blessed with old wine, old friends, and young cares. Cheers."

"Here, here," replied Will Riker, who saluted Picard with his glass and then took a sip, cuing the other guests to drink.

Picard returned to his chair beside Beverly, who sat on his left. Riker occupied the other seat beside her, and past him was Deanna Troi. An empty chair separated Troi from Ezri Dax.

"What an amazing dinner," Dax said, gathering another spoonful of chocolate mousse. "Thank you for inviting me."

"Every new commanding officer deserves to

be treated at least once to a meal in the Captains' Lounge," Picard said with a collegial grin. "Not only is the cuisine exquisite, but the view is spectacular."

His comment turned everyone's eyes to the vista beyond the restaurant's concave wraparound wall of flawless transparent aluminum. Set against a perfect black curtain of star-flecked space was the majestic, looming curve of Mars's southern hemisphere.

The real focus of attention, however, was the newly arrived vessel in the docking slip below the VIP guests' table. The *Columbia* NX-02 was being swarmed over and doted on by a small army of engineers, mechanics, and technicians, who had begun the task of restoring the ship so that it could return under its own power to Earth orbit, completing the ill-fated journey it had started more than two centuries earlier.

Riker sighed with admiration of the vintage starship. "They really knew how to make 'em back then, didn't they?"

Dax replied with mock injured pride, "I think they make 'em just fine now, thank you very much."

"It is amazing, though," Troi said. "To think of how much of history was shaped by the fate of that one ship."

"Like the butterfly effect," Beverly interjected. "One decision today can spell life or death for a billion people a hundred years from now. You just never know."

"True," Riker replied. "Maybe the universe is more like the subatomic realm than we normally think— full of invisible effects and unseen consequences." He smirked at Picard. "What do you think, Jean-Luc?"

"I think perhaps you've all had enough champagne," he said, trying to hold a stern poker face and failing as a smile cracked through his mask of propriety. It felt good to grin and laugh and be the man he'd hidden from view for so many years. He felt as if he had come home to himself at long last.

His friends chortled good-naturedly with him, and then Riker said, "Seriously, though, what do you think?"

Picard permitted himself a moment of introspection. Until recently, he had dreaded such self-reflection, because his inner life had been haunted by the shadow of the Borg. Now, granted a measure of peace and solitude, he thought about the sensations and impressions that had lingered after the Caeliar's transformation of the Collective. He sipped his demitasse of espresso and appraised his newly altered worldview.

"I think that we're all echoes of a greater consciousness," he said. "Cells of awareness in a scheme we can't understand. At least, not yet."

Beverly seemed taken aback by his answer. Leaning toward him, she rested her hand on his forearm and said, "Is that really what you believe, Jean-Luc?"

He arched one eyebrow. "I hesitate to call it a *belief*," he said. "Let's just say it's an *idea* that I'm entertaining."

"Pretty big idea," Riker said, flashing his trademark smile behind his close-cut salt-and-pepper beard.

Picard shrugged. "Why think small? Thinking is free."

Dax folded her napkin and set it on the table. "Sorry to eat and run, but I have to get back to the

Aventine by 1900. We're expecting new orders from Starfleet Command."

As she got up, Picard and Riker stood as well. Smoothing the front of his tunic, Picard said with genuine optimism, "An exploration mission, perhaps?"

"Not likely, I'm afraid," Dax said. "I spoke to Admiral Nechayev before I came to dinner. She told me the *Aventine*'ll be needed to help coordinate rescue and recovery efforts inside the Federation for at least the next few months." She frowned. "Seems like a waste of a perfectly good slipstream drive, if you ask me. Now that it's fully online, I was hoping we'd get to visit a new galaxy or something."

Riker gently chided her, "A *new* one? Do you mind if we finish exploring *this* one first?"

"Don't be silly, William," Dax teased, standing on tiptoes to plant a chaste kiss on his cheek. "That's what Starfleet has *you* for." The sweetness of her smile took the sting out of her jibe. To Picard, she said, "Captain, it's been a pleasure and an honor. I hope our paths get to cross again someday."

"I'm certain they will," Picard said. With a nod at the table, he added, "But next time, you're buying dinner."

"You're on," the diminutive Trill captain said. Then she turned, said her farewells with Beverly and Troi, and left the restaurant in quick strides, without a backward glance. By the time she had finished her exit, Troi and Beverly had risen from the table to stand with Riker and Picard.

"She's something else," Beverly said, with a combination of admiration and exasperation.

"Yes," Troi said. "She's exceptionally sure of herself."

Picard and Riker traded amused glances, and Picard said to the two women, "She can't help it—she's a Dax."

Crusher poked Picard's chest. "And I'm a Howard woman."

"And I'm a daughter of the Fifth House, heiress to the Sacred Chalice of Rixx and the Holy Rings of Betazed," Troi said. After a horrified pause, she added, "And I'm turning into my mother."

"God, I hope not," Riker muttered.

"What was that?" Troi snapped.

"Nothing."

"Mm-hmm."

Sensing that it might be a good time to change the subject, Picard said, "Does *Titan* have its new orders yet?"

"Nope," Riker said. "We're moving to McKinley Station tomorrow at 0800 for some upgrades and refits. We'll find out what's next once we're done with repairs." He shook his head and after a rueful grin, added, "I do love a surprise."

"Listen to you two," Beverly said to the men. She and Troi looked irked with them as she continued, "You talk like the biggest things in your lives are light-years away."

Troi added, "Did you forget your new assignments already?"

Knowing glances of mock dread passed between the two men.

"Parenthood . . . ," Riker began.

". . . the final frontier," Picard finished.

Beverly smirked at their exchange but pretended to ignore them as she asked Troi, "Have you two picked out a name yet?"

"No," Troi said. "You?"

Beverly shook her head. "Not yet. It's been a matter of some . . . contention."

"I know the feeling," Troi said, wrinkling her brow in frustration at her husband, who rolled his eyes.

"We should go," Riker said. He reached forward and shook hands with Picard. Before the elder captain could speak, Riker added, "Don't tell me to be careful."

"I wouldn't dream of it," Picard said. "Be bold."

"That sounds like the Captain Picard I know." He let go of Picard's hand, slapped his shoulder, and added more softly, "Good to have you back." He and Troi bade Beverly farewell, and Picard saw them off with the hopeful valediction, "*Au revoir.*"

Then he and Beverly were alone in the Captains' Lounge, which had been closed for his private event. Sometimes being a famous savior of the Federation had its perquisites.

Beverly took his hand, and they stood together, staring in wonder at the austere majesty of the universe. A grim chapter of his life now felt closed, and a new, brighter chapter was about to begin. Old debts had been settled, and old promises had been kept. His obligations to the past were fulfilled, and for the first time in decades, he was free to contemplate the future.

Wistfully, Beverly asked, "What will you do in a universe without the Borg, Jean-Luc?"

He didn't answer right away. It was not a glib question.

Squeezing her hand in his firm but gentle grip, he met her reflected gaze in the window and said, "I'll hope that our son is born healthy. . . . I'll hope that we can be good parents. . . . I'll hope that he can grow up in a galaxy of peace."

He regarded his own reflection with a smile.

"I'll hope."

Terminat hora diem, terminat auctor opus.

ACKNOWLEDGMENTS

Kara, my lovely and patient wife, thank you for being so good to me, and so understanding even as I spent most of my nights for more than fifteen months secluded behind closed doors writing this trilogy. It would have been unbearable without you.

Marco Palmieri and Margaret Clark, my esteemed editors, I thank you for tolerating my bouts of uncertainty, my moments of dudgeon while I received your eminently reasonable story notes, and my adolescent practical jokes. ("All work and no play makes Mack a dull boy.") I couldn't have done this without you both.

Geddy Lee, thank you for taking an hour of your time to talk with a stranger, and for sharing your lovely anecdote about French vineyards, and the way that vines are like people, in that adversity adds depth and complexity to their characters. I hope you will forgive me for making use of it in this tale, and that you will approve of the manner in which it was applied.

Keith R.A. DeCandido, Kirsten Beyer, and Christopher L. Bennett, thank you one and all for going above and beyond the call of duty to help me vet all three books of this trilogy. My thanks also go out to Michael A. Martin and Andy Mangels, who graciously tweaked their novel *Kobayashi Maru* to track with situations I had established, and for suggesting that Ree ought to bite Counselor Troi. Nice idea, gents!

To revive an old tradition of mine, I wish to thank the composers who helped create the numerous original film and TV scores that serve as my link to my muse while I write. Many of my favorite moments throughout the trilogy were coaxed from my imagination by the music of Bear McCreary (*Battlestar Galactica,* Season Three), Tyler Bates (*300*), Alan Silvestri (*Beowulf*), Javier Navarette (*Pan's Labyrinth*), Thomas Newman (*The Shawshank Redemption*), Hans Zimmer (the *Pirates of the Caribbean* scores) and Dario Marianelli (*V for Vendetta*).

Last, I need to thank author Robert Metzger for having made me aware of the concept of catoms, in an article he wrote for the *SFWA Bulletin*. Astute readers might have wondered if the character of Johanna Metzger in *Gods of Night* and *Mere Mortals* was named in his honor; she was.

Until next time, thanks for reading.

APPENDIX I
2156

Featured Crew Members

Columbia NX-02

Captain Erika Hernandez
(human female) commanding officer

Commander Veronica Fletcher
(human female) executive officer

Lieutenant Commander Kalil el-Rashad
(human male), second officer/science officer

Lieutenant Karl Graylock
(human male) chief engineer

Lieutenant Johanna Metzger
(human female) chief medical officer

Lieutenant Kiona Thayer
(human female) senior weapons officer

Ensign Sidra Valerian
(human female) communications officer

Major Stephen Foyle
(human male) MACO commander

Lieutenant Vincenzo Yacavino
(human male) MACO second-in-command

Sergeant Gage Pembleton
(human male) MACO first sergeant

APPENDIX II
STARDATE 58100
(early February 2381)

Featured Crew Members

U.S.S. Enterprise NCC-1701-E

Captain Jean-Luc Picard
(human male) commanding officer

Commander Worf
(Klingon male) executive officer

Commander Miranda Kadohata
(human female) second officer/operations officer

Commander Geordi La Forge
(human male) chief engineer

Commander Beverly Crusher
(human female) chief medical officer

Lieutenant Hegol Den
(Bajoran male) senior counselor

Lieutenant Jasminder Choudhury
(human female) chief of security

Lieutenant Dina Elfiki
(human female) senior science officer

Lieutenant T'Ryssa Chen
(Vulcan-human female) contact specialist

APPENDIX II

U.S.S. Titan NCC-80102

Captain William T. Riker
(human male) commanding officer

Commander Christine Vale
(human female) executive officer

Commander Tuvok
(Vulcan male) second officer/tactical officer

Commander Deanna Troi
(Betazoid-human female) diplomatic officer/senior
counselor

Commander Xin Ra-Havreii
(Efrosian male) chief engineer

Lieutenant Commander Shenti Yisec Eres Ree
(Pahkwa-thanh male) chief medical officer

Lieutenant Commander Ranul Keru
(Trill male) chief of security

Lieutenant Commander Melora Pazlar
(Elaysian female) senior science officer

Lieutenant Pral glasch Haaj
(Tellarite male) counselor

Lieutenant Huilan Sen'kara
(Sti'ach male) counselor

Ensign Torvig Bu-kar-nguv
(Choblik male) engineer

APPENDIX II

U.S.S. Aventine NCC-82602

Captain Ezri Dax
(Trill female) commanding officer

Commander Samaritan Bowers
(human male) executive officer

Lieutenant Commander Gruhn Helkara
(Zakdorn male) second officer/senior science officer

Lieutenant Lonnoc Kedair
(Takaran female) chief of security

Lieutenant Simon Tarses
(human-Romulan male) chief medical officer

Lieutenant Mikaela Leishman
(human female) chief engineer

Lieutenant Oliana Mirren
(human female) senior operations officer

ABOUT THE AUTHOR

David Mack is the author of numerous *Star Trek* books, including *Wildfire*, *A Time to Kill*, *A Time to Heal*, and *Warpath*. With editor Marco Palmieri, he developed the *Star Trek Vanguard* literary series, for which he has written two novels, *Harbinger* and *Reap the Whirlwind*.

His other novels include the *Wolverine* espionage adventure *Road of Bones* and his first original novel, *The Calling*, which is scheduled for publication in 2009 by Simon & Schuster.

Before writing books, Mack cowrote with John J. Ordover the *Star Trek: Deep Space Nine* fourth-season episode "Starship Down" and the story treatment for the series' seventh-season episode "It's Only a Paper Moon."

An avid fan of Canadian progressive-rock trio Rush, Mack has attended shows in all of their concert tours since 1982.

Having recently fled corporate servitude, Mack now resides in a secret location with his wife, Kara. Learn more about him and his work on his official Web site (www.infinitydog.com) and on his blog, http://infinitydog.livejournal.com.